BETWEEN WORLDS:
» *MALCONTENT* «

An Aetherium Novel

Written by

Paul and Jennifer DK

ZMOK
BOOKS

Between Worlds: Malcontent
Cover from Jason Engle
This edition published in 2021

Zmok Books is an imprint of
Winged Hussar Publishing, LLC
1525 Hulse Rd, Unit 1
Point Pleasant, NJ 08742

Bibliographical References and Index
1. Science Fiction. 2. Other Worlds. 3. Dystopian

For more information on Winged Hussar Publishing, LLC, visit us at:
https://www.wingedhussarpublishing.com

Twitter: WingHusPubLLC
Facebook: Winged Hussar Publishing LLC

For our two children, who have filled our lives with meaning, love, and wonder. And for all the LGBTQ+ kids out there. You are never alone.

AETHERIUM

What is the Aetherium?

For the average person, life is brutally hard. The world is spent, broken, a wasteland. There is drudgery and filth and endless streams of meaningless, menial work. And then there is the Aetherium. More than a virtual reprieve from the urbanized nightmare of the 23rd century, the Aetherium is a digital landscape of countless dimensional frontiers, a virtual reality so vivid as to be indistinguishable from reality itself. The Aetherium, then, is an essential human commodity. Uncountable billions plug themselves in every single day to live out their dreams of a better existence.

⫸⫷ » Chapter One: Home « ⫸⫷

The mag-train pulled into Keral Station Seven, and, just like that, Mal was home. In the only place, at least, that made any sense to call home. Axion Academy, where she had been taken when she was thirteen, definitely did not count, and she had never lived long enough anywhere else for it to be home. When the train pulled up, there was no announcement, no "Welcome to Keral" from the conductor. Through the dirty window Mal could see no crowds, not a single person waiting for a loved one to disembark. The Hub itself, cavernous and forbidding, was made of dark, aged iron that seemed to absorb most of the available light and echoed with emptiness. More than a dozen tracks and gates were arrayed throughout the large domed building; several of the tracks were clearly not in use and instead piled high with decommissioned mag-train cars and other nameless junk.

The compartment door slid open, and Mal stepped out onto the platform and then into a long, tunnel-shaped passageway lined with tables; these should have been attended by Axiom personnel, checking Papers for signs of disloyalty and bags for contraband, but the tables were deserted. Somehow *this is even sadder than I remember.* A bank of obviously nonfunctional scanners, motionless and silent, stood in for the missing personnel. Mal adjusted the pack on her shoulder and exited the tunnel into the dingy sunlight. Outside were a handful of abandoned and stripped ground cars and a large pile of metal refuse that had been cleared into a corner of the lot. Station Seven was the one furthest train hubs from the tall, dark center of the city of Keral, a place of more than a million citizens. The Keral Sprawl, which ringed the city center, stretched from horizon to horizon, everything washed out and gray. The Sprawl itself was broken into numbered Pods, small areas that contained housing, factories, and, in theory, every other kind of zone, such as medical or commercial, that residents would need.

Parked a short distance from the Station's exit was a six-wheeled ground car. A thin, weathered-looking man with gray hair and white but reddened skin leaned against it, clearly waiting for Mal. She walked up to him.

"Mal Turner? I've never met an Agent of Axiom up so close and personal," he said by way of greeting.

How am I supposed to respond to that? Mal looked pointedly at the car, and he scrambled to open the back door. She settled into the transport, her pack carefully on her lap, her hand resting inside it.

"I mean," he said, driving away from the Station, "I've met plenty of Axiom operatives but never an Agent. This is a first for me." Mal did not respond and silence fell.

After a few minutes of quiet driving, he tried again. "I just can't believe there's something going on around here that deserves a visit from an Agent." His voice hovered over the last sentence, turning it into a question, and his eyes met hers in the rear-facing mirror.

"Is that a question?" she asked.

"No. I mean, I have my orders and I know the way." After a merciful pause, though, he pressed on. "So are you on a mission then?" This time, he turned a question into a statement.

"I am."

"Does it have to do with them that calls themselves Nanomei?" He pronounced it strangely, as though it was a word he didn't hear or say very often. Nice touch.

After Mal gave him no reply he glanced back in his mirror and gave her a knowing nod and a little wink. "They sure like to cause trouble, those Nanomei. Always ruining it for those of us loyal Axiom Citizens who like things to be orderly. Hard to keep a schedule when they're always disrupting this or that. You know, I heard last week they shut down every street in New Lagos? For an hour!" His eyes, focused on hers through the mirror, waited for a reaction. "Can you believe it?"

Mal could believe it. Disruption of civic services and infrastructure was pretty much Nanomei's standard operating procedure; in areas where the Axiom Collective owned and operated all the moving parts of society, Nanomei's sabotage was a constant. Their pranks ranged from simply irritating to disruptive to dangerous.

"But... not much Nanomei activity here in Keral. Not much activity of any kind. Can't remember the last time I had a call direct from Control. So, what are you looking for?"

Mal didn't answer.

"You ever been to Keral before?" he tried.

"I lived here as a child," Mal said. Something in her tone, maybe, finally convinced him to stop talking. She looked out the window and a sudden glare from some metal scrap alongside the road reflected her face back to her, and she flinched; the sudden reminder of the disconnect between her appearance and her real self was jarring. She was dressed in black, loose-fitting pants,

10

black combat boots, and a ratty gray poncho that covered her torso. Her short, straight black hair hung loose down to her shoulders. In the Meatspace, Mal dressed to disappear; but then, this body, this existence, did not matter. Not really. All that mattered was the Aetherium.

The Operative drove through the Pod in crisscrosses, making sure they weren't tracked, then pulled in an alley about twenty blocks from her building. "I was told to drop you here." He turned around to look at Mal. "Sorry, Agent. I know I ask too many questions."

Mal pulled the gun out of her pack. "Axiom knows it too." She shot him cleanly in the forehead, and his body fell sideways; he didn't have enough time to even look surprised.

Mal got out of the vehicle. That was it. "Eliminate the driver," Mullen had said. "He has been selling information. Leave the vehicle and forget you ever saw him." Mal's orders were clear, and she followed them as always without hesitation. "For Axiom. Loyalty eternal," she murmured.

Mal started walking. The route she plotted out would take her in a large circle, eventually winding her around to her old building. The Pod she had lived in had not been exactly thriving when Mal had lived there, but it seemed to have completely collapsed during her absence. The sidewalks were crumbling and many of the buildings she walked past were boarded up or in some state of Deconstruction. Deconstruction was the newest industry to deal with the lack of resources; old buildings were torn apart and harvested for parts and materials. Harvested buildings were supposed to be replaced with structures built from newer, more efficient materials, but it looked as though these buildings had long been harvested and their skeletons abandoned.

Banners hung limply from buildings and lampposts: The Crossed Key symbol of Axiom. Efficiency. Loyalty. Axiom was one of a few Collectives that split control of the worlds between them. The Collectives governed the people, employed the people, and produced almost everything consumed by the people. Axiom was the most powerful Collective in Keral and all along the coastal territories and it ruled with precision and order. Axiom was the final stand against total anarchy and disaster. Other Collectives were much less important, and only cared for themselves: Ikaru concerned itself more purely with commerce and Value, Nanomei seemed to exist only to tear down what Axiom was trying to build, and RezX, well, they mostly wanted to be left alone in their weird corners conducting experiments or building odd contraptions. All the Pods in Keral were Axiom-controlled; living in an Axiom city had afforded an advantage, in resources and safety, to Mal's family when she was growing up. Loyalty to Axiom was like one of the old religions, a matter of utter faith and belief that it was only Axiom which stood between the end of civilization and those struggling to stay alive.

11

Mal tried to count the years as she walked. When Axiom had "invited" her to the Academy, when she was thirteen, she was still living as Malven, a boy, as she had been assigned at birth. She had not realized her true gender until she had been away from Keral, where everything felt... stuck. She had attributed her unhappiness to the stagnant feeling, the heavy, dusty air. When she got away from this place, as terrified as she was, she was also able to imagine new possibilities. She was able to breathe and to find herself. The turmoil she had felt leaving home, the new confidence she felt at finally understanding her gender: she had experienced these at the same time. Now, back here, she felt herself floundering, weighed down. Just being home, apparently, could make those old feelings of confusion and uncertainty swirl back around her. Mal stopped counting years. This assignment is going to rot.

Mal walked past an old favorite spot of hers as she approached the residential area. She stopped by the acrylic sculpture of a tree, smudged and dust covered. "Breathe Easy Trees" was emblazoned across the trunk. It stood in front of an Air Purification Center that had been nicknamed Ash Tower. The tower was silent now, its filters clogged and its turbines dead. As a child Mal would come sit under the sculpture, pretending it was real. This had been one of the markers she'd used to tell herself she was getting too far from home. "I know, I know, Mom... not past the Ash Tower," she whispered. She ran her fingers across the smooth surface of the artificial tree. Something was painted on it, some kind of graffiti. As Mal cleared away a bit of the grime on the tree she revealed the outline of a white rabbit sprayed onto the surface. A Nanomei symbol. She felt her heart quicken.

As Mal walked toward the Axiom Housing area of the Pod she could see the entrances of the factories a few blocks off, to the east. The factories were built on lowered ground and connected to the street by bridges. Less damage if there was a spill. Less chance of spread if there was a factory fire. Mal tried to avoid looking at the blackened, burned-out factory, partially collapsed in on itself; it looked as though it, too, had undergone some Deconstruction, but that the process had been abandoned.

Lines of workers entered and left the factories that were still functional, snaking down into and up out of huge ramps leading in and out of the factories from street level. Mal knew their mission. Make enough money, gain enough value, afford time in the Aetherium, for themselves and for their families. What else was there to work for here? Aetherium access cost a slice of Value for every minute logged in, not to mention the cost of hosting programs to use while logged in: House, vehicle, clothing, everything. Paradise was not free. It wasn't even cheap. Mal stopped outside the chain fence that separated her from the workers queuing up in front of the building. Her father had been one of these workers once. They looked haggard, tired. A few glanced her way, maybe wondering if she would join them. Mal's job was so different from theirs, but her goal was exactly the same. Do the job. Earn your time. Get back in. Even if they didn't see it, she was as desperate as they were. I'm just in a different line.

The Rig Parlor down the block was still open; the bottom was a storefront with a dwelling in the floors above. Mal peered through the grease-streaked front window. Inside, there was a single attendant at a desk facing the window, and about a dozen rigs. The rigs were cylinders of brushed aluminum about five feet high with reclined chairs attached to their bases. The headrest of each chair had a hole in it, to allow a cable to run from the chip in the User's skull to the cylinder, or the rig's Core. Most public-use rigs had a keyboard of some sort out of reach of the chair, for an attendant to maintain oversight while the person was logged in; these had simple touch panels on the casing itself, which meant these Patches were operating their rigs themselves. And they were operating unsafe rigs, clearly in need of repair, with parts of their casing stripped away or missing entirely, revealing bundles of wires, cables, and circuit boards inside. Despite all of this each of the rigs was occupied by a person who had uploaded their consciousness into the Aetherium, their minds free and traveling while their bodies, unconscious, waited in the Rig chairs.

The Aetherium was a world between worlds, a new dimension that human minds were able to visit. Users equipped with Interface Chips implanted in their brains could access the Aetherium through the Core of their rigs. The Aetherium was made habitable by constantly running programs that were supported by Pylons, constructs built out of raw computing power pushed into the Aetherium through Meatspace hardware. As a User's mind traveled through the Aetherium their Rig ran programs that created a body, clothes, tools, or literally anything else, for them to use. While connected, a User's senses and perception of reality was completely immersed in the programmed reality of the Aetherium.

The experiences of these Users in the Rig parlor, though, would be muted. These cheap rigs could not create a strong enough connection for their Users to truly immerse themselves. Even the best commercial rigs, specially designed to allow for multiple Users, offered experiences that were mere shadows of what could be accomplished with Single-User models; but at least at the higher-class places the rigs would be better than this. At better parlors there would also be workers to attend the customer's physical needs, such as nutrition and hydration, allowing customers to spend more time in the Aetherium.

Mal felt someone approaching from behind and readied herself.

"Little boy."

Damn. Mal stared at her reflection in the glass. There was only so much she could do in the Meatspace to articulate her gender. One of the many reasons she preferred being in the Aetherium, where her appearance always agreed, effortlessly, with her gender. Mal knew she was female, and so that's how she appeared in the Aetherium. End of story. So easy, there. So right. She ached to log back in.

"Slice for a trip?"

Mal turned, tugging at her hair. No way of knowing how old the man was; he was street-filthy and bent. His eyes were dully feverish and his black skin pockmarked.

"I've got nothing," Mal said.

"Slice, just a slice, slip your Value. I just need an hour." He pressed towards her and held out his hand toward the door. He just wants to get back to the Aetherium. Where everything doesn't hurt. Mal stepped around him then, keeping one hand free and ready, the other keeping a firm grip on her duffel. He spit after her. "Cog."

Mal walked on, breathing tightly. I know how you feel.

⟩⟩•••••⟨⟨

The building in which Mal had spent her childhood was a nondescript Axiom-run Domestic Dwelling, a low, four-story building made of grey ash-block. The Children's Recreational Area next to it, where Mal, her younger brother, and her friends had spent so much time, was empty; the climbing equipment, the swings, all looked as though they were waiting for kids who might never come. Mal could see where the buil ding had been patched with modern materials; Paliscrete reflected more light and it never quite blended with the older building materials. She sat on a rusted bench and watched the building for a while. Every living memory she had before the Academy centered on this building.

It was Mullen's fault she was back here. It had to be. He was the superior to whom Mal reported in Axiom, he was the one who had briefed Mal on her mission, and he was the one who told her she would be staying in her family's old residence. She had felt dull sense of dread wash over her at this news, but she also had a rush of irrational excitement. Foolishness. No one is waiting for me here. Mullen had not offered any explanation about why she was required to stay in this building to accomplish her mission, and a good Agent asks no questions. Mal was an excellent Agent.

She walked up to the front door of the building. Her family had lived in one of thirty Units on the third floor. Mal pressed her Crypto-Card onto the door lock of the lobby and it made an eerily familiar squealing Noise as the door opened. In addition to opening every door she was legally entitled to pass through, her Crypto held her Papers, Value, history, rank, licenses, and privileges within the Collective. Of course, what she carried now was all cover. Faked Papers, fake self. As Mal entered the building and walked to the elevator other residents, like good Axiom citizens, kept their eyes averted and their business their own. The hall itself was narrow, short, cramped. The rubberized flooring matched the walls' peach color which made the whole hall look like the inside of an intestine. The doors were simulated wood, each with the identical woodgrain pattern. Mal recognized that pattern, every swirl, wave, and knot.

Mal walked in and used her card to access the elevator. On the third floor, she pressed her Crypto-Card onto the security panel for Unit 37 and it opened to a silent, empty dwelling. It looked well-lived in. Drab. Functional. And much as Mal remembered: Clapboard floor. Undecorated walls. A barely functioning refrigeration box and a small cooking surface. A ratty couch. A vid screen built into one wall. She dropped the Crypto-Card on the table near the door out of old habit. She felt like a ghost. There should have been some new family here, wondering about the strange presence they could sense in their home. Would they feel the memories Mal was stirring to life as she walked across the floor? Here is where I sat when my parents got the communication from Axiom that I was to attend The Axiom Academy for Gifted Citizens. Her father had been vehemently opposed, but her mother was resigned. What Axiom wanted; Axiom took. Here is where my father stood, in their way, and said "He is not going." Mal traced the patchwork in the wall. The Praetorians had smashed her father with a shield when he stood in front of Mal and refused to move. Mal had screamed. Her mother had grabbed her arm and pushed her toward the Praetorians. "Just take him! Take him!"

Mal had ripped her arm from her mother's grip and ran to her father, who was collapsed on the floor. He was bleeding from a cut on his forehead. Mal could hear her brother crying from the other room. The Praetorian stepped toward her and cast a shadow over her and her father. Mal's father opened his eyes, but they were unfocused. She could not tell if he could see her. She felt the bulk of the Praetorian behind her. "I'll go," she said, standing and turning to face the guard. The Praetorian's eyes were obscured by the polished visor of his helmet and Mal could see herself clearly in its reflection, a terrified boy trying to look calm on the outside and whose insides felt as though they were folding in on themselves. Just a child.

There were two doors off the main living area. One, Mal left untouched. The other she opened, and through it carefully entered her family's Rig room, which had also served as her bedroom, and sat on the bed. There was a stump of dead-ended connections where her mother's Rig had been installed. The cheap Rig she had used as a child to log in to the Aetherium was also gone; in its place was replaced by a new rig, a Brix. Mal studied the new Rig warily. Through a Brix, she could experience the Aetherium in a truly immersive sense; she would feel, taste, smell, see, and hear just as she did in the Meatspace, but compared to Mal's Razor, the Rig she was accustomed to using at Axiom, it would feel outdated by a decade.

When Mal turned four she entered primary school and there she used her first Aetherium Helmet. The Helmet was attached to a huge stainless steel Rig casing that housed the separate rigs for her entire class of twelve; this was the only safe way for small children to enter the Aetherium. Mal could remember her first moments in the Aetherium with perfect clarity. The first time she switched on her helmet and saw the Aetherium's version of her classroom, the rust was gone from the chairs, the board was a three-dimensional holo-space instead of the dingy whiteboard. The other students were represented as simple images, mostly featureless, and uninteresting. But the window. Mal walked to the window. In the Meatspace the classroom looked out on an abandoned lot and the window itself was grimy and rusted shut.

"No, child, that is not programed to open," the teacher had said. But Mal was already figuring out what she could do in the Aetherium. She tugged at the window, and it opened. The sun was bright, and there were real trees outside. Hacking, Mal would later learn, was the ability to modify the code of a program to a person's will without going through the long process of writing that code over. Users who could hack were able to modify, control, and change the very reality of the Aetherium all around them. Mal had wanted that window open so badly she had hacked without realizing it. The rush of possibility, of creativity and will made real, exploded through Mal's mind, and from that moment on, she lived for the Aetherium. Outside the window there was a whole city, alive, vibrant, colorful. Spires in the distance like golden mountains. Flying cars. Someday I will fly.

Back in the present, Mal gritted her teeth and went back to inspecting her Brix. Users logged in with rigs like this all the time. They went about their daily lives, buying vehicles, toys, weapons, jewels, or extinct animals; watching holo-films or tele-serials; meeting up with friends, lovers. These people, everyone Mal ever knew before being taken to the Academy, were called Patches. In the Aetherium they were simple representations of themselves, able to experience the Aetherium but not access the underlying code. They were there to escape daily life; they fueled the economy and sometimes even the very reality of the Aetherium.

Mal's experience had always been different. She was able to move faster, jump further. She could also see, smell, taste, hear, and feel details in the Aetherium that others could not. Commander Mullen gave Mal access to better and better rigs as she learned and grew. By the time she was a second-year cadet she was kitted out in the Blazetech Razor 7000. All of the trials, all of the shit from Mullen, and the fights along the way with Kass, were all worth it because Axiom, for Mal, meant constant, reliable, and high-qual-

16

ity access to the Aetherium. Every job she'd ever done had been while logged in. Until now.

Dammit, Mullen, why? Why am I back here? There were hundreds of places she could have stayed for this mission. Mullen knew Mal, he knew she would have shit to deal with, coming back. She did not feel in balance, and she did not feel ready for an assignment. This put the mission in jeopardy. Which you would never do. So, why?

Mal replayed the conversation in her head.

"This mission is important, Agent Turner."

"All missions are important, Commander."

But when he looked up from his datapad and made eye contact with her she could feel something in his gaze. He was trying to tell her something without saying it aloud. She knew him at least that well. She ditched the attitude and listened hard. But what he said next was not thrilling: "Today, I am sending three Agents out on new assignments. You, Kass, and Dek."

Fragging Kass. Mal struggled to keep her feelings off her face. Kass was her own personal pain in the ass. Every time Mal took a step forward, it seemed, Kass took it too. Every advancement. Every accolade. And now, on the day the Commander was giving her what appeared to be a vital mission, Kass was getting one too. As was Dek, but Dek mattered much less. He was successful, a good agent, solid, eager. He was an obsessive rules follower and completely unimaginative, but that worked for him. Mal forgot he was part of the conversation before Mullen said another word.

"The Nanomei operating in The Drain have become more than a nuisance, Agent. They have become a credible threat to the whole Aetherial city. We believe that they are preparing some sort of major uprising there. Your usual assignments are being cancelled and I am putting you into deep cover. Your mission will be to seek out the Nanomei gang operating in The Drain and infiltrate them. You'll be set up as a code smoother, working for Axiom, but you will also develop a secret identity as a rabble rouser. You should start with seemingly random acts of aggression against Axiom and work up to larger acts of civil disobedience and even violence. Nanomei is always searching out new talent for their ridiculous crusade against us. Develop your cover into someone they would notice and recruit."

"I understand," Mal said. Except that I don't do cover missions, so what are you playing at?

"You will be set up in Keral."

"I grew up in Keral." But you know that, don't you?

"We know that," Commander said without a smile. "We're putting you back in your old home. It's the perfect way to get you in deep. You have history there already."

No room for questions, even though Mal had hundreds. She just nodded.

"Our intel says they need more talented hackers. Show them what you can do. I want dead-drops nightly. Do them through the Meatspace."

"Loyalty Eternal," Mal had intoned, inclining her head before leaving the room.

A knock at the door to the Unit made Mal jump, then curse herself. She had to settle her nerves. But she practically ran to the door just the same. Before opening it, she pressed her palm onto the smooth synthetic wood and tried to breathe. Her Matron was always talking about managing her breath to manage her mind. It was absolutely not working. She opened the door anyway.

"It is you. Malven," a man said. He was dressed in dirty grey coveralls, and an ID card hung around his neck from a lanyard. The man was looking at her expectantly. "Don't you remember me?" He had real hope in his eyes but also wariness.

She stared. "It's Mallory, now. Mal." She said that part without thinking, a reflex action her mouth performed while her brain tried to catch up. She tried to shake off the unpleasant sensation of being called her old name. "Are you...? Of course. Trent." He had the same smile, same dusty-black skin. His youthful halo of black hair was now cut close to his skull.

"That's me."

"Wow." Conflicting feelings skittered around in Mal's brain. "You want to... come in?"

"Nah." He looked a little nervous. "I shouldn't. It's just... this place has been empty for years, and then a few nights ago, I got the communication 'Mal Turner' was moving in. I had to wonder... I work for Axiom now. I'm the Building Supervisor." He leaned a bit against the doorframe, grinning, and assumed an old-man voice. "Any trouble getting here?"

Forget you ever saw him. "No, none at all." she tried a similar old-lady voice, but it cracked.

He hesitated, suddenly looking serious. "Where have you been living? Why did you move back here?"

"Well, code smoothers go where there's Glitch. And with everything going on in The Drain lately they've got a lot of work for me."

"So, bringing you back to your old digs?"

"Axiom efficiency," Mal said.

"Is the name change....?"

"I'm a woman now."

Trent paused for a moment, then nodded. "Remind me if I forget and call you Malven. So where were you living before?" he asked.

"Look, I'm sorry, I'm actually really tired. Could we maybe talk tomorrow?"

"Yea, sure thing! It's great you're back, Mal." His eyes lingered on the Unit, over her shoulder, for a moment. Then he was gone. Impossible to be here and not look back, but impossible to look back. Leave the past where it is. She closed the door to the Unit, firmly. She looked at the second door in the Unit, the closed door, but didn't go near it. She heard Trent greeting someone in the hall and receive an answer in a light child's voice.

Do the job. Earn your time. Too many distractions buzzing around in her mind. She found a tube of protein paste in the kitchen, ate it, and slept that night in a room she had not seen in years.

〉〉••••••〈〈

Mal was awakened the next morning by a loud thud against the door to her Unit. She almost leapt from bed, grabbed her gun from the nearby table, and ran to the door, keeping low. Another thud. She opened the door and swung her body out, keeping her right hand and gun in the unit.

There was a small human in the hall, wearing some sort of helmet. As she watched, he rammed a different Unit's door with his head. He stopped and looked up at her "Hi!" he beamed at her. "Who are you? My mom says you're new."

"I'm Mal," she said slowly. She kept the gun out of sight. Weak light filled the hall; it was morning, but very early.

"Do you wanna play?" he asked.

"I have work," she said.

"Do you work in Meat or Magic?"

"What?"

He looked at Mal pityingly. When he spoke again, his voice was pitched slightly higher and louder, as though he was addressing someone rather unintelligent. "Well. There's Meatspace and Magicspace." He rapped his knuckles against a doorframe. "Some people work in the Meatspace...."

"I get it, kid," Mal interrupted, as he looked as though he was gearing up for a lengthy discussion. "I work in the Magic. I'm a code smoother."

He was clearly unimpressed. "Do you have a kid? Can I play with them? My mom is always jacked in. She's jacked in right now."

Mal felt a flush of recognition. Children this age were usually left to fend for themselves while their parents spent time in the Aetherium. She, her brother, and Trent and the other children of the building had been the same.

"I'm sorry. I don't. I am alone here."

"No, you're not silly, I'm right here," he said. "Watch!" He readjusted his helmet and ran full force at a neighbor's door. The thud was louder out here, and she heard muffled swearing from inside the door he had attacked.

"I meant.... Never mind. I've got to get to work."

"What's your name again?"

19

"Mal."

"That means bad."

"Sometimes," she said, and closed the door behind her. She heard him say "My name's Gibson," out in the hall. She set the gun on the table and went back to her room, determinedly not looking at the closed door.

She had to get back into the Aetherium, no matter what kind of Rig she was dealing with, both for the job, and for her own peace. She sat and stared down the Brix for a while. She heard another series of thuds from the hall.

Mal took a deep breath. "Ok, you pile of scrap. Let's get acquainted." She sank into the worn cushion of the rig's chair. This was a one-person rig; everything was within reach of the User. Her Razor was so large it took up thirty feet, bundles of cables pulsing with light and weaving through junction boxes and coolant tanks, slick with evaporation and stacked in walls. It took three attendants to maintain her Rig during operation: one to keep her body safe and comfortable, another to maintain coolant levels and vent the restrictors, and a third, a "handler," who could act in the world at her direction and feed her information that, for security reasons, should not be delivered through the Aetherium.

Mal ran her fingers over the cool, black heart of the rig: the core. It was a two-foot-wide cylinder about three feet tall and had several bands of wires, cables, and various small modifications in the form of pieces of machines that, to some, would look like scrap metal fused together haphazardly. But she could see that the inverter band held a modified core from an older unit, and it was there just to provide an additional slot for memory. The blink cable had a cross Patch which was not necessary but made it look like it was spliced older cables, which was more realistic, without losing the signal quality of a single filament connection. Whoever had done the work had done an excellent job making it look like a homemade mod.

All the peripherals, bands of wires and cables, were feeding into the core, except for one: the stem. It was a pure platinum cable running from the box itself to the headrest of her chair. The end of it was a half-inch blade that would be inserted into her chip. Mal was shaking with excitement to get back in. She had let her fear of the Brix hold her back. She flipped a few switches, settled into the chair, and slid the blade into her chip at the base of her skull, just behind her right ear. The keyboard lit up and swung into place. She closed her eyes, took in and released a deep breath, and gave the final command, the one that always came directly from the mind of the User. Login.

Logging in with her Razor felt like a rush of motion from and in all directions and then a crack of lightning in her mind. Using the Brix, time felt painfully disjointed. The transition stuttered, froze up, reloaded. By the time Mal's consciousness had left her body and reformed in the Aetherium, she was nauseous and disoriented. As always, she had skipped the white room, a place she could ground herself, load programs, and make adjustments. She usually bypassed the white room because, when she was this close, she just wanted to dive into the Aetherium. Besides, she could make many of the changes to her programs directly in the Aetherium that others needed a white room to accomplish.

Mal was in the same access point that she had last logged out of in her old gear, just a subway, littered with blowing paper and filled with Patches going up and down the stairs as they entered and left the Aetherium; but the normally sharp details were fuzzy, the sounds distorted, and the colors less intense. Damn this rig. I'm crawling where I used to fly.

The Razor had flawless data and sensory gear and had an overlay over her vision that she could change with a thought. She could analyze, see, and measure almost anything in an instant. She could feel those capabilities in this rig, but when she accessed her Heads-Up Display, and tried to see how many people were in the area, she could feel the Rig searching and counting. She gritted her teeth in frustration. Part of the high of the Aetherium was the constant rush of information, the knowledge that she could count the bricks in the side of a building, track anyone, compute probabilities, in heartbeats. Mal tried to quell the wave of panic rising inside her. It has what is necessary. It will be enough.

Mal stopped next to a building plated in a titanium and studied her reflection. And this will be enough. Mal's face had narrowed; her tawny-beige skin was smoother and brighter, her black hair hanging in gentle curls down her back. Her eyes were a deep honey color. Her body was a woman's, as it should be. Mal felt a sudden burst of euphoria. She had not realized how it had felt like moving through tar, stuck in a male body in the Meatspace, until she was free of it. She was wearing her knee-high red lacquered combat boots, her absolute favorite footwear program, a short black skirt, and hoodie. She grinned at her reflection.

Mal practically hopped up a set of grimy concrete stairs, her long hair bouncing against her shoulders, out of the subway terminal onto a crowded street. Walking in the Aetherium felt just as corporeal as anything she experienced in the Meatspace. Mal could hear the murmur of hundreds of people moving about their business and smell cooking street food. She could taste the salt of sweat from the crowd on her tongue. She was in the Aetherial City known as The Drain.

The Drain straddled the Quantum River, a river of concentrated Quantum Noise that flowed like water across a nodal plane. All of the Aetherium contained Quantum Noise in varying states, mostly a plasma-like mix similar to heavy mist. All Quantum Noise was toxic to the human mind and the denser the Noise the more dangerous. Nodal planes were places where the Quantum Noise was least dense; it was still dangerous, but at these planes Pylons were used to reduce the Noise and make the space livable. Beyond keeping the Quantum Noise at bay, Pylons also hosted all the programs used to create the world around the people in the Aetherium. Every object, building, street, everything in the Aetherium was a program. To sustain such complex work, Pylons all contained an Artificial Intelligence (AI) which maintained the working order of the Programs and kept things running smoothly. Some of these AIs were relatively simple and others hyper-advanced. It was the ability of these AIs which was a prime determining factor in the quality of the Pylon and its ability to remain functional and stand up against fluctuations in Quantum Noise and even resist the attempts of Hackers to change the reality the Pylons enforced. The Quantum Noise River had never been named, beyond being called… The Quantum River. Super-Creative.

Aetherial Cities lived lifetimes of development in just decades: Instant construction, infinite resources, and the time dilation between the Meatspace and the Aetherium, which caused time to move twelve times faster in the Aetherium than in the Meatspace, resulted in insanely quick growth and just as rapid decline. The Drain was no exception. The area along the river was called The Trench. These were some of the oldest Pylons; they were battered by Quantum Noise, failing power structures, and countless turf battles for control. Damaged Pylons allowed programs to degrade, and the human mind interpreted faulty programs as rust on cars, crumbling buildings, and structural decay; The Trench had become a no-person's land along both banks of the river, a double band on each side a few city blocks deep. On the north side of the river was the Commercial District. People called it The Mall; it was the size of a small open-air city and jam-packed with everything Value could purchase or lease. Nestled in a smaller part of The Mall was a place called the Old Drain; that was where Mal logged in. The Old Drain's Pylons were, as the name implied, old. They had once been the pinnacle of high tech and owned by some of the wealthiest residents, both private and corporate, in The Drain. Most of those people had migrated off to the most distant area of the Drain, though: The Spires. A virtual mountain range of ultra-high-rise buildings and sky cafes, The Spires were a place of luxury and decadence.

At the convergence of the Old Drain, the Mall, and the Spires districts was the Seven-Sided Cube, a club that was the social hub for more than The Drain: it was the center of the social world, especially for powerful Users, across The Aetherium. The Cube served many purposes but the primary one was as a safe place for normally opposing groups to meet without fear of attack, subterfuge, or sabotage. The Seven-Sided Cube was true neutral ground.

South of the river, beyond The Trench, were only two areas: The Grind, which was the name the workers had given the industrial area of the city, and The Burbs, low-cost housing space in the Aetherium adjacent to both the Trench and the Grind. Bordering on both The Burbs and The Grind were

The Docks. Travel in the Aetherium was rare, usually reserved for science vessels, or short-range flyers or hover cars. But the Docks were often home to a few ships willing to make the dangerous trek into the Noise for other, often shadier, reasons.

Spanning the Quantum River were four marvels of Aetherial Engineering: The Bridges. Even though air and hover cars were ubiquitous for the wealthy, nothing could fly near the Quantum Noise River as the interference given off by concentrated Quantum Noise would degrade program vehicles too quickly, and so bridges had been built. Two of them linked The Mall to The Grind. Those roadways were kept relatively safe and well maintained. The third of these was called the Praetorian Bridge and it connected the Old Drain to the Burbs. The fourth bridge was reserved for the residents of The Spires, who almost always flew in their vehicles where they needed to go. The fourth bridge had a single off-ramp for The Grind, for the most upper of managers to come to check on their Cogs once a cycle. Its main purpose was to give The Spire direct access to The Dock.

Mal opened her communications package and pinged her oldest friend, Tok. The result came back with an auto-reply Tok often used. "In the Noise. Back at you soon. Ever onward." Mal sighed. She had been in the Meatspace preparing for the mission for three days, which meant that in the Aetherium about a month had passed. Tok was captain of a RezX Noise Ship. It was one of the few ships able to spend any considerable time in the Quantum Noise. She was completely brilliant and full of enough hope and good energy for a dozen people. Mal had not seen her since Valcor Six, a small Aetherial Outpost where she had had a quick mission three Aetherial months ago. Mal did not leave a message, knowing that the ping would stay registered until Tok made it back to civilization.

As Mal traveled from the Old Drain and towards the Mall, the Pylons became newer, more well maintained. The schema, or area hosted by a Pylon or set of linked Pylons, was modest and hectic; collections of little business and restaurants, mostly stalls and carts. There were no vehicles on the road, which was teeming instead with people, their bodies anywhere in the world, their consciousnesses all here in The Drain. Many of the stalls were three or four customers deep into the street and were probably owned by individuals rather than groups. These stalls were rickety and could have been from a holo-vid from the twentieth century, in some Asian city, from before the Monoculture Wars. They were smaller and more frail than corporate-owned stores, but the thing that really set them apart was that those hawking their wares were Patches: real people logged in through a rig. Most of the large, shiny megastores, those selling the wares of the thousands of subsidiaries of the Collectives, were self-serve kiosks with consoles built into the displays to allow instant purchase, customization, and delivery to a consumer's rig. Mal pressed past dozens of people all heading to their own destinations with urgency, and what Mal guessed most people would see as chaos. But crowds had always been easy for her. Not to join, but to read, to feel the ebb and flow. The entire area was hung with the black vertical banners of Axiom, the familiar orange crossed keys on a solid black field.

Mal continued down the street, looking for a good, wide alley between buildings. She had to find the limits of this Rig and the capacity it had to support her level of hacking. When she found an alley between a Pacific Rim eggroll shop and a little toy store, she entered it and climbed the fire escape a few floors to the roof of the restaurant. The rooftops were empty; a few buildings away, she could make out some kind of clandestine meeting taking place, complete with furtive glances and lurking in shadows. She could see the jagged outline of The Spire, several miles to the North, but here in the Mall, the buildings were only three or four stories high. This looks safe. Safe-ish. Safe enough. She looked down at the street below and lined the toes of her boots up with the edge of the building. She thought hard about her wings, the pure freedom of flying. She called up the program that gave her wings. She felt them stretch out from her shoulder blades, flat semi-transparent blue panels, felt the warmth of the reinforcement code she'd built into them, and tingled as the mods for speed kicked in. She leapt.

And fell. Mal lost connection with her wings entirely and was left scrambling in the air for a moment before a terrifying plunge to the street below. The wing program Mal was used to using had grown very complex with all her modifications; this lesser Rig was clearly not prepared to run a program that complex smoothly. Or at all. The program had failed utterly, and her wings had derezzed. Mal slammed into the pavement. Her entire body was jarred by the impact and the disruption of the connection of her consciousness to her body left in the clutches of painful, scary, Glitch. Blue energy arced through her body, stinging like a thousand tiny bites. Glitch was the dissonance between the Pylons and the conscious mind; after a mistake or a failure in the Aetherium, that Glitch could burn a person's very consciousness, causing damage to the connection, the rig, or in the worst cases, the mind. Mal deactivated her failed wings and forced herself to her feet, shaking and twitching as the Glitch ran its course. Even after the lightning stopped, Mal could feel the Glitch burning in her, a short between her and the Pylon's reality trying to reach her. Mal steadied herself against the wall of the building and pulled her hoodie up over her head with her other hand. I am so fragged. Desperately hoping she had not been seen, she started walking, trying to shake the feeling that, at least for now, she was not in sync with the reality of the Aetherium.

》 **Chapter Two:** Drain 《

There was a tentative knock on her door the next night. When she opened it, Trent was already walking back to his Unit. Luckily, the Glitch from the previous night had diminished to little more than a headache.

"Trent?"

He turned around too quickly, almost spilling whatever was in the two tin mugs he was holding. "Thought you could use a drink."

"That's not…"

He grinned. "It is. Dad's old still. It keeps breaking down, but I manage to get it back up and running every time."

Mal opened her door wider. "Come in."

He paused for a moment and then entered, offering Mal a mug of clear liquid. Trent's dad's still was built in the non-functional cooling device in their unit. It had been an endless source of fascination for Trent and Mal, who as children, had snuck drinks from it one ill-advised afternoon and spent the next night sicker than they had ever been.

Mal took a tentative sip from the mug as she and Trent sat down. She winced and laughed. "It's like if burning had a flavor."

Trent laughed. "And this is after I improved it."

They sat in companiable silence for a while.

Trent had to ruin it with talking. "So, what's the story, Malven? I'm sorry, Mal?"

"Not much of a story. Academy, then job. Moved around a lot."

"More of a story than me. I never moved."

"Is your dad…"

"Still alive, believe it or not. You'll have to come say hello. He doesn't leave the Unit much these days." Silence fell, uneasily this time. "I was really sorry about your dad, Mal. He was great."

"That part of the factory is still just… burned out, hollow. They didn't even finish tearing it down."

"It wasn't cost effective to rebuild, I guess, so they just gave up clearing it away. It seems to collapse a little more every day. Three hundred and seven souls."

Mal's eyes went to the bedroom door that had so far remained closed. "Trent, I think we should drink as much of this as our bodies will allow."

He leaned over and clinked his mug into hers.

〉〉‧‧‧‧‧‧《《

The next morning, Mal strapped herself into her chair and ran a thorough diagnostic and login. After connecting to the rig, she closed the contacts on the board and blinked. When she opened her eyes she was standing in a white space with black lines a meter apart forming a grid on floor, ceiling, and walls. She was in her rig's white room. The console, the Aetherial representation of her Rig, was the only object in the room. White rooms were where most Users did any coding, changing of settings, or accessing parts of the Rig they needed to do. Mal preferred to code within the Aetherium, which required using a console in the Aetherium, running off a Pylon. Her cover persona would not have been wealthy enough to own a Pylon-based Console, and so she was stuck with the white room.

Mal stripped out most of her progs, opening up some storage slots to improve the function of the progs she really needed. She kept the essentials: wings, sword, knife, Heads-Up-Display, basic Comms package, simple first aid. She could always pick new progs up in the Aetherium; they would not work as well as the ones stored in her rig, but they would do in an emergency. The current emergency, though, was that she needed to be able to fly.

With everything set, Mal thought the final command: Login.

Rezzing into the Aetherium from a white room was a slower process than jumping straight in. Mal could feel the core programming of her Rig interfacing with her mind to create an image of herself. The cosmetic programs for clothing, hair styling, and physical form loaded in first in wireframe transparency and became more real as she materialized. As she stepped fully into resolution, she saw others doing the same. She took a swift moment to appreciate the feeling of being in her right body, and back in her candy-red boots, a long, silk coat that rippled out behind her in the breeze, jeans and a white tank top, her hair loose and full and falling to her shoulders. She stopped where she was and took and released a huge breath. Here, in a woman's body, she could breathe all the way in. She smiled to herself. She was in the subway station, in a large matte-grey tiled area.

The Drain was a busy city; at any given moment, dozens of Patches were using each Access Point Pylon. In the Drain, these were almost all public transportation terminals. Mal worked her way through the people coming down the stairs to logout and got to street level. Her red-painted nails glimmering as trailed her hand along the wall as she went up the stairs. She had chosen to login where she had because of its proximity to Ming's House of Noodles. She needed to get some work done, and Ming's was the place to do it. Eating was of course not necessary for Aetherial bodies, but it was a social act, and gave reason for groups to gather. It was also pleasurable; it would be nice to remember a bowl of Ming's later, in the Meatspace, eating her protein paste.

An hour later, her eyes watering from the spice levels of the Death Angel Noodles, Mal was thinking through the first real steps in her plan. She let the steam from her bowl bathe her face as she thought. She needed to create a persona who hated Axiom. Trouble was, there isn't much an ordinary Citizen could do to express those feelings. The Collective controlled all forms of media in cities it controlled, to avoid the spread of misinformation or divisive content. Vid screens in public and home spaces offered a steady and reliable stream of information and news direct from Axiom. Holopics and other entertainment media were all Axiom-approved. It was common for Users to create fliers and hand them out to crowds, and there was always that one crazy person yelling at the street corner, but neither of these possibilities would exactly set the right tone. But her stupid, Axiom-hating persona needed to get her message out.

Mal took another huge bite of noodles and looked out the window. Of course.

Across the street, a kid was using spray-paint to deface a building. He was spraying a blue skull with red eyes and under it a string of numbers. The numbers probably referred to his score in the I-EX games. Mal wiped the noodle-induced tears from her eyes. It was time to make something new. She began by coding a simple wire-wrapped cylinder; once it appeared in her hand, she created new strings of code and wrapped them around and through it. She sat in her back corner for most of the afternoon, ordering more noodles, surrounded by glowing green and blue symbols in long, twisting strings like digital double helixes. She wrapped them into the can, building the Core and mods; she built in back doors to make the code more malleable to her hacking. When she was done, she had a can of spray paint.

She left Ming's and scanned the area. If she hated Axiom.... It was difficult to even think about. There was a reason anti-Axiom sentiment was rare, and why Nanomei was a disorganized and understaffed nuisance. Axiom protected people by maintaining what was left of civilization; in a dying world, Axiom kept people alive. Mal knew she could not immerse herself in the role she needed to play. Whether that meant she would blow this mission remained to be seen. Kass, your mission had better be as hard as this one. I guess you, too, Dek. Whatever.

There was an Axiom Supply Center down the street. The whole point of a Supply Center was to distribute needed materials. Who could hate Axiom for that? Mal needed to start somewhere, though, so she pulled up her hood and ducked between the Supply Center and pan dulce stand next to it, which was closed for the day. She stared at the wall of the Supply Center. Do the job. She raised her hand far above her head and sprayed the outline of her own pulled-up hood. The slick black paint adhered easily to the concrete wall. She traced the side of her hoodie downward and drew the outline of her skinny jeans, legs in what she hoped looked like an imposing stance. She did all this work in black, adding at last her arms and hands out at her sides. She let the paint set in a realistic manner, soaking into the wall and binding there. Then she added wings, spread out from behind the black silhouette, larger than they were in life, and Quantum Noise blue. This paint she let pull from the wall and hover, making the wings sway and swell slowly. Lastly, she put a golden key in each of her hands, representing the crossed keys of Axiom, then signed her work: Death Angel.

Swallowing her Axiom pride, Mal marked up a trail through the city moving from the Trench and out, away from the river, into the Old Drain. Mal stepped back to admire her work. Or be horrified at it. As she sprayed, she hacked the paint program and the can helped provide a stable conduit to the Pylon's basic refresh matrix. Mal had always found hacking, the ability to create, destroy, or modify existing programs in the Aetherium without the long process of coding, to come naturally, even joyfully for her. It was even easier when she had built the original program, in this case the can, she was hacking. The end result was a can of spray paint that, in her hands, could be used to make really lasting marks. That would have been the end of it if she had been content to let the paint fade when the Pylon refreshed. Instead, Mal placed her palm on her own image and felt the code of the concrete and the code of the paint. Pressed her palm through both. She could feel her hand take on the qualities of both and started to weave them together. The code of the paint was made for this, for the hack she was performing. It was an effort of will, intense and almost painful. They Pylon was strong, and pushed back, hard, but as she pulled away her hand, she knew the image would last. If Axiom shut down the Pylon that the location was on and rebooted it, it would clear, but shutting down Pylons was expensive and dangerous. Eventually the code would fail against the unrelenting pulse of the Pylon's reality, which did not include her vandalism. But until then, her artwork would remain visible. This would be impressive. Hacking like this was rare. Come find me, Nanomei.

〉〉 • • • • • 〈〈

A few nights later, Mal printed a report from her Rig onto a tiny chip which she wrapped in a sheet of static plastic and carried with her in a twisting path through the Pod. Just a few empty doors down from the Rig Parlor, in the darkness between two buildings, was an old tube, the kind that was once used to send messages among buildings. Mal pulled the chip from her pocket and inserted it in the tube and closed it. After a moment of waiting, she could hear the chip get sucked away. She started to walk away but found herself needing to open the tube and peek into it just to be sure the chip had really gone. This felt archaic. But if Nanomei was really focused so heavily on The Drain right now then sending messages from her cover-Rig could certainly be more of a risk than a dead drop in Keral. She walked away from the dead drop and along a meandering path through the Pod, letting her thoughts wander with her. Unlike some Agents, Mal had never bought into the idea of hating the enemy. Axiom provided a bulwark against a dying world and demanded only obedience and loyalty. Axiom functioned like a machine and served the citizens and kept peace and safety and productivity going against all odds. Nanomei threatened to change those odds for the worse. Mal saw them more as a sort of cult of chaos. The sorts of people who did not only want to watch the world burn but wanted to douse it in fuel first. And light the match. And then dance as everything went up in flames. It was her job to stop them. It was that simple. Mal was turning for home when a ground car pulled up and the rear passenger door opened. Sitting in the back seat… Mal caught her breath. It was Kass, her super-bright red hair flowing down her back like water, framing her face and her angular eyes, which were brimming with laughter. She loved surprising people. Mal looked around the street and ducked into the car.

The air in the car was conditioned and cool and the seat was soft.

"Kass, what is this?"

"Drive," Kass said to the Operative behind the wheel. The car went smoothly into motion and they were driven in a seemingly random pattern through the Pod.

"Kass…"

"I'm not supposed to be here. I'm not here."

"Okay." Mal wanted to grab Kass and pull her into a hug. She quashed that feeling, assuming that in ten minutes she would want to shove Kass from the moving car instead.

"You know I'm on a mission."

"So am I. So is Dek."

"Who cares about Dek? I thought I'd come give you a little help with your assignment. This isn't exactly your area of expertise. Don't they usually just have you hacking things until they go away?"

"I can do other work. I can do a sleeper mission."

"Sure you can," Kass said, laughing. "I want to help. You'll never get this done without a little extra push."

There it is. "I don't need anything from you." Even as she said it, Mal heard the doubt creep into her own voice.

Kass leaned forward, and suddenly all Mal could smell was flowers. "Ramos is the key."

"That's wonderful for Ramos."

"Dammit, Mal." Kass had a habit of saying angry words without looking or sounding angry. It was adorable and irritating. "Don't turn down free information because of your silly pride." Kass slid across space between them, from her seat to Mal's. "You know Namomei has no command structure, no organization. But what we'd call field commanders rise and fall, charismatic cults of personality rising up and flashing out of existence just as fast. Ramos is on the rise. And he's coming to The Drain. He's intense. He has big plans. He could use you."

"Cover story me, you mean."

Kass reached an arm out to Mal, leaning closer, until Mal could feel Kass' breath in a cloud against her face. "Kass…"

Kass pressed a button on the side of the car behind her, and the Operative's voice echoed through the comms. "Agent Durand?"

"Pull over." She smirked at Mal, who scrambled internally to appear casual. "It's Ramos, Mal. Find Ramos."

Mal slammed the car door on the way out and walked away without looking back.

〉〉 • • • • • • 〈〈

Mal logged in the next day and started her day by checking on her tags. Most were still intact. Some had people nearby talking about them. The tone wasn't kind. "What sort of scum would do this?" one man was saying, wildly gesticulating at the winged icon behind him to general noises of approval from a handful of gathered Citizens. Another tag had drawn a little crowd, who were waiting around it tensely, presumably until it could be taken down. At other locations the paint had already been removed, and a few were just quietly existing, their wings slowly pulsing just off the surface where the rest was sprayed. The trail of her tags had Mal her into the Old Drain and the last tag had been placed on an Axiom Civic Center. The tag was in the process of being cleaned off by a cleaning crew using a Pylon Interface Tool to remove the image by scraping the wall down to its base code. Chunks of plasticrete were sloughing off and clattering to the sidewalk.

Mal went to see Mollo, a data trader and overall waste of a person. He'd sell any bit of info on anyone to anyone. His place was a dusty old art gallery in the Trench. Mal had seen archival footage of this gallery in its glory days, when it sold actual art. This place had been famous for a while, fancy, sought-after. But the art ran out, or the luck did, and now Mollo sat in an empty building, its walls covered not in art but in small brown packages with encrypted labels written in slap-dash black marker. Mollo's art was secrets now, which was much more dangerous.

"Now that's a face I haven't seen in a rat's age," Mollo said as Mal entered. He'd let himself go. His skin program had Glitch tracing itself through his thick, greying hair and his deeply olive skin was marked with scars. This would take a simple logout at a Pylon to fix.

"How long have you been connected?" Mal asked as a greeting.

"I moved up in the world. Got a full- time nurse. She keeps me plugged in 24-7."

"That's not a good idea," Mal said, though she was a bit jealous. Not having to ever log out sounded nice, but without someone you really trusted to take care of your body it was extremely dangerous, even aside from the threat of Glitch.

"What are you looking for here?" Mollo asked. "Don't pretend you're here to chat with Mollo." He settled back into his "throne," as he was wont to call his ornate chair, made of actual wood, and red, faded, velvet. He could have sold that thing, the last piece of art in his store, for a pile of Value, but he refused to.

"A man."

"Lucky fella. But I thought you were more into the women," Mollo said.

"You know I don't care, Mollo, as long as they're pretty. But this is business. I need to find a Nanomei named Ramos."

"Never heard of him," Mollo said.

"Of course you have. If you decide to admit it, contact me. I'll make good," Mal said holding out her fist. In the Aetherium, a quick touch of hands with the intention of sharing contact info was a simple program hardwired into all rigs. Mollo lazily brought his fist up and the deal was set.

Mal walked out into the street and received a ping from Tok.

"You're finally back in?" Tok asked.

"You too?"

"Okay, I was gone for three Aetherial Days. You've been gone a month!"

"Who's counting?" Mal said. I am.

"I see you're in the Drain. I'm going to be there in a day or two. Maybe our schedules will line up? We could meet up at the Cube."

"I'd like that," Mal said honestly.

〉〉 • • • • • 〈〈

Trent caught Mal that day as she returned to the building and picked up her package of nutrient paste and energy bars from the entryway. Trent was replacing the lock on a door and looked up, grinning, as Mal approached.

"Hey Mal," he said.

"Hey Trent," Mal replied.

The delivery had come in a single, grey Axiom package, the kind used to deliver pretty much everything in Keral and across Axiom-controlled territories. It was a biodegradable package that had the Axiom crossed keys printed much larger than the addressee's name and housing code.

"Direct delivery. That's nice. Does every code smoother get that?" Trent asked.

"I don't know, honestly," Mal replied. "Probably. It's efficient. Gives us more time for work."

"Probably a tough job, though."

"It's not. I just wander around and eliminate stutters in the code. Anything that could cause Glitch, or just isn't running efficiently. It lets me walk around in the Aetherium and get paid for it." Huh. I just said something true.

"Well, having a job where you spend so much time inside must be great," he said, his voice trailing off.

You have no idea. "How was your day?"

"Did a few repairs. Did an intake interview for a family moving in."

"Trent?"

"Yeah, Mal?"

Do you want to come in for a chat? Say it, Mal. Memories stretched out between them like lights on a string. "Nothing. Forget it. Have a good one." Feeling like a coward, Mal went into her Unit and closed the door behind her.

>> ····· <<

Mal decided to log into the Aetherium and spend a night in one of The Drain's shopping districts within The Mall; there was a Prog-Store-Safe location there at which Ramos had been seen, at least according to the rumors skittering around The Drain. If she couldn't get him to find her, perhaps she could find him. She appeared in the Aetherium wearing dark leather pants, her red combat boots, and a sheer blouse. Her hair was piled on her head in a tall ponytail that bounced around when she moved. The streets were dark; this area was lit for perpetual midnight, with neon signs and continually rain-slicked concrete. Mal closed her eyes and breathed it in. The night was humming. People passed her, stopping to scan the vendors' shops or dart across streets, their voices joining together into one murmur that hung around her in the air. Mal smiled, and merged effortlessly into the crowd, riding it to the

Prog-Store-Safe. The shop was shallow, only about twenty feet deep from the entry to the rear and the front of the place was all glass. The three walls were lit white plastic and all along the walls at varying heights were small doors, each a mini storage unit to slot Progs.

Mal stood outside the shop for a time, watching the crowd. No, not just watching the crowd; she attuned herself to it. She could feel a rhythm to it, a pattern. What do you feel when you walk these streets, Ramos? She felt a surge of frustration. Where are you?

"Frag this!" She had said it aloud, but it was barely marked by the people around her. Mal stomped off; she went deeper into the shopping area. In this area, the smaller shops and eateries thrived and hummed in the night. Mal passed a vendor selling motorcycles, six of them set out to touch and feel with a hundred more in boxed form: rectangles showing holograms in miniature. She passed dueling vendors, across the narrow street from each other, both claiming to sell the best shower programs in all the Aetherium. The one on her left was showing a waterfall complete with tropical bird song while the other was hawking one that sprayed the recipient with water from every conceivable angle. Since everything in the Aetherium is a program, all artisans, craftspeople, and builders were really programmers. The good ones tended to specialize and some of the great programmers out there, some of the best coders, were known for their perfect iteration of a certain item. The price of these programs supported the industry of creators and artisans who have expertise that cannot be replicated by an AI.

On one corner a man wearing what looked like a pile of filthy rags stood on a bench, yelling. "The world is the lie! Here we are real. The Meatspace is destroying us!" Nobody was listening. Mal watched the man for a time. He looked blind; his eyes were pure white. She wondered if that was natural, part of him, or if his Rig was Glitching out. Passersby ignored him; there were so many other Patches to push past, so many vendors to see: food vendors, clothing vendors, bars, cafes, experience vendors… Would causing disorder here get some Nanomei attention? What did Ramos want in a recruit? Should she light something on fire? She needed to break through to them somehow. You guys like fire, right?

Turning a corner and dodging a vendor hawking grass programs ready to code into a customer's homespace, she almost crashed into a Patch, who shoved a flier into her hands and pushed past her to get to other Users. It was printed on bright blue nanostock with giant block letters: "BattleDome, Dedicated Gaming Pylon. The Battle is real: The damage is not." She walked towards the Dome's address and found the streets getting more and more crowded. Ahead was a parade of some sort, a celebration of some sliver of culture remembered from the long-ago time when different civilizations and nations existed, before the Monoculture Wars.

She pressed forward and through the crowd. Ahead were a couple dozen people dancing, strange glowing strings trailing from their bodies, neon paint smeared across their skin. Some were definitely male, and some female, and some were both or neither. Their skins were a dizzying array of colors; in the Aetherium, those with the abilities to change their own code, or willing to pay a good skinner, could make real changes to a User's appearance. Skinners were a specialized type of programmer who can modify the physical appearances Users present in the Aetherium. Programs could easily change surface appearances, but they were akin to changing clothes: a quick change that doesn't go very deep. Skinners work more slowly, connect with their client's base self-image as a place to start, and get creative from there. Some of the Users in this crowd had gotten very creative indeed.

The music was throbbing, deep bass and chaotic flights of whimsical chirping noises. As the dancers surged forward, they offered Users in the crowd a small candy in an outstretched palm. As people accepted and ate the brightly colored candies, they too started smiling and dancing. The parade gathered a few more followers, welcoming them with glowing necklaces or other trinkets. A gracefully moving dancer stretched out their open palm to Mal, a bright pink bit of sweetness offered up. They continued to move, bend, and twist the rest of their body in time to the music while keeping their palm steadily stretched out to her. Hesitatingly, Mal took the candy. Maybe it was not about burning anything down. Maybe she needed to embrace some chaos. What would you do, Ramos? Mal popped the candy into her mouth.

The sweetness filled her mouth and then warmed her whole body. She felt... lighter. She could feel the beat of the music in her veins, and her body felt a command from the song that she could not ignore. The coding of mind-altering substances was a favorite pastime of many amateur coders, but this was professionally done. The dancer who had given her the candy was in front of her, and Mal copied their movements at first; the rational part of her brain watched what she was doing in surprise, but the rest of her did not care. She felt a rush of relief at that realization and let herself dive deeper into the music.

As she danced, she felt herself pull her consciousness together, building up to exert her own will on the local Pylons. Gravity itself was her target. She held the truth that gravity was not a real thing here, that the only thing keeping an idea like gravity functioning was that the collective belief of so many minds made it so. And her mind was going to convince gravity that they were just wrong. This was deep hacking: changing the rules that so many believed to be true. The revelers all around her noticed and started to move in great leaps, gravity holding them down less and less. Soon they were all dancing and moving through the air. As she joined them Mal felt herself rise up as if dancing up a flight of nonexistent stairs. She flipped backwards then and let herself float down slowly. Letting herself give in to the moment felt amazing, like slipping into a warm sonic bath and just letting the meter run. Like a hack that clicks into place as if it were the only way the code would fit. The other dancers were testing their new circumstances too and clearly loving it. She got a few appreciative looks as they floated and then the one who gave her the candy soared over to her and pressed their lips against Mal's. They both laughed as they kissed, and the dancer breathed words into Mal's mouth.

"Thank you. You're magic." Filled with a sweetness and fire, Mal and the dancer kissed again once more, pressing harder this time, more urgently. Then the dancer laughed and leapt into the air. Mal started to follow, flinging herself completely free from gravity, but the part of her that remembered the job suddenly reasserted itself, like cold water dousing a fire in her mind. She settled her feet back on the ground. She knew this wasn't the way. Altering her mind was not some magic answer to finding Ramos. This isn't the job, Mal. Do the job.

›› • • • • • ‹‹

The next morning, there was a quiet thudding outside her door. Her first thought was that it was little Gibson, so she went to the door and opened it fast. "Boo!" she said.

A man fell backwards into her apartment. He must have been sitting outside banging the back of his head on her door.

"Whoa there," he said, laying on his back in her entryway. His white skin was sallow and unhealthy-looking, and his longish brown hair was greasy. His eyes were desperate.

"What the hell?"

"I'm Karl," he said, as though that explained everything. After a moment, she realized it did: Trent had warned her about Karl. He was spun; unable to get back into the Aetherium, unable to function in the Meatspace. It wasn't rare, especially among the poor. Axiom had tried to deal with the issue: rehabilitation centers, new Rig technology, drug therapies. But the problem worsened. Access was necessary but also expensive. And loyalty only buys so much.

Mal intended to get him out fast but as she knelt down, he started to cry. Big, fat tears. He was hugging himself on her floor, crying.

Mal felt... uncomfortable. Kneeling down she patted him awkwardly on the shoulder.

"Whatever it is, it'll be okay," she said.

"I just need to get in. I haven't been in in so long," he sobbed.

She stood and walked over to her sink. She poured water into one of her two cups and dropped in a sleep tab.

"Here," she said, helping him sit up. "Drink this. It'll help you calm down. Let me get you to your place," she said.

"You're nice," he said.

"No, I'm not. I'm kicking you out," she said.

"But you gave me water," he said. He sounded like a child. She walked him down the hall until he gestured at a Unit. "This one's mine." The door was ajar.

"Are you going to be okay?" she asked.

"Please don't tell Trent I bothered you. I'm not supposed to bother you," he said. Mal closed the door to his Unit.

Once she was back in her Unit, she stood for a moment outside her bedroom and touched for the other door leading out of the living room. She went in. Her parents' bed was the largest thing in the room, along with a large storage shelf empty now, but where once her parents had kept their meager belongings. She went around the bed, and to the far side of the room. There in the corner was a much smaller bed. She knelt down there. The blanket was the same, and the thin pillow with a yellow sun stitched into it. Mal touched the wall just above the small bed where other planets had been painted in now faded colors.

Mal shook herself back to the present and almost ran from the room, slamming the door behind her. She threw herself into her chair. She didn't wait for the white room, just logged back into the Drain. She wore her black, shorter combat boots, black tights, and black shorts, with a snug black shirt. Her hair was up in two huge ponytails and was bright pink. Ready for action.

The entrance to BattleDome was much like other Schema entrances, more an advertisement than anything else. In a world where everything was a program, most exteriors were little more than a skin or a facade. Entering through a thick metal door was little different than walking through an archway. Often the design of a building matched up with the durability of the Pylon: powerful Pylons tended to have their buildings dressed up as steel, stone, or plasticrete. Weaker Pylons may look like wood or even fabric. This one was designed to look as though she was entering an arena made of huge pieces of rock and wood. Several signs were posted at random intervals along the walls: Specials, deals, features. One of the signs read "NO NANOMEI" in bright orange letters. That was impossible to enforce, of course, more of a political statement than anything; the sign was there as a message to everyone that this place was loyal to Axiom.

Entering the Schema brought Mal to a large, clean lobby full of huge screens showing some of the action going on in the games. There were other boards tracking bets being placed on the results of different battles. The numbers flashed and changed in real time, so fast she could barely understand what was happening. A huge greeting station dominated the far wall, housing a small army of attendants, all wearing neat, blue shirts. A huge red banner hung across the far wall, fluttering in a breeze that wasn't there. Black silhouettes of a huge sword crossed with an automatic rifle adorned the banner under the name Gladiator Games. That name, unaligned as it was pretending to be, was probably bogus. Almost everything in the Aetherium is connected in some way with one of the major Collectives, no matter what they pretended. The workers behind the counter all seemed delighted to see Mal as she approached. She sighed.

"Welcome to BattleDome, citizen!"

"Thanks?"

"Are you interested in entering the Dome?

"Yes. Somewhere I can fly."

"We are having a sale today on entry to any of the advanced combat areas!" Was it her, or was this guy's too-cheerful smile beginning to waver at the corners? "There's a noobsite as well, if you prefer that sort of thing."

"I'll take the advanced area."

"Great! Have you played before?" The crowd around the gambling boards erupted: half were cheering, it seemed, while the other half was booing, cursing, or generally being angry.

"It's been a while. I'm sure I'll remember quickly. It's the same stuff."

"No! Here at BattleDome, the customer is always right! But you are completely wrong in just this one little instance! Advances in this kind of tech occur at blazing speed. In just the last few weeks, we have added the ability to set your level of kinetic feedback and damage! And..."

"The physics still match the Aetherium?"

"Absolutely! Unless you go to one of the special..."

"Where do I sign?"

Walking into the Battle Arena felt different than crossing schemas usually did; more muffled and controlled, probably because of more safety protocols, more surveillance. The weapons she'd been given were contained in a housing program that looked like a tactical vest. That vest held the complexity of these faux weapons so that players' rigs wouldn't be burdened. This sort of thing only worked in these controlled, sealed servers; normally if Mal grabbed a bunch of weapons her Rig would need to handle their code. She strapped on the weapons vest they'd given her, activated her wings, and looked around. She was in a white room, set up as a waiting area where players waited for the game to start. She pulled her most trusted weapon into her hand from nowhere. She frowned and turned the handle over in her palm and it disappeared. More than that, she unloaded it from her memory. It would not be accessible here. Just for a little while, old friend.

There were probably thirty people in the room, some standing alone, some in small groups talking. One particularly irritating group of six was preparing for the game by yelling at each other and crashing their bodies into one another. This was appropriate energy for them; they were here to play. She was here to practice and hopefully improve her relationship with this rig.

The other players were probably all Patches. Some had flight programs, such as jetpacks or rocket boots, or other programs changing their capabilities, like enhanced HUDs, Target Assists, or Appearance Changers, but these, like the guns she'd just rented, would only work here. Their rigs and minds were just not capable of running those programs out in the Aetherium proper: only in this Schema that had a Pylon willing to help with some of the heavy lifting of the code.

The walls around them disappeared. They were standing in a hundred-foot diameter circular area marked off by bright yellow paint in the middle of a broad, open area of grassland. Mal assumed this painted grass indicated a safe zone, a place for players to be sure they were completely logged in and having no technical issues, and where they would reappear after taking enough simulated damage. To the west there was rough terrain, small hills with vertical faces on one side. These would make for good flying practice. There was a ravine to the south with a twinkling stream running through it. To the north was a large, flat, open area. Probably a good place to rack up some quick, early kills. To the east was a tall, abandoned-looking building, at least six stories tall. Mal made up her mind that she would fly to the top of that building before she left this place. That's when she would know she was back. She opened her wings. They arced into form behind and above her. She spread them out to their fullest. She wanted the others to be afraid of her. "Fear is a powerful tool, Cadet," Mullen once told her. He was right. In this context at least. She thought he'd been talking about good instruction techniques. In which case I'm pretty sure you were wrong.

A buzzer sounded, harsh and immediate. A good half of the participants ran north; a large chunk ran for the building. Only three headed for those hills; they ran out of the circle at top speed. They were definitely there as a group, working together, and looking very confident. They were clearly accustomed to winning. Mal flew over and past them, landed in front of them, raised her pistol, and shot twice. Two shots, two blinked-out targets. The third swore and opened up, fully automatic, spraying the area. Like a lot of people shooting while panicking, he aimed too high, looking for a head shot and missing, and then aiming even higher because of kickback from the weapon. She took a quick position on one knee and shot three times. Face, chest, balls. She just needed them gone so she could practice.

The guy blinked away and Mal looked back as oddly gentle chimes sounded, announcing the three players' arrival in the safe zone. Derezzing in the Aetherium usually took time as the mind struggled to keep the connection. But here, in the curated experience of the BattleDome, the mind was shunted instantly back to the safe zone. All three appeared to be swearing at/threatening her, but of course she couldn't hear them through the barrier. She did not engage and anger them further; she leapt into the air, hoping against hope that she wouldn't waver or Glitch. She didn't get much height but still felt stable as she flew low to the ground, and fast. As worked up as they were, she figured they would come after her again, she would take them out again, and then they would leave her alone and go play somewhere else.

She got to the hills, and, skimming the ground, reached the top of one of the taller knolls. She looked back to see the trio, just released from the safe zone, running toward her. One fired a few shots, but the guns didn't have anywhere near that kind of range, so it was more of a symbolic gesture. She had a bit of time. She jumped from the sheer side of the hill and tried to fly up. She ascended about twenty feet before she felt the wings falter and start restoring themselves into storage. She plummeted to the earth. She shoulder-rolled a landing and ran to put more space between her and the three guys gunning for her. Chimes rang out again, indicating that the safe zone had received new players who were faux-derezzing from taking damage; they would have to rest there for a time before rejoining the game.

Mal took some cover and waited for them to blunder closer. She didn't have to wait long. They were exhausting themselves by running at full speed and helpfully yelling to each other about their plans.

She waited for them to pass her and leveled them all; it took four shots. While they were gone, she tried again to launch herself into the air with her usual ease. She was improving slightly, or perhaps not falling down so quickly, when she looked back at the safe zone. It was fairly full, and everyone in there seemed strangely clustered together. As more people derezzed and entered the zone they were being absorbed into the group; this was potentially a problem.

The group rushed out of the zone all at once, and all coming for her. She rezzed a sniper rifle and knelt. Three shots took out three of the group, but the rest were charging her position in the hills. She took out a few more, threw her gun aside, and ran deeper into the hills. Behind her, the group peppered the air with colorful energy blasts.

Mal had not anticipated this coordinated attack. She made her way south through the hills, taking out a few here and there, and suffering a couple of close misses. She was starting to run out of hills, so she looped back. She rounded the base of a hill and almost crashed into a guy wearing a very full assortment of weapons. He was wearing jeans and a tight-fitting camo shirt and looked as shocked as she felt. She blasted him and he popped out, but then a flurry of blasts peppered the air behind her and she caught one in the arm. It stung but didn't really hurt. It was enough to qualify as a hit and she appeared in the safe zone.

Camo shirt guy was already there, of course. He eyed her, appraisingly. "You a pro?"

She laughed. "Hardly."

"You are the coolest girl in here. Wanna team up?"

Girl. It felt so good. Mal laughed out loud. "Absolutely."

Their time in the safe zone was almost up. "Cool! Let's get 'em!"

"Let's go east." She pointed to the building.

"I'll catch up," he said as their timers wound down. Mal burst from the safe zone, raised her wings, and took off. She was getting better acceleration, and better lift, and was reaching for the roof when her wings faltered and her speed dropped out from under her. She stretched herself toward the building, reached out with one hand… and just grabbed the ledge. A few shots hit the near top of the building's wall, close and getting closer as the shooter adjusted their aim. She heaved herself up by one arm. She was on top of the building. "That counts, right?" she muttered. She watched the other players streaming out of the hills. They were coming for her. Mal caught herself grinning.

The battle was long, and she was hit twice more. She did eventually connect with camo shirt guy, who made a great eyes and ears on the ground for her. There were some moments of glory for many of the combatants: the time she took out seven with six shots, the time Morris, a random dude who barely knew how to play, took her out when she'd miscounted the shots remaining on her rented gun, the time where Bella got behind her and attacked with a Ibrahimade, blowing the shit out of Mal and three of her own group in the process.

In the end they jostled together in the lobby, laughing and taunting each other. "Hey," camo shirt guy said. He held out his hand to her. "Contact."

Mal hesitated. "Yea, okay." She bumped her hand awkwardly into his. The crowd burst into a flurry: "Contact." "Contact." As she left, Mal could see herself appearing here and there on some of the betting boards. She left the BattleDome, deleting the contact information as she went.

〉〉 • • • • • 〈〈

That night, Mal saw Gibson sitting in the hall outside of Karl's door. He looked as though he had been crying.

"What's wrong with you?" Mal asked. "Are you injured?"

"I saw Karl. He looks really bad, and my mom said he's burning himself up."

"Yeah. That can happen," Mal said.

"To anyone?"

"No. Not to anyone. Karl has had some bad luck."

"Can anyone have bad luck?" Gibson asked.

Mal hesitated then sat on the floor next to Gibson. "Not this kind. You have people who care about you. They'll keep you safe and make sure everything's okay."

"Karl doesn't have anyone like that?"

"I don't think so," Mal said.

"Do you have people?"

"I do. I have a lot of friends in the Aetherium. And a few outside." Doesn't hurt to lie to make the kid feel better.

"Maybe I shouldn't go into the Aetherium. Magic Land is starting to sound frightening. I don't want to break my brain."

"The Aetherium is a place of magic, though, especially if you have the imagination for it."

"But it can be dangerous. It can mess you up," he said.

"Like Karl."

"Like Karl." Was it her imagination or was he inching closer to her?

"Both worlds have their dangers, Little. But the Aetherium is amazing. Especially when you learn how to really play the game."

"Like you?" You don't want to get any closer.

"Like me. And like you. You'll do great in the Aetherium. I know it."

"Oh! I have something for you. A scary lady gave it to me," Gibson said. "She saw me outside and said you'd be happy it if I gave this to you."

Gibson produced a chip and handed it to Mal who took it gingerly. It was an unmarked memory chip.

"Thanks, kid," She said. She went back to her Rig and went to her white room. It was the safest environment to open a mysterious package delivered by a scary lady.

Accessing the chip gave a series of locations on a map of the Drain. A voice narrated as the blips appeared. "A spelunking-gear shop in the Commercial District. The tool-mod shop at the corner of Algiers and Third. Dumpling food cart on Lake. And at a few parks." Kass. Scary lady, indeed.

〉〉•••••〈〈

Mal stood atop a roof in the Old Drain, looking across towards the glowing Quantum Noise River, fretting about the elements of this assignment that did not add up. How does Kass know my mission? Did Mullen tell her? Why would he tell her about my mission, but not tell me about hers? Can't I just shoot someone and move on to a new assignment?

"Hello," a voice rang out behind her, startling her. She leapt up, and backwards, off the edge of the building and into flight, her wings spreading out behind her. The speaker was a man wearing a long coat. His head was shaved bald and covered in tattoos of moving water. His eyes... Damn. Those are some pretty eyes.

He covered one fist with his other palm and bowed slightly. "I am Nama," he said. "I am very sorry to startle you."

"Mal," She replied, easing forward, and landing lightly on her toes while retracting her wings. She looked at the man narrowly, trying to look aloof and irritated, and not flat-out delighted that her wings had worked so well without her even thinking about them.

"Your wings are a wonder," he said.

"They'd better be all this time I've spent," she said.

"I appreciate a good movement prog," he said. "What Core did you use?"

"They're scratch," she said.

"All you? Wow," he said. He reached into the folds of his coat, dipping his hand out of sight for just a moment, and rezzed two lit cigarettes, then offered one to Mal.

She raised an eyebrow and accepted it, waiting to put it to her lips until she ran a simple scan. It was a well-made little cosmetic prog: no substance, just a minor image. She ran a simple and subtle copy program. No use wasting good coding.

"I saw you flying near the river and followed you here," he said.

"That's not a great conversation starter. Unless you're looking to get stabbed tonight?" Followed? Really, Mal?

"I meant no disrespect. I am sorry that I acted inappropriately."

"Apology provisionally accepted. What do you want?" Mal asked.

"I am a pilot," he said, smiling and taking a drag. "I am a pilot for Ei-en-Tousou Corporate and one of the things I do for them as I travel is some recruiting," he said. Mal recognized the corporate name as part of a lower tier in the House Ikaru web. "I believe you are very talented. I believe I have a way for you to make good use of those talents."

"I'm already making good use of them. I like it out here, pissing off Axiom."

"Why fight a losing war that you don't need to fight? Axiom is inevitable. You could live a life of comfort as a programmer for another Collective. We are always looking for inventors."

"Look. Thanks. But I'm not looking to be recruited. By Ikaru or anyone else." His eyes showed no reaction but the water tattoos flowing across his skin became more turbulent. His (gorgeous, soft) eyes never left hers.

"Well then, are you looking for a race?"

Mal smiled.

〉〉 • • • • • 〈〈

Mal was back at Ming's when Mollo sent her a contact message. She found him as usual in his eternal place of rest and squalor, sprawled in his throne, talking with a well-dressed man. His guest was a Spire type, who had excellent programming on his skin, and held himself in a way that meant he was not used to watching his back. After he left, Mal approached and smiled.

"You never smile," Mollo said. "That was upsetting."

"I smile when you're about to give me something," Mal replied.

"You were asking about Ramos."

"I was. I know he's in the area,"

"Yes. And he has a chip on his shoulder."

"What? You get chips in your head…" Mal said.

"It's an old expression. Don't know where it came from. Means he has a bug up his ass."

"A bug? Where?" Mal said.

Mollo smiled, silkily, and leaned back in his throne. "Do you want the information or not?"

Mal bowed slightly. "My apologies, highness. Now, spill."

"I got nothing on Ramos."

Mal waited. The rest was coming, once the dramatic pause was…

"He popped up in a different search. I was working up a file on the Gorgon."

"The… Gorgon? Why?" As soon as she had said the words she realized her mistake.

"You want to know?"

"No. No. I can't afford extra information."

"I thought so. So… the Gorgon."

"Tell me," She said.

"And you will give me what?"

"What do you want?"

Mollo used the pyramid he was making as an excuse for a very long, very dramatic pause. He laced his fingers together into a pyramid.

"I've always admired your sword," he said.

Mal laughed and rezed the handle into her hand. "It's yours if the intel is good." Making copies of programs is hard, almost impossible. This blade, though, was slotted directly into her rig. She'd be able to rebuild the same blade the next time she logged in because she had the source code for it; she'd written the source code.

"So, your Ramos is elusive. Truly elusive. Almost invisible. I was about to give up. But then, there he was. Big as day in the Gorgon's file. There's blood there. Bad, bad, blood."

43

"Really."

"If you need to flush out Ramos, get the Praetorian on the board. Vice versa would work, too."

Mal handed the handle to Mollo and smiled again. If this had been a program purchased, she'd have to buy it again from a vendor but since it was her own scratch code, she'd be able to upload a copy the next time she was logged out and at her Rig. It was a tiny price to pay for useful information.

Mal activated her wings and leapt into flight. She needed to think. The Gorgon was a legend among the Axiom. Though the origins of his name were lost to time he used an image of a woman's head with hair made of snakes to brand himself. That brand meant steadfastness, and a hard line against the enemies of Axiom so it was no surprise that he and Ramos would hate each other. She flew through the Old Drain south, to The Trench, to the edge of the river. It was beautiful. And terrifying. The Quantum Noise was liquid lightning blue and pure, flowing like water, lighting the sky. She looked to her left and saw in the distance the three great bridges spanning the river. The fourth was well beyond those and she could just barely make out the lights from it in the far distance.

She soared over the Praetorian Bridge, careful to stay directly above it. Straying too close to the edge could cause a flyer to be hit with the interference from the Quantum River below, causing Glitch or degrading programs. The bridges were huge: wide enough to hold two lanes of traffic each way plus pedestrians in the median. They were also well lit, and from above looked like four pillars of strength across the dangerous blue glow of the Quantum Noise below. The bridges were a monument to Axiom, to its strength, its ability to protect its citizens from the Noise. She hovered over the fourth one, watching. Those bridges were forever.

She landed along the Riverwalk and walked along it. She had to jump over a few breaks that dropped into the pooling Quantum Noise below. The shattered and broken area she walked through was devoid of most people and she felt she could move freely. She had known, she had always known, it would come to this. That she would have to do something that would hurt Axiom. Hurt her. Now that she was here…

Do the job, Mal. She started, as she approached the first bridge, to think about explosives. Everything she knew about explosives. She started with chemical compounds and physics. She called to her mind the implied power in a bomb that has not yet exploded, the potential energy stored there. The poetry of the perfect chain reaction. Mal was building code and integrating it into the bridge through hacking. Hacking was never a science: it was art, and she was writing a love song to explosives.

Mal lived that song for three Aetherium days, which was about six Meatspace hours. She stayed at the base of the first support for the bridge.

She was building code and shaping it to the bridge support itself, hacking cracks into the bridge and filling those cracks with more explosive code. This big of a coding challenge, alone in a chair for this long, was a risk. She dared not logout though, as the program would not fit into her Rig with her Wings and Sword there already; she just didn't have the slots to hold it. So she remained logged in. This was not ideal. Every time she slipped in her hacking or had to compensate for an unforeseen bit of defensive code from the bridge, she took a sliver of Glitch. She was pushing herself to the edge of her ability, holding too many complex strands of code at once Glitch crackling through her form. She couldn't activate any sort of program for relief, couldn't go to a Pylon to bleed off the Glitch. She felt untethered, like her mind was barely present in the Aetherium, like she was unable to focus completely on the reality she needed to.

She had crafted enough malleable explosive paste to bring down the support. It would not bring the whole bridge down, but it would destabilize it and it would need to be rebuilt. She was not interested in killing a bunch of people by dumping them into the Quantum River.

After the explosives were set in a grey, sticky mass all around the support, Mal moved to a safe distance and waited for the cycle to change today. She wanted to get people walking or driving from the Burb on the south side of the river to the Mall on the north. And she wanted them to be terrified. If enough people were afraid after this attack, if Axiom were furious enough at the destruction, Mal just might get the Gorgon on the board. She decided that this next task, unlike every other thing she'd done, would not be included in her dead drop. This would need to illicit a genuine response from Axiom, not a scripted one. A wave of queasy guilt hit her at that thought: disobeying a direct order.

She brought her senses into contact with the code of the supports, seeing the code as it really was, not the skinned overlay that most people saw; it looked like the sturdy wireframe of the support with her own code crawling up the sided and burying itself in the cracks she had hacked into the form. This was more difficult than normal through the Glitch she was suffering. This was the core of hacking something that existed as such a solid, well-known object as this bridge. The bridge was even more real because all the citizens of The Drain knew that there were four sturdy bridges and they relied upon them. One mind against the belief of all the inhabitant of The Drain. One tiny voice against the chorus. She wove the code of the bomb into the code of the support, not just layered on top, but infiltrated the very code of the bridge with the explosive. She was turning the bridge into the bomb.

She positioned herself a block away on a nearly empty street where she could no longer see the explosives. It was hard for her to walk away from the bridge; she had created such a connection to it that she was drawn back to it, like gravity. But the code was still visible in her mind. She felt it ready to explode, ready to bring the support crashing down. She felt herself ready to explode, too. The bomb was everywhere through her mind. She felt connected at a deep level to the bridge, to the bomb, to the swirling dizziness she couldn't shake. There were a few dozen people walking her and a handful of ground transports. The line between Mal and bridge and bomb was falling away. She threw the explosives into action.

The iron beneath the plasticrete erupted outward, and the whole support exploded, up from the base all the way to the bridge. Mal fell to her knees and screamed. Glitch poured off of her, uncontrolled, shredding her Sync, tearing at her mind. The Glitch coursing through Mal was causing this to go all wrong, threatening a complete loss of control of the explosion. The rumble shook everything. Half of the Pylons in the Trench for several blocks winked out and Mal saw gridlines and blank, featureless space appear as they did. The bridge held but when the support blew the portion of the bridge closest to the shore slammed downward, crushing several buildings it landed on, making a large, steep ramp up to the rest of the still standing bridge. The ramp did not hold. Everything shuddered as the weight of ramp pushed the still-standing parts of the bridge beyond their capacity. Then the whole bridge collapsed in a violent series of explosions, twisted metal and plasticrete, until all that remained were a few dozen people flailing in the Quantum Noise of the river and dying their digital deaths. Nothing at all was left of the bridge. Nothing in the river, nothing in her. She felt a great emptiness where the bridge and the bomb had been part of her.

Mal heard screaming all around her. Users were pushing past each other, into each other; some were trying to see what had happened, others were trying to get as far away as they could. Horror was uniform on their faces. Axiom support vehicles sounded their wailing sirens but could not drive through the crowds. Users started logging out in a panic; alerts of terminals reaching logout capacity were broadcast on public information screens. Fly. Mal, FLY. Mal activated her wings and flew with all speed, just grazing the street level of the Trench. She scraped herself badly, tumbling through the air. She crashed and took off again, stumbling, running, flying in a mad dash to get out. She had to get to the subway station. She tried to take a deep breath but it felt as though her lungs were concrete. Her vision began to blur. She scrambled down the subway stairs and to the access point station. Logout.

〉〉 • • • • • 〈〈

As Mal logged out her senses came to her Meatspace body in a jolt. She struggled with the strap on her chair before falling out of it to her knees, vomiting. She let herself lay back on the floor and kept her eyes closed. She lay there for only a few minutes. One minute is twelve, Agent. She regained her feet and didn't bother to clean the floor. She went to the kitchen, drank water from the tap and spit into the sink. She took a few desperate bites of an energy bar, quietly hoping that they would stay down. She could have slept for days but had no more time to waste in the Meat. She stepped into her chair and logged back in as fast as she could.

Pylons tracked their logins and logouts and became a matter of record. Mal's training and gear allowed a way around this as long as she was not transporting Pylon programs. This meant logging out and then back in was for Mal like resetting herself; there would be no direct detectable evidence that she had blown the bridge. She logged in at the commercial district. Axiom efficiently locked down information that could cause panic or distress; but it was impossible to hide an infrastructure disaster of this size. A sense of fear was stretched through the crowd, which was oddly quiet. They're listening, Mal realized. Listening for the next attack. She stared aimlessly at the flowers in a cart parked along the road. Beautiful. There were several baskets, brimming over with different colors and varieties.

"Crazy, right?" a man said standing near her.

"So many colors," Mal said faintly. The people around her were moving around her as if on automatic pilot; walking, haggling, buying. But their faces were taut with fear, and their voices flat.

The man leaned in closer. "Are you alright?"

"No." Mal stepped closer to a basket of blue flowers. They were huge, like cups holding themselves out to her, light blue on the edges and darker and darker toward the center. Slowly, other voices made it through the fog around her.

"Do you think it was the Pylon?"

"No. I heard it was sabotage."

"No."

"I heard it was Nanomei."

"Of course, it was Nanomei."

"Have they claimed responsibility?"

"They will."

"Or Death Angel."

"There's nothing on the official News Feeds."

"It won't be on the official news feeds. But there's already footage on the e-web."

"I wonder how many Patches died."

Death from loss of connection, or Sync, was not automatic. Derezzing in the Aetherium like that could cause headaches, and problems, bleeds, sure.

But derezzing in Quantum Noise, like those poor citizens in the river, was certain death. Their brains and bodies had died in their chairs.

Mal moved herself away. An alarm sounded; everyone jumped, staring wildly around them, wondering what was next. Three people burst out of an Ikaru shop two or three storefronts away. One threw a smoke Ibrahimade to cover their exit and cried out "Ramos is everywhere!" Another yelled "the Death Angel is coming for you!" They all three ran. Mal scanned the bands for Axiom communication. She found the local data bundles and started a hack. She reached out and felt the data-streams, and slipped their paths, adding a sixty-second delay. Then she ran after them, through the smoke. She crashed into a cart but kept moving. After she got through the smoke she saw that she was not the only one chasing them; there was a man in an all-black, silk suit running after them too. He had light copper skin and his slicked back, black hair and perfectly pressed suit were too well put together to be a Patch. He was also running sideways on the exterior facade of a building, avoiding doing stupid things like running into smoke clouds and crashing into carts. Had to be House Ikaru security. He pulled out a sleek, silver blaster. He was going to take these three out before Mal could make contact.

He leapt from the side of a building to the pavement, his back to Mal, and raised his weapon. Mal tried to catch up. He was taking aim at the three fleeing. Why were they not ducking around a corner? Did they not understand line of sight?

Mal was parallel to him when he took his first shot. Screams everywhere. Mal saw one of the three go down. She sprinted the last few steps to put herself in Ikaru's way then before he could take a second.

"Move!" he yelled.

She didn't. He tried to dodge sideways to get past her, but Mal matched him, keeping herself between him and the kid. She didn't look behind her to see if they'd gotten out of sight yet but she got a solid clue from the swearing Ikaru let out.

He leveled his blaster at Mal. "You have made a mistake," he said.

Mal held her hands up. "Just let me see to the kid." She took a few steps back, and, when she didn't get shot, took that as a yes and turned her back on Ikaru to run to him.

He was derezzing. He was screaming as parts of his physical form transformed into tiny blue-white cubes and then started falling, splashing into thousands of points of blue light as they hit the ground and slowly rising up like a ghost's form.

"What the hell did you shoot him with?" Mal asked.

Ikaru shrugged. "Standard issue," he said.

Mal knelt down. The kid was just a Patch. There were no protections on a Patch's Rig to mitigate this level of sync loss.

Mal grabbed the kid's hand, but it fuzzed and turned insubstantial for a moment. If he was more skilled, not just a Patch, he'd be able to rebuild his sync. But he was fading too fast; he would finish derezzing well before Mal was able to hack a healing prog to repair his sync.

"Look, kid," she said to the derezzing boy, finally making contact with his hand. "Look at me. I will do what I can, but when you finish logging you need to call a medic. Your Sync is gone." She leaned closer. "You said Ramos. Kid, do you know Ramos?"

With her other hand she found her Sync-Stim in her belt pouch. She applied the stim, sticking the contact point to his chest, hoping to repair something of his connection. There was a spark, and he settled a bit.

He tried to say something but Mal couldn't make it out. She leaned closer to him.

"I'm the Death Angel," she said. His eyes widened. "Call a medic when you get out, then come find me. Leave me a message at Ming's."

"That boy's dead," the man said behind her. "He won't make it out." His tone was unreadable.

The boy disappeared, finally derezzed. Mal stood. She knew Ikaru was right. The boy's chances were slim, unless he had means to have a medic nearby. Maybe he'd get lucky.

Axiom guards arrived on foot. Mal didn't want to be here for this. Looking around she saw that a crowd had gathered. She turned her back on the Ikaru man and melted into the crowd.

≋ » Chapter Three: Riot « ≋

The next few days were a sleepless blur. If Mal closed her eyes, she saw the bridge collapse. If she stopped distracting herself, even for a moment, she heard the screams. She tried to keep moving, to keep busy, but she was exhausted and unfocused. She remained logged off, paced her Unit, walked through the Pod around the Dwelling. When she finally tired of this, she dragged herself out to the bench across the street from the Dwelling, huddled in a baggy pair of dark green pants and a grey hoodie, watching people straggle past. The knowledge of what she had done swelled in her chest, making it difficult to breathe. She could not tell a soul.

Living as an Agent was like living in a holopic; it was as if everyone and everything else was just sets, and unwitting extras, for a show she was putting on. Real relationships were impossible. Her parents were dead. Her brother was dead. Tok had no idea she was an Agent. Mal honestly did not know how she would react to the truth. And now she was even cut off from her fellow Agents. At least they knew her, or some part of her. *Kass knows me. Mullen knows me. Dek knows me,* but who cares. *Tok and Cyprus and Tae and Nama and all the others, they only know what I show them. The lies.* A brand new thought started hammering at her brain: *I don't know if I can do this.*

"Do you wanna see someplace secret?"

She jumped. *Of course. The kid. Now I'm letting children get the drop on me.*

"Not really, Kid. I'm kind of thinking here…"

"Follow me!" he said, running to the doors.

Sighing, she followed him back into the building; she thought he was leading her to the elevator but at the last moment he ducked down the hall that led to Trent's residence. Next to Trent's door was a closet which Gibson opened. He ushered her inside, looking furtively around them. Playing along, she stepped into the closet. Gibson joined her and closed the door behind them.

"Gibson, what…"

"Just watch!" So much life in this kid. How does he do that in a place like this?

He reached his hand behind some supplies on a shelf and pressed something in the wall. A hidden door in the back of the closet opened.

Mal was genuinely surprised. "How did you…"

He flashed her a huge grin and stepped through the door. Mal followed.

"It runs all through the building," he said. "You can even see into some of the apartments in places!"

"Gibson…"

"I never look! That wouldn't be okay. Follow me!" he said in a loud whisper.

They came to a narrow stairway heading downward. Mal followed closely and as quietly as possible. Finally, they came to a metal door. It was thick and reinforced, bolted along the seams and edges. But it was not locked.

Gibson pushed it open to reveal a neat and tidy room. Along the wall was an old workbench and shelves. In the center was a reclined chair and a portion of a rig. The Core was missing, though; it would not function without it. The casing of the Rig was set up to house a portable core. A large cylndirical hole where the core would be inserted during use was empty. The core was nowhere to be seen in the room.

"I come in here all the time to hide." Gibson went over to the shelves and lifted one to reveal three ratty old comic books. Gibson climbed into the chair. He knew this was an important find and was clearly proud of himself. "But this is new. It's only been here a couple of weeks. I use it to read these and pretend I'm logged in."

"That's fun…" Mal cast her eyes around the room. "Do you ever look in any of these?" She indicated the shelves and workbench.

"Just a few books. Not comic."

Mal flipped through them while Gibson sat in the chair with his eyes closed.

"Mal…" he whispered.

"Yeah, kid?"

"I'm in the Aetherium… it's beautiful."

Mal smiled at him in spite of herself. "Tell me what you see." The workbench was completely ordinary, grey extruded plastic, a couple of drawers. She opened each one: tools, mostly. Odds and ends.

The kid droned on. "And there are turtles everywhere. I'm swimming in the sea with them…."

"Great, kid." Many of their conversations included references to extinct animals. The kid was obsessed.

She opened the last drawer. Empty. But… she pulled again. It wasn't coming out as far as the others. "Keep talking, Little." She need not have worried.

"I see manatees…." The kid's voice was dreamy. She slipped her hand into the drawer, glanced back at the kid, and worked the mechanism that opened the drawer all the way. In the secret compartment in the back, she found a black journal with a synthetic leather cover and an old-fashioned ink-based writing utensil clipped to the cover. Opening it Mal saw a few pages of carefully penned dates and times, a few with notations. Days and times she'd left the building, one noting she'd gone out in the rain. One noting that she'd ignored him. They matched her movements since the first day she returned. There was no name, only "subject" used to describe. Oh, Trent.

〉〉 ••••• 〈〈

Mal returned to the Trench where the bridge had been destroyed. The bridge supports were not entirely gone, but they were in wireframe: simple blue-green glowing lines outlining where the supports had been. Small monuments had been erected near the site on the Riverwalk: Aetherial flowers, pictures, holograms, recordings. There were engineers and construction programmers on both sides of the river. Rebuilding would take much longer than normal because even though the Node was safe to build on, and there were surrounding Pylons, the Quantum Noise River made it much more hazardous and interfered with other, more distant Pylons which under different circumstances would be able to help the process. It was painful to watch the workers risk themselves to span the dangerous river. They could easily fall to their deaths on the job repairing the damage she'd done. This is disorder. This is chaos. How could this be the world Nanomei wants? Ramos would have to be some kind of monster if this made him happy.

Mal heard angry voices, a swelling of disturbance, in the distance. She went to investigate. On the next block she saw a large crowd of people outside a Praetorian Recruitment Center. A protest. Mal scanned the crowd. They were gathered now in the center of the street, centered around an overturned car; some looked Nanomei, for certain, but she actually thought she might see some Axiom citizens in the crowd as well.

"Axiom promises safety! We obey and they protect! They provide!"

"The bridge! The dead! Axiom must protect its citizens!"

Mal slipped in among the protestors. It was fairly common for Nanomei to start little protests here and there, but in The Drain they were usually inconsequential, drowned out by loyal and loud Axiom citizens or broken up by their studied indifference for the protest. This crowd carried more rage, more purpose, than Mal would expect to see here, and the Citizens on the edges were looking uncomfortable, or angry, but mostly staying silent. As she pressed through the crowd and got closer to the center, near the overturned car, Mal saw some Riot Girls, easily recognizable soldiers of Nanomei, seven or eight of them. She felt a strange thrill as she saw them. Their clothes somehow shouted that they were rebels but unified them at the same time: ripped shirts and camouflage pants, thick black boots, bandanas over the lower halves of their faces. Some had signs, programs that changed their message at a whim. One of them was cycling through a series of images, one of which was her Death Angel tag. A Riot Girl jumped atop the overturned car, her combat boots slamming hard into the metal. In one hand she had a bottle with a large rag burning at the top. Riot girls are like moths to the flame of danger and chaos. To see them here, in The Drain…it hit her like splash of cold. It's me. It's me or it's Ramos. Or it's both.

"Down with Axiom!" The Riot Girl yelled. She threw her bottle which smashed against the Recruitment Center Wall. The flames burned impossibly against the cold plastisteel. The crowd surged forward. The other Riot Girls threw more bottles and rocks. This chaos was something she'd made, she'd unleashed. She felt unclean, sick. No mission could be worth this. As bricks flew at the Axiom walls she cringed as they struck. As the people pushed forward, she was deeply aware of how fragile they were. And, she hated to think, but did: how fragile the system was. If she could tear apart the city, just one Agent…

Mal dodged a rock, which, if it connected, might have damaged a Patches' connection, but not hers; she was only in danger from weapons programs. Like… the ones the Riot Girls just started handing out.

The Pylons nearby started to wink out. Schemas went wireframe in the distance. Axiom must have ordered a Pylon shutdown. The Pylons would continue to protect from the Quantum Noise but they would do nothing to support the programs they normally ran. All around people started to disperse, fleeing the area. For three or four blocks in all directions everything nearby no longer looked "more real than real." Instead, the ground became a flat, matte black field, perfectly level and lined with a grid. The buildings lost their solidity and became wireframe outlines of their previous selves. The only building remaining all too solid was the center itself. Then the Praetorians started to rez in. Each appeared with a ground-shaking thud. Mal held her breath.

The first ten or so were average Praetorians. They wore matte black riot gear and carried large riot shields, transparent from the back and opaque from the front. Their helmets obscured their faces. The last, though, looked different. His armor was similar but lined with spikes. Unlike other Praetorians Mal had seen, he wore no helmet. His head was bare and covered in short-cropped hair that was jet-black with grey at the temples. He shouted "Praetorians!" His ruddy white skin looked like it was hot to the touch.

The other Praetorians smashed their shields' bottom edges on the ground in unison and yelled. The leader rezzed in his own shield. It was also a riot shield, but larger than the others. The front of the shield was carved a woman's head with the hair of snakes. It was him. The Gorgon.

The Gorgon's Praetorians formed a line between the Praetorian Center and the throng. At a yell from the Gorgon the Praetorians charged, their shields raised ahead of them and shock batons in their other hands. They advanced as a wall.

Most of the gathered mob scattered and ran but the Riot Girlz stood their ground, defiant as the others fled, with their signs and other rough weapons held against the oncoming shield wall. One of the Riot Girls yelled "Nanomei!" and she threw a bottle which shattered on the shield of one of the advancing guards. Their shield derezzed and the flames started to consume them. The line broke.

Mal shoved her way through the crowd toward the Riot Girls. Two Praetorians charged at her, and she ducked away, sliding under the swing of a club. As she got her feet, she came face to face with one of the Riot Girlz. She had glowing green paint in three lines on her cheeks and shocking pick hair. A Praetorian ran into view behind her and brought his club down. Mal stepped past the Girl and held her hand out. The club slammed against it, sending reverberations of pain down her arm, but stopped inches away from the Riot Girl's face. Mal's eyes locked with the Riot Girlz' for a moment, and she shoved the club away. The Praetorian grunted and smashed her with his shield, and she flew twenty feet in the air; he must have had a kinetic booster mod on his shield.

She landed near a burning Praetorian. The street was a mess, pavement buckled and on fire. Praetorians stomping towards protestors. Looking wildly about her, she saw that half of the Praetorians were down or burning, and five or six of the Riot Girls were still standing. We can take them. But then The Gorgon bent his will to the field. She felt it. It felt like waves of heat and focus coursing over her. But his hack wasn't affecting Mal; the fallen Praetorians were starting to rise up, the Glitch peeling off of them in torrents of blue energy.

"Run!" the Riot Girl yelled.

"No!" Mal yelled back. "Stand and fight!" She felt a rush in her veins. All the grief, all the conflict, in her rushed to the surface. She cried out again "Stand!"

Mal stood near to a fallen light post. It had to be twenty feet, made of metal and heavy. She poured all of her mind into a hack to increase her strength. Bringing to the hack her deep understanding of motion, physics, and physical mechanics, she bolstered the power of her movements, adding force beyond reason to her kinetic energy. A pair of Riot girls stared as they saw Mal lift the pole. Mal swung it hard into the nearest Praetorian. It shattered his shield into a million blue motes and sent his body flying backwards. That felt good.

The Riot Girlz cheered and charged forward again. The Gorgon yelled too, and leveled his right hand, outstretched at Mal. A great hammer appeared in it and he roared a challenge.

Mal released a wordless battle cry and charged forward. She felt focused, alive, for the first time since the bridge. Three Praetorians blocked the way, and Riot Girls lobbed incendiaries again. The Gorgon was standing amidst roaring flames and Mal brought the pole to bear against two of the three Praetorians, sending them flying, both derezing as they landed.

The third smashed Mal with his shield and she stumbled, dropping the pole. Then he brought his disruptor mace in a wide overhand arc. But a Riot Girl shouldered him hard and fast; he stumbled a few steps away and his blow smashed the ground instead.

Mal shouted a thanks and charged headlong towards The Gorgon, who was standing in a wide, defensive stance, his snake-haired shield held high, his hammer ready. Then Mal saw a drop ship. At least two dozen more Praetorians were slamming into the ground from above.

"We have to leave!" one of the Riot Girlz shouted.

"Ramos!" another yelled, and time seemed to stop.

Mal whirled around and saw a ground car pulling up near the wreckage in the street. A man had gotten out of the car and was standing with the door open, ushering Riot Girls inside. He had tawny, almost golden skin, is black hair, dyed purplish, stood straight up from his head. A voluminous scarf covered the lower half of his face. He wore a thick vest, almost leather.

Mal, forgetting for a moment that she'd been almost toe to toe with The Gorgon stared at him and then took a step towards the car. This was it—

Except that it wasn't. The Gorgon's hammer caught her in the back, and she flew forward, landing next to a derezzing Praetorian. The Gorgon was charging her. She struggled to her feet and spread her wings. Two Riot Girls stood with her.

"Now's the time!" one yelled.

Mal picked up a dropped disruptor mace. "You two go. I'll cover you!" she yelled. And from behind her she heard two huge blasts. Sparks and Glitch flew from the Gorgon's raised shield and Ramos charged him, blasting a sawed-off shotgun with every stride. The Gorgon yelled Ramos' name and charged forward.

As they clashed into each other Ramos dropped his gun and a sword appeared in his hand already cutting through the air in a long arc. The Gorgon blocked the sword with his shield and answered the blow with his hammer. Ramos ducked, and drove his sword into the Gorgon's boot, forcing the sword deep into the ground. The Gorgon screamed in pain and tried to free himself. Ramos smashed The Gorgon's helmeted head with his own forehead.

Mal saw past him at least two dozen more Praetorians smash into the field as well as the rest of the Praetorians converging back towards the Gorgon with all speed.

"Ramos!" Mal yelled.

"Run, you idiot!" yelled one of the same Riot Girlz who had called for retreat earlier.

Everyone ran, Ramos leading the way. He leapt onto the roof of the ground car, and it sped away. There were perhaps three dozen Praetorians now and they were charging as a wall towards her and the last Riot Girlz standing on the field. Mal ran like the rest. The temptation to spread her wings and soar out and above the crowd was strong but she fought it. The ground car had torn away and so Mal and the Riot Girlz started running as fast as they could and ran straight into a mass of protestors. Safety in numbers at this point. Mal tried to reach out and grab one of the Riot Girlz but she saw the girl shift appearance and lose contact. She ran with the crowd into the subway station, people fell down the stairs and scrambled over each other.

After getting through the crowded subway terminal, she pulled the connection from behind her ear and stayed in the chair for a good, long while.

Mal was exhausted. Physical exertion in the Aetherium isn't the same as in the Meatspace. Instead of a User's muscles burning it is their very consciousness. And Mal had been running herself ragged even before the riot. She pulled herself from the chair and walked out to the living room. She tugged on the window, but it was welded shut. She was overheated, dizzy. She needed to get out.

Out in the hall Mal saw a man, crumpled over, against one of the doors. Mal stepped around him quietly. Mal needed space, not conversation. As Mal moved past he stumbled to his feet. "Hey!" he said angrily.

"Whoa, man," Mal said, putting both his hands up. "Just passing through here. You're in the hallway." It was Karl.

"Is this Meat?"

"What?" Mal asked.

"Am I logged in?"

"No," Mal said in a low voice. "You're in the hallway of an Axiom-owned and operated housing structure in Keral." Mal heard a door open behind her.

"Dammit Karl, what are you doing out in the hall?" Trent said behind him. "Mal, I'm sorry. Karl. Get in your place."

Trent came forward and pressed his Crypto-Card onto a locking mechanism next to the door the man had been leaning on. It opened with a click and Karl stared at them.

"Frag you, Trent," he said. "You're nothing. You can keep your fancy ti-tles. Your special job. Watching everybody." He looked up at Mal. "You know he watches you, right?"

Trent shoved Karl the rest of the way through his doorway and slammed it closed. He and Mal walked away. They got to the doorway and opened it and stood outside in the damp air together. Trent offered Mal a hand-rolled cigarette, which she waved off. Mal waited in the careful silence. Would Trent address what Karl had said? Trent shifted, squinted into the night as he smoked. Eventually he coughed a little, then cleared his throat.

"Sorry about that. I'd like to say he's harmless," Trent said.

"He seemed really out of it. More than normal."

"His rig's trashed. He's high on Cadno. All the time."

"Shit."

"Yeah. He was a skinner, and a pretty good one. A Patch, but knew his art."

"Wow. I don't know many Patch Skinners. That's talent."

"A real waste," Trent said.

"Won't Axiom do anything for him?"

Trent sighed. "No. Not enough hours of service to qualify. His parents died young. He showed up here on a grant. But he was already downhill." He glanced sideways at her. "You look horrible. Did something happen?"

Mal just shrugged. Subject shrugged.

She wanted to ask him, of course. Find the rational explanation. Trent would have stories about her... family after she and her dad were gone. He knew things that Axiom wouldn't tell her. Circumstances. Dates. He could be useful. But she turned and walked away. If Trent hesitated, watching after her, almost saying something, she refused to notice. Mal walked through the neighborhood in a pointless pattern. She wasn't getting even the minimal exercise she usually did as part of her normal routine; Meatspace exercise was never her favorite. Mal's relationship with her Meatspace body, which was fragile, limited, and the wrong gender, was uneasy at best. Still, sometimes after a prolonged shift in the Aetherium, the need to move and stretch this useless Meatspace body was undeniable.

The streets were deserted for the most part, so any activity did stand out. She saw a pair of walkers close enough to each other that they kept bumping each other off course and laughing quietly. She saw a thin dog growling at a hole in an alley wall; probably at some rodent dinner it was hoping to snag. She avoided the direction of the factories and the Rig parlor.

As she returned, she saw Gibson playing on the Children's Recreational Area outside of the building.

"Hi, Gibson" Mal said cautiously, stopping at the low fence between the sidewalk and the play equipment. One word to this boy and she could be caught in a very long, and very confusing conversation with no end until she walked away.

"Hello, Mal," Gibson said. He fixed her with his cool blue eyes. "Would you like to play?"

"Aren't there any other kids in the building to play with?"

"Not really. A couple, I guess. But they're older, so they're chipped."

"That rots."

"Yes. But sometimes it's better to play with an adult, anyway."

"It…is?"

"Yes. Kids can be so limited. It's nice to play with someone with a little more life experience."

Mal laughed. It came out without measure.

A woman came out from the building. She was about Mal's age. "Time to come in, Gibson," she said. She looked drawn, haggard. Working too much, probably, trying to afford to get Gibson chipped.

"Aw Mom, ten minutes?"

"Okay. But you leave the other tenants alone," she said. Then, shifting her attention to Mal, she added, "I'm sorry if he's bothering you."

"No. It's fine."

"You new?" she asked.

"Old and new I guess. But yeah, pretty new."

"Are you the code smoother Trent is always talking about?"

Always? "Yeah. Probably," she said.

"That's a good placement."

"Where are you placed?"

"The factory," she said. It had been a stupid question. "I'm Ella," the woman said, extending a hand in a woolen, fingerless glove.

She shook Ella's hand. "Mal," she said.

"It's nice to meet you. I should go," and then she went back to the door, saying "ten minutes, Gibson. Don't make me come back out!"

"OK, mom." He looked at Mal. "Ten minutes. We better make them count!" He ran.

Mal was nonplussed. But she ran after him, and he let out a whoop.

Mal walked the kid in after ten minutes. As she was returning to her Unit she heard someone calling for Trent. Approaching Trent's Unit she heard it again.

"Trent? Need you." It was a scratchy, paper-like voice. The voice of an old man.

Mal approached the door and found it open by a few inches. Unsure where Trent was, she knocked.

"Trent? Is that you? I can't get up," he said.

"Mr. Jacobsen?" Mal asked, pushing the door open. Trent's looked much the same as her Unit and she entered into the kitchen. On the floor, near one of two chairs in the living area was Trent's father so much older now than she remembered him, older than he should have been, considering the number of years she had been away. He was on the ground, his legs underneath him, his arms holding the seat of the chair.

"Oh. Hello," he said seeing Mal come in. "Can you help me, young lady?" See, how hard is that? Mal went in the rest of the way and bent down to him.

"Mr. Jacobsen, are you hurt?" Mal asked.

"No, no, Dearie. I just missed the chair is all," he said.

Mal moved to him and stepped behind his body. "I'm going to reach under your arms, Sir," she said.

"Oh, good, good," he replied. Mal lifted him. He was so light the kid could have gotten him up. "Thank you, thank you."

Mal helped him get situated and then stepped back. His cane was on the floor, and she righted it and leaned it on the arm of his chair.

"You've changed your hair," he said.

"I wasn't sure you knew who I was. It's been a long time, Mr. Jacobsen."

"Well, Trent's been talking about you coming home. Glad to have a Turner back in the dwelling. Your family always lightened the place up," he said.

"That's kind of you to say, Sir," Mal said.

"I remember the Parade of Remembrance. Your brother he stole a whole brick of those snappers and had them all through the building. Drove Trent nuts it did! I had already retired by then, you know."

"How has retirement been?"

"Well, I log in every chance I can get. Trent has been affording us some extra time lately, and my neurals are still great. You should see me in the games!"

Mal laughed. "I'd like to see that."

"What's that?" Trent's voice asked from the doorway.

"Trent! Your friend Mal is here. She helped me up, I'd taken a bit of a fall here," he said. "Offer her some tea, will you?"

"Oh, I couldn't," Mal said, standing. "It was really nice seeing you again, Sir."

"And nice to be seen," he said with a twinkle. "Maybe we'll see each other logged in some time."

"That would be nice," Mal said, moving to the door.

"Thanks for helping him. I was out," Trent said.

"Not a problem, Trent. Mr. Jacobsen always has interesting things to say," she said as she left.

⟩⟩ • • • • • ⟨⟨

Mal soared above the Drain. Flying this high, seeing the Nodal Plane from above the schemas, had always made Mal feel a mix of exhilaration and terror. Not a lot of Patches, not even most Users, can make it up this high, and this sense of being alone is rare in the Aetherium. It was a weird rush, these moments of solitude. To maybe, always be, probably be, watched, yet still alone. To not be pretending. She could see the Pylons glowing in the night, great towers of light and code stretching upwards to infinity, pulsing the reality they created outward from them. The code, from a distance, looked like shimmering motes of light constantly rising from the source itself, venting the light upwards as a form of energy and way to express the reality it is building. Up closer to the column of light, Mal would have been able to see the complex code: fractal flashes, strings of lights pulsing and moving in an intricate dance. Even closer to the physical Pylon and none of the light or code would have been visible. Just the reality that the Pylon created. But up here, too high, and too close to the Noise, the artifice was visible. And so fragile looking. Up here, she could see the way the horizon of the Aetherium bled into the acid blue of the Quantum Noise, which filled the Aetherium wherever the Pylons can't keep it out. Everyone was in a safe bubble in the Aetherium but if Mal thought about it, really let herself think about it, how they were in a tiny pocket of reality in the infinity of the empty and lethal Noise... She tried to not dwell on that part.

Three days of fruitless searching had turned up nothing of Ramos, but the streets were buzzing with word of both him and the Death Angel. Her persona was growing a following. She landed on the top of a building near the porous border between the Old Drain and the Mall, which gave her a view of much of the territory she had been searching.

"Are you looking for a race?" a voice said behind her.

Mal smiled and turned. "Nama. Back for a rematch?"

"I have a few days of Aetherium time on my hands. Thought maybe you were free for a race or two?"

Nama pulled the pole from his back and twirled it with a grin. The pole was a vehicle prog. If he threw it in the air, and leapt toward it, a small vehicle rezzed in around him, a slender tube with a glass cockpit and three elegant fins. Normally this kind of theatricality would annoy the living Noise out of Mal, but somehow, Nama got away with it.

Still, she rolled her eyes for his benefit. "That's pretty, but pretty only gets you so far."

Nama yelled "There!" and flung a pulse dot up at a distant building, one on the edge of The Mall.

He leaped and dove for a few seconds before activating his vehicle prog in mid descent. It rezzed in around him, first the controls, and his seat, then the engine and finally the outer skin, sleek and silver. Mal watched for a moment then hovered where she was just an inch above the rooftop. She tapped the toes of her foot against the edge of the roof and leapt, arms outstretched, relishing the turbulence in her chest and in her belly before extending her wings and letting them snatch her back from the fall. She grinned at the bright engine spark. She gave him two more seconds before she shot ahead, the wind filling her hair and billowing it out behind her.

She cut close to the balcony of a building to catch up to him. "Watch where you're flying!" Nama laughed.

"I am watching! Are you?" Mal made an unnecessary, but very cool looking, swoop with her wings.

Mal reached the first pulse and threw it back to the Old Drain, but northward away from the river.

"Fly no higher than ten meters up," Nama said as he went into a dive behind her.

"You're on!" Mal said, losing ground to him but going into a dive of her own.

Nama swooped lower and the belly of his vehicle skimmed the street, sending sparks and torn duracrete behind him. Mal did a barrel roll to avoid the spray and hacked more speed onto her wings. Straining to catch Nama had become a regular occurrence in these races. His ship was, at its core, faster than her wings so it required more hacking on her part to put more speed into them. This distracted her from manual control and made precise maneuverability a little trickier, which made crashing into things a little more likely and so a million times more fun.

They both tore through the streets, avoiding signage and balconies with sharp turns and their usual mix of grace and swearing. For three blocks their forms, Mal's wings and Nama's ship jostled for position, and as Mal got the advantage she planted a kiss on the glass of Nama's cockpit. That distraction gave her the lead again for another few blocks.

Mal was well ahead of Nama and turned to see where he had gone. She made a quick, light turn. The pulse dot was only a few hundred meters ahead, but the street did not connect, so they needed to go around. Flying at these speeds was exhilarating and the competition of it all made her whole-body buzz. But as she watched both the area ahead and Nama, she saw him do something spectacular. He ghosted straight through the building, not turning, headed directly through and towards the pulse.

"Shit!" she said and hit as much speed as she could, and as she rounded the corner a good two hundred meters from the pulse, Nama was coming out of the building and becoming solid again. He reached the pulse first, grabbed and threw it. Mal couldn't see where exactly it was because she was still too low.

"Last one!" Nama yelled.

Mal took off after him and ended behind him by a half second. They both came to a stop on a rooftop near the Spires.

"I've never seen someone hack a ghost mod like that," she said.

"You're not the only one with skills, Mal," he said with a wink.

"For someone so cool you are so damn lame."

〉〉 • • • • • 〈〈

The next day Mal received a direct message from the official Loyalty Station near her home; it had come to her Rig directly through a proximity message on her Rig setup and flashed across the vid screen in her Unit as well. It was a "request" to prepare for an appointment at Axiom Loyalty Center Four. In an hour.

Messages like this were not uncommon, of course. Loyalty Officers never gave the recipients time to prepare; short notice testing like this, it was believed, generated more honest answers. If a Citizen somehow missed the message and did not arrive where and when they should, they would be located. Being pulled in for loyalty questioning was not a strange occurrence; but did they want to check in with Mal the Agent or question Mal the cover story? Operations especially seemed to sometimes march to different orders; it may or may not have been in contact with Loyalty Division; Loyalty might have randomly chosen her for a Loyalty check having no idea she was undercover. This should be fun. She would be picked up outside her home. She threw on the grey poncho and walked out into the rain. She never bothered much with her appearance in the Meatspace, even to try to express her correct gender. Why dress an echo? Her real life was in the Aetherium.

The Patrol pulled over in a six-wheeled transport, sleek and silver and without windows. The driver would have a heads-up display inside, and so the whole thing looked like a squished silver tube with six large wheels attached on the outside. Inelegant, but functional. It moved its passengers with efficiency. Mal climbed into the passenger door and found herself in the back of the vehicle with five other citizens. Two she didn't recognize, an older Black couple both with grey hair. Another she did. A blonde pale-white girl, about her age, who lived in the building across the way. She looked scared. There was a couple sitting almost on top of each other in the corner of the transport. Both were women; both wore worker's brown jumpsuits, and both had light brown skin. Their main difference was in their hair; each had one side of their head shaved smooth and the other side was dyed dark red-brown; one had shaved the left side of her head, the other the right. Lefty was very nervous, and Righty was trying to calm her down. As Mal looked around, nodded to the other passengers, the door opened one more time and Karl was pushed in.

63

"We're taking you anyway, doesn't matter you didn't see the notification," the guard said as he manhandled Karl into the seat across from Mal. "Fragging cable," Karl spat after the guard.

The blonde girl looked nervous.

"Don't worry. It happens. Prove you're loyal, you get let go," Mal said.

"Or they think you're not and you stay for retraining. Or disappear forever," the girl said.

"You've seen too many holos," Mal said, but she knew the girl wasn't wrong.

"She's right," the older woman said. "Be sure to be honest and everything will be alright," she said.

Her husband nodded, but also rolled his eyes as Mal looked at him.

"I don't belong here," Karl said. "I am a loyal spinner."

"Karl. Stay calm," Mal said.

"Do I know you?" he asked.

The vehicle came to a stop and the back door swung open. "You two," the guard said pointing to her and hair-in-the-eyes. Mal and the nervous girl left the truck and were escorted through a low entryway to a vast grey building. Mal could hear Karl yelling as they closed the door to the transport, the top of which was lost in a sea of fog and black Axiom banners. Flanking the doorway were a pair of very well-armed and armored troops. They wore shining black chest plates and grey camo. They held assault rifles at the ready. The girl Mal was with looked downright terrified at this point. Mal made eye contact with her.

"Just be honest. Be loyal," she said. She could see the doubt in the girl's eyes. Which meant she was in trouble. Once you make space for doubt, you're screwed. Mal shook her head slightly and stopped thinking about her. Once you make space to worry about others, you're screwed, too.

The room Mal was put in was a ten-by-ten square with two chairs in it. One chair was a simple metal folding chair. The other was bolted to the ground, with straps on it for wrists, ankles, waist, and neck. She sat in it and waited as the guard left.

A pair of Axiom workers walked in after ten minutes. *These ten minutes are two hours I could have been logged in.* She did not let that thought cross her face. She remained, outwardly, calm and impassive. Both workers were dressed in grey jumpsuits with the crossed key insignia of Axiom on the chest, and their ranks on the right arm. Neither outranked Mal, and neither mattered. They were only here to prepare her for the Loyalty Officer.

One spoke, while the other unpacked a datapad and series of electrodes. As the first one questioned her the other applied the electrodes to her temple, neck, arms, wrists. They did not apply the straps.

"You are Mal Turner," the Worker said.

"I am," she replied.

"You know why you have been brought here?"

"For loyalty testing," she said blankly.

"Are you ready to begin?"

"I am."

"Are you nervous?"

"No." Mal said.

"And do you have any questions before we bring in the Loyalty Officer?"

"No. I am loyal. I am Axiom," she intoned. This seemed to leave an impression: The one putting trodes on her paused in mid application. After finishing, they both left the room without another word, leaving Mal with her thoughts, which were currently not great company.

It was only a few minutes more before a single person entered: A Loyalty Agent. She was tall and thin and wearing an all-black and unadorned uniform. Her sleeves were rolled up and her boots were polished. She wore a silver pin on her lapel: stylized silver wings. This was the symbol of The Matrons, a group within the Axiom hierarchy. Matrons oversaw the Loyalty Division of Axiom. This Loyalty Officer's wings were silver, which meant that she was still in training. If she proved her loyalty, and her skill enough, she would one day be considered for membership and might even get the gold wings. A single tech came in after she entered, accessed the datapad, and told her it was recording. The pad was placed on an arm of the chair. She could see the readout screen but Mal could not. The tech left.

"I am a Loyalty Agent," she said.

"I am a loyal Axiom Citizen," Mal replied.

The agent smiled but her eyes remained blank. "I know who you are, white fractal."

Mal let out an audible sigh of relief. "White fractal" was one of her trust phrases. There were three of them assigned to this mission and after each one was used it could be re-used. But this told her that this Loyalty Agent had nearly full access to her information.

"Why did you bring me in?" Mal asked. The Loyalty Agent's face registered some small amount of surprise, and more annoyance. She was not used to being questioned.

"Have you had success in contacting Nanomei Criminals?"

"I have had insignificant contact. I have seen some rioters."

"Have you been approached by any Nanomei criminals?"

"No."

"Have you committed any crimes?"

"Yes, of course I have."

"Why do you say 'of course?'" she asked.

"My mission is to be recruited by Nanomei and infiltrate them. They respect those who cause chaos. They respect those skilled with hacking."

"Are you seen as skilled?"

"Yes," she said. No point in false humility.

"Could you attract their attention by your hacking skill alone? Without causing problems for Axiom?"

"Perhaps." Mal said. She breathed in, and out, evenly.

"Why have you not attempted that?"

"I was given objectives, not specific orders. I am an Agent of Axiom, not some cog following a script," she said.

"Do you enjoy chaos, Citizen? Agent. Do you enjoy chaos?" Mal thought back to the riot. To the overwhelming release she felt as she had let go and unleashed that chaos. It had been a rush and if Axiom had been attached through Rig connections, they would have known that. But they weren't. But then she thought about the bridge.

"No."

"Agent?"

"I said no."

"Who is Namaiki?" she asked. The Loyalty Officer's skin was pale, her eyes were pale blue, her hair so blonde it was almost white. Like you could disappear.

"Namaiki is a Pilot for House Ikaru. Also, a recruiter."

"Is he an asset?"

"No," Mal said.

"Does he further your mission?"

"No."

"Did you destroy the bridge in The Drain?"

"No."

"Did you contribute to the chaos of the riots?"

"Yes."

"Did you raise your hand against The Gorgon?"

"That was more him than me," Mal said with a grin.

The Matron cleared her throat. "Back to your criminal activity. Do you plan additional crimes?"

"Yes."

"Will you enjoy those crimes?"

"I enjoy pushing the limits of my skill. These crimes push the limits of my skill." Mal was being as honest as she could be. She had layers. And she didn't want to peel that artichoke with some Loyalty Agent she didn't know, especially a Matron. This is not the time to be self-reflective.

"Does this further your mission objectives?"

"Yes."

The questions were coming faster and faster. She was pressing Mal. The trodes were pulling so much data Mal could almost feel them heating up.

"Do you know Ramos?"

"I know him by reputation."

"He has no file."

"Reputation. I did not claim to have read his file."

"Do you admire Ramos?"

"By reputation, he is skilled."

"Do you admire skill?"

"Yes."

"Did it take skill to destroy the Praetorian Bridge?"

"I did not destroy the Praetorian Bridge," Mal said.

"Do you admire Ramos?"

"He is skilled. I admire skill."

"Does your admiration of his skill cloud your judgement?"

"I have applied no judgement to Ramos."

"He is a criminal Nanomei."

"He is one of many. I plan to infiltrate the Nanomei. I do not know what else will be asked of me. But whatever it is it will be done. As is my mission. If it were my mission, I'd rip these trodes off my skull and strangle you with them.'"

The Loyalty Officer stepped forward and struck Mal across the face. She hit hard and the pain echoed in Mal's skull. Mal did not move but she smiled internally. *How easy to make you lose your resolve?*

"You are in the seat of an interrogator. I am a Loyalty Agent, and you are an Agent of Axiom. I know full well what your mission is. You run the risk of being corrupted by the rebels. This attitude is doing nothing to assuage the fears of Control!"

"I am no common—"

"Silence, Agent! Now."

The Interrogator stood over Mal, her fists balled.

"Are you capable of completing the mission?" she finally asked.

Mal felt an almost physical snap deep inside. "I will follow my orders," she shouted. The Loyalty Agent took a step back at the rage in Mal's voice. Mal could feel herself breathing too fast, too shallow. She had let the Loyalty Agent throw her off balance.

The Agent did not ask another question. The sudden stop of the fast-paced exchange startled Mal. The silence that fell was strange.

"You have many things to answer for," she said.

"I am an Agent."

"Agents are still Citizens. You will spend a great deal of time with the enemy. Watch that you maintain your loyalty." She paused then and looked Mal directly in the eyes for perhaps the first time. "Don't worry, Citizen. You have passed your loyalty test."

"Good to know. Would you tell me if I had failed?"

"No."

Mal stood from the chair, the trodes falling away.

The Matron's face was expressionless. "You are excused, Citizen."

"Ever loyal," Mal replied.

>> • • • • • <<

As Mal was released she was taken to a garage. The group that had ridden together was pacing about, mostly avoiding eye contact with each other. The older, grey-haired couple was quietly holding hands.

Karl looked positively delighted. He was grinning. "Can I go now? Get my own transport?" He asked the guard.

"Suit yourself. We have to wait until everyone's here. Might be a while."

Karl left, hollering for a Meatcab as he reached the garage entrance. Mal watched him, bemused.

"What's up with Karl?" she tried to ask the couple. The man made eye contact and gently shook his head, gesturing with his eyes. Mal tracked his gaze.

Righty was staring down the hall Mal had walked down after her appointment. It was empty. The look on Righty's face was aching. Mal settled into the silence with the others. There's still hope, Righty. But she didn't believe it enough to say it out loud.

After what felt like hours of waiting, the datapad on the guard's arm made a tiny chiming sound. It rang through the air like razors. He checked the datapad. "Well, that's everyone," he said.

"Where's my mate?" Righty asked the guard.

"You came alone. There was no one with you," the guard said.

"No. I know she's still in there. You have to let her out," she said, desperate and shrill.

"Step into the transport, citizen. Everyone's accounted for."

Mal touched Righty's elbow. "You should board the truck now," Mal said. Righty did not move. She was deciding. "If you don't want the same thing to happen to you, you'll shut up and go home," Mal said. The woman broke into sobs and let Mal push her aboard the transport, but she turned again to share hopelessly down the hall as the door slammed in her face. Mal broke away.

"Let's go, let's go," the guard said to the crowd, and they continued filing into the transport.

"I'll walk," Mal said, walking past them. The guards did not question her, and she left without looking back.

She walked through the old neighborhoods and towards home but not in a direct line. Torn up inside and unwilling to go home she kept snaking through the surrounding streets and neighborhoods. She walked, aimlessly, for hours, until she found herself in more familiar territory and saw the busted neon light sign for the Rig Parlor down the block from her dead drop.

There was a crowd outside. The shop was brightly lit in the night, its light spilling out on the faces of the people gathered at the window. Mal walked faster. This was not the normal queue just waiting their turn.

"What's going on?" she asked one of the people in the crowd, a large man who looked the type to be willing to talk.

"Someone got fried," he said.

"Shit." Mal pushed her way through the crowd to look through the grimy window.

It was Karl. He was laid out in a Rig chair, but fully reclined and his arms hung at limp, strange angles from his torso. His shirt had been ripped open and there were paddle burns. They had tried to restart his heart. Mal shoved her way to the door and into the shop. There were three men around Karl as they tried to disconnect him.

"What happened?" she asked, putting on an air of authority.

The first guy looked up and said, "Glitch feedback. He'll be okay." He did not sound convinced. The others did not look convinced. Mal was not convinced.

Mal looked down the row. Four others were twitching, clearly Glitch-burned too. Karl was still; he was either safe and unconscious or gone already.

"We told him this row was out of order. He jumped anyway. Said he'd just got some Value and couldn't wait. He was supposed to wait. Man. Just an hour or something 'til the tech got here. All he had to do was wait." He gestured. He had a multi in his hand.

"You've got to get these people disconnected," Mal told him.

The worker looked at her helplessly. She snatched the multitool out of his hand and pulled the connector hose forward and brought the blade end of the tool to strip the wire. Sparks showered out of the Rig next to them and Karl's body spasmed violently. Someone started yelling down the line. Mal stayed focused on Karl. Glitch was taking him. If his mind did not return soon, it would be lost to the Aetherium to dissolve. His body would die.

"When I say, you pull the plug. Exactly when I say," she said to the worker.

Mal popped open the access panel on Karl's rented rig. It was a patch-work of cables and wires re-worked, re-done, re-cycled. Mal worked fast as more sparks came from the next rigs over.

"Now!" she said as she hiccupped the connection between the third and fourth matrices. She was trying to bleed Glitch and complete the logout; if it worked, enough of Karl's mind would make it back through the connection to the Aetherium. If it didn't…Sparks showered her hand, and several cables, lit with an internal glow faded and went dark.

The worker twisted and pulled, and Karl was free. He moaned and turned on his side.

Mal stood. It was clear: Karl was breathing but not coming around as quickly as the others were. Karl's eyes were flickering and moving but he was not yet coherent or aware. There was nothing more Mal could do here. Either his mind would survive, or it wouldn't. Either what lay on the floor was Karl or just some sack of meat. Mal heard the siren approaching: a medi-vehicle. She moved away into the crowd and allowed herself to be herded with the others as the medics entered and a pair of workers started pulling out a nano-plastic barricade. Then she slipped away from the crowd and down the street alone. Looking back once she saw the crowd still trying to see what was happening. The last thing Mal saw of the Rig Parlor before turning the corner was the crew of the medi-vehicle leaving their van and entering the Rig Parlor. They were in no rush.

⚡ » Chapter Four: Shield « ⚡

Nama was not part of the job, but Mal stayed in contact with him, meeting up for races when they were both able. She had never met another User in the Aetherium who could give her a challenge in flying. Competing with Nama pushed her past where she'd been. Being the best, she could be was part of this, and every job. That's not why I'm going to see him, though.

That night, they were playing a game of tag, tearing through the air at breakneck speeds, when Nama swerved northwards and flew toward The Spires.

"Are you crazy?" Mal said over their shared com program.

"Can't handle the Pylons?" Nama said, sliding the wings of his pod outward and rising on an updraft.

Mal flexed her wings and poured on more speed. As they neared The Spires the buildings got taller and more well maintained. Soon the more advanced, powerful, and therefore harder to hack Pylons of the Spires would take over the reality they were flying through. Hacking more performance out of her wings in most places was second nature again and in places with weaker Pylons, like the Trench or even parts of Old Drain, it was easier than it should be. But she knew in the Spire that would change.

Nama tore between two huge buildings and entered The Spires. Mal, just on his tail, could immediately feel the Pylons' strength, like a wave of heat spreading through her showing her that the Pylon saw her, registered her, knew what she was allowed to do. They both lost speed but neither faltered. They raced among glittering towers made of light and chrome that seemed a whole different world than the rest of The Drain. They spent an hour pulling more and more daring maneuvers before Nama pinged a sky café and said, "Let's land!"

Nama flew in full speed and changed his ship back to the quarterstaff as he landed, and Mal folded her wings back into her black hoodie as she did the same, just a heartbeat behind him. Looking good. The platform they landed on was like a dock, three air cars were parked, floating just a few feet off the brushed bronze walkway. The café itself was a transparent dome with a dozen tables and User servers and food programmers.

As they entered the dome, Mal felt the Pylon connect with her Rig, she was being Value checked. It was an uncomfortable feeling, a sort of soft buzzing. Mal waited for the pleasant ping which would mean she had been approved to enter based on her Value. Instead, the buzzing began to increase in intensity.

Then the buzzing stopped and Mal heard a distorted ding, one which meant that her Value had been insufficient but had been taken care of by another. Nama smiled at her and they found a table overlooking the city below, the Quantum River's glow apparent as a backdrop behind distant buildings.

A Patch came to take their order, dressed primly in all black with white piping along the arms and legs. She was pretty in a plastic sort of way, the sort of skin given out to those who worked in service industries to be both pleasant and unobtrusive looking.

"Your order, Sir?" She said to Nama.

Nama, one elbow on the table and the other hand on his knee smiled widely at her. "We'd like a flight of drinks. Your best sake please." He giggled a bit as he said it.

The server asked if there was anything else that they needed, inclining her head slightly toward Mal. Nama looked at Mal and shrugged with his hands and shoulders, smiling.

"We're fine. Just the flight please." Nama burst into laughter as she said flight.

"Sometimes I wonder if you're a ten-year-old boy," Mal said.

"Forever young, Mal, forever young."

It was mere moments later when the server brought out a long wooden board with eight small ceramic pitchers, and sixteen small glasses, arrayed two to each pitcher all along the board.

"Would you like me to explain the origins and qualities of your flight?" she asked, hitting the word flight with just a slight raising of the pitch of her voice, showing that she was also in on the joke. Nama burst out laughing.

"No thank you. We understand well the origin and qualities of our flight, even if they are not equal," Nama said.

Mal rolled her eyes and the server left, looking confused but playing along and laughing with the customer.

They talked aimlessly for a while, then Nama drifted off in the middle of a sentence. He was staring. Mal shifted in her seat.

"What?" She sounded more annoyed than she had wanted to, but Nama did not seem bothered.

"Are you sure I can't bring you over to our side?"

"House Ikaru? No way, man. I mean, sure you get fancy new toys and seem to have infinite resources but that's no fun. That seems almost too easy," she said.

Nama stared at her. "There might be other reasons to join us."

Mal smiled. "Always lots of reasons to..."

Nama leaned forward. "Please don't stab me."

He waited a moment to see if Mal was going to go for a knife, and then he pressed his lips against hers, and Mal melted.

"Nama..."

"Wait. This mission, this quest that you have. I see it hurting you. Every race, every time I see you, you are sadder. A little more of the light has gone out."

"Nama, please."

"Leave it. Leave all of it. Come with me."

The slow burn of Nama's kiss hovered on Mal's lips. He smelled, some-how, of fresh things. Wood, earth, plants. Was that the smell of calm? Mal closed her eyes, just for a moment. "Nama, I can't." When she opened her eyes, Nama's face was resigned.

"I see you, Mal."

"Nama, no." Mal stood close to him and stared into his eyes. She said nothing. Nothing.

Nama pushed himself back and stood. "Goodbye Mal. I hope you find what you seek."

He left. Mal did not ask how long he would be gone, or if in fact this was their last goodbye.

〉〉・・・・・・〈〈

In the Meatspace, the building moved on around Mal. She spent time with Gibson and watched Trent. Who do you work for Trent? Your subject wants to know. A new family moved in, carrying their things in from the relocation van that dropped them off. She only got a partial look at one of the parents. He looked almost hollow; his khaki-colored skin sagged with the weight of years he had probably not lived. He carried two large boxes in his arms.

She ran into Trent on her way out.

"New family moving in?" she asked.

"Yeah. Gibson will be happy," he said.

"Oh, they have a kid?"

"Two."

"Wow. Expensive."

"I know, right?" Trent said. "They're moving into Karl's old place."

"He's still at the long-term care facility?" Mal asked.

"For the foreseeable future, yeah. Prognosis doesn't look good."

Mal pushed open the main door of the dwelling.

Trent whistled. "It's really raining out there... can't your errand wait?"

Mal had a nightly deadline which she always pushed until the last minute. And now that meant a trip through the rain.

"It's time sensitive," she said honestly.

"Well, try to stay dry," Trent said.

"Hey, Trent," Mal said, standing in the door frame. "Is your dad as sharp as ever?"

"What do you mean? Did he try to get you to login and play games with him?"

"Yeah, that too. How's his memory though?"

"Like a steel trap. His body's frail but his mind's strong," Trent said. "He always liked you."

"Thanks, Trent," she said.

Mall pulled up her hood and walked out into the sooty rain. It wasn't far, the walk to the Parlor and then a few doors down to the narrow alley where the pneumatic tube waited for her drop. She made the drop and headed back into the rain.

"I saw you here when that guy got fried," a voice said from a rain-soaked overhang. Mal spun and saw that in the doorway of the Rig Parlor she was passing was a man in a grey-green poncho. His hood was also raised against the rain and he looked thin and pale, and ragged. His skin and hair were so pale Mal could have imagined the rain had washed all his color away.

"Yeah, I was there," she replied cautiously.

"Can you help me? Do you know a place? I need to stay out of sight a while and there are patrols everywhere," he said.

Trap, Trap, Trap.

"You in trouble with Axiom?" she asked, keeping her tone even.

He looked around in the empty rain-soaked street. He looked strung out and nervous.

He stepped forward too and extended a hand. "My name's Marcus and I'm not dangerous. I just need help." His hand and wrist stuck out in between them, pale and thin, with ropey veins under nearly translucent skin. Mal took a step forward and took his hand, and turned his arm over slightly revealing a faded white rabbit tattooed on his inner wrist. He took his hand back and looked her in the eyes.

"Come with me," she said, trying to sound certain. He looked confused. "Stay close, walk at my side and try to look like you're having fun," she said and started walking. He strode next to her. "You look like you're going to a funeral," she said after a bit in frustration. "Laugh, look like we're enjoying each other's company." He did, sounding semi-hysterical and more scared than lighthearted. Great work.

A patrol car drove by, six wheeled, armored, with lights so bright shining in all directions that the whole street was lit up like noon. Patrols like this were just part of life in Keral or anyplace Axiom held control, but the man cowered. Mal grabbed his arm. "Stay with me, man," she said. When they arrived at Mal's building the halls were empty.

Mal dragged Marcus to her Unit and pulled him inside. He looked unfocused, lost.

Mal went to her kitchen cabinet and took out a fresh tube of protein paste and a clean bottle of water.

"Here," she said, offering him the tube and bottle. He took it and stood there, dripping in his poncho.

"Get comfortable. You're safe here," she said. "I'm going to get dry clothes on. I don't think I have anything that'll fit you, but I can bring you a blanket."

She left him alone in her living space and went into her Rig room. She changed quickly and brought him the thin blanket she used. He'd removed his poncho and stood there. The tube was half empty already and the water gone.

"You can crash here tonight, but what's your long-term plan?"

"I need to get out of Keral," he said.

Mal sat on the thin cushioned sofa and motioned for him to sit on the other end of it.

"I'm wet," he said.

"Couch doesn't care," she said.

"Why are you helping me?"

"Are you Nanomei?"

"I'm. Well, not really anymore. I used to run with them but I'm neurally burned, man. I guess I'm retired," he said. Neural burn happens when a User takes on too much Glitch too often. It can fry their nerve endings and screw with the brain so badly that a User might not be able to jack in anymore. Mal shivered, either from the cold or at the thought of not being able to log in.

"Axiom doesn't forget," Mal said.

He looked deflated. "Exactly," he replied.

"Where are you trying to get to?" Mal asked.

"I need to get to Thresh."

Mal went to her Rig room again and let him finish his paste. She brought out the datapad from her rig. It allowed her basic access to information. The ability to order things mostly. For anything other than consumer activities she would jack in all the way. But this was simple.

"Do you have Papers?" she asked.

"No. I run off grid."

"Shit. Wow. Makes everything hard, that."

"Yeah."

A knock on the door sent both of them into silence and Mal raised a finger to her lips and went to the door. She saw it was Trent through the view-hole.

"What is it Trent?" she said through the faux wood.

"Just checking that you got in okay. Somebody said they saw a strange man in the building," he said.

Mal looked back at the strange man and motioned to the door to her rigroom. He moved quietly and quickly. Mal opened the door. Trent was standing there with a concerned look on his face.

"Everything okay?"

"Why wouldn't it be, Trent?" Mal said, letting some exasperation creep into her voice.

"Just thought I heard voices," he said.

"I thought you said someone saw a strange man."

"That's what got me to patrolling the hall," he said with a weak smile.

"Well, I'm alone. I talk to my Rig when I'm setting up. I have to get logged in, Trent. I have a stutter to smooth in The Drain."

"Oh, well I wouldn't want to keep you from Collective work!" he said, but made no move to leave.

"Thanks," Mal said, hoping that would finalize things. Still, he stayed, his feet just a bit in the door frame.

"You know, I could stick around. If there are strange folk wandering around maybe you'd feel safer if I was here?"

"I'm okay, Trent," she replied. "But, hey, thanks for watching me." She started to close the door. Trent looked as though he wanted to say something else but shifted his feet and let her close the door.

"Goodnight. Be safe," he said.

"Thanks," Mal said through the door, watching as he walked away towards his own apartment. Trent had left wet footprints behind him. Next time change your shoes too, Trent.

"He's gone," Mal said, coming back to the main room. Marcus was already coming out of the rigroom.

Mal's fingers were dancing about the datapad while she talked. "So, where do you want to go?" She asked.

"What?"

"I can rig a ticket to be physical. No Papers required. Or… it'll count as your Papers when you present it. You'll be pre-verified and secure and won't be questioned." As she spoke with Marcus she continued the work on the datapad. Station Seven.

"How do you get around the checkpoints that way?"

"You go out by train."

"But that's too expensive. That's impossible."

"No. I can cover you. The rich don't have to answer questions."

"You don't look rich," he said, looking around. Mal laughed.

"You're not wrong," she said. "But I know a few tricks." As she said this a datastick popped out of her pad. "Here," she said handing it to him. "Take this to the train station. It'll get you to Thresh. Last time I was at the station it was automated. You'll be fine."

"This must have cost you," he said.

"A bit, yeah. But if you need to get away from Axiom, I want to help you," she said.

"How do you know this isn't a loyalty test? Couldn't I be a plant and testing to see if you are a loyal citizen?"

"That's a risk I'm willing to take to help you."

"Why?"

Because I'm pretty sure you are a test... just not from Axiom. "Your reasons are yours and mine are mine. I want to help."

"When's the ticket good for?"

"It'll only last 24 hours. You can sleep here tonight and tomorrow it's not too far to the station."

"You haven't told me your name," he said.

"It's Mal."

"Thank you, Mal," he said.

"You can sleep here on the couch," she said.

"How do you know you can trust me?" he asked.

"I can't. Call it a leap of faith and an unreasonable confidence in my ability to handle you if you cause any trouble."

He laughed but it was a nervous laugh. It didn't sound too different than his fake laugh from earlier.

She brought him out a pillow and gave him the last of her water and paste. She'd order more tomorrow. Same day delivery. So many perks to life as a Citizen.

She left him on the couch. As she went into her bedroom he was already sleeping, his breathing ragged and stuttering. She lay awake most of the night, thinking about the bridge. She finally fell asleep near dawn but woke only a few hours later.

When she woke in the morning, Marcus was gone. The only sign of him remaining was the damp couch cushions. He had been real. But had his story? Test or real Mal had made a choice. Hopefully it was a choice that would bring a step closer to Ramos.

77

>> • • • • • <<

Three days after her loyalty test Mal walked up the subway steps from the login terminal to see a small yellow and brown bird sitting on the back of a bench facing her. And looking at her. She glanced behind her as a reflex, wondering if the bird was looking at someone past her, or waiting for someone, then caught herself and rolled her eyes. It's a fragging bird.

But things in the Aetherium can be more than what they seem. The bird kept its bright eyes fixed on Mal as she approached it. It cocked its head, watching her, seeming to approve as she walked toward it and held out her hand. It swooped down and into her outstretched hand and disappeared. An image, just five words, floated in the air above her hand for just a moment, then also disappeared: "Nice work by the Praetorian Center." Is that you Ramos?

Seemingly in response to her thought question, where the bird had stood was a transparent hologram of Ramos himself. He looked much as he did at the riot.

"Death Angel," he said. "I'm glad this recording has found you. I sent a flock out and was worried perhaps you'd gone to ground after the riot. I am glad you have not. That shows resilience."

Mal looked around herself and moved out of the walkway and sat on the bench. The hologram followed her movements, which was a nice touch. Hologram Ramos sat on the bench with her.

"My name is Ramos," he said after settling into a sitting position. "I, like you, have no love of Axiom. I, like you have certain talents. I would like very much to meet you." There was a pause in the recording. It was possible that it was programed to wait and then modify its message based on her response. She remained silent.

"Good. You know when to listen," the recording said. "I need proof of work if we are to meet, though. I can see from your tags that you are skilled at both hacking and coding. I can see many things about you. What I can't see is if you will follow my command. And so here it is."

The recording paused again, this time, though, Mal thought it was for dramatic effect. The hologram reached forward and offered a data chip. As Mal touched it a datapacket was loaded into a slot on her Rig.

"You will go to the Pylon detailed in that datapacket and disable the security protocols, including the panic button, for the residential units above the sandwich shop. This recording is not going to pause for questions. This is a direct command and if you can follow it, we'll meet."

>> • • • • • <<

Mal went to the Pylon mapped out in the datapacket. It was in a corner sandwich shop. Small Pylons like this were responsible for a building or two, or perhaps just one shop in a larger building. Nesting Pylons like this were the safest way to create redundancy in the system. A Pylon for the whole building but also a Pylon for this specific shop. There were three customers and an AI waitress. She wore a chrome female form dressed in a flower print dress and carried a paper-style notepad. She even had an antiquated graphite writing tool tucked behind one ear.

Mal walked up to the counter and ordered a corned beef, wondering as she often did about what the meal had been like in its original form, and sat at a window table. She tried to decide if she liked corned beef, or if she liked what Aetherium told her corned beef was, and then decided it didn't matter. She looked out the window across the street was a weapon vendor, neat lines of guns displayed in the window. Weapon programs in the Aetherium were complicated; ninety-five percent couldn't use a gun program with their rigs. But they could buy low-complexity skins of the programs as cosmetic items. And since it's not clear at first glance who is a User and who is a Patch, carrying a weapon can give someone a certain sense of power. Even if they can't pull the trigger.

Mal waited until there were a few more customers in the sandwich shop before making her move. Disabling the panic button wasn't difficult, but the message from Ramos had said that the change had to last twenty-four hours. That was the trick. It meant that a simple hack, an act of will, would not work. She needed to access and change the code of the Pylon itself.

Mal approached the counter with her dirty plate and glass. "Thanks," she said to the chrome girl.

"You're welcome, citizen. Is there anything else I can get you?"

"Pie. Could you list all the types of pie you offer?"

"We offer sixty-four distinct varieties."

"I've got time," Mal said, beginning a nice, slow hack. She pulled her will around her and pressed it out toward the AI. She found the edges of the AI's code and checked to make sure she was independent. Some Pylons run an AI as a simple interface, which would have been easier and more convenient; she would have been able to hack the Pylon code from her. But the AI was indeed an independent program. Mal made a few small changes to her as she continued to list pies. To Patches Mal would look like a patient customer, focused on the Serving AI. Any Users present, though, would have seen thousands of strands of blue-white code streaming and cypher rotating across the space between them. Mal cut the connection between the AI's sensors and her own specific image. The AI could no longer detect her. The serving AI would take care of other customers but would henceforth register Mal as empty space. Mal copied her key to the backdoor and activated both hacks at once.

79

The AI immediately stopped listing pies and went to check on a customer, forgetting Mal completely.

Mal walked through the backdoor to the Pylon room. It was larger than she had anticipated. The whole building, which included three or four shops, and a dozen dwellings on upper floors was being run by this single Pylon. She approached the Pylon, which had the form of a black metal cylinder with curved data display screens and holo-boards for access. She hacked away some intrusion countermeasures, which was simple stuff. She had been asked to remove the panic button from this Pylon. Taking out the panic button itself was an easy task any trouble would come from defenses in place but here there seemed to be nothing surprising. Peeling back layers of defensive programs on Pylons was something she'd started training for on her earlier days in the Academy. Eventually someone would notice, but she also left a dormant duplicate of the button so that it would take some real time to figure out what was wrong with it. Ramos wanted twenty-four hours, but without anything calling attention to the button this would last until the next maintenance cycle, which she could see through a simple check of the Pylon's logs was not set for another three weeks.

With the first Pylons handled Mal needed to check in on the nesting Pylons. These could be set up in myriad ways and some were simple to work around, and others were not. As Mal traced the lines of connection to the other nearby Pylons through the Pylon interface-nesting module it started to become very clear that there was nothing exceptional here. The Pylon she had modified controlled a simple residential area of a couple of floors in the building. The Pylon holding that one also housed several other floors, including the commercial space below. A third Pylon governed the neighborhood but still no additional security. Whoever lived in the residential area where she'd modified the panic button did not warrant any form of additional security through the Pylons. They must be common citizens. She walked back out having spent only a quarter of an hour or so. The chrome girl did not greet her and did not say goodbye. She had no memory of the strange customer who had asked for a recitation of all the pies they offered.

〉〉 • • • • • 〈〈

A day later Mal was at an old, exposed Pylon in The Trench; this Pylon was known for being shady in general. She was listening for chatter. It was a vacant, abandoned bar, but the Pylon was still functional in the Aetherium. Perhaps it had been abandoned by someone in haste and still had a viable power source, or perhaps it was a back door maintained by some recluse. This place was a well-known secret among Users like Mal. From the outside, the bar itself looked like a boarded-up, burned-out sort of place on the outside; inside the room was made of red brick which looked new and clean. The floor was matte grey concrete. Behind the bar was an old Pylon, exposed and open for anyone to access; it had been scrubbed of its identity and was a perfect conduit for receiving transmissions from any and all other Pylons. That meant that even though it was in the heart of an Axiom-controlled City it was a reliable place to get unauthorized news. Word on the street, chatter from an unregulated newsbox, these could be very helpful in adding some of that illusive transparency to Axiom decisions. And she was interested in the work she had done the day before at the sandwich place. She had a theory that it had something to do with the gun store across the street.

Mal sat at the bar with maybe six or seven people filtering in and out, a couple of them accessing the Pylon as well. The Pylon was built into the bar itself and was accessed through built-in bubble glass screens. Most of the patrons were hooked in through a standard interface: a simple program that connected to that glass. Place your palm on the glass, run the program and you had access. Mal, though, was using something that looked more in place. She'd coded a low-ball glass of whiskey that she set on the glass and when she wanted more access she drank. As long as the burn was on her tongue or in her belly, she could access the Pylon. And she coded her whiskey with a lot of burn. She wasn't showing off; it was all about immersion for her. Making the Aetherium feel more real than real. A midnight-skinned man with pure white teeth was playing some thumping electronic music and a pale skinned woman seemingly made of skirts was burning incense and dancing. It was dark and messy and the perfect place to stay up to date. Mal was dressed in a short black skirt over black leggings, her usual red combat boots, and a white tank top.

Unlike the slickly produced news of Axiom State Broadcasting, these were unofficial short video or verbal records, passed and curated by those who were able to corroborate some part of them. Mal sat at the bar and flipped through titles of Newsbits in her mind, though the burn of the drink. An overturned tanker had destroyed a city block with an explosion of its contents. A giant bear named Oxna had escaped it's programmed cage and run wild through the streets of Aegis Prime, an Aetherial Axiom fortress city. There were shortages in the Meatspace, solar flares causing havoc with satellites. There was little worry about the news being fabricated: Users were quick to call out fake stories and track down where the fabrication originated. A swarm of butterflies had clogged the air intake at an Axiom outpost. A chunk of city broke free when a Pylon went down, setting a seldom used back road out into the Quantum Noise. Someone had coded the sky to look pink for a whole day and the "sun" changed into a neon sign in the sky saying, "I love Molly." Mal drank her way into a records database and started sifting through residency records for Axiom citizens. It was not hard to do, not even illegal. Since Aetherial Identities and Meat Identities were never linked in public records, very few people cared who lived where. And there it was. The end of residency record for her Mother and Brother. A full two years before the Parade of Remembrance.

She took another drink, and her interest quickened: a still image of the apartments above the sandwich place had popped up. She closed her eyes so she could see the image more clearly, access the story. A slightly distorted vocal track over still images of the place: "The panic buttons didn't work, and six people had been derezzed." Getting derezzed violently is never fun, but in a city, and especially near a good Pylon, you just logged out with a headache. Mal had been on the receiving end of in-city derez many times. But if someone really wanted to crack your brain and kill you, they could in the time it takes to fully logout. All it takes is damage to the connection which can come in the form of any physical trauma to the Aetherial body. Usually, a User's Rig buffered that trauma or at least refreshed the connection regularly, especially near a Pylon, but this was not possible during logout and so a User was most vulnerable then. "At least three were Meat-Slain by accounts and checks with records." Mal pulled her jack out of the Pylon's console. The background sounds of the noisy bar retreated. Everything sounded hollow. Three people. Add them to my tab. She set her teeth against a wave of nausea.

Mal was interrupted by a red blip in the corner of her eye that needed attention. As she focused it resolved into a holographic overlay that only she could see. "It's time to get serious. Meet us at the rooftop across from the Dispensary on the Canal." She unplugged and left the bar through the alley exit. Put the Bridge aside. Put the six aside. Do the job. Earn the time. She pulled herself into the air, her wings flashing out fast. Mal didn't know if this was a meeting that would wait for her. She sped towards it fast and hard, barely taking time to watch her back.

Her HUD scanned the rooftop for her on the way in. There were three of them: The first two were hard light blue outlines drawn over their silhouettes, one hiding behind a pile of trash, one in the huge air vent that curved out of the building and onto the roof. The third was… harder to pin down. It was a few strokes of blue here and there and then gone. They must have been using a stealth program of some sort. Mal pulled her wings in just as her feet met the rooftop. She planted her feet firmly on the concrete of the rooftop and scanned the area. Hopefully, they had not seen the stumble and were suitably impressed with the wings and the serious coding skills it took to create them. She held out her hands, showing that she had no activated programs ready to use, no weapons.

Movement in the shadows cast by one of the piles of debris that scattered the rooftop. Then an anonymous voice: "Scanning." She stood still, swallowing her impatience.

The beam formed a 3-dimensional grid of lights that scanned up and down her body. Mal was confident it would only find what she wanted it to.

"That's a nice knife," said the voice. Perfect. She spawned the knife into her hand and tossed it to the ground in front of her. Theatrics. This knife was just hard enough to detect to make it seem like they'd accomplished something when discovered. Which, of course, left Mal's other programs inactive and hidden.

"Anything else on you?"

"No."

If they revealed themselves soon, this wasn't a trap. If they stayed hidden, it was. The fact that they were still in the shadows was adding to her twitchiness. Enough, Ramos. I've been chasing you through shadows long enough. She hacked a cigarette and put it, already lit, in her mouth, then paused. Thanks, Nama. "Oh, my manners. Anyone want one?" She looked around.

"You can stop showing off," said the first voice. No one approached to accept a cigarette. "We know what you can do."

"Doubtful." Mal took a drag from the cigarette.

"It's not safe to get too overconfident in the Aetherium." A second voice stepped out from behind a huge air vent on the roof. She was presenting as fairly female, black skin with cool jewel undertones, with a shaved head and a dozen or more neon and chrome chips neatly rowed into her scalp. She was wearing a grey-green jumpsuit. She put both palms up and stepped into the grimy light. Mal could see wires trailing from the back of her chips pulled into a bundle and plunging into her spine. She was torn between rolling her eyes at how hard this person was trying and respecting the skill of whoever created the skin.

But then she remembered seeing Chiphead before, in the back of a few crowded places. She had been one of the customers at the sandwich shop. She had been outside the BattleDome. Mal started rummaging through her memory for other times she had seen this person. She missed her old Rig which had the capacity to record, catalogue, and search her visual memories for a month at a time.

"I would not be here if I did not understand how talented you are." Ramos stepped out from the shadows. Tall, with copper skin and black eyes, glowing blue tattoos that swirled up his neck to his right ear. The glow seemed to pulse, slower than a heartbeat, more like the deep bass of some electro-dream rave tune. His hair was still annoyingly pointy and dyed blue-purple. "I'm Ramos."

"I'm Mal. But you knew that."

He circled her. "Your name isn't just Mal," he said. "You're Death Angel."

"How did you find me?"

"I have eyes everywhere."

"Okay, then why did you find me?"

"My group needs Users like you."

"Heh. That's what Axiom said at first."

"I feel like you'd be a better fit with us. I think you'd be happy working with us."

"I work alone," she said.

"Don't we all start that way," Ramos said flatly. "Look, your feelings for Axiom are clear."

"Frag Axiom," Mal said.

"Precisely. You may lack subtlety, but I think what you really lack is support for that hate," Ramos said.

"What does that mean?"

"It means there are plenty of like-minded people out there who could help you."

"I'm doing okay on my own," Mal said.

"But think of what more you could accomplish with people to help you. With safety."

"You can provide that?"

"We treat our best very well," he said.

"Alright, call me interested."

"Are you familiar with Severance Point?"

"Yes."

"Good. I have a job for you."

"It's starting to look like you're just getting me to do a whole bunch of your dirty work for free."

Ramos laughed darkly. "I like you. But you need to do this job and then we will welcome you as you deserve."

Scanner-wielding guy, still unintroduced, with blonde-yellow hair and soft-looking pink skin stepped out of the shadows. He held out his hand; in it was a slim metal disk with a faint blue glow. It was an old-school Crypto-loc. "You know how to use one of these?"

This time Mal let herself roll her eyes. "Of course." It was an incredibly simple program to use, a way of communicating coordinates. Trick was, though, whoever was on the other end could make untraceable adjustments; this meant the coordinates were always as up-to-date as they needed to be, but also made it tricky for the holder to plan too far ahead. All she had to do to see the coordinates was to hold it and concentrate. She took the disk and palmed it. "Anything you'd like me to pick up along the way?"

Ramos nodded. "Funny you should ask. I'd like you to bring me a Praetorian Shield." Chiphead grinned a wide, toothy grin at her.

"What do you want one of those things for?" she asked.

"You don't need to ask-" Chiphead started, but Ramos interrupted.

"No. I understand. It's good to question authority. Blindly following orders is not what Nanomei is about. Let's say I'm trying to piss off an old friend."

Chiphead looked surprised but said nothing.

Mal met Ramos' eyes. "You care how I get it?" *Is this the whole story?*

"Just as long as it's the real thing. And just as long as it's gotten from the Drain."

"No illusions, no hacks," chimed in the unnamed man. He was just a flunky, she could tell. Chiphead was almost an equal to Ramos. If things ever went sour, she'd be the first in the fight and the biggest threat; her loyalty to him hovered in the air around her like a fog. *Mullen's going to be curious about you, Chiphead.*

"Done. I'll see you at Severance Point. What's the clock?"

"No deadline. But if you'd like to impress me with your efficiency, go right ahead."

〉〉 • • • • • 〈〈

She soared above the cityscape's tall black buildings and towers of light; far above the grubbiness of street level but close enough to feel the energy of the city. Her months with this Brix had paid off. Hours of gaming domes and jumping off rooftops and racing Nama was making this passable. It wasn't anything like the Razor, but it was allowing her to fly again and pull off some sweet hacks too, without frying her with neural feedback and Glitch for her trouble. Mal flew lower to compensate for the shorter buildings, watching the streets below her and trying to take the knots out of this problem. Separating a Pretorian from their shield would not be an easy task. Was it as difficult as she thought an endgame test would be? Not really. And that made her worry. They should have come up with something more impossible for the final test. There was an Axiom Recruitment Center near here and that always meant a few guards. Maybe she would get lucky.

Approaching the Center, though, she found what she needed. Circling the Center, a few blocks from it in all directions, were Axiom Checkpoints. Streams of people waited to be scanned before they could leave or enter the area. Axiom was sure to have disabled all logging in and out in the cordoned-off area. Praetorian Guards were checking people through on the walkway, vehicles on the street. She landed in a nearby alley to watch the checkpoint for a few minutes.

There were three Praetorians on the street checking vehicles, and one on each walkway on either side of the street. Praetorians were overkill for this sort of work but after the Bridge Incident they'd become more ubiquitous. They were fully equipped with maces and shields. A properly sized disturbance might separate them. Simple math: one is easier to deal with than five. There was a fair-sized crowd, all Patches, on the street watching the checkpoint, and a few dozen lined up to get through. They wouldn't be trouble. Mal gave herself a moment to think about how strange it was, hiding in the shadows planning to attack a Praetorian. Just a moment.

Mal held her hand out in front of her and concentrated. She pictured the chaos she needed, the Pretorians enraged, the scene disrupted. She needed an explosion. Something she could carry in her hand, and throw… she could feel the reality of the Aetherium pressing up against her. It knew she did not have a Ibrahimade in her hand. It knew, too, that Ibrahimades can't appear out of nothing. she concentrated her will on her open hand. There will be a Ibrahimade here. Blue dots of energy coalesced around her hand, swirling, gathering themselves into a shape. The Aetherium pushed back, but she was already certain. In another moment, a smoke Ibrahimade sat in her hand, solid and real. It was time to move.

Mal peered around the corner at the checkpoint. A few dozen people in line on the walk, three ground cars, low and sleek metal, and glass, on the street. She retracted her wings, clutched the Ibrahimade in her right hand, slipped it into her hoodie pocket, and joined the line. She would need to keep her mind on the Ibrahimade if it was to stay solid and real until she needed it.

The Patch ahead of Mal turned to glance at her as she joined the queue.

"What's the checkpoint for?" Mal tried her best to sound bored and irritated.

The Patch presented as a nondescript worker, someone who moved Aetherial data across from one end of a desk to the other. Inbox to outbox, inbox to outbox, repeat on infinite loop. "Who knows? Who cares?"

The Patch ahead of her turned. She wore a bright blue uniform with the House Ikaru logo emblazoned on it. She was a Kiosk Girl and probably far from home. Her job would be in one of the seven Ikaru Malls in this city, hawking the latest Aetherial Tech. "I heard an unauthorized person tried logging in at the Recruitment Center." Mal looked ahead to the checkpoint. It was as good a theory as any. The Recruitment Center ahead was sure to be marked high security. Axiom would not permit anyone but their own officials to log in there. She squeezed the Ibrahimade in her pocket to reassure it that she was in charge of whether it was real or not, not the nearby Pylon. If this were a real emergency, Axiom would have ramped up the nearby Pylons and a hack like this would have been much more difficult to pull off and to maintain. The guy shrugged. "If Axiom loves their efficiency so much you'd think they could get this line moving faster."

Mal took a deep breath. Do the job. "Maybe this will help." She tossed the Ibrahimade ahead of the line, toward the checkpoint. It went off with a loud crack, and smoke poured out of it, filling the air with a giant smudgy cloud. The Praetorians did not flinch, but shoved their way through the crowd immediately, searching for the culprit. Mal gave the one closest to her a little wave and took off running, back toward the alley. At the entrance of the alley, she chanced a look behind her. There were two Praetorians after her. This was definitely more complex math. She reached the alley, turned into it, slid to one knee and pulled the invisible blade she was carrying from its wrist sheath. She took and released one deep breath, concentrating on how solid the weapon felt in her hand. Mal turned to the face the entrance of the alley.

The two Praetorians were charging into it at full speed. Full chase-down-the-deviant speed. She jumped straight into the air as they entered the alley, side-by-side with their shields in front of them in a wall. She waited until they were underneath her and she dropped faster than gravity strictly required, slashing one across the back with her blade on the way down, landing behind them.

The Praetorian yelled out in pain through his helmet but they both held their ground, spinning in place to face her and pulling their disruption maces out of their holsters. The one she'd hurt had telltale blue arcs of energy crawling over his shoulder: Glitch. It would slow him, make his connection weaker. Mal could take advantage of that.

As they approached, she ratcheted up her concentration, and ran up the wall in an arc to get back behind them, slashing again at the one that was already hurt. Her arc put her about five feet behind them, and her blade strike hit home. He went down to one knee. The other hesitated, probably considering calling in backup. It was clear his ally was about to log out. The Glitch wasn't bad, so he'd be ok if she left him alone while he logged out. Unless he had already taken in Glitch she hadn't seen. Mal looked at the other Praetorian and took a step back. Behind her, she heard the telltale buzzing of a logout in progress. The second Pretorian took advantage of her walking retreat to charge forward. He swung his disruptor mace wide, but she felt confident that her counterstrike…. Before she had a chance to counter, he brought up his shield and slammed it into her side. She went flying and smashed into the brick wall of the building to the side of the alley. She tumbled down the wall and landed in an undignified heap on the concrete. He came at her again. She leapt to her feet and backed deeper into the alley, getting some space between them. Something big moved between the lights of the street and the alley. Two more Praetorians. It was really, truly, time to run.

Mal had been hoping to lure one Pretorian away from the crowd, run a hack, and steal his shield. Stealing programs, though, is not easy; it isn't just a matter of cracking the defenses of the rig, but also the nearest Pylon. A couple of Praetorians bashing her face with disruptor maces were not going to make it any easier. She needed time.

The Praetorian near her was not giving her any, though. He smashed at her with his shield, and, when she ducked away from it, followed through with his mace. She dodged that, too, just barely. "Stop resisting," he yelled, his voice booming through the voice modulation program Praetorians always had running. He swung his mace again, using a lot of strength but not a lot of creativity, and she leapt backward, coming up against the brick wall of a building. Nowhere to go. She pressed her hand into the wall behind her, feeling the cool, rough brickwork under her palm. She felt the code spinning and pushing the idea of wall out into the Aetherium. She twisted that idea and moved the wall. The wall reappeared between her current Praetorian problem, and the other two running toward them, cutting them off. The Praetorian that remained on her side of the wall cursed loudly and took another swing. Her head was still spinning from the hack and she reacted too slowly. His mace caught her in the shoulder and then shoved her into the wall, crushing her between the bricks and his shield. Her shoulder was pure agony. Disruption maces can be used to apply a sort of shove, or just do raw, physical damage. He'd set it to try to kill her.

"Nice shield," she grated.

He raised his mace to derez her completely. She gripped her blade and stabbed it into the soft spot in his armor, just under the arm. He let out a yell of pain and anger and fell to his knees, Glitching in and out. She deactivated her blade and grabbed his shield. When he finalized his logout, the Pylon would try to download the missing shield. She needed a fast hack. She also needed to get the hell out of there, as the other two Praetorians had started smashing at the brick wall. Only a matter of time before they broke through. She was lucky that she was fighting Praetorians; they tended to be far too uncreative to pull off a hack, and her wall would stand up to some smashing far better than another hack right now. The Praetorian was still kneeling on the ground; somewhere in the Meatspace, his body was struggling toward consciousness, in a Rig somewhere, with one hell of a headache.

She had it. It had been a difficult hack; she'd had to move her mind in and out of the code strings faster than usual to make up for doing twice the job. She felt the Praetorian's Rig surrender the shield and immediately the Pylon began to try to derez it from her. No. She ignored the sounds of the wall she'd built being smashed to pieces and completed the hack to sever the shield from the Pylon. This was not a kind of hack that she'd often attempted. Stealing wasn't her thing. At least it hadn't been until today.

The shield was free. The wall Mal had made was crumbling, revealing the other two Praetorians, one yelling "Cease!" while they waded into rubble up to their armored knees. The wall would not have lasted long even without the Praetorian's efforts; but it had served its purpose and delayed them long enough for her to steal the shield.

The shield was heavy and awkward. She needed to stow it but didn't want to stop running. She spread her wings and took to the sky, being careful to angle away from the Recruitment Center. She was moving slowly but she got some air between her and the Praetorians and flew into the night. Axiom protocol would be to send drones. She deactivated the shield and slid it into one of her rig's slots, the shield disappearing into nothingness in her hand.

As soon as she stowed the shield, she felt an immediate lurch. A huge wave of exhaustion washed over her. She felt overcommitted, her cycle time faltering. It was her rig; something was really wrong. The shield reappeared, heavier than before, in her hand. It must have had a safety feature, some sort of dormant virus. It was replicating itself and filling her rig's memory slots, eating capacity. Unchecked, this would lock her in place, unable to move, she would have to lose the shield or figure out what this problem was and fix it. To do better work Mal would need to get to a console to be able to access the code in her Rig more directly. That was limited when logged into the Aetherium without the console. Her blade was already disabled, the alien code burying it under its weight. Her wings started to sputter, and her vision clouded. Her sensory package was compromised. With shield in hand, she would be unable to log out through normal means.

Her vision was blurring out and she started to plummet. She angled herself behind the shield, crouching behind it as she fell. The shield took the brunt of the damage as she impacted in the streets of The Trench. Pain wracked her whole body, Glitch pulsing through her. Struggling to her feet, she hefted the shield, which felt almost an impossible task now. She dragged it towards the nearest building. She needed a place to recover. She heard Axiom sirens. They were searching for her. She stood, weighed down by the shield and staring down the street but an Axiom Air Car, hovering over her, sirens blaring, intense search light shining down on her.

For a heartbeat she considered trying to tell them who she really was but that wasn't possible. Ramos was most likely watching this. Had probably known that the shield would react this way. Was probably laughing his ass off. Mal had no time for talk and needed to get away from this air car. From how the horizon looked when she fell, she was pretty sure she was about five blocks from the river. She gathered every ounce of strength she had, took all buffers offline, and shifted everything into flight. Her wings glowed with a golden radiance, and she blasted off into the air.

"Cease Citizen!" the amplified voice of the Air Car pilot roared.

Mal turned toward the neon blue Quantum Noise river and put as much speed on as possible.

The Axiom car behind her was keeping pace. She was speeding directly at the river.

"Cease Citizen!"

She did not cease.

As she approached the river, she felt the Glitch threatening to gather. She flew straight at it and, looking back, saw that the air car was following. It was already starting to spark blue Glitch from its engines. She dove. Fast.

The car followed; she was only a hundred feet above the river when she pulled up. The car started to tear apart. She was going too fast and at the last minute realized what was inevitable. She plunged into the Quantum Noise.

Her entire body and mind screamed in pain, but she focused on two thoughts. She felt the Praetorian's shield in her hands and the idea of flight in her mind. She did not stop to die. She screamed through the river and arced out of it. She did not look back to see that the air car had utterly been destroyed but she could hear the screams of the Axiom Agent inside it dying. And the echoes of those I threw into the river from the bridge. She rose up, Glitch tearing at her form. She was not going to hold together for long. Her wings were falling apart behind her. She put on as much speed as possible and climbed out away from the river. She was over the Southern Trench district then when she could climb no further. She tightened the grip on the shield and stole a look behind her. Nobody was following.

Then, angling herself towards the Burbs, a few blocks in from the river, she started to fall. She tumbled down in a small residential schema, an area of small gathering spaces like a cluster of homes in the Meatspace. These were simple homes, from the outside looking like little more than grey cubes from a distance, showing their decorated skins only as she got closer. They looked, closer, like small boxy homes made of many different materials, a stone castle-looking one, another looked like a small pink box with a white fence of some kind around it.

Mal landed roughly in the street, her wings shattered and her form failing. She kicked open the front door of the nearest home. She didn't know for certain if she was being followed, or how far behind her they were if they were following her, or what else this damn shield was going to do to her rig. There were programs that could corrupt a User's other stored programs, screw with their senses, or even tag them and start burrowing into their Rig to identify them.

The interior of the house was not powered, so it presented as a small empty room, maybe 30 feet by 30 feet, with black walls, floor, and ceiling, with a vid screen on one wall. Totally undefined. The only light came wearily from the street behind her and barely made it into the room. Mal scanned the walls with her HUD while rezzing her multitool and found the control panel; she ripped it open with her multitool and hacked the controls inside; the power came on and rezzed furnishings into the room; suddenly the barren space was a comfortable-looking room with two big chairs facing the screen on the wall. She accessed the home's console through the screen and spawned in a workbench in the corner with a strong light above it. The choices available in any home depended on the Value of the owners, and what they'd preloaded in. This was simple stuff she was choosing from. Their chairs had been set to spawn in on activation which told her that they were the type to spend considerable time sitting here. This workbench would serve as a rudimentary console for her, something she could use to dig deeper into the code of her Rig and the shield than a hack would allow. She would need access to more complexity than these people had, though. She needed to do something about that quickly: she hacked the panel to convince the Pylons in the area that this house was cleared for much higher complexity.

Her mind was full of Glitch; she could hardly think straight. The pain thudded through her head, but she continued to work. She was running lines of code almost faster than she could read them; the code from the shield was worming its way deeper and deeper into her rig. This was not standard protocol. This must be new tech, or maybe a mod made by the Praetorian she'd lifted this from. She worked carefully. At every turn, as she prodded the code it reacted and continued to replicate. She Just didn't have time or resources to really deal with it and working here was not a stress-free environment. And her head her head her head. The workbench provided a holographic keyboard that shifted, morphed, and moved about in an attempt to help her code, or in this case decode, the shield.

Mal was keenly aware of what this shield program would have done if most Users had gotten a hold of it. Their rigs would have been almost immediately overcome and they would have fallen to the ground. They would have been completely unable to move, change their input or log out. Their consciousness would have been trapped. It's possible that the virus would stack Glitch on the person as they started to rez out, which could easily kill a Patch. But she was not a Patch.

She left the shield on the console and stumbled away. She was starting to lose control of her senses, of her body. She collapsed on the floor and felt the worlds spinning. If she were not physically in Keral right now, if she were at her old posting, there would be attendants there to help her mitigate the Glitch, to keep her body safe. To help her if she became unable to function.

She had nearly passed the point of reason. If she logged out now and left the shield she might escape without brain damage. She might be okay. But then the pain washed over her anew. The Glitch was replicating, and she needed to stop it. She could end the mission. Not just this ridiculous fetch quest, she could call it all off. Summon Axiom with the panic button in this house and they'd come for her. Sure, she'd probably be demoted, or at least lose the possibility of promotion, but she'd live.

She closed her eyes and lay on the spinning floor of the worlds.

She started to hack together a program. Something to smooth the Glitch, to ease the connection. She started simple, a first aid program she'd memorized at the academy. She had one in her rig, of course, but the shield worm had already corrupted it. Her programs were inaccessible, so she'd need to hack together anything she needed here. She closed her eyes and saw the strings of code as she went through the rote memory to recreate, through her hack, the prog. It was harder than it should have been, her thoughts difficult to bring to focus. A stitch here in time argh.

She brought the first aid program online. The hypospray appeared in her hand and she pressed it against her thigh and activated it immediately started to smooth out her connection, This did nothing for the pain and the Glitch but it started to clear up her senses a bit. Then she took the empty spray and started to hack that. Hacking the can, changing it, was easier than focusing enough to start with a fresh hack. To modify it well beyond what it was designed to do. There were advanced programs that could bleed off a small amount of Glitch with each activation. She was crafting one of those. Glitch… go away…. You bitch. Ha! Glitch bitch Glitchbitch Glitchbitch….

Finally, after what seemed an eternity of dizziness and reworking the same code threads over and over, she had the modified program and applied it to herself. The Glitch bled off and she was finishing the repair of the damage the shield had done when the vid screen on the wall flashed to life. "Security Alert: Active Renegade." A picture of the renegade on the screen. "Security Alert: Active Renegade." Beneath these words was a three-dimensional image of a big red button. Everyone in the Aetherium knew what to do in this situation. Watch for the renegade. Using the Security Activation Protocol, report any sightings to Axiom's forces. She looked at the door she had broken on the way in just in time to see the silhouettes of two people standing outside the home, surveying the damaged doorway. She could see past them into the street; it was not lost on her that a 15-foot-tall image of the renegade flashed behind them on a giant vid screen They eyed, in slow motion, the vid screen in the house, turned to look at the one on the street, and then looked at her. The renegade. In their house.

The first man looked middle-aged with warm amber skin, thick greying curls and a thin, hungry frame. He looked calm and ready to deal with the situation. The other was more worrisome: he looked agitated, scared. His dark brown skin was showing glimmers of sweat. They were just Patches, no danger, but they could of course access their Security Alert Protocols if they touched their view screen. Don't ping for help. Don't make me… just don't make me.

"Who…. are you?" Asked Grey Hair. "What do you want?"

"My name is Mal," Mal said. "I just needed a place to work on my rig." She moved slowly toward the door, and they inched away from it to keep distance between them. One was squinting a bit at her, trying to get a better look.

Mal lifted the door back into the doorframe and hacked it back into place. She did this with a little less subtlety than normal. She wanted them to see her power. "This doesn't have to be a bad scene. If you can just go about your business and stay away from your vid screen, I can gather my things and leave. I am sorry but this is just something that had to happen."

They looked at each other. She could see them communicating; the silent language of people who have been through some shit together and don't need words to agree. They looked back at her in unison, but it was Grey Hair who spoke. "Agreed. We don't want any trouble here." He paused and glanced at Worried. "So... can you leave? And take trouble with you?"

Turning back to her workbench, Mal grinned wryly. "Yes." That's me. Door-to-door trouble. They approached their furniture cautiously, then sat.

"I... work at loyalty processing. I am known to be loyal," Worried said. "I bet."

"Is that a real Praetorian shield? How do you have that?" Worried sounded just a little impressed.

"You don't want to know. Remember your loyalty." Mal ran final checks on her rig. It was good enough for travel, maybe not a huge fight but for travel. There was no way to even think about getting the shield hidden, though, so it really was a Noise-Ship she was going to need to get to Severance Point.

"Look. I need two minutes to contact a friend and then I'm gone," Mal said.

There was something inscrutable in Grey Hair's expression. Something he wanted to say? Or to ask her? He did not look as upset at her presence in her home as he should. His expression changed, telling her he'd decided. "Okay. Take the time you need. We will not call for the authorities."

A sense of relief flooded through Mal, and she brought up her telecom package and scanned the Docks, a nearby Schema. She pinged three people she knew could help if they were nearby: Tae, Nama, and Tok.

"Hey Mal," the smooth voice of Tae filled her senses.

"Tae! I'm in a situation," Mal said into her comms.

"I got your ping. I can be to you in three cycles."

"Frag. That's forever!"

"Yeah. I know but I'm out in Belkar and I have a shipment I can't ditch."

"Thanks, Tae. I'll be gone by then."

"Another time, Mal!"

As she disconnected, she received a quick voice note from Nama: Mal. In New Tokyo on Assignment. Can't reach you. Can send ship if needed."

But a third reply came in as well, just a ping, no message. It was from Tok, and the ping came from The Docks.

Mal allowed herself a smile. "Okay. I'm out of your hair. And there's a bright side for you. I recoded your connection to up your complexity. I needed it. It will be there for you to use. It'll stay that way indefinitely unless you mention it to billing. Consider it a thank you." The connection between the local Pylon and a house like this determined the total complexity of programs they could run. The more complex a program the more functional. The more interesting the program, usually, the more complex. This was a quality-of-life improvement that would have taken both of them a lifetime to afford.

Worried opened his mouth, maybe to protest, but Grey Hair quieted him with a look. "Thank you," they said together, taking each other's hands.

"You're welcome."

Mal picked up the shield and stepped out into the street. A bit of a crowd gathering at the vid screen, but no Axiom agents swarming the streets. Yet. She had flown fast and far enough away from the incident that the door-to-door search had not yet reached this Schema. She spread her wings out behind her, took three steps, and launched herself into the air, carrying the awkward and heavy shield the best she could. As the Patches and their neighborhood grew tiny on the ground behind her, she turned toward The Docks and flew to them with all speed.

➤➤ » Chapter Five: Ship « ➤➤

If Mal were taking a normal trip on a normal day, she would simply disconnect and walk out of an approved Access Point attached to a publicly accessible Pylon. Safe, legal, untraceable, and easy. Travelling with stolen goods made that mode of transportation impossible. If she logged out, Axiom would register the program that should have been attached to a Praetorian. They would have immediately found it, and her. Keeping the shield off her Rig meant that she had to literally carry it out in the open. If she had been able to load the shield more completely into her Rig, she could have reskinned it to look like something else. Now she had to hope that others who saw it assumed Mal had skinned something else to look like the shield. Frag this entire mission.

Tok would be able to point her to a ship that could take her through the Noise to Severance Point and her meeting with Ramos. Tok was well known at the Docks; she was a brilliant engineer who worked her way to become Captain and was somehow crazy enough to love travelling through the Noise. Which made her a perfect member of the RezX collective. They were all mad. Super-smart, but mad.

The Docks opened beneath Mal as she circled, the shield dragging on her arm. She kept lookout behind her as she arrived. She wasn't very familiar with this part of the Drain, as she avoided travel by Noise-Ship, because she was not insane. The Docks weren't fancy, all bare metal bones, but no one that frequented them were interested in their beauty. The Docks were there for travelers to rez their ships in or out, or to unload big cargo, or, for the truly stupid or desperate, book passage on a ship headed out into the Noise. No, she thought. Not only the stupid or desperate. There were still true explorers in the world. Maybe the Noise is the last uncharted mystery.

Relatively reassured she wasn't followed, she circled downward, eventually drifting to a perfect landing near the Dockmaster's station. The station was really more of a giant desk, kind of plunked down in the middle of the docks. The Dockmaster, Max, worked for Trinidad, who worked for no human. Trinidad was The Drain's most prominent businessman and criminal all rolled into one. Max was well over six feet tall, had deeply blue-black skin, and wore a grey suit on his broad frame and a heavy, jeweled ring on as many fingers as he could manage. She had never seen Max in person before, but he was well-known in the Drain, and when he was working publicly for Trinidad like this, had a regular appearance he maintained in order to be recognizable. Mal nodded at him, and kept walking, or tried to: Max raised one hand. "Renegade." His low voice rolled out of him like a song.

"I'll be gone in five minutes."

He made eye contact with her, and she froze in place. He seemed to be considering her. "Make it three."

"Three. Yes. Absolutely." He turned away, and she felt free to move again.

"Contact Tok." A tiny picture of Tok with hair from at least three re-skins ago appeared in the upper left of her display.

"Hey there," Tok answered, her voice ringing adorably into Mal's ear-piece.

"Hey. You free?"

"No, but I'm cheap. Are we meeting at the Cube?"

"I'm at the Docks." Mal kept her voice steady, despite the adrenaline churning in her veins. "I need a ride out of here. Any ideas?"

A pause. "My ship is on the far slip about three hundred yards from your position. I'll meet you there. This have to do with your... status?"

"I'll explain when I see you," Mal said.

"No, you probably won't," Tok said, sounding resigned.

Relief flooded her but it was tinged with guilt. "Thanks." Mal disconnected and looked around. She had landed in the primary hub, which was connected to the city by a long, wide walkway made of black metal. Curving around the edge of the Schema that walkway continued and from it jutted long slips where Program-Ships docked. Many of these ships would be for internal use only: moving cargo within or above the city. A few would venture out into the Noise. Every ship here was wildly different. There were maybe three dozen vehicles, all program ships, at the Docks that day. A few had decks protected by clear, Noise-proof fields, like bubbles of air that could move underwater. Some looked like private airships, small and unnecessarily fancy covered in rare metals and decorative flair. A few here looked like they had a strong need to defend themselves; they had mounts for guns and obvious armor plating modifications. Most of these ships were surrounded by people working on them, modding them up and preparing them for work, flight, or fight. The RezX ship towered over the others, at least six or seven times larger than the other ships docked around it. It looked like a vast tube of bronze and punctuated with half-domes of darkened blue glass. Mal walked towards it steadily. Confidence is the best camouflage. She felt outside of herself, disconnected; the Glitch was still affecting here, creating a tiny lag between thought and action.

The RezX Collective built and operated the safest of these deathtraps; their tech enabled them to build mobile Pylons, allowing travelers to log in and out on their ships. Having a way to log out on the ship is really the only reasonably safe way to cross the vast expanse of the Noise, but even then, there's no guarantee. It always takes some time to finish logging out, and if a User started logging out at a Pylon that was destroyed or damaged, they could end up just as scrambled as if Glitch knocked them out of the Aetherium.

"Isn't she beautiful?"

"Tok." They embraced, Mal still holding the shield in her left arm and hugging Tok firmly with her right. It had been a long time. "Love the hair."

Today Tok's hair was styled in a bright green pixie cut. She visited skinning parlors regularly to change her appearance; even though she had some programs to change her looks in the Aetherium she liked visiting the shops. "It's the artistry," she was fond of saying. She was wearing the leather smock of an Engineer, covered in blast marks, and creased by a wide leather belt that had at least a dozen tools that Mal could not name hanging from it. All of this over and in stark contrast to the khaki uniform beneath.

"Thanks. Love the…" Tok waved her hands appreciatively in Mal's general direction. "Let's talk." She walked toward her ship and Mal followed. "I have to assume that giant and very illegal shield had something to do with your urgent need to get out of here."

There were a dozen questions in what Tok was saying. Mal couldn't answer a single one of them. "I need to get to Severance Point."

"That could be on our path. We're heading out pretty deep, and it doesn't really matter which way we go to get there."

"Pretty deep," Mal shuddered. "Any chance I can get on board?"

"I can squeeze you in." Now, closer to the ship, Mal could see it in all its… beauty? Tok gestured toward this ship with both of her arms. "This is Aura." Mal had the strangest feeling she should say something back to the ship, but she refrained. A huge antenna array piled with haphazard-looking scanning equipment jutted out from one spot and several of the domes looked as though they were in the final stages of being repaired. A dozen or so workers were crawling over the hull, some working with bright arc welders, others using a sort of gun that seemed to be fastening hull plating. It was loud and active yet somehow not at all chaotic. It was a dance.

It's kind of lucky that we connected." Tok gave Mal a sidelong glance. "It's been a while."

"You know me. So lucky." They were at the gangplank. Their footsteps rang on it as they walked, metallic and hollow.

Tok stopped and turned to Mal. "If you want on, and want to get off at Severance Point, you'll have to do a torpedo drop."

"Seriously?"

"That's the catch. Isn't there always a catch? The Collective ceded docking rights to Ikaru in a really complicated trade agreement three months ago. I can't dock there even if I wanted to."

"OK. Fine. I'll do it. Let's just get on." Mal felt like a blazing flare standing in the open with that giant shield at her side.

Tok led her through the open doorway of the ship. The clatter, voices, and mechanical sounds of the docks faded away, replaced by the lush murmurs of a skilled crew and the hum of RezX tech. The entryway was dimly lit by gaslight globes dotted along the walls. The interior was paneled in a dark, polished wood. Fixtures, such as the gaslight holders and the door handles, were all in brass. Mal smiled to herself, Super-smart, mad, and snappy decorators. As they walked deeper into the bowels of the ship, they could see more crew, moving in a coordinated way she couldn't understand, foul-mouthed cogs of some great clockwork beast. They all wore the same close-fitting, pocket-covered khaki uniforms, complete with belts and sashes upon which various tools and weapons hung. After Mal bumped into a few of them and was summarily cursed, Tok managed to get her and the shield down a narrow side hallway into a small cabin.

"Stay here," Tok said with obvious relief. "Once we're underway, I'll come get you and we'll take a walk around the ship." She grinned at Mal and scampered off. Mal had not known a grown person could scamper.

The cabin was glowing with that same deep brass color scheme. It was basic, with a bunk, a desk and chair, and no windows. A small lamp on the desk cast a gentle glow. Mal propped the shield up in a corner and collapsed onto the bunk. This was a welcome chance to recover, finally rest, and feel safe, if only for a short time.

Mal reached out with her mind, feeling the Aetherium at work around her. She could feel the pulse of the ship's Pylon Drive, pressing the reality of the ship into her consciousness. This was a much different feeling than that of a normal Pylon. Most of her life in the Aetherium Mal had spent time in Aetherial cities which layer Pylons upon each other, keeping the Quantum Noise several Pylons removed. And the Pylons she'd lived near and had been accustomed to were built on Nodes, places within the Aetherium where the Quantum Noise was less dense, like islands of relative safety. Pylons enhanced that natural safety. This Pylon, though, must be strong enough to stand on its own, and not on a Node. The intensity of the Pylon made Mal feel like less of a User, less like she could Hack. It made her feel cut off from herself, isolated within this place but also isolated from herself. She caught herself imagining just how hard it would be to hack against this Pylon. It felt like a constant drumming in her head, the beat deep and intense, echoing the thought that this ship was secure, this ship was secure, this ship was secure. This Pylon would protect the ship as it traveled out beyond the borders of any Node or other Pylon. This was going to be an interesting trip.

She was not tired physically; after all, her actual body was still in the Meatspace, still jacked in, physically at rest. But her stress levels were exhausting her. And guilt was wearing on her. So many dead in the wake of this mission. And Tok. Tok was saving her ass, here, but would she go to these lengths for an Axiom Agent? Every word Mal said to her was on some level a lie. Mal tried to sleep. The bed was comfortable and the hum of the ship reassuringly monotonous, just at the level of hearing. She let herself drift off.

Mal dreamed. She was at the Academy, in her dorm. Her Rig was just on the other side of the wall. She did not go to it. She sat and concentrated on her breath and started to float just about an inch off the ground. Then she gave the command in her mind without connecting to the rig. Login. She rezzed into the Aetherium. Everyone around her there moved slowly, deliberately. She was in a city, near to a great Pylon, its orange beam of light a pillar in the sky. Mal flew up into the sky. There were no programs on her; her physical form itself was in the Aetherium. Mal flew in spirals and caught updrafts and soared straight up along the edge of the beam of light. Reaching out with just her fingers she traced a line up the beam. Quantum sparks flared to life along her arm. She flew higher and higher, towards the eternal Quantum Noise. Scraping the Pylon as she continued upward, she felt her physical form start to deteriorate, blue sparks erupting from her body. She pressed onward, higher, and higher. Finally, she broke free and appeared back in her room, which was on fire. She could hear screaming. Axiom agents everywhere were running and burning. She stood among the chaos, not knowing what to do.

A loud whooshing sound and then a muffled voice, some kind of announcement, broke into her rest. It took her a moment to realize where she was and to orient herself to the ship. She never dreamed in the Aetherium. She barely dreamed when she slept in the Meatspace. Sleep in the Meatspace was never long enough or deep enough to create any dreams; she would not have thought her short sleep cycle in the bunk would have either. I am drifting here.

What had the announcement been? They were out of Dock and in free space, plummeting through the Noise. Mal could feel the active Pylon Drive's reality close around her like a glove, both comforting and claustrophobic. The Pylon would work hard to protect passengers on the ship from the Noise, but in doing so would cement its reality around them so hard that hacking would be difficult if not impossible. Mal spent a frustrating hour trying to sleep again, to no avail, before she heard a brisk rap at the door and opened it to find a beaming Tok. Tok loved it out here, that was clear, and she was brimming with energy. "Let me show you around."

99

Their visit to the bridge filled Mal with a mix of wonder and terror. The front of the bridge, across from where they entered, was the inside of one of the huge blue domes Mal had seen from the outside. From this side, though, the dome was completely clear and transparent so she could see the way the ship was hurtling through the Quantum Noise at ridiculous speeds. Mal imagined those first people finding this world without the protection of Node or Program, their minds ripped apart by the Quantum Noise. Mal felt a little sick, standing in this dome.

At the center of the Bridge was a battered-looking workbench, one that had been merged with an old-time computer, with keyboards, dials, and a box of several small levers. There was an important looking but empty chair, there. The captain's chair, surely. There was a man hovering at the station, but not sitting in the chair, who nodded at Tok as they entered. He took a bit of a shuffle away from the chair as they talked in.

"The bridge has five stations," Tok murmured in Mal's ear. She pointed to an elegantly haphazard arrangement of screens and monitors of different shapes and sizes. "That's Echo Station. It shows the Noise in all directions. That's the Fuse, or the weapons station."

Mal nudged her with her elbow. "Who names these stations?"

Tok grinned. "Captain's prerogative. That's the Stick, which controls the throttle. It funnels power from the Engine Room to the Bridge." The Stick really was just a large lever and some readout dials, round and brass with glass faces. "And the wheel, of course." The wheel looked like the iconic images of the wheel of a sailing vessel but with several more dials and switches installed upon it's polished wood surfaces.

"That's only four stations," Mal said.

"The Chair," she said in a purr. "My personal station. Mine. Just mine," she added.

After the Bridge, they ducked briefly into the crew quarters. There were a dozen bunks. A few other crew members were here, a trio at a small table playing cards, two lounging in their bunks. Tok introduced her and Mal promptly chose to forget their names and identifying features.

"You'll really like this," Tok said as they slid down a ladder and into the deeper bowls of the ship. Though there were no signs posted, Mal knew immediately that they had entered the Engine Room.

The room made the Bridge look open and airy by comparison. There was more gear and equipment in the room than there was open space. In the very center of the room was a huge brass-ringed cylinder containing intense blue light. "That's the Core, the Pylon itself," Tok said in a hushed tone. "All of this equipment helps the ship function," Tok said, "but this," she put her hand on a more contemporary looking data console, sleek and silver, attached to a bronze arm mounted on the cylinder, "this is the heart of the operation. The direct connection to the Pylon." As Mal stared at the Pylon she could have sworn that it was somehow staring back at her. Tok was still talking, but Mal was wrapped up looking deeply into the Pylon. Mal could feel it confirming her own existence in the ship. Mal could feel it maintaining this whole structure against the Noise. Mal also knew, standing there, that the mind inside of that Pylon was beyond her ability to comprehend. It was so far beyond the AIs of the Pylons she'd encountered up to that point. It almost felt as though this Pylon had a distinct…personality.

"You can see her, can't you?" Tok said in a whisper. And for just a moment Mal could. Standing in the blue light Mal saw the form of a woman, tall and broad-shouldered, looking deeply into her eyes. All Pylons have an Artificial Intelligence inside of them that runs the Pylon itself and is inseparable from the Pylon; but Mal had never seen the AI in this way. As more than coded intelligence. As though…

Then she was gone.

"Yeah. I saw her," Mal said.

"Did you fall in love too?" Tok asked.

〉〉 • • • • • 〈〈

As they continued the tour, Tok showed Mal down a long hallway. She pointed out small boxes attached to the brass pipes running the hallways.

"Notice that the air isn't stale and yucky in here?"

Mal nodded. She had, actually.

"I added these. They mix in a bit of code that makes the air feel fresher."

Mal looked at her blankly.

"I modded out the sound dampening in the walls, and the wooden floors, so that the interior of the ship was quiet and free of the roar of the Noise outside and the constant footfalls of the crew. You should hear what it normally sounds like in here," Tok said, reaching for the box.

"No! It's alright. Thanks. I appreciate your work without the demonstration."

As they walked on two people were running towards them, jogging with plenty of room in the corridor for passing.

Tok grabbed Mal's hand and then put them both into the center of the passage, directly in front of the joggers. She was holding the brass bar with her other hand. The joggers were not backing down but coming straight at them; Mal tried to pull away but Tok's grip was tight. The joggers passed straight through them.

"Like it?" Tok asked. "If you hold the brass bar other things can clip right through you. I made that. They're installing them in all the ships next month," she said, nodding to a polished brass bar running along one side of the corridor. She let it go and they continued.

Tok ended the tour in the mess, pushing Mal ahead to a long, polished wood table, busying herself at a side table and a crazily constructed coffee pot (also clearly modded out, Tok-style), and returning with two mugs of coffee.

"Why are RezX coffee programs so much better than everyone else's?" Mal asked. "I mean, aside from your invention there."

"We have the most complete database of what those plants were really like in their natural habitat…"

"Ever have coffee in the Meatspace?"

"Stim drink, sure. Real coffee from beans, nah. Every slice of my Value rating goes straight to my ship." She said, gesturing around her.

Mal raised her tin mug to her. "Amen."

A crew member stopped while they were talking. "Captain Tok? Daniels says that the Noise dampers on the starboard side are off again. Can you help?"

Mal half-listened, and let her eyes wander the mess. There were a few crew members at the cook station, at the far end, chopping piles of fruit into bits and arranging them on a platter. Mal had to admit Tok was right; RezX had some good food programs. Mal could see apples, peaches, melons, and even some she did not recognize: a dark purple fruit that oozed sticky-looking juice as it was cut, and something pink and green with wicked-looking spikes. Mal listened idly as Tok rattled off some words Mal didn't understand in an order that made them no clearer. From the look on the young crew member's face Mal had to assume this was at least partially true for him as well. Mal grinned. Hard to keep up with Tok on any day, but today she was drinking coffee. Mal got up to wander around a bit. Some welding marks crisscrossed the wall of the mess, which was on the outer edge of the ship. Most of it was rubbed by age to match the bronze metal of the hull, but there were a few marks, four long slashes, that had a new shine to them. They were recent work. They were about eight feet long, parallel to each other, with a bit of curve to them. Mal put down her coffee and crossed the distance to the wall. Mal placed her palm against it. She felt Tok beside her. "If I didn't know better…"

"They are."

"What? How?"

"Noise Beasts."

Mal turned to look at her. Her face was deadly serious and a little guarded, as though she were sharing trade secrets not meant for Mal's ears. "Noise beasts…." Tok glanced around them and Mal lowered her voice. "Noise beasts are this big!" Mal held her hands out, about a foot apart. "Seriously!"

"Some are." Tok nodded toward the table, and they returned to their coffee. "They are mostly bodies and arms or legs. Some have hard carapaces.

They're more varied than we are. They look like hybrids of some sort... cybernetic bugs. But on our last run we were attacked by something much larger. With claws. It tore clean through the hull in six places and the Noise just... poured in."

Mal tried to block that image from her mind forever. "Why have I not heard anything about this?"

Tok shook her head, her green cascade of hair sliding back and forth. "Axiom and Ikaru don't want citizens freaking out, so they're trying to dismiss the information as rumor. They seem to think if they choose to ignore science it goes away. It does not." She looked again at the slash marks and a shadow passed over her face. "There's worse."

"I cannot imagine worse."

"I think the ones that attacked us were intelligent."

Mal felt her insides chill. "No."

Tok leaned forward. "They weren't just mindlessly attacking like I've seen them do. This was organized. A flock of littler ones came in first and wrecked the sensor array. They were so small our weapons couldn't touch them. When the sensors were down and the weapons were useless, two big ones came in and went for the hull. The bridge got a lucky shot at one and they retreated."

"Does anyone else know?"

"This whole crew does, that's for sure. Off this ship, most of us RezX Captains know. We're calling them the Rhommox. We lost three crew members to the Noise in the attack."

Tok went off to do Captain stuff. Mal spent the next hour in an observation bubble, staring out into the Noise, wondering what was out there and how badly it wanted to eat her. She tried not to think about how good it was to see Tok again, even in these guilt-ridden circumstances.

〉〉••••••〈〈

When Mal left the bubble, she felt strangely reluctant to return to her cabin or the observation deck. Moving through the passages and past rooms she had not yet seen, she wandered. Mal realized that she was walking with purpose, but it was a purpose she did not understand. She stopped for a moment and rested her hand against the wall of the ship. What am I looking for? Mal rapped her knuckles against the wall of the ship. That's not it. I'm not looking. You want to show me something, don't you? Mal needed to stop wandering and start exploring. She needed to get deeper into the ship.

But, of course, first she had to get distracted. A doorway on her left stood open and voices were drifting out into the hallway; interestingly, the voices were discussing her.

"I hear the captain smuggled some lover onboard."

"I hear it's some renegade."

"I heard it's a spy."

When Mal peeked into the door, she saw a group of four women in various stages of peeling off brown rubber Noise Suits and changing back into their ship uniforms. These were Sirens. Mal had heard of them. They worked on RezX Ships, making repairs and modifications from the outside. It was one of those jobs that only gifted hackers could perform well; the hacker also had to be crazy enough to step out into the Noise.

"I'm none of those things," Mal said.

The one who was mostly back in her RezX shipboard uniform stepped forward grinning. "Hey. I'm Kay. These are Sindara, Lily, and Wanda. You sure you're not some juicy gossip?" Kay's hair was impossibly long and braided, and she was tucking it into a complex knot as she spoke.

Mal shook her head. "I'm Mal. Just boring Mal."

"Welcome aboard, what's your gig?" Kay asked, finishing her hair.

"Code smoother out of the Drain."

"Working stiff, eh?" Wanda grinned a wide, toothy grin. As she finished belting on a clanking toolbelt stuffed with program tools.

"Nothing as exciting as Siren work."

"You ever taste Noise?" Lily asked. There were a few glances passed around the room. Lilly was by far the smallest of the Sirens and looked much older than the rest by at least a few decades. She was wiry and lean and her skin resembled the suit she had just sloughed off.

"Most of us don't jump out into the Noise on purpose," Mal said.

Three of them laughed.

"There's stuff out here that we sometimes need to fight," Kay said, buttoning the top of her uniform while she leaned against the lockers.

"Out there? As in, Axiom? Pirates, what?"

"You'd have to ask the Cap." Sideways glances went around the room.

"Noise beasts?"

"No sense in wagging our tongues over it, though, eh?" Lily said, closing their locker with a slam.

"Aw. She runs a tight ship, eh?"

"Cap is Cap," they said. It sounded like they said it a lot. Kay smiled and sighed.

"So are there always four of you and do you often speak in unison?" Mal asked.

Three of them laughed at that but it was a harsh laugh. "We're down three," one said.

"Like they're off duty?"

"Like they had to disconnect and get medical aid," another said. The rest started to shuffle nervously at the mention.

"That's not something you're supposed to tell, eh?" Mal asked.

"How do you and Cap know each other?" Sindara asked her, changing the subject.

"That's classified," Mal said to a chorus of laughs.

The Sirens were mostly finished dressing by then when Kay put her hand on Mal's shoulder.

"You're a friend of Cap's so you're a friend to the Sirens."

"We are going too fast to take you out with us, but if you're still here when Capt'n stops running us like a torpedo maybe we could suit you up," Lily said.

Nothing in all the worlds sounded like a worse idea. "I get off at Severance Point," Mal said, trying to sound disappointed.

"Another time," Kay said. "If we finish our dive before Severance we can sit and talk Noise Beasts to your heart's content."

"I'd like that," Mal said.

"Ever onward." Kay said and was joined by a chorus from the others. Mal smiled and ducked out of the doorway.

Leaving the Sirens behind, Mal walked through a bit more hall and a room and found a hallway she had not seen before. She still felt that sense of a need for exploration, as though there was something on the ship Mal desperately needed but could not find, or even name. Mal followed the hall to a long, thin room with six porthole windows looking out to the Noise. The room was lit by the eerie blue light from the Noise beyond glowing through the windows. Along the wall opposite the porthole windows was a line of six pedestals. On each one was a physical model of a Pylon. The first that Mal came to looked like the ship drive that Mal had seen with Tok, though without her modifications. As Mal moved down through the room, the models were depicting older and older versions of Pylons. All the way at the end was a Pylon from the earliest days. It was tall, like a giant spike driven into the world. It was round and slightly askew on the pedestal. Made of some sort of crystal that had been surrounded by a latticework of chrome, the Pylon's control panel was shaped like a chair that could be used to log in from the Meatspace.

Mal exhaled slowly. This was the history, the story of RezX's early attempts to conquer the Noise. The RezX were the first to really get Pylon Tech right. House Ikaru was busy making the rigs, the interfaces, better and better. But it was RezX who were pioneers in the Aetherium itself, and even though Pylons exist in both the Meatspace as huge server farm-like clusters of computers and in the Aetherium, as physical objects pressing reality into shape, most of the finesse of making the programs actually function must be done Aetherium-Side.

RezX is also the only Collective to have mastered the creation of Pylons that were mobile in the Aetherium... their ship drives. Were you calling me?

Great. I'm talking to rooms now. But then the room talked back and Mal's vision swirled.

Mal saw the AI from the Pylon standing there, luminescent, and beautiful, made of light and dreamstuff. She reached forward and touched Mal's forehead. Mal did not flinch away and felt the cool press of the Pylon's fingers on her flesh.

"See what I have seen," the AI said.

Mal saw a landscape made of enormous black cubes arranged like buildings. And a battle raging all around. Then she was there, standing with the Pylon AI at the center of it all.

"Reverse the entirety of the net," a voice said. "Draw power from the AI. We need the ship to stay close." Then a ring of code more complex than anything Mal had ever seen swirled like an impossible tornado all around her, making the ground become the sky and the sky become the ground. For just a moment she saw Ramos' staring at her, no at the ship. It was unclear exactly what was happening but Mal could hear the screams of what she knew to be thousands being cast into raw Quantum Noise. She heard them all dying. She pulled her hand away from the gyre of code and then she was standing in the room with the models again, alone. This is what you wanted to show me.

>>••••••<<

Mal heard footsteps approaching and turned toward the hallway. Tok was striding towards her looking like nerd on a mission.

"Problem," she said as she entered the room.

Mal put her many questions aside for later. "What is it?"

"A distress call. RezX Research Vessel. It sounds bad."

Mal followed Tok to the bridge. "What do you want me to do?" Mal asked as they hurried forward in the ship.

"I don't know yet. Stay close."

The bridge was buzzing. There were officers everywhere, all with expressions of quiet intensity. One was activating a large table that sprang to life with a three-dimensional rending of the outside of the ship and the ship we were approaching.

"There's a beacon on the ship," someone said.

"I'm not picking up any pings. I don't think anyone's left," said another.

"I've got movement!"

"Yeah, but that's not..."

Tok grabbed Mal's arm. "We are going to have to fight," she said.

"Wait, what? Fight what?" The room was suddenly alive with alarms.

Tok met her eye, and that connection felt like a sudden oasis of calm in the frenzied room. "There are Rhommox on that ship, and they're coming for us."

"I don't see anything," Mal said, pointing to the table display which showed only the two ships getting closer and closer to each other.

"They evade our sensors. But there are enough signs. The ship we wanted to save is being eaten by creatures and they've sensed us. There's no way to outrun them and fighting at speed is more dangerous than standing our ground. Our Pylon can help us move or fight but not both."

"I've got six, maybe seven. I think they're all Rhommox. Looks like mostly drones!" someone yelled.

"What can I do, Tok?"

"I am sending out the Sirens," She said. "You could suit up with them. We're down three. I know you have zero training, but I've seen you hack. Out there, in the Noise, you'll be worth a dozen Sirens."

Mal gave herself three seconds to let the pure terror of this idea wash over her. Then she nodded at Tok. Do the job, do the job, do the job.

"Captain Tok! We could abandon ship. We may have time to logout before they destroy the hull."

She and Mal both looked at the officer who said this.

"We abandon ship and we lose out on the last three years of modifications to my ship. She hasn't been disconnected in all that time. And the cargo. What about that? You're a good pilot, kid," Tok said. She left the rest unsaid, but everyone on that bridge heard it. A brief silence followed, broken only by the alarms. Mal knew that it was more than that, but ship decorum seemed to keep them from giving voice to the real threat. If the ship were to fall to the beasts and Quantum Noise rushed in it would be too late to log out. People would be logging out and very much vulnerable to both the Beasts and the Noise. People would die.

"I'll find the Sirens," Mal said to Tok. "We're going to get through this," Mal said and put a hand on Tok's shoulder.

>>••••••<<

The Sirens helped Mal get into one of their suits and within a few minutes, she had been given a crash course in operating two very important pieces of equipment: first, the suit that would serve as protection from the Quantum Noise, and second, the tether, which hung in the form of a rod at her belt and would keep her from drifting into the endless Noise. Wanda went over the use of the tools and rod, while Kay made sure she understood the dangers of the Noise. If Mal needed to get back to the ship all she had to do was point it at the ship and activate the rod. "You need to be within about a hundred yards, though," Wanda told her. "The rod holds a shard of the ship's Pylon. Activate it and it will bring you home in a relatively straight line and fast," she added.

Kay said, "When we're out there, in the Noise, we are not fully protected by the Pylon."

Mal stared at her and stopped walking. The rest of the Sirens continued on and started climbing into a narrow hall, which ended with a porthole out to the access port. They noticed as a group that she was not with them and turned back to get her.

"You mean to say that there will be nothing limiting my hacking?" Mal asked.

Kay grinned at her. "Almost nothing. That Rod keeping you connected to the ship also keeps the ship's protections close at hand."

Numbly, Mal allowed them to drag her along. They joined the other Sirens in leaving through the portal from the ship. Mal had never felt such a combination of terror and exhilaration. To be untethered.... But out there in the Noise... she just hoped she didn't vomit into her suit as she took one hesitant step out of the airlock. It was strange that it wasn't strange. The Pylon's influence reached the hull of the ship and so she could still feel the Pylon supporting her, wrapping her in safety, in warmth and the smell of coffee. That's the stuff. The Sirens, six of them, surrounded her. Some she had not yet met but there did not seem time to get acquainted. Mal stood on the hull of the ship and looked around.

Water metaphors are used to talk about Quantum Noise across the Aetherium, but here it was clear to Mal that the areas between Pylons was much more like what she imagined space to be. Great emptiness with a swirling swarm of blue electrical mist. Mal remembered seeing old images of distant nebulae and galaxies. This is what the Noise looked like out this far. Out several hundred feet away Mal saw the disabled ship. The ship was failing completely, already broken into three main pieces. Streams of code were pouring out into the Noise. Standing here, on the very edge of reality, pulled Mal's mind a thousand directions. For the first time in the Aetherium she was genuinely afraid.

A swarm of creatures streamed from the wreckage of what was once a sleek, silver ship. They were a meter across and winged and far enough away that Mal could see little else in terms of details. They moved as if flying in random zigzags; Mal could see no pattern to their movement. The Sirens started rezzing weapons: Wanda a large gun, Sindara a sword and shield, Kay and the rest spears.

Mal spread her wings and tried to measure her breaths. The Quantum Noise itself was mere feet away from her and Mal was about to be engulfed in to. On purpose.

"Stay close to the ship, Tok will bring us in, wait until we push off to fight."

Mal didn't know which Siren was saying these things but she appreciated the direction. These women were a fighting unit and one of her main goals here, aside from not dying out in the Noise, was to not get in the way of their work. Mal ran a diagnostic on the suit she'd been given and brought up the controls. It was possible to use the suit for flight out in the Noise and her wings would work with the suit to make it faster than it was designed to be.

"These things, the big ones at least, are almost impossible to kill. We need to do enough harm to them to drive them off. Mal. Tok says you're some sort of Hacking prodigy. Feel free to impress us," Kay said.

One of the blue domes on Tok's ship halved itself and opened to reveal a gun. Sort of. It was small, the size of a person, perhaps, and made of a large copper coil with a bundle of multicolored wires wrapped down the middle and braided through the coil itself. When it fired the copper glowed blue-white and then a ray shot out the color of a sliver of the sun. The gun fired and the swarm dodged away, and towards the Sirens.

"There's something in the wreck," Kay said.

Mal could see that there was indeed something there, something large. It was nothing more than a shadow among the other darkness. The Quantum Noise rippled blue around its vague outline.

The Sirens gathered themselves around Mal for a moment and then bent their knees and launched themselves towards the approaching Drones. Mal wasn't ready. She felt unstable. Mal could feel the edge of the ship's Pylon all around her protecting her. They had just leapt away from that protecting field of reality, launched themselves headfirst into oncoming dangers known and unknown.

Mal stood her ground, making as ready as she could; she swiped all the feeds to full on her suit's wrist control panel and drew out her invisible sword. Over her head, about a hundred yards away, the Sirens engaged the swarm in an arhythmic dance, stabbing, swinging, shooting, and fighting. The Sirens worked together like clockwork birds. One dove towards a pair of oncoming drones, and sliced to the left, drawing their attention while two other Sirens attacked with their spears and another swept past, raking with a torrent of darts from some hidden weapon.

Drones swarmed all around, but the Sirens answered blow for blow, dodge for dodge. Wanda took deep, echoing shots with a long gun; after she fired a few times, the Drones homed in on her and started to tear at her with multiple passes. Each pass, one of the creatures lunged a bit off their swarm's path. They were working in unison, in concert and with intelligence. They did not let up and though several other Sirens came to her aid, but she was clearly hurt. One of her fellow Sirens wrapped her arms around Wanda and pulled her back toward the Aura.

Mal launched herself, but did not fly, strong and graceful, as the Sirens did. She tumbled end over end. Tok's ship was rotating in and out of view, the Sirens battling in a cluster, surrounded by drones. Moving in the Noise was nothing like moving in air or in water. She felt free and yet every movement made her more and more aware of the strange nature of the world around her. Every breath in the contained skin of the suit was full of terror.

Kass, of all people, came into her mind. They had zero-g training at the academy. Mal had never done well with zero-g, but Kass had taken to it as a natural. "Close your eyes," she told Mal once. "You need to reconcile that there is no horizon." Mal had closed her eyes and immediately vomited. Mal could still hear Kass laughing. It was shortly after this that Mal had thought to start constructing wings. That night, in the dorms she stayed up, logged into her console and Kass' laugh played through her memory all night as she built the first alpha version of her wings.

Mal closed her eyes. Emptied her mind. She saw Kass standing at the edge of the Academy roof and heard the promises they were making to each other. We will climb these ranks together. We will travel to the forbidden continents. We will learn to fly without programs. We will be free. Mal opened her eyes and was still. Tok's ship was behind her, the swarm and fight with the Sirens ahead. Mal reactivated her wings and pressed herself forward.

Mal launched herself straight ahead. She flew between two drones, slashing them both as she passed. Kay was tossed by a blast of energy from a drone and Mal grabbed her hand, spun with her, and threw her back into the battle. The battle was fast and fierce, the Drones eager to rend flesh or blast with their beams of concentrated Quantum Energy. Their hard-shelled, fast-moving bodies repelled a great deal of the Siren's attacks, the energy beams reflecting at angles off the shells of the drones. A few direct hits cracked the armor instead, shattering the Drones. Mal made her share of graceful strokes and worked in concert where she could. Her blade too glanced off the smooth shells, but she was still able to make a few solid strikes, piercing in through the armor. Mal also felt in the way at times, and started to fight in a more isolated way, moving away from the main group to engage with stragglers from the swarm.

One drone flew straight for her, a cold calculating intelligence in its dozen eyes; Mal was able to hack a net into existence without a second thought. It was made of green glowing strands of energy. Mal whooped with joy. Hacking had never felt so easy or come so unbidden. No gathering and focus of will, just pure raw improvisational creation. She summoned a shield and found the code dancing at her command. The shield glowed with intensity and the weight of heavy steel as she transposed it between a Siren and an incoming attack from a drone. The drone smashed at full speed into the shield and blasted itself to bits with the impact.

110

As Mal fell behind the Sirens, she hacked a platform to jump off from to gain more speed; it appeared in a heartbeat under her feet, and she sprang full speed away from it. I make my own horizon now. Wanda took a hard hit from a pair of drones and Mal, some sixty feet away, hacked together a rope and threw one end of it shooting through the air to the wayward Siren. Mal modded the rope as Wanda grabbed it and pulled, shooting the Siren back into the fray. Mal shouted with glee as she hacked these things. Mal heard Tok swear over comms as a drone tore a large gash into one side of her ship. Mal flew along behind the drone, just out of reach of the ship's Pylon. Mal pushed her newfound freedom in hacking to reverse the effect of her blade. It became a blade of bright light that Mal ran across the tear, sealing the gaping hole as she went. Mal heard Tok's "Holy shit, Mal. How are you doing all this?" through the main comms shared by all of them in the battle. This felt amazing; Mal was building reality itself with no rules.

The ship's gun was smashing into the wreckage of the Ikaru ship and the beast inside it. And the swarm seemed to be well in hand when Mal heard the roar. It shook all of reality from the ship to her bones.

Almost as one, they all turned toward the sound. The creature that had made it looked like a sort of lion, but with huge, leathery wings and claws like scimitars. It was huge. It roared again and landed on Tok's ship.

"Mal, Tok here. There's something really big coming at you."

"Thanks for the heads up," Mal said, staring.

"The creature over at the Ikaru ship is nearly destroyed. How's the swarm?"

"Sirens are on the swarm. I'll handle this thing," Mal said.

"Is that smart?"

"Definitely not."

The lion spread its wings. Are you jealous of mine?

Mal swooped back to the ship and readied her sword. She hacked more speed into her wings to make her approach even faster.

Mal swooped close enough to the Lion to swipe out with her sword. Mal slashed hard and sliced into the beast's wing. It screamed in pain, a sound that was partly organic and partly technological. The beast pounced towards her and Mal ducked out of the way of its huge claws with no more than an inch to spare.

Getting this close to Tok's ship hindered her hacks a bit and her wings slowed down. But it was not the harsh reality of the Pylons she was used to interfering with her; It was more comforting somehow. The beast was on her. Mal turned and her wings and back scraped against the hull of the ship as the creature clawed at her and pinned her to the ship. Pain ran through her right shoulder as the beast's claw pierced her Siren suit.

All hell broke loose. The Sirens and swarm were still fighting, and the derelict ship exploded completely, leaving nothing behind but a million tiny particles each derezzing in flashes of blue light. But that wasn't the hell of it. Hell was the fact that the Siren suit Mal was wearing was now punctured. Mal could feel the program trying to seal itself, but it was failing. Its connection was crashing, and the Noise was flooding into her suit. She didn't understand the suit well enough to hack a new one into place. She felt panic wash over her in a wave of heat. The Noise burned, tore, electrified. She smelled ozone and tasted acid on her tongue. The beast tried to bite her, but Mal dodged away, and it snapped above her head.

Mal was struggling to bring her sword upwards to the beast but could not. The creature roared again. Her suit started to disintegrate. Panels flew off, and reinforced undercoating eaten away as if by a strong acid. As she moved more of the suit broke away and flared into nothingness. Mal was in raw Quantum Noise. The Noise shielding from the ship was keeping the Noise mostly at bay and still it was tearing into her mind. She could feel it eating away at the connection keeping her in this world. She was running the very real risk of violent, even fatal, disconnect.

It was like Glitch, but worse. Glitch was localized pain and moved through a body. Quantum Noise was inside her, tearing her apart from the mind outwards. This is what I did to those people on the bridge. The beast roared again, and it was as if the Noise in her responded. Mal was swimming in acid, electricity streaming through her mind. She screamed in pain and blacked out.

›› • • • • • ‹‹

"You up?" Tok's voice was gentle.

"What happened?" Mal felt as if she'd been torn apart and put together roughly. A child's toy cobbled together from pieces that didn't fit.

"You did good," Tok said. Her face was large in her field of view and behind her Mal saw the inside of the small room Mal had been given in her ship.

"How'd I get back inside?" Mal raised her hand, closed, and opened it in front of her. There was feeling there but it was numbed by the pain. Even in trying to focus enough to move her hand hurt.

"The Sirens brought you in after they took down the beast."

"Did we lose anyone?" Mal thought about sitting up but decided against it.

"No. A few were hurt, but the Pylon has healed them."

"How'd it end?"

"You were moving so fast we couldn't track you," she said. "Great wounds opened in the creature."

"My sword. You can't see it," Mal said.

"I know that. And the beast started anticipating your moves and got a hold of you for just a moment. Its teeth tore your suit."

"I don't remember this."

"Then it took off with you. I don't know how, but you activated the rod and it tethered you back to the ship. I sent the Sirens after you. By the time they found you the beast was dying, and you were in bad shape."

"They risked a lot, coming back for me."

"I would have kicked their asses if they hadn't. Come on."

"I would like to not go anywhere, please. I like this bed."

"Come on, you baby."

Tok half dragged, half cajoled Mal out of bed and led her to the Engineering room. Every step was painful for Mal and required intense concentration. They walked to the polished bronze of the Pylon; Tok took Mal's hand, and, keeping her hand on the back of Mal's, pressed her palm against the cool metal.

"Close your eyes," she whispered. Mal obeyed.

With her eyes closed Mal focused on the feel of the cool metal on her palm and the heat of Tok's hand on hers. Then the metal felt as if it started holding her hand, lacing smooth metal fingers through both Mal's and Tok's. Mal's connection was suddenly surging, fireworks in her closed eyes. Her sync burned like raw fire in her belly, and Mal felt as connected more deeply into the world of the Aetherium than she had ever before. The pain melted away and was replaced by comfort, energy. Mal turned and Tok's face was close to her own, their eyes locked for a moment. Mal didn't know if there was a cost to this, did not know what really was happening, except that she had been accepted by the Pylon in a very personal way. "Is this what it means to be part of your crew?" Mal asked.

"No, silly," Tok said. "I've never let anyone else get that close to her."

>)) • • • • • ((

Mal sat cross legged in her room, alone, on the small cot. She closed her eyes and tried to call back that feeling from the Pylon. Tok's hand. The Pylon's hand. One of the core functions of a Pylon was to replenish connection. But Mal had never experienced anything like this. She let herself wonder if it was the nature of the mobile Pylons, or if it was some RezX secret. Or maybe Tok had something truly unique here.

Mal's sync was still incredibly high. She sat and looked inward. Self-reflection was not one of her talents, but some kind of pause was called for. She closed her eyes, feeling more than a little foolish. Tae had tried to get her to meditate with him once, but quickly gave up. Mal wondered if it was the eye rolling or the giggling that had done it; either way, he refused to ever try again. She tried to remember what he had said. *Focus on your breathing...* her Matron was always saying that, too. Instead of focusing, she felt her mind drift. Hacking out in the Noise had felt like that first day in the Aetherium when she opened the window. *What window was she opening now?*

Mal heard a whisper. "You should join us."

Mal knew it was the Pylon, literally, speaking to her, and was not surprised.

"I can show you wonders you can't imagine," the Pylon continued.

"I believe you," Mal thought back.

"She trusts you," the ship thought, spoke, whispered... Mal couldn't tell anymore.

"She is safe to trust me. I would never hurt her," Mal said. Mal felt a skip in her heartbeat as she wondered as to the truth of that statement. *For a mission?*

"I know."

Mal felt herself fall asleep, was fully aware that her body had tumbled to the floor. Mal let herself sleep. The Pylon showed her visions. The ship, new and glorious, streaking away from the shipyards of The Museum. A hundred voyages into the Noise, six captains, countless horizons visited. And all from the point of view of the living heart of the ship.

Her last vision brought her back to the Pylon room. She knew she was not really there, but it felt real. More real than a dream less than the Aetherium. The Pylon stared out at her.

"Like seeks like," one of them, Mal was never sure which, said.

〉〉••••••〈〈

Though Tok was back running the ship full time, and had suggested she rest a bit, Mal couldn't rest, could not seem to stay in her room. Every time she returned there, she stood in the doorway and then left again. *She had felt this before, as she'd come aboard. She was calling to me even then.* Mal felt as though her skin were humming after her time in the Noise. The unfettered hacking... Mal could see why the Sirens went out there. Mal was beginning to see the allure of this form of travel. She paced the ship, no real destination in mind.

"Hey!" Mal jumped. "Oh, sorry!" It was Tok, of course. "You lost?"

"Nah. I found what I was looking for, thanks. Now I'm just wandering around your awesome ship."

Tok's head was tilted to the side. She was considering her. "I know you're weird. But...." She paused, then made a decision. "I want to thank you for what you did out there."

"Don't get all mushy on me."

"I'm serious, Mal. I know you're a badass hacker, but I didn't realize... I mean, you are a force to be reckoned with."

"Thanks," Mal said. Mal wanted to ask about the ship, about the Pylon, about what they shared.

"When you do your drop, you'll have to keep the torpedo shell intact. Those things don't stay together well but you shouldn't have any problem keeping it together. Simple hack, for you."

"After fighting Noise Beasts, it sounds easy."

"Where did you learn? I mean, you've obviously had some really advanced training."

The question hung in the air between them. Tok and Mal had been friends for about three years, and in all that time, as much fun as they'd had together, they never asked questions like this. Mal had always presented herself as a random person in the Aetherium, no affiliations, making her way by way of odd jobs and attitude. Mal felt suddenly awful. How would Tok react to the truth?

Mal could see it in her eyes, too. The fact she'd never asked. The reality that Mal knew everything about Tok and Tok knew nothing about her.

Mal tried a laugh. "Here and there, Tok. You know me."

Tok's face was serious. "Do I?"

The odd whooshing sound that preceded a message came through the loudspeakers. Mal heard the announcement: "Thirty minutes to Severance Point. All systems should remain operational, including the Noise Dampeners. Please maintain maximum readiness."

Maximum readiness. Is there any other state of being?

"Guess it's time for my drop."

"You don't sound scared about that anymore," Tok said. They both laughed.

"Yeah, I've tasted Noise now. A torpedo drop is no big deal," Mal said.

〉〉 • • • • • 〈〈

They stopped at Mal's room to pick up the shield and then headed straight for the shuttle bay. What Mal was looking at was a hollow torpedo in which she was to lay flat. The shield barely fit in the with her. Thin, narrow, cramped. Mal settled into place and looked up.

Tok bent over her and planted a squishy kiss on her forehead. "Be safe, Mal. Ever onward."

"I'm more worried about you than I am about me."

A tech bent over her. "I'm not going to kiss you. Hope that's ok."

"Your loss."

"I'm going to seal you in. About ninety seconds later, you'll be launched. It will feel like a free fall and be over before you know it. You'll land in the Severance Point Docks where our people will help you disembark."

"Okay. Tok said I'll have to keep this thing together. Anything I should know?" Mal asked.

"The torpedo shell is a simple program. It won't stand up to the Noise for too long. They're really only good for very short-range shots. We can't get in that close to the Point. Once it's out of range of the ship's Pylon, you'll have a bit of work to keep it together. But everyone's talking about what you did out there. Shouldn't be a problem for someone like you," he said. "Good luck!"

"Thanks."

"Thank Captain Tok."

Mal looked for her face, to do so again, but the door was already closing and Mal was sealed in. She took a few breaths. The inside of her torpedo lit up and Mal had a very clear view all around her. Tok was already leaving back through the thick doors to the main body of the ship, and the tech had moved over to a console. As Mal lay there, she could see all around her, as if the Torpedo was completely transparent. The shield was heavy and uncomfortable on top of her. While Mal waited to be launched into the Noise she opened her eyes to the code of the Torpedo, learning how it was constructed, getting a sense for how to bolster it later.

Then Mal launched, and the scene around her turned into streaks of color and movement, and it felt as though her insides remained behind in the hangar. After the initial rush of the drop, the speed of the Torpedo stabilized, and Mal could see more clearly. Severance Point was sprawled out below her, a dozen Pylons reaching their light into the sky. Severance Point was heavily Axiom-dominated, so the skyline was a deep glowing orange.

Mal stared at the Noise around her for the first time with little else to do or worry about. She could see why some described it as pretty; it was if you didn't think too long or too hard about how it could kill you. It was like being inside a color. Or a hundred colors. Every shade of blue a sighted person could imagine, swirling eternally. Lethally. It was already difficult for Mal to believe she had been out in it. Her exhaustion started to tug at the edges of her mind and joined with the swirling colors outside to lull her into a kind of sleep. Her mind drifted, almost out of her control. Out there, in the Noise, what was possible? In the uncharted reality away from the Pylons, Mal could be or do anything. If only she could survive it. Mal pressed her hand against the shell of the dead drop ship. I know what it's like to fly free of a Pylon.

When she was growing up, the Aetherial city she logged into for school had only three Civic Pylons, so its stability was always in question. Sure, the buildings and such, held by various Collectives and corps were supported by more, but the infrastructure was spotty. Children whispered to each other when the Noise burst through the world or hovered at the edges of it. The adults warned them. It was like a story, a monster or something that could hide behind a corner and get them. Stay away from the Noise. Stay away from the Noise. Mal whispered it to herself, now, hurtling through it in a see-through coffin. Mal remembered the looks on her parents faces when they talked about the Noise.

Half in dream, half-aware, Mal remembered the day the Noise crack in the pavement at the edge of the alley where Jackobi, Trent, and Mal walked during their lunch hour at school. Just a couple of feet wide, but enough to be scary. "Stay away from the Noise," Mal intoned, as though chanting some kind of ritual from long ago in the Meatspace. The Noise so close to a school meant a program was damaged and they were too far away from a Pylon for it to repair itself.

"I can jump it," Jackobi said.

"So can I, then." Had her response been so immediate? That's the way Mal remembered it. The lure of the danger, of doing the opposite of what her careful parents wanted. They were all around nine or ten, swinging their lunch pails at their sides.

"No way, guys. Let's go around," Trent said.

Mal and Jackobi looked at each other. Which one was first to set their lunch pail on the ground? Mal remembered her heart pounding. Fear? Excitement? Pure adrenaline? Mal remember loving the feeling. They were about 50 feet away from the rift. They both started running.

As Mal approached it, the rift seemed to stretch and grow. Mal knew she could jump it, she knew it, but she suddenly realized Jackobi would not be able to. In that moment, Mal saw him stumble. Mal thought about stopping, calling out his name, but her feet seemed to have taken on a life of their own, and something in her was too afraid to stop. Maybe he would make it, but if Mal tried to stop him, he'd fall.

They both reached the rift at the same time and pushed off with everything they had. Mal sailed through the air and landed several feet past the rift, and skidded to a stop, turning as she landed.

Mal saw him go in. Trent did too.

Jackobi was flailing around, his form Glitching badly and phasing in and out, his body jerking as if in and out of time: it would be in one position, then another, but the movement in between the two positions would be cut off. The blue energy of the Noise started to bleed into his form, as though it were acid eating away at him. He became a half-person, half-Noise creature. He was screaming. Mal just stood there. Mal watched. She did not look at Trent. Eventually Jackobi stopped struggling. His connection was broken, but his mind was probably trapped. The Noise was eating through his thoughts. Then he was gone.

In school the next day, the other children, of course, wondered why Jackobi wasn't in school, but people disappeared in the Meatspace, without explanation, every week. In the end, he was just one more of them. His parents faded away, then they were gone too.

A warning buzzer brought Mal's attention back to the present. The ship was well behind her already and she was nearing Severance Point. The Torpedo was starting to lose integrity. She pressed her palms against the inner curve of the torpedo shell and concentrated. She heard Jackobi's screams. She heard those who had fallen from the bridge. She closed her mind to the screams, called to mind the code of the torpedo. Tried to keep the memory of the taste of the Noise out of herself. It was easy, too easy. As she fortified and kept together the torpedo her senses touched the noise. Though she was safe inside the Torpedo's shell she was, at the same time embodying the shell. The Noise overwhelmed her senses until her head spun, and she started to replay the scene of Bridge again and again but now it was Jackobi falling from the bridge. Not once but hundreds of times. Over and over, Jackobi fell.

"Hey, you ok?"

Mal was startled out of her vision. Her vid screen had disappeared. A semi-concerned face was peering at hers, oddly in the same position Tok's was right before she kissed her. Mal was in her torpedo, on the docks.

"Yeah," Mal said. "Can you get this thing off me?"

"Sure," he replied. He grabbed the edges of it and pulled, then looked at her, surprised, for a moment, but continued to lift. A girl in a hoodie carrying an object that both looked like a Praetorian shield and was as heavy as one... I guess I'm still not the weirdest thing he's seen today.

"Thanks." Mal stood up. She was in Severance Point.

≈ » Chapter Six: Delivered « ≈

The docks in Severance Point were smaller than those in the Drain, just a few landing areas huddled together under a metal roof, walls of sorts patched together with bits and pieces of other buildings. There were only a few ships here, and they looked as though they were not fitted for the Noise. Mal shook off the RezX guy and walked quickly through the crowds. Severance Point was huge and chock-full of a variety of schemas, a haphazard quilt of a city. Mal hefted the shield, muttered a few choice curses at it, and started walking.

Mal crushed the Crypto-loc from Ramos and coordinates swam up in front of her eyes. As Mal wove her way out of the docks and toward the coordinates, she was surprised when the streets opened up to a pleasant plaza, with a fountain at the center, a wide expanse of green grass, and even some healthy trees lining the path. People strolled at a relaxed pace. The buildings surrounding the plaza were built of the same black concrete as most Axiom buildings, with the same orange highlights, but were more open, with windows and glass and even balconies.

Mal walked out of this Schema and through the gate. The coordinates led her almost a mile away through the city to a small stretch of bars, food stalls, and skinning parlors. Mal found the Slapdash Pickle and pushed through the door, which was really just like a couple of shutters. The bar was decorated like the Ancient American West, a long wooden bar dominating the length of the place, with bottles of alcohol lining the shelves behind the bar man. On the bar, eight huge glass jars of pickles in various brines. There was a pool table in the back, and a juke box. The skin job on this place was impressive. Mal felt her nose twitch. They'd even programmed dust to float through the air. Someone who knew what they were doing had spent idle time here, tinkering with things. Mal asked the bartender about Ramos.

The bartender nodded and spit on the floor. "He'll be around."

Mal waited for a better answer, but none seemed forthcoming, so she ordered a "Clumsy Cow" and took it to a corner table, leaning the shield awkwardly next to her and angling her chair so that her back was to the wall. Mal watched people come and go for more than an hour; it seemed a fairly normal place, aside from the over-the-top skinning. People coming and going, meeting up, doing business. Finally, a door at the back of the bar opened, and Ramos stepped in. There was a shift in the room. There were only a handful of patrons, but they all noticed when he entered, and they kept noticing him. He walked straight for her table, extending a closed fist over an outstretched palm, a greeting typical in the Aetherium. It represented a hand willing to take action, and a hand free of weapons. He fixed his eyes on the shield and grinned as Mal returned the greeting. "I knew you could do it."

"I should think so by now."

"Look. I want to trust you. I could use someone like you. We could," he added. Interesting slip. He sat down at her table and continued. "We've been watching you for a long time," Ramos said. "You've obviously had training. Your skills are off the charts, and you run a good rig. So, who are you, really? Some of my people think you're too good to be true."

"If something appears too good to be true, it usually is," Mal said.

He laughed then, a big, hearty laugh that felt as though it shook the table. "You're quick. But I need to know more about you," he said.

"Not much to tell. I don't have any family left. I was scooped up by Axiom when I was thirteen," she said.

"I bet you were. They wanted you for the Academy?"

"They did. I went for a year. Could have been an Agent, they told me. Of course, they told me that on the way out the door with expulsion papers. I ended up smoothing code for a living. It's a better wage than most and lets me have plenty of time logged in."

"And gets you into some interesting places. Code smoothing is a good gig. So where did Death Angel come from? Why all the rage?" Ramos asked.

"I have it good as a code smoother. That doesn't mean I can't see the truth of what's going on around me?"

"You're a hero then?"

"No. Just don't like seeing the way Axiom takes what it wants and leaves the rest of the world to the scraps. They decide how to use the resources of what's left of a dying world while demanding obedience, worship."

"That's nothing new."

"It's bad enough in the Meat but word is they're going to do it here more and more. This world was going to be a new horizon. So much promise. I've seen what Hacking can do what we could make the Aetherium be for everyone. And Axiom would parcel it up and place limits on what can be done here. Pylons could help Patches experience this reality in better ways, more like Users. Patches could be free to explore, thrive. Even here. I guess you could just say I'm not one of the believers."

Ramos was leaned back in his chair, watching her. "I like you, Mal. I think we could work well together."

"Good. I do too. Let's get started."

"We'll contact you," he said and sat back slightly in his chair.

"Are you serious? I removed that panic button. I've killed for you. I'm supposed to sit tight and wait for you to call?"

"I wondered how you were going to feel about that. That was an internal affair. One of our own, selling secrets to the Axiom."

"And the others who died?"

"His family, of course."

"Do you see my eyelashes?" Mal asked.

"What?"

"Do you see them? I didn't blink. I didn't bat them. I have done everything you wanted."

"We know you're skilled. We need to know you're a good fit."

Mal stood and finished her drink in one smooth swallow. "Let me know when you're serious about this." Mal touched the shield one last time, offloading it from her Rig and severing all connection to it. "This is yours," she said.

Mal was three steps from the strange door before he called to her. "Don't go."

Mal turned back. Two men were carrying the shield back through the door and Ramos was smiling wide. *You're used to that smile getting you what you want, aren't you?* "Let's walk a bit," he said, striding forward and extending his arm like some old-fashioned cowboy who would have fit in at this bar. Mal kept pace but let him keep his arm.

"What do you want, Mal?"

"I want to break Axiom. I want to be free from their control. I want to give people their choice back."

"That felt a little rehearsed."

"Of course, it is. I have been figuring out what I'm going to say to you the whole time I've been traveling with this shield."

Ramos laughed again, his big, booming laugh. "Let me show you I place I love to walk."

They walked in silence for a while through busy streets that were closed to traffic but teeming with people. They walked down a street littered with small carts and stands selling all manner of celebratory items. Frozen treats, light up swords, tiny lizards that obeyed verbal commands, three-dimensional hover puzzles, and more delights were displayed brightly. Moving through a crowd, they approached a kite stand. Small children and young lovers were all having their Value checked to take one of the intricate and beautiful kites from the stall and fly them in the nearby park. As Mal watched them, Ramos rented a kite. There were probably two dozen in the air already, swooping and diving. Happy sounds and conversations were carried on the same wind. Mal closed her eyes breathed it in, deeply. She let herself slip into the code, as if she were about to hack it. Mal could see the wild blue fractals all around, see the complexity of the algorithms. She felt invigored, excited. Seeing the code like this, the care with which it had been constructed filled her with a strange feeling. If asked to put a name to that feeling she would have been hard pressed, but she would perhaps have called it hope.

Mal followed Ramos to the center of the park. He let the kite loose and it sailed on an updraft.

"Some might say if we give in, if Nanomei stops resisting Axiom and lets them control the entire Aetherium, it would all look like this." Mal glanced sideways at him. "We'd have peace. But you must not believe that."

"Of course I don't. Why would I fight if this were the whole truth about Axiom? If we could trust Axiom with the sacred duty, they're claiming there would be no reason for war."

"Many believe this is the whole truth. Fervently so." Mal noticed Ramos' kite was flying faster than the others.

"With a state like the Axiom Collective how can we ever be sure that there is a truth? The demand of unquestioning loyalty to a secular religion is too hard a pill for many to swallow."

"How is that different from Nanomei, or Ikaru, or any other Collective?" Mal waited as a pair of Patches came close enough to cause a pause in their conversation.

"It's an issue of what we worship. Ikaru would have us worship objects. Wealth. RezX wants us to worship science and discovery. Both of those Collectives have their faults but they're at least asking us to believe in something other than themselves."

"Doesn't Axiom just us to believe in order, loyalty and obedience? Aren't those things to worship, just as science, wealth?"

Ramos smiled out across the park, completely at peace. "If it was just order I'd be fine with it. It's the obedience I have a problem with."

"Do you really think you can ever affect them? In a real way?"

"I do. One bad Pylon can bring down a schema, and a fallen Schema can topple a Node. We don't have to fight them head-on, Mal. We don't have to fight them all at once, either. My methods might be a little more... physical than other Nanomei operatives, but it's all the same principle. Small, focused attacks. Surgical strikes. The right place, the right time."

He looked around him and took a deep breath. "Look at them. They have no idea. One wrong move on the part of the people here and it's over for them. They're standing on the edge of a precipice and don't even know it." He turned to face her. "Like those in Breakwater."

Mal fell silent. No one knew for sure what happened in Breakwater; it was a perfect Node, much like this one, safe and pretty and secure. Full of families, kids. Then one day it was gone. Just... gone. Not by accident, rumor had it. Rumor said Axiom ended it. They had somehow gotten a hold of every Pylon in that Aetherial City and turned it all off. No warning, no explanation. So many lives lost.

"No one knows for certain Axiom pulled the plug on Breakwater." You sounded as though you are defending Axiom. Careful, Mal.

Ramos' voice was low. "I do."

Mal waited, but he did not say anything more. His kite moved higher, swinging wildly from side to side, and dashing between the other kites. The other kite fliers were more careful and controlled, but this hardly mattered. Ramos avoided tangling his own kite, but others were crashing into each other in the wake of the chaos he caused. He was starting to draw looks and conversation toward him. He let out another of those laughs and eventually handed her the strings.

"I want you in," he said plainly. "As soon as possible. Where are you?"

"I'm right damn here." The park was all around them, people talking, kites going back into the air.

"That's not what I'm asking." His eyes were trained on Mal's, unrelenting. "We don't let people in unless we can count on them one hundred percent. Especially people as potent as you."

Mal hesitated. "My body is in Keral. But you already knew that. Marcus told you that, didn't he?"

Ramos' eyes glinted in the sun, but he did not respond to her question.

"We'll be to you in three Meat days."

"Should I pack my Rig?"

"What are you running?"

"A Brix 1100."

"That's too big to travel. Scrap it for parts and we'll get you fixed up."

"I guess I'm recruited, now?"

"Not scared? The Nanomei are coming to your house. This was the sort of thing with which good Axiom Citizens frighten their children."

"Sorry, but it takes a hell of a lot more than you to scare me." That was honest, at least. Mal handed him back the kite string, feeling more than a little foolish.

He nodded and grinned. "Good to hear. Now that's arranged, there's something I need your help with here and now." Ramos deactivated his kite. He started walking and Mal stood there for a heartbeat watching him go. He, apparently, was just assuming she'd follow. He really was used to getting exactly what he wanted. She caught up to him.

"What if I had said no? If I had left?"

"You weren't going to do that." The certainty in his voice rankled at her. We'll settle that one later.

They walked together in silence for a while until they had cleared any sign of crowds or green grass. The buildings here were taller, more imposing and mostly gray concrete, all pillars and crossed-key banners.

Ramos stopped on a corner.

"I usually do my work from rooftops," Mal said.

"I've noticed," he replied. "This is no tag I'm going to ask you to do. And no test either. This is the real thing," he said. "No turning back."

"Anything you need," Mal said.

"That building there is new. It replaced an old Axiom warehouse a few days ago," Ramos said. "And it's got a very high level of security for just an admin building. Walking past it you can feel the intensity of the Pylon inside."

"It doesn't look like a fortified position," Mal said. There were no windows on the building but there were no other indications of high security; it looked more to Mal like a mid-level administrative building. Which did not track at all. *How much do I know of the truth of Axiom?*

"No. But it's got high level Pylons and it draws no power from anywhere else. It's self-contained and it's not what it seems to be. Problem is I can't get in alone," Ramos said.

"We want to get in?"

"You can't just blow up all the problems. I need to know what this place is. It's in my back yard and I don't like it."

"If we blow it up it won't be in your backyard anymore."

"Knowledge is power, Mal. I want to know."

"Do you have a plan?" Mal asked.

"Well, getting in is the hard part. Spoofing IDs is difficult. Fighting our way in is problematic at best."

"You're waiting for me to say, 'but you thought of something brilliant,' right?"

"No. I was hoping you'd think up something brilliant while I talked," he said with a smile.

"Come with me," Mal said, walking out along the sidewalk. She did not bother with any sort of stealth. Ramos followed. She toyed with telling Ramos she could not break in; there was a very high and horrible probability that they would meet resistance inside. *I have killed enough for this mission already.* Their path took them across the front of the building. The street here was empty of traffic and nobody walked here. It was eerily quiet. It was a corner building, and they followed the corner along another face of the building which had no doors.

"I've looked around the whole thing, there's only the one entrance."

"We'll make that work for us," Mal said. She walked to the alley between their target building and the place next door. Another Axiom building, though with lower security and windows. Mal switched sides with Ramos, so she was walking alongside the building they hoped to enter. She ran her

124

finger along the concrete, trying to get a feel for the Pylon. It was incredibly strong. She felt a super-fast refresh rate and felt the intensity with which it maintained its programs. This building held or would hold soon something important to Axiom.

She stopped at the midpoint of the alley and unfolded her wings.

"The roof is secure as well. No entrances," Ramos said.

"We're not flying," Mal said. "I saw a friend do something pretty cool once," she said. "I didn't admit it to him, but I've started using it myself."

Ramos raised an eyebrow. "This isn't a test," he said. "I want this to work. You don't have to impress me."

"You'll be impressed when it works," Mal said. Her wings flared to life, glowing a bright blue, and she hacked the ghost mod into them with strands of what looked like ephemera, pulling her will together, knowing that the Pylon they were going to try to enter was well maintained and powerful. She worked fast and intensely.

"I'll be finished in a second. Be ready. I'm going to grab you," Mal didn't bother to check for his reaction. She finished her hack, held onto Ramos as if she were hugging him and wrapped her wings around him. Then she stepped backwards into the wall.

And through it. She felt the concrete slide through her form, felt for a moment as if she were the concrete wall, felt the Pylon resist, felt pushed away or maybe pushed into becoming concrete herself, but the Pylon was not prepared for a focused assault of her will. She pressed herself backwards and stepped right through the wall and into the building. She let go of Ramos, riding a wave of relief; she hadn't exactly been certain she'd be able to carry someone with her through the wall. Ramos was coughing.

"I wasn't ready for that," he said.

"You can be caught off guard?" She folded her wings back into her hoodie and they both crouched down and looked opposite directions down the corridor they had entered. It was a T-junction, with a door at either end of the hall and about twenty feet ahead a left turn, open leading deeper into the complex. The walls and floors were black marble, shot through with lines of bright quartz. This was different from the usual drab low-contrast greys of most Axiom buildings. Even more strange than that was the lack of sound. It was completely quiet. Mal got the feeling that they were alone.

"This way," Ramos said in a whisper and walked towards the door he had been facing. Mal followed. The door was not locked, and they entered quietly and quickly, Mal closing the door behind them.

"Will the Pylon find us?" Mal asked.

"I have a stealth field up on us," Ramos said. "It won't stop visual detection but the Pylon itself won't register us unless we do some shit."

"Well let's not do any shit then. Let's get going," Mal added. The room they were in was small, about twenty feet square and piled with crates. "We're clearly in a closet."

"Well, I wanted to get somewhere safe first and then figure out a plan."

"I thought you Nanomei folks would just grip it and rip it."

"We like to plan it and live."

Mal shrugged. "This is a fascinating closet you discovered but this isn't telling us what we need. Let's go back into the hall. This place feels empty. And if this hall is a dead-end hall that lead to a closet I doubt the other door on this T is all that impressive. Let's head towards the middle of the building," she said.

Ramos opened the door, stepping through quickly while Mal followed.

"Weird lighting. Why are the lights so dim in here?" Ramos wondered aloud.

"Maybe it's in standby? You said it's a new place. Maybe they're still moving in."

"Maybe," Ramos said. "Not very efficient to be powering an empty building." They got to the T section and turned left, towards the center of the building. The hall came quickly to an intersection, but Ramos strode forward. "Up ahead, it feels like it opens up more," Ramos said.

As they continued Mal felt it too. There was a gang plank railing in front of them. Their hall had taken them to a large, central square room. Across to the other side of the room, and a level below them, was a large double door, probably out to the main entrance. The catwalk ringed the whole room at the level they were on, about thirty feet above the floor of the central room. The floor of that main room was fairly empty, with a Console, a pillar about three feet tall with controls and a holo screen on top, at the center. There were four opaque white cubes, about twenty feet to a side, positioned around the Console. There was a single ladder going down to the main level and a few other halls at the level they were on leading off to other parts of the complex.

"Best way to see what's here is the Console," Ramos said.

"My thought too," Mal agreed. They walked around the gangplank to the ladder. Ramos started down and then slid the rest of the way. Mal just climbed down quickly. The lights here were also dim but as Ramos approached the Console the lights went up in the room. Still not fully lit, but enough to see. Ramos accessed the Console through a thin cord he hacked into being between his palm and the cool black metal.

"What's there?" Mal asked, watching the room carefully.

"Not much. Wait," he said. He made some sort of adjustment, and the opaque cubes became transparent. They were hollow and inside each were human forms, five or six in each, wearing orange jumpsuits and severe, thick metal collars. Their skin was thin, literally thin; Mal could see their muscles and veins beneath the surface. They each had the Axiom Crossed Keys brand-ed onto their foreheads. Their eyes were orbs of white and grey static. The forms shuffled slowly around the interiors of their cubes, sightless, mindless. Even with these things in the room Mal still felt alone.

"What are they?" Ramos whispered.

"I have no idea," Mal said.

Ramos was moving fast through the Console. "There are prisoner ID numbers here."

Mal moved towards the cube.

"They're in the meat. In prison," Ramos mumbled.

"Why," Mal whispered.

Ramos stared. "It can't be."

"What?"

"I think… there are rumors… The Deleted." He looked genuinely shak-en. "They say enemies of Axiom, taken as prisoners in the Meatspace, some-times end up like this. Their minds are broken to extract information. This is what's left." As he spoke, Ramos interacted with the Console. His eyes told Mal that these rumors were confirmed.

He left the Console and walked between two of the cubes, staring into one of them. Mal just stood there.

"They are mindless, unable to act on their own. If the rumors are true, they are bound to a powerful User who can control them. They are deadly and do not have the free will to care what happens to them. The story is they can-not be killed. If they are derezzed they simply come back. Their brains already so damaged that it doesn't matter."

They both stood there for long moments staring at them shuffle mind-lessly. When one brushed against another a minor, seemingly instinctual, course correction occurred. There seemed to be nothing behind them or their movements. No thought. No intent.

Mal went to the console, leaving Ramos at the cube. Accessing the Console was easy and flipping quickly through subdirectories was second nature to those trained in layered information structures. Each cube held a different User's group of these destroyed people.

"The facility is waiting for Users. Whoever is going to control these… We should leave," Mal said. And it seemed like Ramos was about to agree. He turned and started to walk back toward the ladder. Mal watched him go, his shoulders slumped.

Then Ramos stopped dead in his tracks. He turned sharply and looked in the cube on his right.

"I know that man," he said in a hoarse whisper.

Mal approached him, the Deleted not registering her presence. "That's not a man anymore. That's just a mind projection. A tool. There's nothing left of the man you knew." Mal reached out and touched his elbow. She wanted badly to leave.

"His name was Simon," he said.

"You're right: Was. Past tense. Ramos, we have to get out of here," Mal said.

"He disappeared one day. He was part of a cell I worked with a year ago. We were in the field, and he just logged out. Gone. No contact. I heard from his husband almost a month later. Axiom had come to his house, taken him."

"Ramos."

"Simon. He was always making the worst jokes. At the most inappropriate times. He was not funny but that made it funny."

Ramos took a long, deep breath in and strode back the way he'd come, back to the Console.

"Ramos, what are you doing?"

He reattached to the Console and said, "I'm opening Simon's cube."

"Ramos, don't be stupid. There are six of them in there. We don't know what they'll do," she said.

"We're getting him out of this," he said.

"Ramos, they have him in the Meat. They have his body. There's nothing-" Mal stopped short. Ramos had derezzed the cube Simon and five other Deleted were in. They did not change their behavior. It was haunting how little changed. The cube was gone but they just shuffled about aimlessly as before. Ramos disconnected from the Console and walked over.

He walked up to the one he was calling Simon and took him by the shoulders and shook him.

"Simon, it's me, man. It's Ramos," he said. The creature in his hands did not react. It swayed slightly, moving weight from one foot to the other, but its static eyes did not change, and its mouth did not form words.

Mal stepped forward, among the Deleted. They brushed against her as she made her way to Ramos. She stood behind Ramos' shoulder and watched. She saw no responses.

"He's trapped in there, Mal," Ramos said. "I need to get him out."

Mal put her hand on the thing's shoulder and tried to see its connection through her HUD. Nothing. She started a hack. Closing her eyes she could hear Ramos' breathing, hear the quiet shuffling of the Deleted near her. She could feel them jostling her.

Then she found the connection to what stood in front of her but in that there was no neural connection back to the body. Instead of seeing a bright stream of neural activity coursing through a latticework of code she saw almost nothing. A void that she could both see and feel was emptier than anything should be. She pressed out a code ping, bright and blue into that darkness and there was nothing. The blue light was swallowed.

"Ramos, there's nothing to save here. He's not in there," she said.

"Would a gun fix this?"

"No, Ramos. He'd drop for a minute but then he'd be back. It's not your friend anymore. It's something else."

Ramos turned then, the three of them standing close among the other shambling and shifting Deleted. "Can you end this for him?"

"I can try," Mal said.

Ramos shifted out of the way. He was looking around the room, looking like a man who needed something to do.

"Keep these things from bumping me. I need all my concentration," Mal said.

"On it," Ramos said, sounding relieved.

Mal pressed both of her palms onto the thing's temples and closed her eyes. She saw what was standing before her in the revelatory form of the pure code. It was strong. There was no personality here, no memory. Not on the surface and not anywhere she could sense.

She pressed further, hoping to find that stem back to the chair, hoping to find something to sever. This was something different than someone whose connection was Glitched and broken. This was foul and wrong.

As she had become the bridge and the explosive as she had for just a moment felt as though she was the wall as she ghosted through it she felt trapped for just a moment, a prisoner, someone who had no will of her own someone who was there only to obey Axiom. Simon are you in here? She started to see code structures laced through what remained of his mind. She kept her eyes closed and visualized herself hacking those ribbons of code away, pulling them from soft matter. Time flowed by with no meaning as she struggled and pulled on strands of sticky code like a giant spiderweb She stood among discarded, sloughed off pieces of neural matter, thoughts, memories. She was searching for him still. Some trace. Simon are you in here? The strands of code, commands, and formations, and pack tactics, and programs were both falling away from what was once Simon and trying to adhere to her. Simon are we in here?

She continued the hack, completely unaware of the Aetherium around her. Completely oblivious to any sound or sensory input from anywhere. We can't live like this. She started a Hack meant to destroy programs. She ripped away at everything, not only the command code. She tore great pieces of neural energy away from some dead core. It was not enough. She opened herself to a torrent of Glitch to power her efforts, to drive this exorcism. She pulled and peeled away layer after layer until she stood there in a room with three cubes full of these creatures and Ramos and five more of them still shuffling mindlessly. She was out of breath.

129

"He's gone," she said between breaths and fell to one knee.

At that same moment she heard a voice that was not Ramos'. She looked up and saw that an AI was spawning in the room, coming from the Console behind Ramos. Ramos stared directly at her, he looked transfixed.

"Ramos, behind!" Mal said, as she activated her sword into her hand. She did not go back to her feet though, it hurt too much, and she was too spent. She saw the AI take a glowing semi-transparent, bright orange female form.

Ramos spun and saw the AI, and rezed a shotgun into his hands, firing twice as he did. The shot flew through the AI harmlessly.

"Cease, Citizen," the AI said in a chillingly calm voice.

"Mal get up!" Ramos roared as he fired two more ineffectual shots through the AI.

Mal dragged herself to her feet.

"I have contacted Axiom Control. You should stand down and await their arrival," the AI said. "You will deactivate all weapon programs now."

The AI took a more physical form, completing her entry into the room. Ramos fired again but as the shot hit her, they disappeared into tiny rings of distortion and reemerged blasting through one of the Deleted, spraying blood from its chest backwards across several others.

The rest of them activated. Their eyes went from the silver-grey static to bright orange. Two grabbed Mal before she could react, and another balled up its fists and smashed them onto her shoulders. It hurt like two hammers striking her.

The other two, wounded from Ramos' gunshot strode towards Ramos who fired again, a multitude of shots. He was retreating, though, as he fired, stepping back towards the ladder. One of the two fell but the other did not.

Mal twisted her sword hand and severed the wrist of one of the two holding her and tugged herself away from the other. But they were savage and fast and clawing at her form. One hit her so hard in the side of the head that she staggered back to the ground, slamming down onto her hands and knees. They smashed her back with balled fists and kicked her in the ribs and stomach. Over and over, they attacked, viciously, and so intensely that her Sync was bleeding fast, and she was in danger of losing connection completely. Glitch piled up on her as they pummeled her. This was not her, not someone who anything got the better of in combat. As they smashed her again she felt as if she were becoming someone other than herself. Some Death Angel.

She heard Ramos yell something indistinguishable. She collapsed fully and lay flat on the cold marble floor. The creatures left her then, heading for Ramos. She rolled onto her side and saw Ramos at the ladder, shotgun still firing, four on him. He was yelling but she could barely hear.

130

The struggle to her feet was slow and painful. First to her hands and knees, the cool black floor offering no comfort, no stability. Mal struggled one leg forward so her foot was planted on the ground and then stood the rest of the way more-or-less upright. The AI was directing the creatures at Ramos and didn't seem to notice as Mal swayed and fought to stand. She brought her blade down through the AI, but instead one of the Deleted was cut and fell to the ground. Only three more were standing.

The AI turned to her. "You cannot hurt me," she said.

"You only have three more," Mal spat as she dropped another by cutting the AI three times in quick succession, her arms burning with pain and the stress of moving, her head swimming.

Ramos felled another, and the last leapt towards Mal, leaving Ramos. Mal did not have the strength or speed to bring up her blade or any other defense. But as the creature approached fast and unrelenting, she heard like thunder Ramos' gun and the face of the creature exploded towards her, shot from behind by Ramos.

Mal turned to the AI readying another blow and probably a smart-ass quip when she saw the AI smile and the three other cubes opened, the Deleted within each ready to spring, their bright orange eyes glowing.

"We can't take this many, Ramos," Mal said weakly.

"Agreed!" he shouted and ran to her. He grabbed her around the waist as if he was going to sweep her away like some hero from a holo-pic but he looked at her and said, "Please get us out of here."

Mal deactivated her blade and brought her Wings back online. "Hold on tight, I don't have the strength to carry your big self," she said and leapt. Ramos held on and yelled. Mal for her part leapt forwards towards, she hoped, the same side of the building they'd entered through at first. She hacked the ghost mod back in place and slammed through the wall.

Walls. The first wall was one she ghosted through, but it turned out the way they went they ended up smashing through a ceiling and three more walls. They left holes. In the end, Mal and Ramos landed in a heap back in the alley, the AI still calling for them to cease. There were no sirens or alarms outside of the building though.

"You're hurt. You need to logout immediately. I will stand over you as you go. Keep you safe. Logout now!" There was real urgency in his voice and Mal felt that force of personality that great leaders share.

She started the logout process. The last thing she saw were a handful of Deleted appearing in the hole she'd made in the outer wall and the last thing she heard was the ringing of Ramos' shotgun.

〉〉‧‧‧‧‧‧〈〈

Coming out of the Aetherium is never fun, but this reentry was worse than normal. Reality slammed back into her brain. The Glitch followed her, and her head was spinning. It was like licking a fuel cel all over her body. Mal pulled the trodes and yanked the connection from her chip. When Mal stood up, she vomited, her left-hand pressed palm flat onto the cool plastiwall. The world continued to resolve itself all around her. Her deep cover room, the rig, the door to the main area of the apartment. Mal was unable to focus her thoughts or stand without leaning against the wall. Before going undercover Mal had attendants. A perfectly ergonomic chair, and a damn bucket ready if she vomited. I need my old life back. There was a knock at her door: harsh, repeating, percussive.

"Fuck off," Mal said quietly through the haze.

More knocking. "Fuck off!" Shit. Could be Gibson. She stumbled towards the door.

Was this them already? Was this Nanomei extracting her? Mal brought her time piece to her sight, raising her arm, which hurt.

Mal had only lost about a half hour in the chair. It couldn't be them yet. She opened the door and looked worriedly into the hall. There was a shabbily dressed pair of people wearing work jumpsuits. Worker level.

"Hey!" one said, a scruffy looking man.

"Hey?" Mal answered weakly.

They came in and the woman closed the door behind her. Mal moved to the thin cushioned couch and sat, misjudging a bit and slamming down harder than she wanted to. Her head was still spinning.

The man moved to the single window and looked out. "Clear," he said. The woman went and made a quick check of the bedroom, then reappeared to nod at the man. "Clear," she reported to him. She went back to the door and reopened it. "We're clear," she yelled.

Mal pressed her hands against her forehead. "Guess we're clear."

A few moments later, two more people came in wearing Axiom guard uniforms, black cloth with orange piping along the legs and arms and the crossed keys of Axiom emblazoned on their chests. Following them the last to enter the room wore the distinctive garb of Matron. The Matrons wore all black with orange piping down the side of the sleeves and pants. The material of their uniforms though was smoother, softer than the rest of Axiom. The Matrons were vital; they were the group in charge of maintaining loyalty.

"Sim," Mal said, surprised, half-standing. "Why are you here?" Sim had been a valued Axiom Labtech when she and Mal had first worked together. Now she was training to become a Matron and was often assigned to psych evals and debriefs for agents. She and Mal had developed a rhythm of conversation, that, while not friendship, felt comfortable and welcome.

Sim sat on the couch next to her. "Please stay seated," she said crisply. "Because you look like you'll fall over otherwise," she murmured more quietly.

"We got your message. Commander Mullen determined the risk was worth one last meeting before you go deeper."

Mal blinked. "What message?"

"It was only semi-coherent. You said that they were coming for you. To extract you."

"They are."

"Mal, we need to do a psych eval. Before they take you in. My presence here should show you just how important this mission is to Axiom at the highest levels." It was true, Sim only had ever met with Mal at larger cities, the Academy, Aegis Prime, once on a train when they'd had to set up Mal's rig on the move- focus Mal!

"Seriously? I'm pretty messed up right now."

"This evaluation is not optional. Mal, you're going into even deeper cover. That's huge. You've only ever dealt with the enemy in the Aetherium. This is the real world," she said, patting the ratty couch cushion for emphasis.

"They're both real." This was an old argument between them. Mal always took a specific position when it came the Aetherium. For her, the Aetherium was real. More real than real. Everyone in the world structured their Meatspace time, their value, their goals, hopes and dreams, around getting out of the Meatspace and into the Aetherium. In the Aetherium, everyone was well-fed, rested, could breathe. The colors were brighter, the environments hyper-detailed. What was that, if not reality? But Sim's brand of logic disavowed the idea that the world of the Aetherium could be real as it could only be accessed through and from the Meatspace. That oversimplification served Sim well.

"OK. They're both real. But you'll be out of communication longer than you've ever been. And they are coming for your real body. The one that can't just rez wings and fly away if things go sideways."

Sim was right, of course. The risks of the Aetherium were limited; in there as long as Mal was careful, stayed out of and away from the Noise and logged out in safe spaces, she was relatively safe. If the Nanomei knew the location of her Meat body, the danger became much more real. And permanent.

"Fine. Evaluate me. Ten minutes." Mal sat on the edge of her couch and placed the soles of her feet flat against the floor. She could still feel the Glitch running through her.

Sim opened her case and pulled out an electrode on a wire. She attached one end of it to Mal's arm with a sticky pad and plugged the other into a datapad. "I'll keep this as quick as possible."

"Good. I want to get some sleep before they get here. Like maybe for a whole day." Sim glanced up at her from her datapad, and the look she gave was more calm than Mal was feeling. Which was to say, Sim was clearly detecting her bullshit. Mal closed her eyes tightly, fighting another wave of nausea.

"I'll start with the baseline questions. Whom do you serve?"

"Axiom. I am ever loyal, and ever vigilant for disloyalty," Mal replied in a monotone.

"Mal. This is serious."

"I am serious." Sim didn't reply. "Oh, fine. I am loyal to Axiom."

"Why?"

"Because they raised me up in ways my parents were unable to. Because they provide order and service to the people. I am proud to be part of that service." Mal could have recited this part in her sleep. Her voice sounded hollow.

"Good. What is your true identity?"

"Mal Turner. Child of Angela and David Turner. My education is Axiom Academy. Highest honors. I am an Agent of Axiom First Degree."

"What is your current mission?"

"To infiltrate the Nanomei. Become one of them work alongside them. In so doing, I can serve Axiom. I can be an efficient, valuable asset in the machinery of order that is Axiom."

"How is your mission progressing?"

"Well. I have gained the trust of a Nanomei cell leader. Ramos. I have been working toward this goal since the start of my mission. Now I await further orders."

"Are you proud of your success?"

"I am."

"Are you aware that most agents have faster success, and have cleared more missions, in their first five years of service?"

Mal stilled her breathing and closed her eyes. This was a requirement of the test. Try to elicit a negative response, see what happens when Mal is thrown off guard. How Mal handled herself. "I'm the best hacker Axiom has at my level. I am doing work that few others at my level could do."

"You sound angry," Sim replied. A scripted part of the test, meant to be included if the last question had made her visibly upset. Mal opened one eye to peek her interviewer. Sim was smiling primly. "Only a few more questions and you can sleep."

"Good. I'm tired."

"I know," Sim said, reaching out and touching her hand. Mal opened both eyes in surprise. Part of the test? Connect personally with the interviewee? Another attempt to rattle her? Mal didn't think so, so Mal took her hand for just a moment. She, like all of us, is just doing her job.

"Go ahead. Ask your questions."

"What will you do if the Nanomei uncover your true motives?"

"Escape if possible. Fight if necessary."

"What is the nature of your service?"

"Based on loyalty. Axiom is the most stable of platforms."

"Do you have any feelings of loyalty to the Nanomei or their cause?"

That was the real question. The whole test was about asking this one question. Even hearing this question would upset a good Axiom agent. Mal took a moment, which Mal knew Sim would see and include in her report, but it would be a mistake to answer too quickly. Mal met her eyes with her own, hard. "No. My loyalty is to Axiom. Only Axiom."

She glanced down at Sim's hand, still resting on the couch, close to her own. Sim pulled it away with a closed look on her face. "That's the last question."

"Good." Mal pulled the electrode from her arm with unnecessary force, trying not to feel the shaking in her hands. "Go away and let me sleep."

⚙ ❯❯ **Chapter Seven:** Threshold ❮❮ ⚙

Waking up the next morning, Mal was struck immediately with the fact that she had no control over when she would get back to the Aetherium. She was waiting on the Nanomei to come to her door, and they would get here in their own time.

Restless, Mal ate some protein paste, dressed in her baggy khaki pants and loose black shirt, packed her duffel, and waited. Mal paced the apartment. She kept going into the Rigroom and staring at the Rig. They'd given instructions to strip it for parts, but once Mal took this Rig down she wouldn't be able to log back in. It was the last lifeline she had. She had left some elements laid out, the connectors ready for reattachment, their settings in place. It was a comfort to know that given an hour or so she could reassemble the Rig.

Mal did not want to go out in case she missed them, and she did not want to set her Rig back up in case they showed up. She was well and truly miserable. A thin grey blanket wrapped around her shoulders, she stood in the kitchen over the sink. She had scrubbed it clean on the first hour after taking down her rig. In fact, the whole place was rather too clean now. It looked fresh and new, or as fresh and new as a place like this could ever look. Some stains can't be scrubbed away.

A triple knock on her door, fast and loud, interrupted her. Mal almost ran to the door and opened it without looking to see who it was. There were two people standing there in yellow work jumpsuits marked with the grid utility logo: the Crossed Keys of Axiom with lines radiating out in eight directions. One was standing behind a dolly with a large metal case strapped to it. Trent stood behind them, clearly suspicious.

"We're here to assist in decommissioning your Rig for transport," one said.

"You didn't say anything about this to me," Trent interrupted loudly. "You're leaving?"

"Yes. I didn't have time to tell you. It's ok, Trent." Mal gave him a little wave. Trent nodded at her but did not leave. He looked worried, almost panicked. Just because I'm moving out, Trent?

"Come in. I'll show you," Mal said to the pair in jumpsuits.

They followed her in, Trent watching as Mal closed the door. One was about her height, meaning short, seemingly female, with soft, brown skin and a bright pink dreadlocks cascading down one side of her head like chips, a few strands blocking part of her face. Chiphead. Sometimes people look so much like their presentation in the Aetherium it's easy to recognize them in the Meat. The other presented as male. He was broad, copper skinned with a scarred face and head of dark corkscrew curls. His neck was covered with dark blue tattoos crawling up from beneath his shirt. He started toward her.

"Ramos," Mal said. She stepped forward. "I'm Mal."

Chiphead stepped between them.

"That's close enough," she said.

"Relax, relax," Ramos said.

Mal raised her hands ironically in front of her. "I don't want any trouble," Mal said to Ramos, not Chiphead. Mal felt her bristle.

Ramos laughed. "We're here to pick you up, Mal. No trouble." Ramos's eyes were piercing. Mal felt her heart racing.

"That's good," she said.

"Let me see your Papers," Ramos said. Mal handed him her Crypto-Card. A Crypto was not only keyed to open all doors for which the person had clearance, it was also encoded with a person's history: value, job, home, everything. Mal was never sure why they were called "Papers." Ramos pulled out a reader, smooth and black, about the size of his palm. Mal couldn't imagine how he'd gotten his hands on one. He slapped the Crypto against it and read the screen.

"This is good, but we need to scrub it to blank," he said to Chiphead. "We'll take her to the Barn." Then, turning to Mal he asked, "You have your Rig all set?"

Mal gestured toward her Rigroom door; Chiphead walked over to it and peered in. "Looks like she hasn't finished it yet." Chip paused and looked back at her.

Ramos said, "Get the Rig taken down. Scrap as much as you can."

Chiphead pulled Mal toward the Rigroom with a look. When Mal got there, Chiphead was eyeing the rig. She whistled when Mal got to the room.

"I already took the core bits, everything else isn't worth moving," Mal said.

"You must have built up some pretty good Value with that code smoothing."

"That and a bit on the side," Mal said.

Chiphead knelt near the rig's core. "This is really good work," she said admiringly. She ran her hands over it almost tenderly and then with a single, swift motion, tore the link cable out, a cascade of sparks showering out. Mal couldn't stop herself: she gasped. Chiphead looked back at her and grinned. "Weird. An emotion. It's almost like you're a real live human," she said.

Mal reestablished her calm, feeling strangely defensive. "I am."

Chiphead was expert and efficient in disassembling the rig. Ramos wheeled the large metal case in on the dolly. "Pack it in good," he said and then walked out to the main room.

"We do a lot of trading and modding. We should take as much as we can. Gives you more bargaining power. The parts you took already plus what we can fit in here. It'll help. There's a place we go to on the way."

"Will I be able to use Value there too?" Mal asked.

"With some vendors. There are other places we can go, but Axiom will freeze your Value after you stop going to your job. Depending on how quick they are with that, you may not have any Value to spend."

As Mal stuffed the parts into her only other bag, a black canvas bag, Ramos came into the doorway. "You ready?" he asked.

"Yeah."

"Okay. We're going to leave. And head two blocks over, on 7th. There's a white van."

"Give us ten minutes and follow," Chiphead said. She held out her hand for the bag. Mal handed it over, hoping Chiphead didn't see her millisecond of hesitation. Chiphead put the bag on top of the case strapped to the dolly and started rolling it to the door.

"Give us ten," Chiphead said to her. "Then follow."

"Okay. Ten minutes and I'll go."

"Good," Ramos said, "now walk us to the door and thank us, loudly, for our service. The Building Supervisor of yours seems a bit suspicious."

〉〉 • • • • • 〈〈

"Where are you going?"

Mal spun around. Damn. She had been hoping to leave without running into Gibson. He was standing in the hall in thin grey pajamas, his hair mussed and his eyes a bit foggy.

"I… what are you doing up so early?"

"You have your stuff. That's what you came here with. Are you leaving?" he said.

"I am, Kid. I have to move," Mal said.

"Why would you go so soon? You've only been here a little while."

"Yeah. It's the job," Mal sounded unconvincing even to her own ears. Why is it harder to lie to a kid than a Matron? She took a few steps, leaving him behind.

Gibson dashed around to cut her off. There were tears in his eyes. "I know you're lying. I always know when people lie to me."

"I'm not lying. I am moving because of my job. And I don't have any choice," Mal added. And I don't have any time. Why am I debating my life with this kid?

Telling Gibson she didn't have a choice ended his resistance. Everyone in the Meatspace was familiar with "I don't have a choice." His face fell. "Gimme your contact info so we can find each other after you move," he said.

Mal held her card out to him, feeling weirdly unable to meet his eyes.

He pulled out his, dangling from a cord around his neck, and tapped it to Mal's. "I get chipped soon," he added. "Maybe we can meet up in the Aetherium?" I'd actually love that, kid. Mal did not let that unbidden thought cross her face.

"I'm sorry, Gibson. I have to go now," Mal said aloud.

He started to cry. He didn't say anything else, didn't beg her to stay. He was resigned to his grief. Mal turned around. Trent had been behind her, watching.

Mal walked to the elevator. Trent followed and stepped into the elevator after her.

"Transfer? I didn't hear anything," he asked as the lift doors closed. Mal pressed her card to the controls and the lift started to lower. The sounds of Gibson crying faded away. There is a question in there, somewhere, Trent?

"Yeah. Last minute thing. I have to be out of Keral today," Mal said. All true.

"Do you know where you're going?" he asked.

"No. Honestly, they told me to get to the train station and my ticket would proc to my card," Mal said.

"That's pretty strange," he said.

Mal considered a confrontation. Looked him up and down.

"You know Axiom. When they call, you answer."

"And you have to leave immediately? No time in between assignments?"

"None," she said.

Trent whistled, low and slowly. "Damn. There's that direct Axiom control," he said.

The lift doors opened, and he put his hand over the door's sensor to keep the doors open so Mal could pass.

"It was good to see you again, Mal," he said. "It's really too bad you have to go again so soon."

"Yeah. I'm glad I got to come home for a bit," Mal replied.

"I wish you could have stayed."

I wish you hadn't been spying on me.

Mal stepped off the lift and watch the doors close. She took a long, shaky breath, then turned and left the building. Mal heard the door click shut behind her but did not watch it. Do the job. Earn your time. Get back in.

〉〉 • • • • • 〈〈

The walk to the van was uneventful, and the van itself nondescript. A side door slid open as Mal approached, and she climbed in. Ramos was driving, and Chiphead was in the back with her, perched on a metal box. Mal found another box and sat down. The rest of the back was scattered with scrap and parts. Ramos started the engine, which roared to life grudgingly and loudly. The van must have been ancient. The back section seemed to be made entirely of rust. Ramos was singing something as he drove, but Mal could not hear any specifics over the Noise of the engine.

"Where to from here?" Mal asked Chiphead.

"We need to get you out of the city. We're going someplace called Outpost."

"Why?"

Chiphead looked ahead into the front seat. "First, we're going to someone who can scrub your Papers."

"What's wrong with my Papers?"

"Nothing. But we're going to erase your history. So, you're safer. So, we're all safer."

They drove in silence for a while. Chiphead watched her. Mal tried not to mind. "You feel it yet?" Chiphead finally asked, leaning toward her.

"No. What?"

"That feeling of freedom."

Mal leaned forward, almost tipping the box, so she could look out past the front seats and out through the grimy windshield. Mal could still see Keral's city center. They were headed closer to the center but seemingly going around it rather than into it. Tall buildings loomed ahead, a few dirigibles with streaming lights sweeping the sides of skyscrapers. Mal had assumed they'd be headed out, away from the center, towards the Ring Wall. "I'll feel free when we're away from here," Mal said.

"Where we're taking you, you'll be free. More free than even if you just left. If you left on your own, where would you go? How would you log in?"

"I suppose real freedom requires some level of support, if only for that."

"There's other reasons for that support too. Nobody can make it on their own in this broken world."

I can. "Well, I'll still be glad to get out of Keral."

"Was this home for long?" Chiphead asked.

"Yeah. Where I grew up. Came back after Academy." When Mal had lived here the Ring Wall was newer, well maintained. Now drones swarmed over it, creating a virtual observation wall where the physical one had crumbled.

"You must have been good in Academy, what with your skills."

"Yeah, but I didn't fit in too well, which kept me from performing at my utmost efficiency."

Chip laughed hollowly at the joke. "How are you with loyalty, then?"

Mal hesitated. Answer her.

Chip laughed. "I'm just giving you shit. You're here, aren't you?"

Mal smiled back but did not relax. "Yeah. Right."

Chiphead yelled ahead. "How much longer?"

"We got about a half hour more," Ramos yelled from the front.

Ramos drove them around the edge of the city center. The glittering black spires of the upper city loomed gracefully into the sky and cast deep shadows. Most Axiom cities looked like this: a gleaming center surrounded by wasteland. The further from the center, the more deserted the land became. Ramos drove them into a tunnel. The city itself had built itself ever upwards, burying the lowest levels like sedimentary soil. The low classes and poor lived here, in the neon-lit tunnels and underpasses. They drove down a few more ramps, passing an endless array of grimy street food stalls, rickety vendors, and little crude shops, mostly set up on the crowded sidewalks: a sort of indoor city beneath the city of gleaming towers above. Mal wondered where people ate, slept, logged in. The streets were connected via ramps, and the walkways were eternally crisscrossing on raised platforms, stairways, and fenced-off paths. The sun didn't follow them down there; it felt like entering perpetual night. Some sections of street seemed in a continual rain as liquid dripped down from the higher tiers.

They made their way through the dark tunnels of the undercity for half an hour and finally came out of the tunnels and into blinding light. They drove in a long arc to the very edge of the city, to the sprawl at the inside curve of the Ring Wall. Here the buildings were smaller, and most were crumbling. Some were rusted metal skeletons, others unidentifiable heaps.

The city still loomed to their right, but the area ahead was brighter, more open. After a time, a huge grey building loomed ahead; it may have been red long ago. It had huge doors one narrow side and a roof that came to a sharp point. It was the front facing building of a complex of strange industrial building shells in various states of ruin. Nothing was near except for the rusted-out towns of days past which had been abandoned as the populations had dwindled. There were no cars in sight. Ramos parked in front of the large doors, off to one side. They all got out of the van and Mal looked around. The huge ring wall of Keral was near, and in the distance the city center.

Ramos walked up to the gaping hole in the rotting barn doors and disappeared into the darkness. "What is this place?" Mal asked as they approached the dark entryway. Chiphead stood to the side, waiting for her to enter. Mal took a deep breath, fighting the fear downwards. The doorway loomed before her. Mal felt puny. No wings here. No invisible sword. And crossing this threshold felt… final. She stepped through.

Inside the Barn, there was low, purple light. At the far end was a man in a standing rig. He wore a full immersion suit and helmet. Ramos approached the rig. The rest of the barn was empty, swept clean and free of clutter.

The man in the Rig twitched and a three-dimensional hologram was projected between the Rig and the rest of them. The hologram was not an attempt at reality: the figure was made of oscillating-colored lights, mostly red, indigo, and violet. The physical form of those lights was a bare-chested man with the body of an ancient athlete.

"Ramos," the hologram, as he spoke, changed to look like a tall man with skin black as night, with slicked back hair made of rainbows. "I foresaw your arrival."

"Yeah, I called you an hour ago. We need your skills, oh great one."

The hologram threw his head back and laughed. "I see you have her with you. Hello, Mal. Hello Deja. It's good to see you again, and to meet you, in inverse order. Sorry. The time dilation makes this awkward."

"Been there. it's a pain in the ass from your end," Mal said truthfully.

"Can you help us?" Ramos asked.

"I got you, Ramos. I'll scrub those papers clean. Give me about five of your minutes to get her situated."

The hologram's eyes went blank.

"Do I owe him anything…?" Mal asked.

Ramos turned. "You owe no one, Mal. Niro does this for the cause." Mal nodded.

"Go keep a watch. I don't like being here. He's safe here," Ramos said, pointing his thumb at the person in the rig, "but we're not him." Mal didn't understand this because being in a Rig is a usually a very vulnerable situation. Ramos must have been referring to some other form of safety.

Chiphead motioned her to follow. They took up a position at the edge of the barn, looking out to the highway. The low buildings here were a maze of rusted out frames and piles of debris. There was an odor in the air that Mal couldn't place but didn't want to ask about.

"You can get from here to the city center without seeing the light of day," Chiphead said. "But chances are you'd get lost for weeks trying it," she said. "The places where it looks like the buildings are ruined have often been carved out inside, tunnels through the wreckage and tunnels under the ground, connecting ancient basements, subbasements, steam tunnels. It's a real labyrinth. What took us two hours to drive could take weeks to walk through."

They saw them in the same moment. Three large black, wheeled Axiom transports barreling down the highway towards them. "There's nothing else around here, is there?" Mal asked hopefully.

"Absolutely nothing," Chip said. She touched her ear. "Ramos. Axiom. Gotta ditch. She paused to listen, then added "Okay." She sounded resigned.

"Ramos says Niro isn't done. He also said we should get the hell out of here for now. The Barn is off limits to them, but if they know we're inside they'll wait us out like a siege."

They ran around to the back of the barn. They could hear the Axiom warning sirens approaching. Behind the Barn they were able to get into some of the rusted-out industrial buildings and start fleeing. Mal immediately imagined being lost in these connected tunnels and buildings for weeks. Hunted like rats who couldn't log in. Two long, low buildings made of corrugated steel and old timbers, sagging in the middle, were the closest buildings. They dashed toward them.

"Ramos will catch up. You stick with me," Chiphead said as she ran. They all-out sprinted for a time, but neither of them was used to the physical exertion and stopped, panting together after a few hundred feet. "If we get separated, Ramos' orders are to return here in 48 hours. Niro won't let them stay, and they'll give up if they don't catch us." She reached into her jacket and pulled out a gun. It was Ikaru-made, better tech than Mal had assumed Nanomei would have. Getting caught with something like this as a citizen would be a death penalty. Chip handed it to her. Mal must have looked shocked, because Chiphead added, "Don't get all misty-eyed. You're an investment and no good to us if you get taken. Or killed."

Then an Axiom guard ducked from around a corner, his rifle raising as he yelled. "Stop right there!"

"Split up!" Chiphead yelled to her, pressing the gun into her hand. They both took off in different directions. Mal ran as fast as she could, the gun tight in her hand. The building was full of catwalks and rusted-out metal gangplanks. The metal grates were noisy to run on. Mal ducked into a side room littered with the discarded husks of machinery and hunkered down. She heard someone run past. In a fight in the Aetherium Mal would have a thousand options. In the Meatspace she was fragile, slow, human. Mal shook off a disgusted feeling in her own body and tried to think of a way out of this.

After a few minutes of silence, Mal stowed the gun in her hoodie and crept out of the hiding spot. If she was going to circle back in 48 hours, she needed to find a place further away and safe to hide. Mal moved through the abandoned industrial building and to a narrow alley between two other outbuildings. Mal was not sure she wanted to look for tunnels and sub basements. Staying close to or on ground level seemed safer. She found a tear in the corrugated metal of the building and slid inside, moving as quietly as she could, and walked directly into a room that two Axiom Guards were searching.

They leveled their weapons at her; green energy gridlines appeared from attachments on their rifles, taking a holographic recording of her. In the Aetherium she would be able to take these two in a heartbeat. Crank up her cycle speed, maybe put on a little Glitch, and derez both before they could pull their triggers. Here Mal imagined what the bullets would do to her body as she stood there.

"Don't move," one of them ordered.

"Check him," said the other. Mal's first reaction was one of revulsion, discomfort. She hated being misgendered, even unintentionally. It made her feel even more acutely the need to log back into the Aetherium.

The first speaker advanced, his gun still trained on her. "Show me your Papers," he said. "Now!"

Mal lifted her card toward him and squeezed the biometric access corner to allow a secure reading. She knew that Niro was still working on it and had no idea how that would affect it being read here. Mostly she needed time to figure something out. The chip reader embedded in his glove flashed information about her and her chipped identity.

"Look. I'm not who that says I am," Mal said.

They returned blank stares. Mal needed to be out of this situation, and she needed that now. She looked around them. No sign of Chip. "I am an Axiom Agent. My clearance code is Zeta-71232-5121. Run that now."

"Lies," the first speaker said. "What are you doing here?" He took a swift step forward and backhanded Mal hard. She fell to one knee with the impact and felt blood in her mouth. She spit it on the ground. Pain thudded through her head. Mal stood, moving back a bit, trying to get some space between them. She did not make a move for the gun in her hoodie. The guard who had hit her took a step closer.

"No, wait. She's the real deal. It came through," the other one said.

"No shit," Mal said.

"Oh. I apologize, Agent. We were looking for Nanomei scum," he said. He straightened his stance and looked as if he was now caught mid wince.

"Yeah. Well, you're letting me go now. Get back to your transport and report you saw nothing."

"Right away," the first one said. They left without looking back. Loyalty. Obedience.

Mal snuck through the building and across several city blocks of rusted-out, hollow buildings and ruins. She found a room with only one entrance and started to drag some old, crumbling pallets into a sort of semblance of cover.

"Mal," a voice said. Mal spun and saw Chip, standing with her gun pointed at her. Mal's heart stopped. Everything stopped. She couldn't breathe. How did you find out? Then Chip grinned. "You are not good at this," she said, holstering her weapon.

"This isn't my arena," Mal said. Breathe. Fucking breathe.

"Yeah, yeah, I know, hot shot. We'll get you logged back in soon enough."

They walked together for a time, away from the Barn, wanting to put space between it and them. Mal held her gun at the ready, unwilling to be surprised again. Chip mocked her for it, but Mal didn't let that stop her. It had been a few hours now since the raid on the Barn. They weren't in contact with Ramos; Chip said that Axiom could well have drones overhead monitoring communications.

They started talking a bit as they moved.

"So, you get chased by Axiom a lot?" Mal asked.

"Probably not as often as you'd think. Almost all the job is in the Aetherium," Chip said.

"What's up with The Man in the barn? How is he safe?" Mal asked.

"Oh, Niro? With enough Value, and the right connections Axiom won't touch you."

"That can't be true," Mal said.

"Sure it can. What, did you think it was a meritocracy? Or that Value couldn't buy special privilege?"

"Well, it's supposed to be and no it shouldn't."

Chip laughed.

They were both keeping our eyes forward where they had heard something. That's when they saw the transport on the street ahead. A pair of Axiom Guards were entering. It looked like they were packing up.

"Don't move," a voice said.

They both looked to their right. There was a single Axiom Guard. His rifle was aimed at them, and he looked incredibly young. His uniform was pressed, his bone-white skin even more pale in the face. He looked as if he may throw up at any moment.

"You. Drop your gun. And you, put your hands up. Now!"

"Hey, listen, guy. We're not who you're looking for," Chip said, moving her hand towards her gun.

"Stop!" He shouted. He was shaking. Mal could tell that he wanted to take a hand off his rifle to contact support. Maybe he was worried he'd drop the rifle. He was a merc or a fresh recruit. He was jumpy and dangerous not due to intent but because he could be easily startled into action.

Chip put her hands up. Does she sense it too?

"Drop your weapon!" he repeated. His eyes darted from Mal to Chip and back. He would either kill one of them or bring so many reinforcements they'd be finished. The tiny green light on his earpiece flashed to life. He listened for a moment and his eyes widened, looking straight at Mal. Time seemed to slow long enough for Mal to realize in stunning clarity: it was her, or her cover.

Mal shot him. It was a clean shot the impact of the bullet with his skull making more Noise than the firing of the weapon, and Chip gasped as the bullet tore through the Guard's skull. He dropped instantly, his rifle clattering to the ground.

"Run," Chip hissed. They ran together for what seemed an eternity. The muscles in her thighs burned, her lungs rasped, as they ran. The sun had set and lit the ever-present haze of the ruined sprawl alight with brilliant reds and golds. They sat in the basement of an abandoned fuel depot a good three miles from the Barn.

They spent the next whole day there. Chip shared a few nutrient bars she found in her pack. They tried to take turns sleeping, but neither of them could relax enough. Axiom protocol would mean that the personnel outside would stand down and leave; their Field Commander would not allow them to interfere with an Agent's work. Mal's main worry was that Chip would understand that this had been too easy, that they had left off their search too soon.

"So, anything you can't do?" Chip asked her, suddenly, after a few hours of silence.

"That was a lucky shot. Don't be impressed."

"Well, it tore the top of his head clean off. You're a damn assassin."

"I was aiming for his chest," Mal lied.

Chip laughed at that. Mal watched her closely and wondered if she always laughed death off so easily. Or was she faking it for her benefit? Mal forced herself to join in. This had been different than killing a traitorous driver. This had been killing a young guard doing his duty. They were still laughing when Chip held her hand up and brought her other hand to her ear.

"Ramos says we should make our way back to the Barn. The transports have gone."

They gathered their stuff and Mal traveled with the gun in her hand. They walked slowly. They'd been filled with adrenaline and were well-rested the first time; this time they were sore and tired. They moved carefully and saw no sign of Axiom patrols.

"You'd think they would have stuck around," Chip said as they moved closer to the Barn. "You killed one." Chip's voice, when she talked about the death, was still unreadable to Mal.

"I don't know. Does this Niro have that much power and influence?" Mal asked.

Chip looked at her sideways. "I suppose, maybe."

Said too much. Watch yourself. Mal would have liked to feel she did get herself together, but that would be lying. There were more than a few shifting debris piles and at least two rats Mal almost shot as they moved on. Her breathing was rapid and too shallow, and her heartbeat thudded in her ears. Finally, they got back to the buildings behind the Barn. Mal kept thinking about that kid — that's what he had been — just a kid. They moved through those more quickly and still saw no sign of Axiom.

Ramos met them behind the Barn.

As they walked into the Barn Ramos touched Chip's shoulder. "Any trouble?"

"Yes. We had to kill one. Well, Mal did."

She wasn't sure, but Mal thought she felt a shift in that moment. Did Ramos relax, just a shade more than he had before? Did he stand just an inch closer? Had Mal gained more trust?

Chip told him the story.

He smiled. "Well, an ace shot out here too," he said.

"Like I said to Deja. Lucky shot."

"Never underestimate the importance of a bit of luck," Ramos said.

They walked into the main area of the Barn. Niro was waiting for them. "Welcome back, finally," he said.

"We had a bit of a problem," Chip said.

"They took care of it," Ramos added. "Now, let's get to this. Mal needs her Papers," Ramos said.

"Step forward there, Mal. I need a better look."

Mal obeyed, putting the gun away for the first time since killing the Axiom Guard. Mal held out her card to Niro.

Intricate light-lines formed a sort of holographic cuff around the card and her hand, transparent and lit up in bright greens and yellows. The lights started to slip and move around her wrist faster and faster. Mal felt nothing but started to sweat. This was a core change to her Papers, her very identity. Mal would not be able to quietly prove who she was to the next set of Axiom guards. She was not herself after this.

The process took only a few minutes.

"You are rewritten, clean," Niro said.

Ramos and Chip both clapped her on her shoulders, each keeping their hand there for a moment, creating a triangle of them standing in this ancient place. If she were really entering into the Nanomei, Mal understood, this moment would be significant. This moment would mark a threshold. She was one of them. Or so they thought. The hologram smiled and then disappeared. They were left alone with Niro's body in the rig, motionless, standing there, his mind off somewhere in the Aetherium.

"Now," Ramos said, "We need to see if that worked. We need to get you out of the City. We're going to the Outpost."

>>·····<<

The drive to the Wall from the Barn was long and always a movement towards light. The shadows cast by the city behind them as they traveled gave way to the sprawl, desolate and underpopulated. Finally, as the great ring wall loomed larger and larger ahead, they entered the wastes. A few miles between them and the wall there was nothing. Keral had once been full to the walls. Now these miles in a ring around the city were scrap heaps, emptied settlements, abandoned vehicles. As Axiom had risen to fill the void and fall of other governments it had swelled but had been, in many places, contracting for decades.

"There are no tunnels here. This is pure junkland," Ramos said, loudly to make himself heard over the engine, as they moved along the still-clear highway. The edges of the highway were piled high with debris, metal, rusted out old machines, some cars.

"The plows come through regularly, though, even here," Chip said, as Mal stared out the window.

They drove past a few active encampments. Surely illegals, scraping out a meager life. The gridnet couldn't possibly reach them here; Mal couldn't see a single tower. And remote access rigs were well beyond the means of even average, job-holding citizens. These people were not connected to the Aetherium. Maybe they never had been. If they had, maybe they would never get back. Mal wondered what it must be like to be trapped in the Meat without the escape of the Aetherium. Without Value. Without security or safety. What would make people live like this?

"There are a few main highways left out here that are useable," Ramos roared over the engine. In the wall, there's the train and two highway exits. The other doors were closed years ago." The highway was wide. Turning onto it from the arterial roadway meant driving up a long sloping ramp up, eventually, several hundred feet. The wall did not have a ground-based exit; the only way out was through the highway cutting through the wall.

The highway provided a good vantage point from which to view the emptiness all around them. Out the grimy back window, Mal could see the towers of Keral looming behind them. There were very few other vehicles on the highway and ahead the wall loomed. Behind them, and headed the opposite direction, one of the great tractor-plows scraped the edges and kept the highway clear. The hole in the wall was surrounded by lights bright enough to see during the day's eternal haze and smog. Axiom's control of the City Center, Ringwall, and Highways was much stronger than it was in the Sprawl, especially in this area of ruined pods. At least they still patrolled in Mal's home pod. As they approached, they fell in line behind a few cars waiting to be processed at some kind of facility. Mal had never traveled via ground car into or out of an Axiom city. Mal knew the procedures though: they'd be removed from their vehicle and put on a moving walkway. They'd be scanned, X-Rayed, and eventually interviewed. The interviews were to last no more and no less than sixty seconds per citizen. While all of this was happening, the vehicle would be inspected, scanned, and checked by humans and AI. From the moment of scan to being returned to their vehicle should take exactly ten minutes. This was a short amount of time but the Axiom workers in the Aetherium would therefore have two solid hours to verify and vet each person's Aethereal identity and make sure they were who they claimed to be.

If all went well, they'd be reunited with their vehicle at the end of the walkway. They would have given detailed descriptions of their business in Keral and about their destination. The real decision would be made behind the scenes, in the Aetherium. This was procedure.

The reality was different. The lanes were narrowed to a single lane going out by heaps of rusted out cars and debris. As the van entered the funnel, they were the only vehicle leaving. Two guards came out of a small DropShack. These were prefab units meant to be deployed in hostile territory in emergency situations. They were meant to be highly disposable. This one looked like it had been in place for years.

Ramos opened his window.

"Cards," the guard said in a monotone.

"Shall we get out of the van and present them?" Ramos asked.

"No. Pass them up here." The guard seemed disinterested.

Mal and Chip passed their cards to Ramos which felt strange to Mal. Letting go of your Crypto-Card was something Citizens were taught not to do.

The guard scanned the whole stack at once and passed them back to Ramos.

"Move along. Move along," he said.

〉〉 • • • • • 〈〈

"That was too easy," Ramos said as they drove off.

"Did you pay them off?" Chiphead asked.

"No!" Ramos laughed loudly. "I was ready to! There was no need!"

"I don't think they were Axiom trained," Chiphead said.

"You're right, I think. We got a merc shift. We were lucky."

"Did we waste all that time on my Papers, then?" Mal asked.

"No. The point of that check was just to scan for criminals."

"That's the problem these days. Can't even count on Axiom to be the authoritarians they're supposed to be," Chiphead said.

"Well," Ramos said with a smile. "We saved a bit of money, and we know Mal's card was clean." They all laughed. A good Agent does not question authority. There must be reasons for Mercs being used, for the lack of security. Resources and logistics are not simple equations to balance no matter how powerful the AI assistance. But something itched at the back of Mal's mind. This should have been harder.

"Next stop," Chip said. "Station Nine-Twenty."

"What's that?"

"Scrap shop. Trade Spot. The Rig you'll be assigned at Outpost is going to need work. Outpost runs a tight crew with minimal resources. There's a Rig Core waiting for you but it's going to need parts. Try to get pretty much everything you'd need aside from the Core here if you can." Chiphead explained what parts were waiting for Mal at the Outpost. It wasn't many. She'd need to trade for a lot at this place.

"Good ol' Nine-Twenty," Ramos said in a booming voice. Here, outside the city, his voice was even louder.

>>••••<<

The Nine-Twenty was an ancient refueling station. Refueling stations had not been used for at least three decades, but those that weren't decommissioned and recycled were sometimes still used, Chiphead told her, as clandestine trading posts. The main building had a curved, metal roof, and cheap corrugated steel siding.

"Let's make this relatively quick, please," Ramos said to Chiphead.

"I have something of a reputation," Chiphead said to her with a grin and a shrug and quickened her pace to get past Ramos.

Ramos handed her the black canvas bag of parts and winked. "Get some advice before you trade away your scrap," he said, pointing a thumb at Chiphead. He went off then, looking like a man with a purpose. His black clothing stood out here among the sea of earth-tones. He stood out in other ways, too: Mal hated to think it, but there was a force to his personality. People noticed him and moved out of his way physically even while they noted him. They watched him. Shit, wait, I am too.

Mal scanned the area: there was a rusted-out old building, and three or four stalls filled with junk traders and their wares. The refuse of hundreds of years of tech was available. Wires, casings, boards, chips; the piles of junk were endless. It all looked to be in horrible shape. There were a few dozen others haggling, browsing, and milling about. The people here looked hungry and washed out. Their clothes were, in many cases, scraps.

Mal shouldered the bag and approached the area with vendors. The sounds she encountered in the Meatspace were not surprising, the sights less so. Sure, the Aetherium offers full sensory immersion, but the worst smells are not usually programmed there. The area smelled like dust, rust, vomit, and some sort of alcohol or fuel. Mal's nose burned, and she sneezed several times.

"What'cha got?" a vendor with fewer teeth than fingers said to her as Mal approached. "What'cha got n whatcha want?" he said.

The vendor's stall looked to Mal like the gear in her bag outpaced whatever was available here by far. Which meant that the few things Mal had managed to bring with her could get a full setup, if Mal was willing to take lesser parts. Mal smiled absently at this vendor and hurried to catch up with Chiphead. She needed that advice.

Mal haggled with Chiphead at her elbow giving her cues for an hour, moving from vendor to vendor. Memory Sticks were easy to come by. As were three of four boards she needed for an inverter matrix, and a teardrop reverb, and a pair of transduction nodes. Near the end of their tour, Mal approached a vendor who had much the same scrap as the others, but as Mal approached pulled out a large, flat wooden box. She opened it and her eyes flashed.

Inside the shallow box was packing straw were three red apples. Mal had seen apples before, and even tasted them, in the Aetherium. But she had never seen them in the Meat.

"How much for one?" Mal asked.

She smiled. "What do you have to trade? Or do you have Value?"

Mal pulled out her card and pushed it to the outstretched reader.

"Well," she said, sounding fake-shocked. "You have no Value at all!"

"Yeah, we scrubbed you, remember," Chiphead said.

Mal looked at her and frowned. "I thought…"

"It needed to be completely clean," she said. "Those apples were going to be overpriced anyway," she added looking at the vendor.

"Suit yourself, girlie. I'll find a buyer with some taste," she said.

"Doubtful," Chip said. "Let's move on," she added to Mal.

〉〉 • • • • • 〈〈

After a half hour more they were ready to go and Ramos summoned them to the car with several long blasts of the warning horn. People all around muttered their irritation and Ramos just waved happily to them all. They gathered, Mal's bag a bit heavier.

"Get comfortable back there," Ramos said. "We've got a three-hour drive in front of us, with good conditions."

"What are bad conditions?" Mal asked.

"Dust storms, blocked roads," Chiphead said. She checked her sidearm, though, and that spoke to other dangers she had not named.

They drove for more like four hours, after passing through their fair share of bad road. Mal's geography wasn't strong enough to know where exactly they were. Mal had spent much more time learning non-linear geography as it applied in the Aetherium than maps of Meatspace, which moved, strangely, in straight lines. The city they approached also had a large wall, and they seemed headed straight for it. It looked more intact than Keral's wall.

"Here," Chiphead said, reaching toward Mal.

Mal took the small linen wrapped parcel she offered. Unwrapping it she saw that it was an apple. When Mal looked to Chip to thank her, Chip had started staring out the window, avoiding eye contact. Mal stowed the apple.

"This is Thresh," Ramos said. "We aren't going in. The Outpost is built in its shadow."

They drove among the sprawled wreckage of the outer city, everything outside the wall: a long stretch of junk piles, ancient machinery, and refuse. They approached a huge wall of scrap metal. It looked like flattened, crushed, ground cars used like giant building blocks to build a sort of wall, almost like a castle from some old story.

At the front of the wall was a gate, a long pole with rusted spikes, stakes, and razor wire. Sitting casually next to the pole was a single person, dressed in rags and tatters and covered in grime.

A sign behind them proclaimed "Brice's Junk-Post: Finest prewar scrap." Which war, Mal wondered. There had been so many, stacked atop each other, overlapping trauma dominos.

Ramos pulled the car up and the man in rags stood. "Welcome back to Outpost, Ramos. We're expecting you," he said while he waved to some unseen compatriot at the wall. The gate rose and Ramos drove them in slowly.

Past the wall was an open area with a few broken-down cars and a small shack with a barred window with a heavy black mat on the ground in front of it. Several dumpsters lined the scrap-block walls.

They continued driving past the shack, then through a sort of maze of tight turns and narrow passages. The maze walls were made of rusted-out shells of ground cars, some crushed, some just crushed by the weight of time. Mal saw a few gun emplacements hidden among the junk, wires, and refuse.

Finally, they entered a large courtyard. There were no other vehicles here and the ground was clear. There was a large table in the very center of the courtyard, a fire pit with chairs gathered around it, and small garden with a few scraggly plants. There was a group at the table, eating, that stopped to watch as they approached. When Ramos exited the car, several of the group stood and yelled his name.

"Ramos, come! Sit! Drink with us! It's been so long!" Mal exchanged a glance with Chiphead, who rolled her eyes but looked proud, too. "He's something of a celebrity among us believers," she said. It's a cult.

Chiphead and Mal got out of the car.

"Glyph," Ramos said to a young person with pale white, freckled skin and straight brown hair and did not clearly present as male or female. Mal decided to assume neither for the time being. "Come and take Mal. Show her around!"

Glyph walked toward them and nodded awkwardly.

"I'll show you around and then we can get you something to eat," Glyph said.

Glyph took her to one of three doorways evident in the courtyard. Aside from those three, only two other exits were apparent: the one they had driven in through, and a last one, wide enough for a small truck.

"I don't know if you were paying attention that back there was Willits, Larson, and Q. You came in with Ramos and Deja."

"Heh, I call her Chiphead in my brain."

"I get that," they said. "So, Willits, Larson, and Q are Meats. They never login and take care of the grounds. Keep guns working, maintain generator, that sort of thing."

"Never, log, in?"

"It's a choice," Glyph said.

"Wow."

"Yeah, not a choice I'd ever make either," they said.

"It sounds like hell," Mal said as Glyph opened the door.

"This is the mess," Glyph said as they passed through the first room off the courtyard. The room was carved from the junk-blocks. There were three large refrigeration units, some brushed steel worktables, and an assortment of boxes and crates, mostly unmarked. "We eat outside unless there's a dust storm. Willits is the cook. Don't break his rules. He's insane."

Then they took Mal through a narrow corridor cut into the junk slabs, which opened up into a long hallway with black rubber flooring and canned lights connected via exposed wires above. Each door was closed that they passed, until the last one on the right.

"This will be your place to sleep," Glyph said, standing aside so Mal could see in. It was a tiny room with a simple bed and a footlocker. There was nothing else in the room, no window, no closet, no other exit. No rig.

"Where are the rigs?" Mal asked.

"That's the best part. Wait 'til you see this!" they said.

They led Mal through a few more narrow corridors, one of which had a severe slope downwards. A young man in all grey with a shock of blonde hair sticking out in a handful of ways was passing by them.

"Hey Rat," Glyph said. "This is the newbie."

"Oh. Hi," Rat said. His eyes looked different, unfocused. "I need sleep," he told them conversationally, and continued on his way towards the surface. Glyph smiled shyly and shrugged.

"Rat is the best Engineer we have," they said.

"You can always count on Rat!" Mal heard him yell from down the hall at his name.

Glyph continued downward, and the path never veered or switched back, which meant that they were below ground, and at least a hundred meters away from the entry of the Outpost. Then they were at an airlock. It reminded her of entering Tok's ship. Three doors segmenting a single tube-like corridor.

They went through the last doorway and entered a room the shape of an octagon. There was a central Core feeding six of the eight rigs. Thick, black tubes, wire bundles, transformers, all connected to the Core of to each of the six stations. Each station a reclined, ergonomic chair connected to a rig. Two of the eight looked nonfunctional, one missing a large portion of its casing, and the other being more a bundle of wires with no place to go. Two of the functional ones had people logged in.

"This is our Leader, Vala," Glyph said, motioning to a woman jacked into a rig. "The other one is Shadow, he's our best in the Aetherium," they said. "And that's the physical server Core for our own Pylon." They motioned to the center of the room, which is really where Mal's attention had been all along.

"Wow," Mal said. A Pylon in the Meatspace: rare and impressive for an outfit this size. This was the hardware side of an Aetherial Pylon. Most of those were owned and controlled by whatever collective controlled that portion of the Aetherium, where Mal spent time that usually meant Axiom, sometimes Ikaru. And sure, she'd seen that RezX possessed mobile Pylons… but that Nanomei had one was news to Mal. There was a deep bass hum coming from somewhere below this room: the processor farm supporting the Pylon. The rigs themselves were cobbled together scrap. Piecemeal rigs made by desperate people.

"Nice, right?" Glyph said.

"I can't believe you have a Pylon."

"A small one, but discreet. Allows us to log in and out without anyone knowing or logging it."

"How?"

"It wasn't easy getting it, but Ramos works wonders. He has deep connections in every Collective. You should see what he's done at the CoOp." This caught Mal's attention.

"Which of these," Mal asked motioning to the rigs, "is going to be mine?"

They walked over to the chair that had the fewest connections, and a very incomplete rig. "This is you," Glyph said.

It was broken in several places, but it was not dirty, not disheveled. Merely in need of repair and renovation. And replacement. The connector stream cable was broken and Mal would need a new one. Mal approached the Core of her new Rig and started making an inventory of what she would need, trying not to let her disappointment show on her face.

"You arrived without much warning, or we would have had a chance to get you more set up. What you need is Rat," Glyph said.

"I need more than a good tech. What I brought with me isn't enough to get this up and running." A heat spread across the back of her neck. Suddenly the Rig back in Keral was an impossibly wonderful thing that she was already missing.

"This is Marcus," Glyph said. That shook Mal out of the downward spiral of the impossibility of getting this Rig up and running any time soon. She looked up and saw the same man she had given her couch to.

"We already met," Marcus said, holding out his hand to Mal.

She took this in stride, and his hand in hers, again, turning it to show the white rabbit.

Before they could exchange words, a loud, low buzzer went off somewhere else in the base but echoed through the metal walls.

"I've got to get back to it," Marcus said giving Mal a sly wink. He started to prepare one of the rigs.

"That's food," Glyph said. "Follow me." They led her back to the outdoor table. Rat was the only one Mal recognized, and Mal was glad to see him. Mal would need his help. He still looked tired, and his movements were twitchy. "Everyone, this is Mal." The three at the table exchanged unreadable looks. "Mal, this is Simone. She finds us the supplies we need and organizes who goes where when."

Simone nodded. She wore large goggles on the top of her head which was otherwise covered in impossibly curly, fiery red hair. She wore a tank top and her pale white arms seemed to quiver whenever the sun came too close. The look she gave her was not unfriendly, exactly, but it wasn't welcoming.

"This is Willits," Glyph continued, "who runs the kitchen." Even sitting, Willits towered over the others at the table. He was shirtless, and his tanned skin was covered in a thin layer of sweat. "And Ibrahim." Mal had seen Ibrahim guarding the initial entrance as they were coming in. He was still dressed in ragged brown poncho and a hat that flopped down over most of his head and face. His grin was broken, and grey teeth and his deeply weathered skin covered in stray hair and scars. Ibrahim smiled in a more friendly way and indicated the seat next to her. "Come. Sit. Eat this terrible food."

Willits, glaring at Ibrahim, handed Mal a plate: a piece of rough bread spread with a thick paste.

"Sometimes it's two pieces of bread," Rat said with a smile, taking a seat.

"I can't wait," Mal said.

Mal fielded many questions of the sort she had expected: What are your skills? Hacking. Lying to people while eating.

Who are you?

Why'd you join up?

Q and Larson joined them but Marcus, Shadow, and Vala were in the Aetherium.

This would be nice, maybe, conversation and (bad) dining, but Mal had to make up answers that maintained her cover. It was exhausting. Mal hoped any stress she revealed was interpreted as nervousness about meeting her new crew.

"So, you lived in Keral?" Q asked.

"I did, yes."

"I was there once. When I was little. My parents were moving for jobs. I never left the train station, but I was there."

"What about family, got any?" Larson said.

When Mal didn't answer immediately, Willets stepped in, "Damn, Larson, give her some time before you start interrogating her."

"Ramos spoke highly of you," Simone said. Her eyes were calculating. Mal took a big bite of bread.

"You're his pet project. He's been talking you up for months," Simone said. This didn't track with what Mal knew. Ramos had been aware of her earlier than Mal thought. It made her wonder if Ramos was a step ahead now somehow. I don't have the whole story, do I, Ramos? Not that I can complain.

"So, he had you move the shield to a different city?"

The table got quiet, and all eyes were on Mal.

Mal held her cup in front of her, stared at the surface of the water. In an Axiom mess Mal would be confident that boasting would raise her social standing. But that didn't feel right here. In Axiom, everyone wore their power where it could be seen. Axiom wanted Citizens to get in line, but Agents were expected to get to the front of that line. Among the elite everything was a contest. Especially with you, Kass. These people had a different way. Mal just hadn't figured it out yet.

"Yeah. That was me."

A barrage of questions came then about refresh matrixes, mod limits, and more. There was considerable interest about the Praetorian Shield Ramos had asked for. Apparently, he'd made the same request of most recruits. Half of them never made it and a good recruit was usually defined by how they handled Ramos and telling him it was impossible. Only Chiphead had also retrieved one, but nobody would tell Mal more about that. Mal tried to pull any information she could about Ramos but Mal was the new kid here; they were only looking to get info from her. It was not a give-and-take. Not yet.

"So how's your Rig coming together?" Rat asked as the others started to filter out. "I know you've been here for less than an hour but that would be my priority. Login is life."

"That's our que to get gone," Q said to Larson. They took their trays and left with nods to Mal.

"Still a few things I need. A feedback inverter and a blink cable. Other things too, of course, but to just get it up and running. I need those two before I can even get in. The rest I think I handled at the trade depot on the way here."

"I heard Axiom didn't even check the van at the border. You could have moved your whole Rig with you," Ibrahim said.

Mal just stared.

Rat whistled. "Yeesh. That's a tall order. Sure, a blink cable they could piece together maybe. You'd have some signal loss, but you don't really neeeeed it to get through the connection cycle. But running without a feedback inverter is literally impossible."

"Think anyone at camp has one for trade?" Mal asked.

"Doubtful. There aren't even any hosed ones waiting for repair. Those things are supposed to be indestructible. There wasn't one you grabbed from home?"

"No. I had an integrated Rig pulse inverter."

"Oh, yeah. Those are better. But you sure couldn't transport it. Unless Axiom just let you through the wall without inspecting the van. Did that really happen?"

"Yeah. I'd rather not dwell on the fact that an overabundance of Nanomei caution cost me my Rig and access," Mal said bitterly.

"Hey, who says we're Nanomei?" Ibrahim said.

"I heard Nanomei don't exist," Willits said.

"Hey leave her alone. It's rough being rigless for those of us not moron enough to want that," Rat said. "Now let's get back to getting you hooked up," he said, turning his full attention to Mal.

Mal could swear he was enjoying the challenge. "What do you suggest? Glyph says you're the guy to talk to about parts."

Rat waited for the last of the others to leave the table and didn't say anything until he had watched them walk out of the courtyard.

"There's a Recyclery just on the inside of the wall," he whispered.

"You mean on the other side of the wall? As in an Axiom-controlled city?"

"Well, technically, yes. But the wall has a breach in it. One of the exhaust ports is blown and the fans aren't running. We can get in through there," he said.

"So why the secrecy?" Mal asked, looking around.

"Vala says it's off limits," he said.

"What does Ramos say?"

"Ramos says get the job done whatever it takes," Rat said.

"But you listen more to Vala?"

"It's mostly because if I say out loud that I'm going to go to the Recyclery I'll end up with a "Rat-Get-Me-A List a mile long," he said with a sense of bravado. "But I go every few days and bring stuff back. You could come along and look for what you need," he said.

"I'm in," Mal said. To which, Rat's reply was a wide, sincere smile.

〉〉 • • • • • 〈〈

Mal spent the next few days working on her Rig and keeping her head down. Ramos and Chiphead had gone and Mal didn't want to draw attention and she didn't want to disrupt the rhythms of this place. Eating with these people and spending time in the Outpost was teaching her a lot about at least what this group of Nanomei was really like. Mal learned that there was a tension here, and at least two distinct factions that seemed to orbit around Ramos. Vala, Shadow, Glyph, and the Meats seemed to speak of Ramos differently than the rest (Marcus, Simone, and Rat). It seemed to Mal after a few days that Vala, as the leader of Outpost, did not like it when Ramos rode in handing out directives and bringing new recruits. The other group seemed to lap up whatever Ramos offered and so had been more welcoming to her as Ramos' pet project. Having only three people in the group that welcomed her made her feel off balance. She was resented by the others, or worse. She wondered how far Vala would go to prove that Mal was a bad idea.

Mal made it a point to take a sandwich out to Ibrahim on most days ever since he mentioned his bum hip and how he hated walking all the way through the maze every day for lunch.

"Thanks my lady," he always said, smiling around a bite of the sandwich.

Mal knew to keep out of the mess when Willits and Larson were both there, sometimes avoiding it for hours at a time. Their arguments about ancient poets were just not something she wanted to get involved with.

〉〉 • • • • • 〈〈

Rat was always around but seldom for long, often flitting about to the next project. Mal learned quicky that if you really needed him to do something you had to interrupt him doing something else.

Mal felt herself in that orbit struggling to understand what these people wanted and what motivated them. But it wasn't getting her closer to Ramos, he was never around. Worse: Mal was not logging in. She was also, strangely, missing the dead drops which had always been a nuisance but now were something she would find comforting.

159

On the third night, Mal heard a furtive noise outside her door that may have been a knock. "Uh, come in?" It felt like an experimental response, but the door did actually swing open. It was Rat.

"So, you wanna sneak out and break some rules?"

"Now?" She asked.

"Yeah, now. I packed sandwiches," he said.

"Sandwiches? Well, then. Let's go," Mal said, swinging her legs over her bunk and reaching for her poncho. As Rat turned to go, she slid her gun into her pocket.

The easiest way out of the camp was to climb a part of the scrap wall near the back of the place. There were handholds that Rat pointed out.

"You've done this before," Mal said in a whisper as they climbed.

"Yeah. You can't keep Rat locked down!" he said too loudly for her comfort. Maybe some bragging does go on in Camp Nanomei.

After getting over the wall and out of Outpost the trip was only about an hour's walk through the maze of scrap and waste piled high against the wall.

They snuck past a group of people from Outpost, gathered around an old oil drum fire. They were sharing stories.

"Axiom took everything from me," Q was saying. "But the worst is that I don't know where they were taken."

"I know. Information is impossible to get," Ibrahim added.

"What about what they did in Golden Cluster?"

"I hadn't heard. I knew it was repopulated recently though. They were looking for feeders."

"It was Axiom. I knew a man in one of the cities that logged in to Golden Cluster. The Meatspace cities burned."

"Plasticrete doesn't burn," Larson said.

"Well, this city did."

"What was the casualty rate?"

"No numbers but I'd guess half."

"Shit."

Mal felt dragged toward the fire. They were talking about the Golden Cluster Event, something Mal had heard from the Axiom side. Golden Cluster had been an unstable system because of rampant Nanomei and other insurrectionist groups. Axiom had had no choice but to come down hard to stomp out the corrupt portions of the area: surely some loss was worth that purity, that order. Part of her wanted to listen longer but Rat pulled on her arm. "Let's go," he said.

The Outpost abutted the outside of the wall of this city and it was not a great distance to the place where a valley opened up in the trash and junk layers. A stream of filthy water poured from an outlet, and above that, a good ten feet up, was a vent covering about twenty feet in diameter that was askew. The casing was bent and there was plenty of room to climb in.

Rat pulled out a length of rope with a hook on the end.

"I bet those do not work like you think they do," Mal said.

"Yeah, this going to be a disaster," Rat said cheerfully. Mal could not help but make a face at this.

"I'm ready. Let's have a disaster," Mal said. Her pulse quickened a bit. Mal was feeling pretty intense about getting these parts for her rig, but if she allowed herself to be fully honest, that wasn't the only reason her heart was racing. The night roared past them, and the road ahead of them was dark and full of possibility. No one was watching her. It had been five days since her last dead drop.

They managed to stay relatively quiet as they ineptly made their way up the wall with the help of the grate, Rat's rope, and a good dose of whispered swearing. The inside of the ventilation shaft was large and wide, and they could both stand inside easily. Rat clicked up his light which cast an all-too-wide and bright beam. Mal remembered a time that Kass and Mal had snuck out of the Academy dorms. It was just before they were set to graduate and get our assignments. One last night sneaking out together. "Who designs these things?" Kass had laughed at how easy it was to sneak in and out through oversized ventilation shafts. They had gone out through a similar ventilation shaft.

They crept through the ventilation system and eventually came to an access door which led to a long series of small corridors, doorways, and turns. Rat guided them through the path from black markings on his forearm, a sort of code that led them through the maze. He'd done this before but not often enough that it was rote memory yet. Ahead was a small passage that split in two, one left and one right. Mal focused completely on the path they took, and the choices they didn't take. Rat was talking but Mal filtered it out so she could focus on the path. She was confident that if she returned here, she'd remember the way.

"Up ahead is the only spot where we might have trouble," Rat whispered to her without looking at her. "The one on the left," Rat whispered, "is where we wanna go. The one on the right is a guard station. Sometimes there's nobody there. Sometimes."

Mal pulled out the pistol Mal brought with her.

"Whoa, whoa… what's that?" Rat asked in a hushed panic.

"It's a gun," Mal said plainly.

"This isn't that kind of place," he said urgently.

"What do you mean?"

"I mean we're here for supplies. These are regular folks here. Paid working guards, not Axiom goons," he said. "Put that thing away." Mal made a show of flipping the safety and put the gun back in her bag.

"Now, stay quiet and let's, you know, not kill anyone," Rat said.

"Then what do we do if we get caught?"

He looked at her and grinned, but didn't answer, and took off ahead of her.

They walked together quietly and took the passage that branched to the left. As they crept along the corridors became less and less hospitable. There were steam pipes, hosing and air vents every few steps. Always something to duck under or shimmy around. Mal would not want to be chased through here, she thought, and as she did, she realized she had probably sealed her fate to someday be chased through here. Dammit, Mal.

Rat stopped at a small door. "This is an access door to one of the sorting bins," he said.

"I'm ready," Mal said.

"It's big," he said. "Just be prepared for the bigness." Rat pushed open the door and a stream of warm air came from behind them.

"You are not wrong," she said. The access door opened to a room the size of a stadium, stretching into the haze. It was all electronic junk, scrap, refuse.

"This has been sorted?" Mal asked, looking at the mountains and heaps.

"There is no organic matter here, so yeah, it's been sorted. And cleaned."

"Then what's that smell?" Mal asked.

"There are bins of what they cleaned off it connected via vast conveyor belts about a hundred feet above them. They aren't operating right now. We'd hear 'em," he said.

"How are we going to see anything in here?" Mal asked. "How do you find anything?"

"Who do you think you're with? Name's Rat, have we met? You can always count on Rat." he said with a toothy smile.

"Okay, I'll follow your lead," Mal said.

Rat hopped into the pit; it was only five or so feet down from them at this point, though he created a rolling hillside of trash when he landed. Then Mal noticed that there were other people here. That was a real shock to her. Mal thought this was a clandestine operation.

"We're not alone," Mal said.

"Yeah, try not to shoot anyone," Rat answered. "I know some of these people," he added. None of them were close enough to them for her to get a good description and people seemed to stay away from each other as they slowly searched for their treasures.

Rat and Mal got to work moving the scrap from one place to another, checking each piece looking for tech she could use. It was not easy nor was it methodical. The vast majority of what was here was nonfunctional. Rat had brought along a few bits of diagnostic gear to test things. It was a long, painstaking, and headache-inducing process.

After several hours they stopped to rest, sitting with their backs against a large pile of tubing.

"You've got some focus," Rat said. "Usually if I bring someone here, they get bored or give up way sooner than this."

"I've found some good blink cable, if we splice some together," Mal said. They talked, both of them enthusiastically about the few pieces they'd found in those hours. Rat had found a reverb chip, and she'd found a bundle of synth mod wiring. These would not do much for her own Rig but, Rat told her, they would be really helpful for some of the other rigs. "I still need a feedback inverter, though."

"Yeah, that's gotta happen," he said, handing her a sandwich of the crusty bread and protein paste.

"You really made sandwiches," Mal said appreciatively.

"You can always count on Rat," he said.

Mal smiled and reached into her poncho, pulling out the apple.

"Holy balls," Rat said.

"You can also always count on Mal," she said, tossing him the apple. They ate quietly for a few minutes, the sandwiches and passing the apple back and forth. They'd been at it for hours and it looked like hours more ahead. There was no question of leaving before they found what they needed.

"What else has Vala told you not to do that you're still doing?" Mal asked.

"Well, she doesn't want any electrical engineering experimentation."

"Oh. Say more," Mal urged.

"Well, a few months ago I tried to strip an inverter Core down to wire and then re-coat it with
impact resistant gel."

"What were you trying to do?"

"Trying? I cut latency by 1.5 nspc."

Mal whistled. "Why would that bother anyone? You can do that to my Rig any time."

"Well, it melted the recumbent relays and fried the buffer."

"Don't ever touch my rig," Mal said, and they both laughed. "What else doesn't Vala like, aside from, you know, ruining perfectly good rigs?"

"Nothing really to tell. She doesn't like that I take risks in the Meat. She's all about risk in
the Aetherium but she always holds back in the Meat and especially with Rig work. Simone has no problem with it though, so it happens under the radar. She's logistics which helps."

"Is Ramos often at CoOp? I'd think he'd be in your corner on this." Mal asked. That fell on silence, though. He didn't answer. They got back into it.

After a few more hours, Rat let out a triumphant cry.

"This isn't an inverter, but it's worth three of them," he said, holding up a small chip he'd just pried up from a larger, broken board.

"That's great, but nobody wants to get rid of an inverter. They couldn't connect," Mal said.

"Yeah, but we could take it to a trade depot."

"Does the group leave Outpost often?" Mal asked.

"You're looking at a few weeks," he said.

Mal twitched. She needed to get back in and sooner than a few weeks.

"You go back," Mal said somewhat more shakily than she had wanted to. "I'll stick around," Mal said.

"You can't stay more than another hour. They'll be turning on the conveyors and everything here will be under a few more meters of this stuff. You don't want to be here when that happens," he said.

"Yeah."

"Let's spend a bit more time. Maybe we'll find one and get you back inside," he said. He reached out and touched her hand then. Took it from the top and squeezed. Mal looked at him and he let go. She was not sure what her look had conveyed. Don't get attached, Rat. You won't like where this is headed.

After a handful of hours Mal felt Rat's hand on her shoulder and turned. He was holding the slender black form of a feedback inverter. It looked beat up but whole and was attached to a chipped-out grid matrix that would need to be removed…

"You can always count on Rat."

She almost put her fist out, as if to share contact in the Aetherium but stopped herself. Mal threw her arms around him, freaking both of them out. What the hell, Mal? We do not hug on a job.

"Whoa there," Rat said, in an echo of what she just thought to herself. But he still hugged her back.

⋙ » Chapter Eight: Reset « ⋘

The next three days went by in a haze of activity. Glyph and Mal worked with the broken-down parts of the Rig that Mal had been allocated, the parts Mal had traded for, and the ones Rat and Mal had collected. Other people stopped by with words of encouragement. Rat came by with terrible sandwiches a few times.

"You two haven't rested in 36 hours," he said.

"That's an exaggeration," Glyph said, laughing. "We both slept for three hours yesterday."

They laughed and Rat spent the next few hours doing some grunt work for them, mostly soldering the connections they'd roughed in earlier. Probably about a hundred of them.

After those three days they were finally ready. The Rig was complete and in operational condition. Mal sat there alone. Others had gone to sleep or were logged in and unaware of their surroundings. Mal sat by her Rig and sobbed, so relieved to have a gateway back in. Mal needed to get back in but she was stone cold tired, and even in this desperate state, too smart to log in while this exhausted. Mal didn't have a memory of going to her bunk but that's where she awoke early the next morning.

But it wasn't. Mal had apparently slept a complete day. She stumbled out of bed thinking it had been only the next morning. She wandered out to the kitchen to find Glyph sitting at the table.

"Nobody woke me. I had kitchen duty this morning," Mal said.

Glyph laughed. "No, hun. You had kitchen duty yesterday."

Mal squinted and approached the table. "What?"

"You slept a whole day. Finally caught up to you."

"Well."

"Well, nothing," they said. "I've run the diagnostics. Your Rig is all ready for you. But you'll have to wait to go in," Glyph said.

"What?" Mal said, bolting out of bed.

"Ramos is back early."

"What's wrong?" Mal asked, grabbing her poncho and stepping out into the hall with Glyph. They walked together quickly towards the courtyard.

"He's waiting," Larson said in front of them, waving them to follow.

They walked into Ramos' meeting in progress; he was in the center of the mess, surrounded by about a dozen followers, who were sitting on the benches, counters, or leaning against the walls. All of the people Mal knew from Outpost, and a few she still did not know, were here.

"Look, all I'm saying, Ramos, is that she's new here and we need to start her off slowly," Vala was saying.

"I did not bring her in to have her waiting for parts. I came here to set her on a path. I need her on the grid," Ramos said, his voice calm and even.

"Her rig's ready," Glyph said from next to Mal.

A few people murmured. Ramos looked at Glyph and let his eyes rest on Mal for a moment.

"Good, Glyph," Ramos said. "I told you,"he said to Vala, "I need my best fighters in to get this done. We are making moves that will require all of our best be logged in."

"I know that's your plan. I still believe we need caution here, Ramos," Vala said.

"Caution has not done enough. Blockades and inconveniences are no longer enough. Taking the odd Pylon to just lose it again the next week isn't enough. We need to make them start fearing that their casualties will be real, Meat deaths."

"We are making progress," Vala said.

"Too slowly!" Ramos yelled.

There were murmurs but only one voice piped up above the rest. "Yeah! Too slowly!" It was Rat.

"You'd follow Ramos into a flooding Node," Glyph said to him.

"Yeah? You wouldn't?"

Chiphead stood straight from a leaning position.

"Ramos. I'll get things in order. You tell us what you want to happen. We'll get it done."

"Excellent," Ramos said. "You'll stay here when I leave. Get Mal up and running. Vala, you'll come with me back to Co-Op." Vala shot daggers with her eyes but Ramos either didn't see or didn't care. But one thing was clear about the command structure here. Ramos was in charge.

"Alright, then," Ramos said. He took a deep breath, looking for a moment almost nervous. "This cell has been focused on disrupting Axiom's precious order – which just means control – in the Drain. We have had great success. I would like to hope that we inspired whoever it was that took down Praetorian Bridge."

This was met with cheers. Mal closed her eyes and remembered the screams. When she opened them Ramos was looking right at her.

Ramos calmed the crowd with a raised hand and started again. He said, "It's time to get real. We need to engage Axiom's Users, not just its systems. I want you to derez Operatives, Agents, and other official Axiom personnel in any way you can. Leave the Patches alone, they're who we fight for. But I want Axiom's people to feel outnumbered. Unsafe in the Drain."

"Will you be joining us on this, Ramos?" Rat asked.

"Soon. For now, I am watching a few Users I may want to try to bring into the fold. For now, I need you to do as much as you can."

"Let loose?" Rat asked.

"Let loose. Don't go for kills, but a little brain bleed and Glitch would send just the right sort of message. And if we end up killing a few then so much the better!"

"If it's territory we want, shouldn't we go for the Pylons?" Ibrahim said.

"I know that's how we've worked in the past. But that's not the plan this time."

The mess erupted. "Isn't this reckless? The Drain is where a lot of us operate!" Shadow said.

"What are you doing for risk mitigation?" a chorus of voices started to erupt. "When did we start getting so aggressive?" "People we get hurt. Is this what we want?" The objections piled on top of each other. Vala remained silent; she was scanning the room, it looked like for help. Once she seemed to be about to pipe up and Chip stopped her with a touch on her arm. A heavy look passed between them and Vala remained silent. Everyone seemed to have moved past her reassignment and was concerned more with this new change in marching orders. It because more and more clear to Mal as the chaos of the meeting took over that Nanomei had no strong directive. No overarching directives or people in charge. No stated plan of action. No goals beyond the whims of local, seemingly disparate leaders. How do these people manage to be such a threat to Axiom?

"This is a change, I know. Don't change operational parameters outside of the Drain. In the Drain, though, it's a new game. I want every Axiom operative in The Drain to be afraid to login."

"They're just going to bring in reinforcements. The Drain will be packed with them," Glyph said.

Ramos' eyes glittered. "I'm counting on it."

Vala turned away and said something to Shadow and Mal couldn't make it out. Ramos spoke to Vala quietly and then she turned and stormed off. With a nod, Ramos sent Bix and Del, two of those who traveled with him, following her.

"Mal, walk with me," Ramos said as the meeting ended. Chiphead gathered Rat and Simone and headed to the Rigroom. Ramos and Mal walked out together. There was a cold annoying rain. They stood together under the awning over the table.

"I'm sorry," he said.

Mal must have looked confused. Mal was confused. It was always nice when her cover emotion matched what was underneath. That didn't happen often. Heh. Emotional dysphoria.

"I wanted to get you out into the field as soon as possible."

"Me too," Mal admitted.

"I'm glad to hear you're set now," he said. "Vala will come with me. Deja will be in charge here."

"Thank you, Ramos," Mal said. "You won't regret bringing me in."

"Listen, Mal. I know who you are. I know what you're capable of. I want to leverage that," he said. "You'll be up and running soon and when you are I want you to follow my orders. I don't know if Vala will be back, or who will run Outpost, but you and I are a direct connect. While Deja is here, she speaks for me but if she gets replaced or if Vala returns, it's you and me."

"I get it," Mal said.

"They are nervous," he said, pointing behind them with his thumb. "They're not used to this direct of an approach. What do you think?" He sounded for just a moment less than fully confident.

"I think if you're trying to take over The Drain this is the way to go. I trust your vision." You're a damn fool.

"This isn't going over as well as I'd hoped. Vala hates... this plan." He glanced sideways at Mal, clearly hoping she would press him for details.

"Vala commands a lot of respect here," Mal said.

He sighed. "Just remember, Mal. If you have a problem, come to me."

"I understand, Ramos." Ever Loyal.

〉〉 • • • • • 〈〈

Login.

The Outpost's Pylon's access point was a small room, about thirty feet square, with a Console along one wall. The Console looked like a work bench for someone who would be using metal and wood. Not high tech at all. It was a pleasant aesthetic overall and it felt safe. The Pylon itself looked like an old-fashioned boiler furnace of black iron and felt stable as hell. Mal ran a quick sweep of internal info in the room. There were two doors: one, which looked like an interior door, led into a small dive bar. That bar was also part of the Pylon, according to the schematics. It was hidden, safe. Probably used as a staging area and meeting place.

It felt amazing to be back in the Aetherium. The grime of the Outpost was forgotten, the scratchiness of everything there, the grit, it was all gone. She coded herself a quick change of clothes. A short black dress, spiderweb leggings, glossy purple platform combat boots. She felt giddy as she touched the door to the outside.

The exterior door led out into an Aetherial city; Mal could tell by the way the edging of the doorframe looked a bit too crisp. It was designed as a portal between a city and a safe place. Mal opened the door eagerly and walked out into The Drain. The exit point opened into The Trench, north of the river. From here it was a block to the Quantum Noise River and a short walk up northward to the Old Drain District. Mal could see the wireframe reconstruction work being done on the Praetorian Bridge, looming in the distance some thirty blocks away, along the river.

Mal walked a while. She knew her orders: harass and derez Axiom operatives, cause fear. Throw them off balance for whatever Ramos had in mind. Ramos seemed oblivious to the risk of turning the people against him, of turning Axiom citizens against him. Most followed Axiom by choice and they believed what Axiom told them to about Nanomei. This would be doing the Axiom propaganda machine's work for it. I wonder how other cells feel about this evolution, Ramos. I wonder how the whole Outpost crew would feel if they understood your plan. I wonder how I would feel.

Mal headed for the nearest public access point. The old subway station looked much the same with its grey-green tile walls and concrete floors. Through it Mal was able to re-access any public Pylon in the City; she could log out through one of these and log back in in almost any Aetherial city, but her movements would then be public information. And public information was always a liability to someone in her profession, or even in her cover profession. Travel as a Nanomei was much more fraught than as an Axiom Agent. But it was also freer. Whatever that means.

>> • • • • • <<

It was less than an hour before Mal was walking back through the same turnstile with her sword and wings safely stowed. Mal had spent hours weaving those two items into her rig. For now, they were her programs and with her. Eventually, Mal would need to hardwire them to this Rig but that would take time in the Meatspace.

Mal had one more task, one no one in Outpost could know about. Mal wasn't sure about the sort of surveillance the Outpost cell used for people accessing through their Pylon; to be safe, Mal had just passed through two public Pylons and she would be able to travel about for a few minutes at least without Outpost's Pylon picking her back up.

"Once you're picked up and unable to make dead drops, you'll need to make contact through one of your slimy contacts in The Drain," Mullen had said. So, she was following orders when she started out for the only place that she could do the business she needed to do: The Seven-Sided Cube. Okay, it wasn't the only place. There were plenty of guys who could do what she needed, and plenty of meeting places. But getting back in was cause for a little indulgence. And the Cube was exactly that.

From the outside the Cube looked like a shimmering, gigantic silver cube spinning slowly on one of its corners. That corner rested about ten feet in the air. There was almost never a line; the Cube was a near-infinite space inside. Mal walked up following the empty swirl traced in the duracrete beneath the corner. The entrance was a circular portal just beneath the slowly spinning point of the Cube. Mal stepped into the portal and was transported inside. It was called the Seven-Sided Cube because it had ultra-rare Level Seven security protocols in place. That meant that Users could do almost nothing there. Hacking was next to impossible and activating programs was not allowed. The rules were enforced by one of the strongest Pylons in all the worlds.

Inside, the Cube was divided into three main sections. The bar stretched along a huge, curved wall, currently serving maybe a hundred people with room for many more. Bartenders staked out their own territory and patrons swelled to the best of them in crowds. The energy of the bar was one of excitement and possibility, a warm buzz that made Mal want to spend some time doing absolutely everything. The second area was the club seating and dance floor. The dance floor was a teeming mass, and a Spinner was playing something new enough that Mal didn't know it; it was a mix of human screams and deep base thuds all mixed together with classical orchestrations of twenty-first century pop music. Laser lights pulsed to the beat and abstract visual illusions played through the smoke just above the dancers. Hundreds of hands reached up, brushing the illusions with the tips of their fingers. The third space was tables where private business could be handled. Anyone entering through the set of velvet ropes had their identity scrubbed; they could sit at a table with similarly anonymous people and have the most private conversation in either of the worlds or anything in between.

Mal crossed to the bar. Most people put on their best skins or rented fancy ones for a trip to The Cube. The bartenders here were real, and the drinks programmed with the neurochemistry to make them feel as real as any mind-altering substance. One of Mal's favorite bartenders was here. Noor. She was everyone's favorite bartender and so Mal had to fight to get to the bar itself and lean. Her eyes were like clouds set among tawny skin which glowed with rose-colored tones when she laughed. After jostling her way past several much larger people, Mal caught sight of her. Noor was never seen in the same outfit twice and wore shoes that changed themselves if she stomped down hard enough on her left heel. She wore a top hat with a white ribbon, slightly askew atop her luxurious waves of black hair. Noor was tuned in to the Cube like few others. She knew everybody and everybody who knew her would use the same word to describe her: Fabulous.

"What can I get you, Darling?" Noor asked. Mal was transfixed by Noor's outfit of the day. She was wearing a tight golden dress with vines of roses climbing up one side of her body, the roses animated and dropping petals slowly and reblooming as she stood there waiting for Mal to order.

"Something with a cherry in it. And I need to see Pongo."

Noor slid a tall, narrow glass full of a clear iridescent liquid across the bar. She'd cut the cherry into a tiny rose which floated at the top, red juice trailing out and playing across the surface like blood spilled in water. "I'll put in the word. It'll be a few minutes, he's busy. Now get out there and dance, girl."

Mal sat at the bar and drank patiently. Being here was nice as long as she didn't think about how it was almost impossible to hack inside the Cube. She looked up. Noor was watching her.

"I'm going, I'm going." Mal moved onto the dance floor and let herself get lost for a time in the music. As peoples' bodies started to brush against hers, Mal felt herself remembering the parade; almost unconsciously, she tried to hack less gravity just as she had then. It was common knowledge that the Pylon here was so strong that it made hacking a monumental feat. Most believed it was just not possible. Mal, being Mal, had tested it a few years ago and found the common knowledge to be correct. Today felt different. Mal felt the resistance as something with some give, not the unforgiving, immovable sort she'd experienced before. Mal was toying with the idea of a small hack just to prove to herself that she was able to do it when a voice snapped her out of her thoughts.

"Wanna dance?" a voice behind Mal said.

Mal turned and there she was.

"How the hell?"

"Just dance with me," Kass said as she moved in closer, close enough to speak freely, to feel the warmth of each other's dancing bodies. Kass was wearing a snug fitting dress the color of the iridescent skin of a blown bubble.

They didn't dance long before Kass pulled away without warning.

"I need a drink," she said. "I'm going to get a table. You'll know me," she said.

"I always do," Mal replied. She watched her go past the velvet rope and went back to the bar for a drink.

171

Noor smiled broadly as Mal returned. "Pongo's not ready for you yet, darling. But you seem otherwise occupied anyway," she said.

"Just need a drink, please Noor. She's a friend."

"She was asking about you. Waiting for you. She's quite the dancer," Noor said with a smile, shaking a fresh drink for Mal.

Walking through the rope was a strange feeling, one that Mal didn't particularly enjoy. The weight of the Pylon here was intense: Mal felt it wrapping around her, filling in all of the space she did not; it was as if she were walking through a solid instead of air. Mal slid through the space looking at the tables. At one table two people dressed in black trench coats were leaning in close to each other even though the protections kept their words secret without the dramatic show. At another three people were drinking and gesticulating wildly. Commiserating, complaining about something together. At the third table Mal came to a woman in a freshly pressed Axiom uniform with shockingly smooth porcelain white skin. Blonde hair falling in waves and a face with a pointed chin and pouty lips. The woman smiled at her.

Mal had not bothered to change her own skin. She didn't play games with her appearance.

"You're always you," Kass said.

"And you never are," Mal said.

Mal couldn't even explain why she did it; was it attitude? Spite? Her ever-present, maddening impulse to impress Kass? She approached Kass sitting at booth with a plain white table: a White Room table. Other people had chosen a theme or look with which to skin their tables, but Kass had left hers blank. As she reached the booth, Mal tried a copy hack. Time froze for her, all around nothing moved. Kass stared motionless, the code of the level seven Pylons flashed to life, she could see how the code here wrapped everything tightly, bound it in layers of the reality as it was written. There was room given for cosmetic programs but little else. Seeing the place like this it looked to Mal as if she were walking amongst thousands of spider webs of blue light, strung throughout the entire area. Each person was connected, wrapped in the code webbing.

Mal brought all of her will to bear on the drink she was holding. It was not a mere cosmetic program. It was a drink program, relatively complex in terms of coding, the tastes, aromas, neurochemical effects all wrapped into a small and complex glass of code. There is one drink. Mal reinforced to herself that she was holding the one drink with two hands. One drink two hands. She took a small step forward, the code webbing moving with her, her step making hundreds of other webs move. The Pylons sent more webs to the drink in her hands, connecting to it from multiple other points. One drink, two hands. Then, as she took another step through time and towards Kass she changed her mind. One drink in each of two hands. Thousands of webs descended upon her but she pulled apart her hands as they did and as they attached they attached not to two hands holding one drink, but to two hands each holding a drink.

She'd done it. Hacked in the Cube. She felt the euphoria wash over herself but tried to hide it, focusing instead on Kass' reaction. Kass was leaned back in the booth, studying her. As Mal sat, the table pulsed white twice and the surrounding tables and people blurred out: they were in their own private world.

"Nice trick," Kass said and took a drink. Yeah, she's rattled. "Now that you've moved out of Keral it's harder to track you. We can't get messages to your Rig directly anymore."

"And you have nobody to watch my coming and going," Mal said. She had not really been sure until she said it that Trent had been working for Kass.

Kass just shrugged in response. "He was useful, for a while."

Mal took and released a deep breath. She'd put this aside, for now, along with everything else she someday wanted to call Kass on. That particular datapacket was getting full. Mal took a long, slow sip of her drink, in part to remind Kass what she'd just done.

"The base is called Outpost. Just that. No other moniker. It's in a junk heap outside a Meatspace city."

"Good. They're bringing you deeper in. You're brushing up against my own mission."

"What are you doing?"

"I'm tasked with finding a place called the CoOp."

"Ramos knows where it is. He goes there." Mal took a long drink.

"Maybe I need to brush up against you more often," Kass said. She took a long drink without breaking eye contact.

Mal smiled against her will. Kass had a way of making her do that. They both drank and sat together for a few minutes. Kass was leading up to something, Mal could tell.

"I do know," Kass said, "something that should interest you."

Mal kept her tone light. "You're going to have to be more specific. I'm a naturally interested person."

Kass kept her eyes on Mal's. "I have it on good authority that a position has opened up above Agent."

"Above Agent? There's not even a classification for that," Mal said.

"But there are those who operate above that designation."

"A promotion would mean even better tech," Mal mused aloud.

"This doesn't happen often. There's not much room at the top," Kass said.

"Shhh. Let me think about the tech for a minute," Mal said.

Kass tapped her fingers on the table.

"Okay, okay. Who is in the running?" Mal asked.

"Dek," Kass said. "Definitely Dek."

"I shouldn't stay in here long. Anything else?" Mal asked.

"We never just talk anymore," Kass teased.

"I do miss the rooftop of the Academy," Mal admitted.

"It'll be good when this mission of yours is over. This isn't what we were trained for. I don't know what Mullen's playing at putting you in the field as a damn spy." Is that genuine worry?

"Yeah, I'm an assassin not a spy," Mal said.

"No doubt," Kass said. "Just be careful. The Nanomei are up to something."

"They always are."

"Take care of yourself, Mal. Don't let the Nanomei get in your head."

"Ever Loyal," Mal said and left the table.

Mal didn't go far, just back to the bar.

"He's ready for you," Noor said. "Take him this," she said sliding two drinks across the bar and pointing to a small table in one of the many corners of the place.

Mal approached slowly. Pongo was a young man with pink skin that looked freshly scrubbed in a shiny golden racing jacket sitting alone. He smiled widely at her as she approached.

"Sit down! Thanks for the drink," he said. "Do we have business?"

"We do," Mal said. "I need you to get a message to someone. Pays on delivery."

"Who's the someone? Someone dangerous? Illicit? Hard to find?"

"No. Easy as anything: he's an Axiom Commander."

"Easy to find, sure. Not so easy to deliver to unannounced."

"That's why I've come to the great and powerful Pongo," Mal said, sliding his drink over to him.

"And I get paid only on delivery?"

"That's how it has to go," Mal said.

"Pongo needs something up front too," he said.

"I don't have much," Mal said.

"You are known to me. Trinidad knows you. Noor knows you." At this he moved his hand across the top of the table and a large, silver coin appeared. "You know of Pongo's coins?"

"I've heard of them," Mal said.

"Then make contact with the coin. It is the cost."

"I've heard that these coins can be turned in for pretty much any favor the owner asks."

"True."

"How do I know you won't trade this to someone?"

"You don't. But I promise I won't."

The deal was easy to agree to. Mal needed a secure way to get a report to Mullen directly. Giving over the information was harder. Mal thought about what Commander Mullen could do with this. An airstrike, a drone strike... swarms of Axiom... Do the damn job, Mal. Mal sent her first report to Mullen since leaving Keral. In it were a few pleasantries but the heart of it was the geolocation of the Outpost Base.

"Done," Mal said, pressing her palm onto the coin. An image of her face and several strings of code appeared on the coin, hovered there for a moment and then embedded themselves into the cool, flat metal.

"A sincere pleasure doing business with you," Pongo said.

"I'm sure we'll talk again soon," Mal said.

"Count on it," Pongo said as Mal stood and walked towards the door. She blew a kiss to Noor on her way out.

>>······<<

The next day Mal woke and went through her morning routine: helping in the kitchen for an hour, making bread, stacking things in the pantry. Mal also wiped down the rigroom and helped Glyph with a code block they had going on. Code block was pretty common; it was the result of too much hacking. The bits of the code can clog the relays in the rig, making everything move slower as the Rig tries to reconcile the varying realities.

Mal was setting up her Rig up to log in when a young man walked in. He looked about her age, perhaps younger. He was fit and his umber skin shone in the Rig lights. His hair was black and buzzed close to his skull. He had an intense, overly serious look to him. "I'm Shadow," he said, extending his hand to her as he closed the space between them.

"Mal," Mal said.

Chiphead walked in directly after him. "Mal, you've met Shadow," she said.

"You are always so spot on with your detective work," Shadow said.

Mal allowed herself a laugh.

"Mal is the one I was talking about back at CoOp," she said.

"Ramos' find," he said. "I know. She's been here a few days now. I'm not always plugged in, you know."

Chip rolled her eyes.

"So you've been to CoOp?" Mal asked.

Before Shadow could answer Chiphead interrupted. "Mal, Shadow here is a combat expert and I want you two to get to know each other." Chiphead said. "He fits in well with Ramos' new approach to things here. He's far better at fighting than the more subtle stuff. Get to it. You're supposed to be putting the fear of Death Angel into these Axiom pricks."

"I can, yeah. I have the drop on an Agent who walks the same path every day. I am hoping to get my shit integrated into the Rig though first," Mal said.

"White room crap," Chip said.

"I was thinking I'd use the console in the Boiler Room," Mal said.

Chip raised an eyebrow at her. It was rare for Users to be able to really be able to code their rigs well in the Aetherium. Most used their White Rooms for that. Or even did it in the Meat. But Mal had always been even more capable in the Aetherium than in a White Room and had no plans to change her tactics now.

Mal logged in and spent a few hours working on her wings, updating the neural connections and tracing a few new pathways to take advantage of the Rig's larger processing matrix. People passed through as they logged in and out. She saw Shadow go out, and then Marcus, and watched Simone return. Mal put her wings out on the old-fashioned workbench and pulled out strings of code the lengths of her arms; she manipulated the code in great sweeps of her hands, restructuring modifications and enhancements for her new rig. Several of the code strings were taking more and more solid forms, changing from glowing wireframes to code chunks that were almost programs in their own right. Mal was trying to get more and more speed from them but also tweaking the maneuverability. She was hoping to modify them to allow her to pass through solid Aetherium matter as a matter of course. Building a ghost mod into the wings was going to take a long time; it was complex code and any program can hold only so much complexity, so much code before it starts to crumble under its own weight.

Holographic bits of code and subroutines swarmed around her, faster and faster.

"That is some impressive shit there, Mal," Rat said behind her.

In the Aetherium Rat appeared shorter than he was in the Meat. He also seemed more confident; he radiated a quiet sense of conviction that felt steadier than his twitchier Meatspace identity.

"You want to help?" she asked. Rat's eyes widened.

"Yeah, what do you need?"

"How much code can you hold at once?" she asked.

"A couple dozen flops," he said.

"Good, here, hold this," she said, pulling a bundle of code strands from the wings with a flick of her wrist. More than a dozen connections to the wings remained in the bundle she then handed to Rat. He held it and focused on his task with a determined look on his face.

"No more than this though," he almost whimpered.

176

"I know. They're complex," she said.

"I've never," Rat started but trailed off. "I can see what most of this is for but what about those four in your hand?" he said, asking about brightly glowing strands of code slipping and moving as if of their own volition in Mal's hand.

"These are going to hold the Ghost Mod I've been working on. It's not ready yet, still need to strip and format these connectors. That's today's goal," she said.

Rat watched with a look of awe plastered across his face.

"They're working again, and I don't want to have to register them on a Pylon I move through. So it's worth the effort. Hand me that part back," she said.

They worked together for about an hour moving strands of code, preparing for the Ghost Mod. When Rat was finally no longer holding any extra code, he noticed the sword hilt on the workbench.

"Is this..." he said.

"Yes. It's not loaded on my rig right now, you can pick it up," she said, still distracted by her task.

"Ramos told me that you'd made an invisible blade. But... wow."

"Try it," Mal said, paying attention with half of her brain at most.

Rat picked up the handle gingerly. Mal heard him gasp as he activated the blade. She smiled.

"We're not what you expected, are we?" Rat said, sounding twice as sincere as usual.

Mal thought for a moment before answering. "No. you're not."

"What's the biggest difference compared to what you expected?"

"There's less command structure than I imagined, that's for sure," she said.

"We seem organized from the outside?"

"Well, yeah."

"That's mostly accidental. Nanomei isn't a ship with too many captains. It's a flotilla made of a bunch of junk rafts with a few luminaries so crazy awesome at what they do that they gather a bunch up for a while and make a big boat."

"Luminaries like Ramos," Mal asked.

"Exactly. He's got a pretty big boat, but there are questions. People who oppose him, don't like his methods. But Ramos always gets his way and now you're his way." Mission accomplished.

"Reckless is a word I've been hearing," Mal said.

"Yeah, that's a good word for it. Don't get me wrong, we need some reckless around here."

"I hope people don't equate me with that," Mal said.

He swooshed the blade around the room, supplying his own swooshing noises. Mal could tell he didn't want to talk about it anymore.

"This is impressive work, Mal. You should be an artificer," he said.

"I know you meant that as a compliment but it's not what I love," Mal said.

"What do you love?" Rat asked.

"Flying. Moving. The chase, the hunt, the fight."

"Well. Ramos' new orders should suit you then."

"Yeah. As soon as I have my gear wired hard into my Rig, I'll go do some hard-core engagements. Straight for the throat type stuff. I plan on just outright derezzing some without any reason or buildup. That should shake some of them," Mal said.

"Freedom, any cost."

"Any cost," Mal replied. Loyalty Eternal.

$$\rangle\rangle \cdots \langle\langle$$

Mal leaned against the corner of the alley as a group of four Venari approached. She'd followed them, tracked their movements and flown ahead to lay this trap. She had painted a huge mural on the wall of an Axiom Recruiting Center of the Axiom crossed keys where the top of each key was strangling a citizen as they struggled for freedom. They were reaching out for help from the dark, blue-winged figure of Death Angel. Where the graffiti used to be the point now it was just the bait.

"Explain yourself, Citizen," one of the Venari said. The speaker stepped forward and the other three gathered their rifles into position.

"Freedom, any cost," Mal said. And she launched herself into the air. There were shouts of surprise and fear from the surrounding Patches as Mal leapt, her wings spreading for just a moment to carry her over and land her behind the Venari. None had time to fire as Mal flew overhead. As they turned, Mal cut their legs out from under them, and brought her blade slashing up through their chests, their tight-fitting Kevlar crumbling all around them.

Mal walked away, obscuring her form first in a cloak of mist, and unfolding wings. Then she let a thousand small golden keys spill out behind her which all broke as they clattered to the ground. Satisfied with the image, she spread out her real wings and flew away from the onlookers. All told, ninety seconds of work.

She landed several blocks away. She liked rooftops and kept watching those coming out of the terminal. If Ramos set his people on Agents, there would be deaths. Agents, Nanomei. More blood on her hands, where there was so much already.

Just as she was about to get up and log out, she was pinged. It was Tae. "Hey Tae," she said.

"Mal. You in the Drain?"

"Yes," Mal replied. "You need something?"

"Can't I just be social?"

"I don't know, can you? Who am I to talk, last time I pinged you it was for a favor…"

"So, you sort of owe me one."

"But you didn't do the favor," Mal said, sitting down and letting her legs dangle off the rooftop.

"Details, Mal. Just details."

"What do you need?"

"I have a lock that needs opening."

"Where is this lock?"

"I have it with me. Can bring to you…"

They arranged a meeting near enough to the Boiler Room if there was need of a quick escape.

Tae showed up a few hours later, finding Mal waiting on a rooftop near the Boiler Room.

"What's your thing with rooftops?" Tae asked.

"I'm elitist," Mal said.

Tae approached, bowed slightly and then they hugged. Tae was on a very short list of people with hugging privileges.

"You have not been in communication much. Intense mission?"

"You have no idea. Under cover," she said.

Tae laughed, "But don't they know you're not made for subtlety?"

"They know. They just don't care," Mal said.

Tae produced a small glowing cube from his belt. Mal liked Tae's style but knew she could never pull it off: he wore a flowing silk robe with four slits up the side and an emerald green embroidered jacket. When she asked about it once, he said, he wore it to remember his roots and to differentiate himself from his mostly Nipponese associates. "China is a land from before the Monoculture Wars. Its people were the first to invent many things. Including explosives," he had said once.

Mal took the cube and knelt down in front of it on the rooftop. Tae knew her well enough to remain silent.

As Mal focused on the cube she saw the locking code swirling around it at a very fast speed, its orbit close to the surface of the cube. The code would be invisible to most, even to hackers. It was well made and looked pretty smart too.

"This isn't going to be easy," Mal said softly.

"If it were easy, I could have done it," Tae said.

Mal looked around. They seemed to be alone. "Where does this come from?"

"Better if you don't know," Tae said.

Mal let that go and started to gather her will. She visualized the code slowing and pressed her hand onto the surface of the cube. The code started to tangle around her hand. Tiny spikes erupted from the bits of code and started slashing across her palm and climbing up her forearm.

She didn't move, struggle, or make a sound. To an outside observer she was just kneeling at the cube, toughing its surface lightly.

To her sight, though, the code was struggling to attack her, slipping towards, and being rebuffed by her defenses. This was not typical intrusion countermeasures. It was a learning AI and it had learned she was the enemy, and her defenses wouldn't hold for long. She had to break through.

She pulled her will close and imagined the code stopping entirely, freezing in place. Her breath let out a bit of steam like on a cold winter day. And the code froze, just for a moment. But that was all that she needed. She forced her will then to hack the lock out of existence. That wouldn't last long, it would be back but it was long enough for her to open the cube.

As she did so Tae gasped and a blue mote of light floated up and out of the box, hovering two feet from the ground. Tae put his palm out and the light flew into it. Then Mal picked up the cube and threw it as far as she could.

"You're amazing," Tae said.

"I know. What was that?"

"The box or the light?" Tae asked.

"The box I understand," she said. "It was an advanced learning AI, probably designed internally by House Ikaru. Did you steal from your own people?"

"I will answer one of your questions. Do you want to know that answer or what the light was?" Tae asked, putting on a playful voice.

"The light. I saw it but I couldn't see its code. I can see everything's code."

"That was a gift from a Dzen Hotaru."

"The mystics?"

"The very same. The light was the spark used in creating their wonderous lanterns," Tae said as if that explained everything.

"I've heard rumors. Is it true they walk the nodes without programs? I heard that they login through meditation. Is that real?"

"We don't have time. I'm sorry, I must go."

"You must tell me more when you have the chance," she said.

"I owe you." This was something they said to each other but neither ever collected. The debt washing back and forth between them without account. In the end she only had two people in the world that close: Tae and Tok.

"What are you working on now?"

"You know I can't tell you that," he said with a wink. "But soon you will have to go on than mere

rumors of the Dzen."

Tae took his leave then and Mal felt exhausted, but it had been worth it. Tae would be necessary for a mission someday, just as Tok had been. Performing these small favors had to be part of the job. Because we're not supposed to make friends.

〉〉 • • • • • 〈〈

Mal was tinkering with her Rig a few days later when Simone came in, almost running, and flipped on the holo-display. "Ramos has a job for us. Now!" Rat, Shadow, and Chiphead were close behind her. They all ran to their rigs and prepped them.

Ramos' face flickered to life in the holo-display. "A group of protesters has been rounded up and are making a stand inside of a small building… part of a Schema that took up the whole block. This means that Axiom can't just cut power to it to force them out."

"What is the size of the Axiom force?" Shadow asked.

"Unknown," Ramos said.

"Agents?"

"Unlikely. This isn't really worthy of Agent attention. Still, get in and out fast."

"Our goal?"

"One of the protestors is a man I've been watching for a while, a possible recruit. You'll know him by his active fire virus. Help them all get past Axiom and get out safely but pay special attention to him. I don't have to tell you how rare it is for a non-aligned citizen to be able to control a fire virus. I've been watching him for a while. He's a possible valuable asset."

"Hey Mal, that's exactly what he called you once!" Chiphead shouted as the machines started whirring to life.

"Yeah, look how that turned out," Mal shot back.

Ramos had had more to say, it was clear, but Chiphead cutting him off seemed to remind him that they were in a hurry. He looked stoic in the view screen for a moment and then reached to terminate the connection.

"Any cost," Ramos said as he faded from view.

As each of the Outpost crew finished their final adjustments they climbed into their chairs. Mal reached across her body and turned the last dials up to max and threw the buffers into standby mode. Before this assignment, Mal had grown accustomed to relying on attendants for this. She

181

was starting to relish doing it all on her own. She felt more connected to her Meatspace body when logging in on her own. Looking around Mal saw Chiphead hold up five fingers and then do a countdown to one.

Login.

Logging in all at once felt full of potential; a group arriving in the Aetherium at the same time opened up waves of possibility. They could all feel it, appearing in a boiler room in the same moment. They were poised on the edge of what happens next. The work bench was empty, and the doors closed.

Chiphead was wearing a grey trench coat, her hair a silvery blonde, worn off to one side, a dozen rows of glowing blue chips the color of Quantum Noise along the shaved side of her head. She was holding a long, thin piece of metal that she carried like a staff. Rat was wearing many layers of brown, cloak over cloak and cape draping over poncho. He looked alert, on edge. Shadow was wearing a black tank-top just a few shades darker than his skin. As always, he wore a skin modification that caused him to have a dozen eyes across his bald head. They were all functional and focused independently. It was disconcerting. He had not rezzed a weapon. Mal was wearing her black hoodie and skinny jeans, her wings tucked away for now, invisible sword stowed safely where she could get it in a flash.

"We go in fast and agile. Get the Fire Wielder and then others." Chip said. "Let's do this."

"Thanks for the motivational speech," Shadow said.

"She's no Ramos," Rat said, and they all laughed.

"We should be grateful this mission was so urgent, or he'd still be talking," Shadow said, grinning.

They followed Chiphead into the alleyway. They were moving quickly and quietly. There were very few Patches about.

They walked to the street and Mal brought up a HUD map. They were only a few blocks away. If they could get the Axiom soldiers away from the building the protestors would be able to escape. This was going to be a delicate dance: Mal needed to complete this mission for Ramos but also felt the need to maintain as much order as possible. How dangerous was it to allow another highly talented person join Nanomei? But dangerous to the mission to try to stop them from getting to this new asset. Do the job. Mal couldn't shake the feeling it wasn't that simple anymore.

"Mal, you go ahead, fly. Get there before us and let us know the situation."

Her wings were activated and spread out behind her before Chiphead finished her sentence. Mal launched herself into the air. The public announcement system was transmitting a lock-down order for the area: "Citizens. Remain sheltered in place. Do not enter the streets or a public schema. Remain where you are. Logout if possible. Maintain order." The roadway was clear and wide, and the storefronts were powering down; the street was almost deserted. It was a strange, eerie effect in the usually crowded Commercial District.

Mal flew swiftly to the disturbance. Six Axiom Guards had grouped themselves in front of the main doors. One was clearly in charge; she was shouting orders to the others.

One stepped forward and a flash of fire erupted from the building.

"Six Guards. Standard issue, not Praetorians and not Venari. Nothing I can't handle," Mal said.

"Wait. Do not engage, you're on recon. Watch for others to approach. We need you in the sky."

"Copy that," Mal said reluctantly. Mal swooped to the top of the building across the street from the entrance in question. None of the Axiom Operatives noticed her, as far as she could tell.

"We're on the next block," Chip said through comms. "Any change?"

"No change. I am not reading anything approaching," Mal said. If she were on the other side at this moment, what would she be doing? Waiting for bigger fish.

"Something doesn't feel right," Mal said over comms to just Chiphead.

"What've you got?"

Damn, damn. Why did I say that?

"Nothing solid," Mal said.

"Take to the skies, look for anything. We're coming in hard on the group at the door."

"Acknowledged. And…. Be careful." Who am I worried about? Chiphead did not answer, and Mal flew back into the sky. She ran every possible sensor scan through her HUD, but the Agents she was suddenly convinced were there remained hidden. Or not there at all. Mal saw Chip and Shadow run from around the corner. Chip came around the corner with two fast-shooting machine pistols, emptying entire clips as she ran to the door. Shadow was keeping pace with her and charged at two of the guards she had not mowed down. One of them brought their baton down as Shadow smashed into them, electrical energy sparking off it and encasing Shadow in light. He cried out in pain but still managed to bring the guards to the ground.

Then one of the guards flanking the leader went down. Mal hadn't seen Rat sneak up behind but there he was now. Mal wasn't sure what he had done to the guard, but it had been effective. The guard was making no move to stand again. Derezzing violently does not necessarily end in death, Mal reminded herself. But it certainly can.

Her sensor sweep finally turned something up: there was a login in progress. It was an emergency login; the HUD showed Mal exactly where a small group of Users would appear, so she was watching as they appeared.

"Three Agents! On the roof!" Mal yelled. Three agents were too many for rounding up protestors. Is that you Kass?

Mal veered towards the rooftop, disregarding a warning from Chip and drawing her sword as she swooped.

One of the Agents saw her and raised a silver handgun, firing twice as Mal approached. Mal did not recognize any of the three Agents. Both shots missed and the other two Agents jumped down the hundred feet or so from the roof and landed on the street.

"You have two on the street!" Mal yelled into comms. "Get out of here!"

Mal engaged the Agent on the roof without a pause, slashing his wrist with her blade, and catching his pistol as she landed and rolled past him, her wings folding into a ready-but-tucked state.

The Agent rezzed a blade; it looked like an old school katana with a bright white blade and a jade green handle.

"Nanomei Scum!" he yelled as he charged towards her. She ran at him too, without hesitation. She didn't like the feeling that this was getting easier.

The fight was fast and vicious. He was good, faster than the average Agent, but there was just no way for him to match Mal. In a few seconds, he was laying on the rooftop derezzing. He'd probably be fine once he logged out all the way, but he wouldn't be able to log back in quickly. One down.

Mal ran to the edge of the building and threw herself off; she got a quick glance at the street below as she fell. She didn't see the Agents. Chip and Shadow were helping the people from the building to flee. *Where are you, Kass? I know you're part of this.* The protestor with the fire virus was standing almost a block away looking as if he was trying to decide what to do, not fleeing, not fighting. His hands and forearms were wreathed in blue flames. Mal's mind raced. *What will you do for Ramos if he gets you?*

Mal swooped down to him; he jumped in shock as Mal landed.

"You're Death Angel!"

"It's the wings, isn't it?" Mal said. "We're here to get you out of here. Get moving. You can't take an Agent."

"I can help!" he said and turned toward the Agents near Chip and Shadow.

Mal grabbed his elbow and spun him back around. Then a quick hack and his fire virus was disabled. "No. You need to get out of here. You're why we came. Get moving!"

He nodded quickly, clearly eager to please, then ran. He just had to make it past three Axiom guards who were near him. Mal looked around to be sure none of the Nanomei were watching. They were all engaged. Firehands was still running. Mal hacked the road beneath his feet; it grew hands and grabbed him to the ground. He barely had time to call for help before the guards saw him and unloaded their weapons into him. The damage was so intense he derezzed immediately in a cloud of Glitch and screams.

Mal glanced at Chip and Shadow, still occupied. They had the civilians fleeing and had positioned themselves between them and an Agent who was closing in and rezzed in a blade as he approached.

"Where's the recruit?" Chip yelled as she fought.

"He's down, they've derezzed him!" Mal yelled.

"Everyone out!" Chip yelled. "Mission abort. Get back to the access point! Now!"

"Agent, Agent, Agent!" Rat yelled into comms.

"Rat, get out," Chip said over the channel.

"He's chasing me! I'm on Third Street!"

"I'm going after Rat," Mal said into comms and started running. Mal couldn't see Rat, but Mal could see the Agent chasing him. Mal ran him down, but she was not close enough when the Agent pulled a gun and aimed at Rat. Everything around Mal slowed. The Agent was still raising his gun and Mal was still running at full speed. Mal saw Rat. He'd stumbled. No: he had been grabbed. The Agent had hacked the street the same way Mal had moments ago to form arms and hands and grab Rat who was struggling to escape at nearly the same cycle speed as Mal was moving. Get creative, Agent, the hands were my thing. Mal started a hack to destroy his gun.

Rat looked up at the Agent and Mal could see him also meet his eyes. "Mal," he said. The Agent fired twice before Mal's hack melted his gun. The shots tore into Rat's form, sending blood and blue shards in all directions.

Rat screamed.

"Mal. Get gone. Shadow is down and a transport of eight Agents just arrived. Go now," Chip said into comms.

"Eight?! But Rat."

"I know. He may survive the logout. You can't help him if those other Agents catch up to you," she said. "Get gone now! That's an order!"

Mal drew her sword as the Agent turned to see who had melted his gun. It was a molten mess covering and burning his hand, dripping white-hot and orange lava. He rezzed another gun in his good hand. This one was smaller, probably a personal weapon. Mal leapt toward him, sword slashing invisibly out, cutting a deep gash into him. Mal landed on the ground and skidded to a halt, turning as she did to keep the Agent in front of her. Mal was only about ten feet in front of where Rat was derezzing.

"You can't save him," the Agent said.

Mal answered by dropping into a fighting stance, blade ready.

The Agent shot three times and Mal moved almost imperceptibly, blocking all three shots with flicks of her blade. Then Mal realized he wasn't shooting at him. He was shooting at Rat as he derezzed. If he hit Rat he'd pile on more Glitch. The guard was trying to give Rat permanent brain damage or even kill him.

185

"You shouldn't have done that," Mal growled. The Agent raised his gun again. Maybe he thought Mal had just been lucky. Three more shots, three more parries, and Mal had closed half the distance in a calm, even walk towards him. He started looking worried. Who was Mal to put her mission so high as to attack a fellow Agent? Who was Mal to face down a person dedicated to the same ideals to which Mal was pledged?

"Get out of there!" Chiphead yelled again into Comms. "They're here. Agents came out of nowhere! They just splattered Shadow's brains on the duracrete. I'm a block away and they're only two blocks behind me. They're going to catch up to you."

The pit of Mal's stomach dropped out. When she logged out there would be a dead body in the rigroom with her.

"Rat's not out yet. I am waiting here until he finishes logging out. Mal out."

"No!" Chiphead shouted. "This mission is failed. Get out before we lose you too!"

The Agent was concentrating hard now; he'd thrown his gun down and cleared away the molten metal. He was trying to hack something together. Perfect. Mal reached out and found the Pylon controlling this area. Mal turned her whole will to it but kept walking. The Agent's face strained as he struggled to complete his hack. He was still struggling as Mal brought her sword down through his body from the right shoulder to the left leg. The Agent began to derez immediately. Mal raised her sword then but Chip was suddenly gripping her arm.

"We have no time," she said.

Mal turned to Rat. His form was still lying on the ground twitching.

"They're right behind. We need to leave!" Chip said.

Eight Agents stepped into view from around the corner. They stood in a line across the width of the street. Their weapons were not drawn but they were obviously ready for a fight.

"Stay at Rat's side," Mal said. "As soon as he's clear you tell me and I'll bail." This, they both knew, would save time, because of time dilation. If they waited to get word from the base it could be a minute or more of extra time. If she watched closely here, they'd know as it happened, as soon as it was safe.

Mal put her sword away and walked towards the Agents. They stood their ground.

As Mal approached she thought of her possibilities. She could engage them, which would probably be fatal to several Agents, maybe even herself. She could try to let them know who she really was which would ruin her mission. She could try to stall. That seemed the most likely approach. Behind her was a derezzing Agent, and Rat, and Chip.

"Stand down, Nanomei scum," one of the Agents said through a voice amplifier program.

"We don't have to do this," Mal said.

"You're right. Turn yourselves in and no further harm will come to you."

"That's not going to happen," Mal said.

"They're stalling," one of the Agents said.

Three of the agents started to bring a hack into place, and two others drew handguns.

Then she was there. Kass rezzed in just behind the other Agents. She was wearing a black version of the usual Agent uniform and stepped between two of the other Agents, who moved aside for her.

They lowered their weapons.

She stepped forward. Mal matched her.

"What are you doing?" Chip said over comm.

"What are you doing?" Kass asked her, over a personal comm channel.

"I am not leaving this place until the Nanomei who is derezzing is out," Mal said.

"There are too many of them," Chip said.

"There are too many of us. You cannot stand against us," Kass said.

"Numbers don't concern me. Nobody is getting past me. Not eight, not one. Not until he's out."

"This is madness," Kass said.

"Maybe," Mal admitted.

"This is one of Ramos' favorites. He knows about CoOp. You know how much we can get from someone in one of interrogation rooms," she said.

"I'm telling you he logs out," Mal said.

"I lost the Burner. I need blood for blood."

"You can't have his," Mal said.

"He's out!" Chip said.

Mal spread her wings and leapt into the air. The Agents instantly had their guns out and were firing. Kass watched but did not fire. Mal felt Kass' eyes on her as she flew away.

〉〉 • • • • • 〈〈

Coming out Mal ripped the connection cable from herself and stumbled out of the chair. Mal felt hands on her but pushed them aside. On the next Rig over, Rat was sitting on the edge of the chair, blood staining his ears and neck.

"Rat's going to be okay," Chip was saying as Mal tried to steady herself.

"Shadow wasn't so lucky," Simone said, standing next to his lifeless body on the chair. "Look," Simone said as she came at Mal, crossing the distance in heavy stomps, "I get that Ramos thinks you're the hot shit but wake up!

187

You're nothing special and you disobeyed direct orders to bail and get back home safe."

Mal balled her fists but said nothing.

"It's bad enough we lost Shadow but you put yourself in danger with your stunt," Chiphead said.

"I lived through my stunt. My stunt kept Rat alive. Without me he'd have been abandoned by the Nanomei! Another casualty left in the field."

"He knows the risk! He's not some princess in need of saving."

"No. I like the saving. Save me any time," Rat said weakly.

"And he's alive."

"You need to follow orders in the field!"

"So write me a demerit or whatever you do here but back off. I saved his damn life and if I had a reset and the opportunity to do it differently I wouldn't."

"The mission was over as soon as that many Agents showed up," Chiphead said.

"And I'm someone you should be listening to in the field, Mal! Hell, everyone here has more experience. You should listen to any one of us in the field."

"No. Someone stood up to them," Mal said, defiantly. "I'm sorry if my default action in a fight isn't to run."

"I have orders. I gave you orders!"

"I have friends. And I saved one of them."

"You were the one I was ordered to keep alive. Ramos believes you're so damn special you are at the top of every mission priority checklist. Keep Mal safe. Let her do what she wants. Let her sneak off to the Recyclery. Let her fly around like an idiot but always bring her back."

"Well, fuck Ramos and his rules."

Breathing heavily, Mal turned her back on Simone and tried to leave, but Simone grabbed her arm. Mal's balled left fist hit her square in the jaw and a follow up half step and sweep with her leg and other arm put Simone on her back with a hard thud. Mal turned and practically ran from the Rig room.

⟫ Chapter Nine: CoOp ⟪

It was a few days after Shadow died that Mal was alone in the Aetherium. She was feeling like a spy and had dressed like one: a short black skirt with ripped fishnet stockings, black combat boots, and big dark sunglasses. Not exactly regulation spy-ware but it made her feel just right while following an Axiom Operative who had just logged in and was walking through the street running random checks of Patches. He was checking their Papers for any possible infraction. Mal Hacked the scanner and had the scans come back as impossible results: famous Users, wanted criminals, long-dead historical figures. Mal watched him stop a dozen people in a row, getting increasingly frustrated and confused by his results. It was oddly satisfying to watch. Beyond that, though, it was ticking all of the boxes from Ramos' new mission: Sow fear and terror among the operatives of Axiom. She'd derezzed dozens of operatives and several Agents; in response, Axiom had sent more and more personnel to The Drain. In a few more days she would attack an Agent with a hack from the shadows, disabling his abilities, locking him down and letting him be found stripped of program and power by his superiors. Missions from Ramos were still coming in without pause and with increasing intensity. Instead of blocking a street with a burning dumpster program, Ramos wanted them to steal and use an Axiom Armored Transport. Where he had once asked for minimal casualties, now he seemed to be trying to rack up as many as possible. Collateral damage was accepted readily now as well. It was already possible to see Axiom operatives starting to act differently. They had started moving around the city in groups and looking over their shoulders and there seemed to be more and more each day. There's an old Axiom saying: When one falls three rise up. And still Ramos kept the big picture to himself.

Mal followed the Agent through the crowds to the arts section of the city. The arts section was full of skinners; their work was on grand display on hologram models, which looked as real as anyone else in the Aetherium. One looked transparent but contained multiple swirls of color bounded by a human form. Another was matte black with streaks of lightning and a quiet rumble of thunder as the form moved. Another was a skin-tight white suit which constantly displayed text versions of the wearer's thoughts.

This Agent Mal was following was looking twitchy. By the time he followed a random Patch around the corner and into an alley he looked terrified when he came face to face with Mal instead. Mal sliced his hand off before he drew his gun. He started to derez after her second stroke broke the entirety of his sync. "It's you," he said, his voice strangely digitized by the damage to his connection. As he derezed Mal brought him up to her, pulling his face to within a few inches of mine. "I'll see you again, if you return to The Drain," Mal whispered. Best way to draw more Axiom is to tell them they shouldn't be here.

After derezzing the Agent Mal headed for Mings, the old noodle joint she'd haunted earlier in her mission. She went in and ordered. Sitting alone at her corner table Mal brought up her sword program and started fiddling with it. Mal was not going to get any real work done on it without a console but Mal did not want to be in the Boiler Room right now. Things with Simone had been tense since she had put her on her ass and fighting Axiom was starting to wear on her.

"Can I sit?" a Patch asked. Mal looked up. A completely nondescript Patch presenting as female with unremarkable features and dirty brown hair.

"Yeah, sit," Mal said.

"This place is crazy," she said. "I just didn't want to eat alone."

"Eating alone isn't so bad," Mal said without bothering to hide the irony of her reply.

"It's amazing here," she said.

"What do you mean?"

"Have you tried the fries?"

"Um," Mal said, pointing at her tray with fingers from both hands.

"I mean, it's amazing that you can taste things in here!"

She was a noob. Someone recently chipped. Probably a very poor person to be new at this and as old as she was.

"Is this your first time in?"

"Yesterday. Or maybe that was today."

"Time feels weird here, you're right," Mal said.

"Do you know how hurt you can get?"

"Didn't you run a tutorial?" Mal asked.

"Couldn't afford one. Nobody I know is chipped," she said.

That's when Mal thought about Gibson. He'd be chipped soon if not already. Mal suddenly had a very real need to know how he was doing. This took her by surprise. It came to her mind that she could push this curiosity aside but for some reason Mal fought that. Why do I care?

"I have to go," Mal said, slipping her sword handle back into her rig. "Thanks for the talk!" the noob said to her back.

>> • • • • • <<

Mal did not know if she was going to find him today but there he was dangling from a rock wall at an Axiom Child Recreation Area. He'd given her his direct contact information and with her skills it was easy to break through the normal protections and find where he was without pinging him. What were the chances that their logins would line up like this? A few hours off in the Meat could mean twelve times that in the Aetherium. It was hard to accidentally run into people. But he was in The Drain, in a large, grassy park. A large, flat piece of land covered in soft grass was occupied by a handful of older folks. The park itself had play equipment and a large climbing wall. This place had normal gravity and some extra safety protocols. There were a few dozen kids in the park. Gibson was on the rock wall. His mom was sitting in the sun and reading a book. Mal tried to step towards the park. It was not easy: Mal stood a long while watching. This was not part of her mission.

Mal was no skinner but she hacked together a program to modify her appearance on the spot Mal shortened herself, changed her hair, her face. Mal went full little girl. Freckles and some baby fat in the cheeks, space buns in her hair. Mal was hiding herself, protecting herself. Selfish.

Mal ran up and started climbing the rock wall too. As Mal neared Gibson she reached up and hit his heel and yelled "Tag!"

Gibson squealed and looked down, almost falling.

Mal let herself fall; the play equipment's safety code handled the impact for her. Gibson jumped after her. She rolled aside and he giggled uncontrollably as he smashed his knee to the ground where she had just been. Mal swung herself back up and around a bar and Gibson did his best to follow on her heels. They played for almost an hour.

"You're fast," he said as they played.

"Yeah, you're pretty fast yourself." This was a compliment, especially in the Aetherium. Neurokinetics showed themselves easily in a User's movement speed.

While they sat and rested a bit, Gibson asked in a hushed whisper, "So, do you hack?"

"Whoa," Mal replied. "Do you?"

"Nah. I'm faster than my friends but that's about it. I can't change things... yet."

"Hacking's hard and it can really screw with your brain if you do it wrong," Mal said.

"Well, I wanna learn. Mom says that she may get a promotion and then we'd have better rigs and then maybe it would be easier."

"It is a little easier to hack in a better rig. And safer," she added.

"Come on. You talk like you know how to hack," he said.

"Okay. Some little thing. Here," Mal said. And pulled the code of the play equipment into the visual spectrum for Gibson to see.

He made impressed noises, somewhere between "whoa" and "zionks."

The code appeared in a circle of runes and subroutine links. Simple, civic code. Nothing fancy, no security on it. She could write this code into pretty much whatever she wanted.

"What should we change?" Mal asked.

"Gravity!"

Mal smiled. A kid after my own heart.

"See, this," Mal said, pulling a subroutine folder into view. The circle fogged out and showed only the subroutine, which was column based. Seventeen columns of code. Simple. "Here, we take this piece and move it here, and there's the gravity slider. It's easy to change this because it's already slightly altered for safety reasons," Mal said.

She closed down the code and they tried it out. Thirty percent less gravity meant a much different play experience. They launched themselves upwards, spinning, laughing, and leapt through the air, holding onto the bars to keep from floating off. Other people were less ready for the change and chaos ensued. Mothers struggled through the air to grab their children; one teen just started spinning crazily and laughing.

Mal returned gravity to normal and they all floated to the ground.

"That wasn't hacking," Gibson said.

"You got me kid. That was just straight up coding."

"How'd you get that code to appear, though?"

"That was the hack," she said.

"Thanks...Mal" he asked.

Mal froze.

"Mal, I know it's you," he said.

Mal was dumbfounded. "You're.... you're kidding me. How? When?"

"Pretty much the whole time," he said. He hopped down from the wall, and they walked toward a bench.

"Gibson. How?"

"I dunno. I could just tell. But I wanted to make sure it was you. I have something to tell you."

"What's that?" Mal asked.

"Trent came to our Unit last week. He asked my mom a ton of questions. But they were all about you. Where you were. How he could find you. The super-weird part is that he asked if she knew if Code Smoother was really your job." Shit. Shit. Shit.

"What did your mom say?"

"She hardly knew you. She didn't have anything to say."

"What did you say?" Mal asked.

"Nothing, Mal! I'm your friend. But Trent isn't. He works for Axiom."

"Of course, he does. He's the Building Overseer."

"No, I mean he works for Axiom like you do." Shit. Shit. Shit. Shit.

"What do you mean, like I do?"

He just looked at her, sitting quietly.

"It's okay," Mal said, measuring her tone. Mal thought she had every angle handled in this mission. Why didn't Mal look closer at Trent? Why was Mal here in this park with some kid? Is this mission coming apart? Am I?

"Thanks for telling me, kid."

"That's what friends do," he said. "Do you have some time for tag?"

"I sure do," Mal said. He deserves some play time after that bit of intel.

Gibson slapped her ankle and yelled "Tag!" as Mal was distracted for a moment.

Mal spun and started to go after him. He ran to the rock wall and started to dash up it. Mal followed but instead of climbing, she leapt to the top. Gibson's jaw dropped.

"How?" he whispered, looking at her with wide eyes.

"Anything is possible in the Aetherium," Mal said.

"Can you teach me?" he asked.

"Someday."

She balanced impossibly on the top of the wall and knelt down. She touched Gibson' shoulder lightly. "Thank you, Gibson," she said.

"For what?

"For being my friend," Mal said.

〉〉 • • • • • 〈〈

Mal was headed to the Boiler Room, the entry to The Drain from the Outpost Pylon, when she glanced at a 3d holo-board advertising a new zero-g experience. Something on it snagged her brain. It was just an ordinary holo... No. There it is. Three fuzzy dots at the bottom right of the sign. They were a sign that she'd worked out a long time ago to show that there was a message hidden. She focused for a moment to see the underlying code of the sign, and there, woven in as a thread, a simple message. A set of coordinates and a time to meet. That time was in ten minutes and the place a nearby rooftop. The message could stay hidden there for days, without knowing what those three dots meant nobody would bother to look. The three-dot signpost was something Mal had shared with only one other person: Kass.

"Finding you isn't easy now that you're on the inside," she said as Mal got to the roof.

"Yeah. That's kinda the point of being Nanomei," Mal said.

"Pretending to be, you mean," she said.

Of course. "How did you find me?"

"I didn't. I left signs for you in a score of places, all pointing here. And here," she said bending to pick up a concealed program, "Is a ping just waiting for someone to come up to the rooftop."

The two stood there looking at each other for a long time. This was a thing they'd done since they met. After any sort of argument or discomfort they'd reduce the time between getting over it by staring each other down, silently. The longest it ever lasted before one broke was an hour and a half. It only took Kass three minutes.

"You could have let us get the other one too, you know. You didn't have to make that ridiculous stand," Kass said.

"It cemented my position there," Mal said.

"Did it make you feel like a hero?" she asked.

"What do you mean?"

"I mean," Kass said with an acid tone, "that you seem to be enjoying this mission."

"I enjoy serving Axiom," Mal replied.

"You enjoy being Nanomei. Just watch that you don't disappear so far into the role that you can't see your way back to living like an ordered, well-regulated Agent."

"Is that all?"

"No. I'm here as a professional courtesy."

"What is it?"

She held out a chit and on it appeared the image of a base of some sort. It looked to be in the Noise. There was a ship docked at the base, a RezX ship: The Aura.

"We've found out that this ship has some sort of connection to CoOp. It's RezX so officially it's off limits."

"Officially?" Mal said.

"Well, I'm going to hit it. I need to find out more about CoOp. I'll get the crew to tell me what they know. Finding the CoOp is technically Dek's mission but mine has been so fruitless that Mullen is letting me help the big oaf."

"Even if you can do this and not get caught: that's a full size RezX ship. How the hell are you going to take it out?"

"It's at that base for repairs. Something about Noise Beasts or some such," Kass said, taking a few steps away and half turning.

"Why are you telling me this?"

"Well, this is one of those points where our three missions brush up against each other. And I don't want you getting hurt."

"How?"

"This ship is tied closely somehow to CoOp and so is your target: Ramos. This feels like we're working the same thing from different angles."

"What is your mission?" Mal asked.

"I told you, it's coming up empty."

"Yeah, you said. But what was it?"

"My mission came down from the Matrons. They thought there was a disloyal Axiom Agent in our midst. I've been hunting." Mullen said he was sending out Agents.

"Did you ever think it was me?"

"Maybe for a bit," Kass said but she also winked. "Anyway, enough about my failures. I need to gain some favor back and I've talked Dek into running logistics while I take the glory job of getting that ship."

"Is this a RezX base?" Mal asked.

"No," she said. "That's why this may be possible. It's a base pretty deep in the Noise and it is just serving as a safe dock for the ship. No Aetherial City, no local law, just a nice dock."

"Is there any other way?"

"Aww are you worried about me?"

"Sure." and Tok.

"Good. But the mission is set. I got my hands on the docking schedule. They're planning on being there two dozen Aetherium days. It's costing a fortune to get the dockmaster to allow me to login there with as many Agents as we'll need. Time to reciprocate: What do you have going on?"

"You know my mission. I'm at Outpost. I work often with my primary target, Ramos. I'm building trust."

"That's it? All this time and that's it?"

"I got Mullen the physical location of Outpost," Mal said defensively.

"Shit. That's something at least. Guess you're not asleep in the rig. Heard anything else about CoOp? Maybe the both of us can swoop in and take Dek's mission from him."

"I'm working on it." They stopped turning around each other.

"Well, honestly, I hope you have success with whatever Mullen ends up wanting you to do with Ramos. Or Outpost. Or whatever."

"I'm in with Ramos. I'm on my way to the CoOp. If I get any intel that I think will help you I'll make contact."

"We strike in three days."

>> • • • • • <<

Mal's message to Tok was simple: We need to talk in a secure location as soon as possible.

"Hey Mal. Got your message," came the ping from Tok.

"Where can you meet?" Mal asked.

"You still operating out of the Drain, or are you at the Point?"

"Drain."

"I can meet you at the docks in two clicks," she said.

"I'll be there," Mal said.

Tok had wanted to meet at the Docks, even though Mal knew her ship was elsewhere. She was taking precautions. Is everyone on to me? Mal saw Tok walking up from the street level, she must have arrived like most non-Aethership Captains do, via access point. "Hey."

"This feels like another one of your not-so-social calls," Tok said.

"Yeah. Do you feel like I use you?" Mal asked.

"Just in a good way," Tok said.

They started walking, looking out over the expanse of the Noise.

"Tok. There's a lot I haven't told you," Mal said by way of starting.

"That's honest." Their walk took them to the emptiest part of the docks, no ships were in any slips or sockets for a hundred yards.

"Yeah. I haven't always been."

"Look, Mal. I don't know your story. I know you're invested in Collective politics in some way. You never talk about it. People who aren't buried in it, we talk about it. From you there's nothing. But beyond that, well, I kinda just don't need to know," she said.

"Don't need to or don't want to?" Mal asked, suddenly afraid of the answer.

"We all know the Axiom/Nanomei war, Mal. It's in our daily lives. Those of us with some rank in RezX feel the eyes of Axiom on us, too. It's… unsettling." She turned to her with an almost pleading expression. "We're here for the science, Mal. We're here to explore. We just want to be left alone."

"So you'd align your people with Nanomei, then? If you had to choose a side?" Mal asked.

"It's not that simple."

Tok paused. A House Ikaru short range ship had just come into the docks. It was a glossy white ship of curves with fins off the back and appendages in the front. They both watched it morph its landing gear out and take a spot down at the end of the docks.

"Both Nanomei and Axiom both think short-term and win-lose. I am thinking in the larger, sweeping history of our species. There's this boundless frontier of a new world and it may have the answers we need to figure out what the hell to do about our screwed-up world."

"Is that why you're RezX?" Mal asked.

"No, silly. They just have the best research grants," she said.

"Well, look. Axiom is after this," Mal said, holding up the Chit. It was an image of the secret dock, and her ship.

"That's my ship," Tok said.

"Yeah. It's going to be raided by Axiom."

"That's hard intel to get at," she said.

"I have my ways," Mal replied.

"Wait. How do you... you're Axiom?"

They locked eyes for a moment.

"Yes," Mal finally said.

"I never thought... I mean... I've never met Mal, have I?" she asked. She looked genuinely hurt now. "Not really." She didn't take steps back and away, but she started moving around the area where they were standing.

"No. You have," Mal said, not knowing if what Mal was saying was true. Have I even?

"Is that even your name?"

"Yeah, actually, it is."

"Are you an Agent?" Tok asked.

"Yes."

"But that shield..." Tok said, holding her arms out in the approximate size of the shield Mal had taken onto her ship.

"Tok, I'm deep under cover. Deep," Mal said.

"So, you're running with the Nanomei but you're Axiom? You turn on your... friends?"

"I'm trying to help a friend," Mal said.

Tok seemed to make some sort of internal calculation. Tok looked at her and held out her hand. Mal gave her the chit.

"They're coming for you and your ship soon. They know you're connected somehow to a place called the CoOp. That's their concern."

"I've never heard of CoOp. I've got cargo some people asked me to move," Tok said. "But I offered to get that to them while my ship repairs. They said to wait to deliver it myself, on my ship."

"That's weird, right?"

"They said it was precious cargo and they didn't want it logged on any Pylons. I figured they know my reputation as someone who hasn't deactivated her ship in years."

Mal thought for a while. "I don't know, Tok. I don't know why the Nanomei want you. I know Axiom wants you. They think you're connected to CoOp. They're coming for you. And your crew," Mal said.

"How long?" Tok asked. She did not have time for Mal's crisis of conscience. She had people to protect.

"Three days."

"Shit, Mal. My ship's half torn apart doing a complete overhaul after what those damn beasts did to her."

"Can you get it together in that time?"

"Yeah."

"We'll have to. There's no way we can repel a full-scale assault by Axiom."

"Can't you just call RezX Command or something?"

"No. That wouldn't help. In a situation like this they'd probably just tell me to derez my ship and stop spending so much time outside the Collective. We're not a fighting force, we're a bunch of explorers." Tok paused and stepped closer. "You're putting yourself at risk for this?"

"Not too much," Mal said.

Tok rezzed a small glass orb into her hand and offered it to Mal. Mal took it without question.

"That's a Beacon," she said.

"Tok..."

"It leads to my ship. If you ever need a safe place, if things go south and backwards and inside out and you just need to get out, break the glass and you'll end up on my ship."

"That's..."

"Pretty stupid to give to an Axiom Agent, I know," she said. "But I'm not giving it to an Axiom Agent, I'm giving it to my friend."

"I was going to say that's amazing tech and why don't we know about these?" to which Tok laughed loudly and with a little snort. Tok reached out and touched Mal's face with her hand, pressing her palm to her cheek. Her palm felt like a soft, fragrant breeze against Mal's skin.

"You wrecked my heart today, Mal," Tok said. "But I love you."

>> • • • • • <<

Mal gave herself another hour of Aetherium time, just to fly above the city, watching life unfold below, feeling the wind in her face. Mal let herself get lost in the experience of it, a sort of in-flight meditation. The world was falling apart around her and she felt empty inside, as if she was made of corrupt code. Finally, Mal landed and logged out through the Boiler Room. When Mal opened her eyes in the Meat Mal saw her rig's display showing her that she'd been in 18 hours longer than she thought she had. Mal was sore and tired and drained. She went to the kitchen to make one of those disgusting sandwiches. Or maybe just squeeze the paste directly into her mouth.

Chip came to the kitchen where Mal was spreading a thick layer of protein paste onto some hard bread.

"You look like shit," she said.

"I feel it."

"I've seen what you've done: you derezzed almost a dozen Praetorians, you forced multiple agents to flee the scene, and I can't even mention that squad of operatives you ambushed without smiling. Your mission completion rate was insane last week, so you must be exhausted. And all that happened right after we lost Shadow and you stood down nine Agents all at once."

Mal stared down at her plate. "Do you ever think that everyone in your life doesn't really know you?" Mal asked.

"Every single day," Chiphead answered.

"I just need some sleep," Mal said, honestly.

"Well get some sleep now because I need you to log in in five hours. We're going to CoOp." She left the kitchen after she said that and Mal just sat there. CoOp.

Her mind was racing but her training kicked in hard. If Mal needed to log in there may be some sort of final test before they took her to CoOp. She'd need her strength and focus. Mal went to her room, closed the door, and went to sleep.

>>······<<

Chip and Mal logged in alone to the Boiler Room. Almost as soon as they were finished logging in there was a hearty knock on the back door.

"He's here," Chip said.

Mal opened the door and saw Ramos standing outside, alone.

"Come on," he said. "We've got to get going."

Chip and Mal joined Ramos in the alley. The three of them walked to the street where a ground car was waiting.

Mal got in the back seat and Ramos drove, his knuckles taut with stress.

They drove through the city slowly. Not many vehicles were on the road, then it started to rain.

"Is that us?" Mal asked.

Chip turned to sit sideways in the front bench seat. "Yeah."

"What is it?" Mal asked.

"We are busying the Pylons," Ramos said.

"To keep them from doing what?"

"From tracking us."

Ramos opened a console on the dashboard of the car, revealing a thick handle on a cylinder of green lights contained in a clear acrylic. He grabbed the handle, pulled the cylinder out partway, twisted turning the lights blue, and then pushing the whole thing back in. As this the whole car shuddered and as they drove through the streets were suddenly sinking, deep into the roadway, beneath the city. They drove until the road formed a solid roof above them.

Out the window Mal saw the Quantum Noise high above and stared off into it.

"Your car windows peel away the sky image program?"

"We like to see things how they are," Ramos said.

Then the whole world started to spin slowly along the axis of their travel. They were under the Aetherial city, and though it started out above them, it was rotating and rotating while the car remained level, until the underneath of the city was below them. The deepest basements of the City were now towers they drove around. The streets were still clear, and the buildings all around featureless and smaller by far than the towering cityscape to which Mal was accustomed. It was like they were driving through an ancient virtual reality: black blocks representing buildings, opaque and unreflective.

Chip looked back at her looking, Mal think, to read her reaction.

Mal shared it. "Holy fuck."

"Yeah, that's what I said the first time I saw it too. What's above us now is really under the city, and these black cubes are the basements of the Pylons. We're under the city."

"How are we not being torn apart by the Quantum Noise?" Mal asked.

"You'll see. If we weren't close to CoOp we would be."

They drove then in silence. There were no people here, no activity. They were the only ones here. They drove down a main thoroughfare and turned a few times. Finally, as they neared what Mal could only imagine was the very City Center of The Drain the Quantum River came into view. The physics and neuro-cognitive implications of a Noise River was beyond most people, hell, beyond most scientists. All Mal knew was that it was relatively stable if still in motion Quantum Noise. From the city side it was beautiful, like shimmering, glowing waters. Of course, anyone who fell in was destined for a quick and painful logout which could certainly result in death, or worse. Mal turned away from that thought.

From this side of the city the river looked more like a storm contained in an organically shaped tube of some sort, roiling, and flashing with Quantum Noise and energy. They drove alongside it for a moment. Mal figured they must be under Water Street at that point. The sky above most cities is programmed to look natural. Here, the sea of Quantum Noise hovered overhead, threatening, and beautiful.

That's when Mal saw it. Ahead, between several of the basement-towers, was a string of lights. No: a thousand strings of lights. Chip rolled down her window and Mal could hear music and laughter.

"Welcome to CoOp," Ramos said.

200

They pulled under the lights and left the car among the six or seven other vehicles here. In the space between the otherwise featureless grid-towers they'd been painted vibrant, beautiful colors. There were small homes that looked like they would belong in the past in some sort of rustic fishing village. There were some that looked like glass domes, some that looked like townhouses.

They got out of the car and twenty people came at them with smiles, arms held wide. All with the same message in a dozen ways and as many languages: Welcome.

"I thought CoOp was some Pylon-less Node off in the deep," Mal said to Chip as they were taken towards a part of the area that looked a lot like a street with brown brick buildings and stairway porches. It looked as though it were lifted from some child's show from the distant past.

"There is a place like that called CoOp but it has nothing to do with this place," Chip said. "It's a decoy in the chatter. Something to throw Axiom off what this place really is."

And there it was. She could beat Kass and Dek both to this information. The Co-op was on this side of the curtain: in the Aetherium. It was a central place here, in the Aetherium where Nanomei could do coding work, staging work, and more. It was not a retreat, a sanctuary: it was a base behind enemy lines. At first Mal thought that the anonymous Pylon at Outpost would be her greatest find but this overshadowed that. Even with this win, Mal sensed there was something more to this. Some great destiny hung over this secret place. It was being prepared for something big. Shit. I'm missing the big picture here.

Ramos and Chip walked up the steps to one of the doors and knocked. Mal stayed back a few paces which kept her on the stairs. Many of the people who had greeted them were standing on the street watching but others were going about their business. Small stalls lined the street, but it lacked the commercial feeling that hovered over most Aetherial places. A group of musicians were playing a few blocks away. There were maybe three dozen Users here all moving through the street, the steady buzz of socialization and connection engulfed her.

The people here were far more varied than in the parts of the Aetherium in which she'd spent her life. A few of the people sported large feathery wings, others horns or scales. One of the people here seemed to be made of shards of shifting and moving glass, another looked like only a shadow, moving along the ground in two dimensions. Some of these forms would meet too much resistance from other Pylons, but here it seemed like there was no pushback for them. A User who was as wide as at least five people, grey skinned, with huge horns instead of hair lumbered toward her. They were eye to eye because Mal was up six feet of steps. Mal looked at him as Ramos knocked and the huge guy winked at her.

"What's yer name?" he asked.

"I'm Mal," Mal said

"I'm Grey," he said.

Mal felt a sort of tunnel connected them, as if they were along among the throng. It was like comms but something deeper. Mal knew that the two of them were the only ones who were hearing this exchange even though he was not using her rig.

"This is a neat trick," Mal said.

"We have lots of tricks," he said with another wink. "Stay a while and we'll teach you," he added.

That's when the door opened. Mal nodded to Grey and turned her attention back to the doorway.

Niro from the Barn was standing in the doorway. He looked like a sculpture of Indigo light, with magenta tips at his extremities. His hair was long and a rainbow. "Ramos, you old devil, welcome home," he said.

There was a huge cheer from the crowd. They cheer for Ramos. They cheer for Chaos.

"Come in, come in," The Man said.

Ramos and Chip stepped through the threshold, making room for her, and taking off their shoes. Mal wiggled out of her combat boots and set them straight against the wall, on a mat made of some kind of thick fabric.

They walked into the place and found a comfortable if archaic living space. It was bright and airy. The walls were painted a cheery ocean blue and the woodwork was white. Shelves lined most of the wall space and held an array of glass baubles. The windows were open and Mal could hear and taste the ocean. Not an ocean of Quantum Noise but an ocean of salt water.

Niro sat on a puffy yellow chair and Ramos went to a different room. Chip and Mal sat on a couch.

"So you're Mal," he said. "We've met of course, but never in the Light." That was a strange way of saying in the Aetherium, but Mal went with it.

"Niro," she said. "Are you the leader of CoOp?" Mal asked.

"I made the CoOp but I don't lead it. It's my place and I guess I've gathered some like-minded individuals to me," he replied.

"Niro is one of the Nanomei Leaders," Chip said.

Niro half-shrugged, half-bowed to Mal. "That's what some people call me. You probably have other questions."

"Why was I brought here?" Mal asked.

"Good question," he said. "Ramos believes strongly that you are a valuable asset," he said.

"Is that enough for an invite to the CoOp?"

"Mal, I have heard the reports of your ability to bend the Aetherium to your will. Hacking is the term, I believe," he said. Mal didn't know that there was a different way of saying it.

"It's something that's always come naturally to me."

"But you've exercised it, yes?"

"Yes. What is this place?"

"Our position here," he said, "gives unique advantages. Surely you can see that."

"I can." And Mal could. There were so many possibilities here. Behind the enemy lines, this could be the knife's edge against Axiom. Instant movement and transportation would bring the guerilla warfare aspect of Nanomei into the light.

"From here we could do great things," Niro said.

"You could use it as a hub for moving people safely, a behind the lines depot, a supply station, a forward base, yeah, I can imagine some uses."

"But I doubt you can see the CoOp's true purpose."

Ramos reentered the room. "Oh, we're already to True Purpose times," he said with a smile.

"The CoOp is nearly complete, and when it is we will change The Drain forever," he said.

"How?" Mal asked. Something big.

Niro and Ramos shared a look and a nod.

"Ignore them," Chip said. "It's simple really. The core of Axiom's control of the city is a series of central Pylons in The Drain. Though their buildings are scattered around the whole city, they are linked. They create a sort of subsystem within the network of Pylons that makes up The Drain."

"Sure. That's common for Axiom controlled AE Cities, right?" Mal asked.

"It is," Ramos said. "You see. She is getting there on her own," he said.

"I'm not a child and don't want to play at guessing," Mal said. "What's the end game?"

"Well, the CoOp is also a subsystem in the Drain. Under it, really. And shielded by powerful Pylons to keep the Quantum Noise at bay in a way that the Pylons from the normal side of the city would never need to."

Click.

"That's why you've been drawing as many Axiom to The Drain as possible with your whole reign of terror and chaos thing," Mal said.

"See! I told you!" Ramos yelled.

Niro stood and the rest of the room stood with him, including Mal. "You see then. We will run a powerful hack and flip the subsystems. The CoOp will rez onto the city surface and the Axiom-controlled Pylons will be displaced to the underside."

"And because they do not have the special shielding required, they'll be destroyed almost instantly."

"The amount of time past instantly is nominal, yes."

203

"Every Agent, every Axiom official logged in through one of those Pylons…"

"Would violently disconnect in the Quantum Noise under The Drain," Niro interrupted.

"Die," Mal said. The weight of this revelation silenced Mal for a moment. She felt Ramos' eyes on her. "A lot of Axiom Patches, regular folks, log in through Axiom Civic Pylons."

"Some, yes. The majority of The Drain's Patches will be unaffected."

"You said you were almost complete. What do you still need?" Mal asked.

"This morning two things were missing from the equation," Niro said calmly. "The first was you: your hacking ability will be necessary to pull this off. Ramos is good but he can't do it alone."

"And second?"

"We need a Sentient, Mobile Pylon."

"Tok," Mal whispered. "You got to her through me. You used me. You made me drag that shield all the way to Severance Point through the Noise because you knew I'd need her ship."

Ramos smiled. "You're not wrong, Mal."

Vala came running in from the other room. She was about to say something and saw Mal and froze for just a moment.

"What is it, Vala?" Ramos asked.

She seemed to shake the shock off. "It's the ship. We just got a distress call from it."

"Niro," the Hologram of Tok started. "This overrides the communication from earlier today. We are under attack. Now! The dock login has been disabled. We need immediate assistance! Axiom Agents have gained entry to the ship!"

"What the hell? What did you tell her?" Mal asked.

"She thinks she's bringing us cargo. But it's the ship we need. The Pylon Drive."

"She doesn't know that?"

"We planned to take the ship from her when she arrived," Chip said.

"Yes, Mal," Niro said smoothly. "That is another reason why you are here: To smooth the way between the RezX Captain and our need for her ship."

Mal swallowed some very hurtful and angry words.

"What does Axiom even want with the ship?" Chip said, turning toward Ramos.

Ramos was about to answer when Niro answered instead, "That does not matter. We simply cannot allow Axiom to keep the ship from arriving here."

"There's no way to get there," Niro said. "The dock is days' travel by ship. The only way was to login as we were planning on doing," he said.

Mal held out her palm, on it rested the beacon.

"Can you copy this?" Mal asked.

Niro looked at it. "No. That is not possible."

"Then I'm going," Mal said.

"What?"

"The captain from the Aura, Tok; she gave me this," Mal said.

"There are too many," Chip said.

"Send the captain with her ship here," Niro said.

"We need the ship. Do what you will with your friend. But bring us that ship," Ramos said.

"You would not have an exit," Niro said, "not unless you won."

"Then I won't lose," Mal said, crushing the orb. The last thing she saw was Ramos throwing a fast hack at her, it felt as if he was trying to follow along. For a moment she had an image of the two of them tearing their way through scores of praetorians and agents. Together.

> > • • • • • < <

Mal had never used a beacon before; it was a very strange sensation, like a cross between logging in and flying at a high speed through a mesh laser filter. When Mal materialized, Tok was standing in front of her captain's chair. She looked rattled. The Bridge was frantic with crew members. Mal grabbed her shoulder, dizzy from the beacon. "What's happening?"

If Tok was surprised to see her she didn't show it. "They're already in the ship. We're still not able to move under our own power. We need time!" she said. "There are at least a dozen Praetorians in the ship! They're in my ship!" Tok yelled.

Mal said. "Be ready to fly!" Mal said and ran toward the Pylon room. A pair of Sirens fell into flanking positions with her as she strode forward.

Mal approached the Pylon, placed her hand on the hot metal and pulsed her consciousness through the ship, "Kay, Wanda," Mal said.

"Tok sent us to support you," Wanda said.

"Tell us what you need," Kay said.

"Stay here, guard me," Mal managed to say as the AI appeared and Mal stopped seeing anything else. The AI looked frayed, her form less well resolved as the last time Mal had seen her, her eyes duller. Mal approached her and she looked at her like Mal was the most welcome sight she'd ever seen.

They embraced. "Trust me," Mal whispered into her ear.

As they embraced Mal's senses were suddenly everywhere within the ship, even outside it: anywhere the Pylon could see Mal could see. Anything the Pylon felt Mal felt. Or was it the ship? Ship, Pylon, Mal were all one for that time. Mal felt like a child's hand in an adult's glove, her mind insufficient to fill all of the corners and curves of the form presented by the AI. She felt the code of the AI in the Pylon wrapping itself around, through her. The Pylon AI was whispering to her, her lips brushing Mal's neck like a kiss.

Then Mal felt the control deepen, her awareness started touching everything inside the ship as well, every User. She was aware and connected to every person on the ship. The Praetorians roving around trying to take the ship, Tok on the bridge, the Sirens guarding her, the ensign cowering in a closet, the rest of the crew all at once Mal embraced the crew as tightly as the ship. All were one, Mal, ship, AI, crew. Everything belonged and everything was one and all at once Mal felt the revulsion that the AI felt at the Axiom presence here. Part of her mind screamed not me not me not me, but the AI knew this already, embraced her fully. Showed Mal the possibilities. In that moment, Mal rejected everything Axiom within. Within the ship, within her, within.

The effect felt foreign and familiar all at once, as if her body was pressing outward and meeting no resistance at the same time that it was bound to the smallest space imaginable. It took only a moment, but the end result was exactly what Mal had wanted. Everyone in the ship was where they had been but everyone who did not belong in the ship had been shunted several hundred feet upwards and into the roiling mass of the Quantum Noise, their forms derezzing in a storm of flashes and raining down.

Mal saw them die with the dispassionate observatory powers of the sensors. Felt their absence as the alarms in her quieted. She even felt the few of the Sirens who had been guarding her body at having seen Mal disappear. I'm still here. Mal was able to appear, then, from any point in the ship but stepping back into herself felt lonely, even as she stepped onto the bridge in front of Tok she felt as if she were giving something up, coming into the cold air from a perfectly hot pool of water.

"What was that? Never tell me. No tell me. No. Don't," Tok said as Mal finished appearing. All of the crew Mal could see looked disoriented but seemed unharmed.

"We can't take off yet and Axiom has control of the Pylon in the dock base. More will be coming through. And you're going to have to tell me how you did that some time. Or not."

Kay and Wanda who had been guarding Mal's body arrived and looked confused but ready to help.

"Keep your Captain safe," Mal said, raising one hand. "The ship is clear of intruders, keep it that way. I'm going to the Dock."

"We can help you." Which one?

"Keep Tok safe. I've got the guns," Mal said as she left.

Mal ran from the bridge and down the boarding ramp. There were two Sirens, Lily and Sindara, guarding the ramp, but they were not under attack. Yet. Mal heard gunfire in the dock base. A lot of it. Mal kept running and activated a penetrating scan.

Blue light pulsed out in front of her, and the dock base was laid out before her. It was a small, round, three level structure. Each level was a few hundred feet across and divided up into personal labs and workspaces. The center of the lowest level was where the dock's Pylon was housed. That would be Mal's target. She needed to knock out the Pylon so Axiom couldn't keep bringing more and more force here.

As Mal approached the base, Mal saw the ruins of an Axiom transport derezzing, huge battle scars from Tok's cannon and probably the Sirens' work shimmering like digital smoke. The transport was crashed against the far side of the structure. The Pylon was pressing a livable reality about a hundred meters out from the structure, so they were not also having to fight the Quantum Noise. With the Axiom ship down, unless there was a backup ship coming, the Axiom here would either be on a suicide mission or need to take Tok's ship to escape once they destroyed the Pylon.

Mal flashed her sword to life and ran towards the building.

"Mal," Tok's voice was in her ear as she neared the building. "There is at least a squad of Praetorians in there."

"Any idea about the Agent?"

"No."

"How long until you can get your ship out of here?"

"A few more minutes!"

"What don't I know?" Mal asked as she approached the door. She ran a quick check of her ready programs. Sword, wings, knife, HuD, Comms.

"I was just about to ask you that," Tok answered.

"I don't know why they're hitting you so hard or early. I was told it was a mission to get information out of you. Not destroy the dock and the ship," Mal said.

"What about this cargo? It's off-loaded in the Dock storage bay."

"The cargo's not important," Mal said.

"But I promised to deliver it to The Drain. To Niro."

"No! You can't go anywhere near The Drain, Niro, Ramos, any of them. They want your ship. The Pylon."

"Mal?"

"Axiom wants you for information you have because they think you know about the Nanomei plans. Nanomei wants you because your ship is part of their plan, part of their weapon."

"Where do I go?"

"When you get launched you get clear and get yourself to a RezX Base. Someplace safe. The Museum maybe," Mal said.

"Damn it, Mal! They just rezed an Axiom ship in through the Pylon. I have to fight," Tok said as contact was lost.

Mal pressed her palm to the door and hacked her senses past it. The building's circular form was maintained inside. A single hall bisected the whole level, in the center of that hall a lift from one floor to the others. Her vision couldn't go any further without significant effort and time she really did not have.

There were three Praetorians rushing towards the door. Mal pulled her consciousness back and opened the door into a wide, white-tiled hallway.

One yelled and the three charged, bringing their shields up together, a spiked wall coming towards her. Mal wasn't here to impress anyone. No tricks this time. As they closed the distance Mal reached out with her left hand and pressed it against the wall. The Pylon was already weakened and so the hack was relatively easy.

Mal narrowed the hallway as the Praetorians approached. They started smashing against its sides and were eventually pushed into single file. Mal cut the legs out from the first, hurdled over him as he fell and attacked the second. Mal spun him and squeezed past, cutting him across the back. The third stood his ground and readied his shield as he took a fast swing at her. His stun baton clipped her left arm, sending that numbing chill of sync damage from her arm to her mind. In rage, she lashed out and screamed. Her blade cut his shield in half diagonally and it derezzed into a thousand black shards that scattered around them.

He made the mistake that Praetorians are trained to make: he reactivated his shield. But Mal was so much faster that she severed the whole of his sync before the shield completed its return. Mal left the three Praetorians derezzing behind her and let the hallway return to its normal width.

Mal ran ahead, ignoring the doorways along the hall. Mal was headed to the Dock Pylon. If she could control it Axiom would stop sending ships and maybe she could get reinforcements.

There was a melee at the lift. Mal flashed her sensors up and took stock as she entered the central circular room containing at its center the cylinder of the lift itself. The lift was not on this floor; the indicator said that it was on the bottom floor.

There were a dozen people fighting. Eight were Praetorians, two were clearly dock guards, and the other two were not identifiable by visuals alone but her sensor package identified them easily enough: they were Agents.

The Agents were moving faster than the others present, both fighting the quickly moving dock guards. There were five or six more guards derezzing on the floor. The Praetorians were using the bottoms of their shields to further damage the derezzing guards: something that would almost certainly kill them in the Meatspace.

Mal tore through their armor, blurring herself with speed. The Agents cut down the last two guards as Mal finally came to a stop. On the floor were all of the Praetorians and guards.

The Agents, who both wielded swords, stood and shared a look before one spoke. Mal could tell, though, that they were both ready to pounce.

"Stand down, Citizen," one said.

"You two match. That's so cute," Mal said.

"You made quick work of our Praetorians," the other one said.

"Praetorians are over-rated," Mal said.

"Agents are not," one said.

"There's no way you're getting that ship or her crew," Mal said.

"That is inevitable," he said.

"Tok. I need to know if we're going to get out of here."

"I'm trying to take off but there's another transport incoming! I can maneuver close by but we aren't ready to flee into the Noise yet. We'd get torn apart! They just used the Pylon to let in another transport. You need to blow the Pylon!"

"Keep the other ship off me and I'll take out whoever's here and try to blow the Pylon. Do you have anyone to spare me?"

"Three Sirens are outside the dock, ready to cut their way in on the top level."

"Have them recover the bodies here to get them safe. When I blow the Pylon they need to be on the ship. Agents are coming through the Pylon. I am going to stop them from getting to your ship."

"If an Agent gets in here, we're finished. I'll be back in five minutes. Be ready," Tok said.

As her senses returned fully to the Agents Mal saw that one had taken the opportunity of her distraction to begin a hack of some sort.

The other was watching her; Mal could tell that he was ready to intercept anything she launched. One interesting thing about Agents, though. They're not trained to work well together. But taking out Agents was not like taking out Praetorians. They were just as fast as her, and well-armed and Rigged. Mal could feel the hack coming. He was weaving a grip of code around the handle of her blade. He was good and Mal chose not to fight it. It wasn't worth the expenditure of will it would take. Instead, Mal threw the blade aside. Both Agents looked surprised.

Mal leapt into the air, towards the one who had been hacking. He was caught off guard, but his partner was not. The partner redirected Mal's knee with his arm just before it was going to crush his nose. He threw her across the room, but Mal landed against the wall with her feet firmly planted there. She hacked the gravity as she landed. They were not expecting that and fell towards her, landing at her feet, on the wall.

One struggled to his feet while the other rezzed in a handgun. Mal pummeled one with a quick flurry of fists and elbows until she heard a crack in his neck. He fell to the wall and disconnected. The other fired two shots at Mal, one finding its target. Pain stabbed through Mal's shoulder as she was spun in the air before landing back on her feet. She stepped towards him and flipped the gravity back to normal. He swore as the gravity was reversed back and they landed in a tangle and traded blows, the Agent smashing her wound hard. Mal rolled away from him, his gun in her hand. Mal unloaded four shots into his face.

Mal keyed the lift and it opened. It was empty. Mal tossed the Agent's weapon on the ground and held out her hand for her blade. It sprang across the room and into her hand and she stepped backwards into the lift.

"There are two guards on the main floor at the lift," Mal told Tok.

"I'll relay to the Sirens. What's your status?"

"I'm going to the Pylon. I am going to blow it or it's more Axiom ships. They won't stop."

"You have two hundred seconds until I'm back at the landing ramp. Go!" Everyone derezzing here would die if Mal blew the Pylon. But then Tok would have only one ship to deal with and could get away. That's really hard math.

Mal lowered the lift and as the door opened Mal saw the worst possible situation. The room was empty except for a pillar of code. The outer shell of the Pylon had been stripped and someone had been attempting to access information from it. This can't be good. Kass stepped into view from behind the pillar. Hey! I was right!

"You warned them," she said, "didn't you? Why are you here?"

"I'm here to give the people time to get away," Mal said.

"And what are you doing here, in this room?"

"Well, I attacked a shit ton of Praetorians and just derezzed a couple of Agents. And now I'm going to take the Pylon so I can help my friend defend her ship and get the hell out of here."

"You're going to kill them?" She said it as though she were challenging an errant child.

"What? No. I'm locking down the Pylon so you can't bring more reinforcements."

"Look, your mission's over. Just log out and let it go. Come home," Kass said.

"I have no choice, Kass. You're not getting that ship."

"You have a choice. This is your way to gain favor. Sure, you didn't bring down big bad Ramos but helping me with this is enough. You did it."

"No. I've cut through enough Axiom today and I'm letting Tok's ship go."

"Idiot. I'm here now. And you're not getting through me. I require information from that ship. Axiom requires it."

Tok's voice came back, loud and clear through comms. "Mal. We're here. I took care of the ship. Let's get the fuck out."

"I can't leave here right now," Mal told Tok. "Can you get away now?"

"Yes. You gave us the time we needed," Tok said.

"Go," Mal replied. "And stay away from The Drain. They are going to try to use the Pylon Drive to do something horrible."

"Great but I'm not leaving you here alone," Tok said.

"Can you handle Axiom ships chasing you?"

"We're set here, they can't follow us into the Noise. Hey. How close do you need me to get the ship to do that melding thing you did with my AI?"

"Pretty close."

"Give me sixty seconds." Then she signaled out.

"That's my ride," Mal said to Kass.

"Make your choice, Mal. End your mission, help me. You've done enough." They were circling each other as they talked, back and forth.

Mal hesitated.

"You can come home now. Prove that you've remained loyal. Help me get that ship."

And that's all it would take. Mal could log out through this Pylon and give over this to Kass. She'd wake up back at the Outpost. Maybe they wouldn't even know. She could end the mission. But she had raised her hand against all these Praetorians and Agents. There was no reason she had had to do that for her mission. This had gone too far. She had betrayed Axiom.

The only way now to keep Axiom Command from knowing that would be to blow the Pylon and let it destroy the minds of everyone here. Nothing would remain. She'd log out and be back among the Nanomei. Maybe she could make a go if it with them for real. But she couldn't do either of those things.

"Let's get out of here," Kass said, holding her fists ready.

"No. I'm leaving," Mal decided as she said it. She stepped towards Kass then, almost so they were touching. "I am going. Do what you will," Mal said.

"Now!" Tok's voice came through the comms.

Mal reached upwards with everything she had, stretching her consciousness, senses, everting, her right hand outstretched, her left hand held up, warning Kass to stay away. And though she could not see it, she imagined the AI's hand reaching down from the ship. She felt the cool touch of her fingers and then they were one again for a glorious moment. But the AI was busy powering the ship and getting it out of harm's way, so Mal moved herself with all speed to Tok who was waiting in the Engine room.

"You made it," Tok said.

"Thank you," Mal said, embracing her.

"What are you going to do? Are you going to be safe when you logout?" Tok asked.

"I have no choice. They have my body. I need to go back. I don't know what they'll know. I don't know what they'll do."

"You saved my ship, Mal, me," Tok said.

"You saved me."

⟫ Chapter Ten: Choice ⟪

Mal came out of the Aetherium smoothly, her eyes flashing open to see the lights down in the Pylon room, which was unusual. Chip was there. She had a grey duffle with her. Mal pulled the trodes from her temple and disentangled herself from the wires.

Chip stood there silently.

"What's happening?" Mal asked.

"We know who you are, Mal. We know. Ramos is coming here. If you're here when he gets here, I don't know what he'll do."

"What do you think you know?" Mal asked.

When you left to go save the ship, with the beacon," she started.

"Ramos hacked me," Mal said flatly.

"He was trying to follow along. To help. But instead, it created a conduit. We stood in CoOp watching everything. Hearing everything."

"How long do I have?" Mal was suddenly empty, a void sucking all emotion away, a cold pit of nothing.

"We should go now," she said.

Chip offered her the duffle.

"This is your stuff from your room," she said.

Mal stood uneasily and took the bag. As Mal walked out of the room the hall was lined with Nanomei. Each was wearing a white rabbit mask and standing with their hands folded in front of their chests.

Only Chip did not wear a mask. She walked behind Mal to the edge of the Outpost, to the gate where even old Ibrahim who watched the gate in his disgusting outfit stood wearing the mask. He did not say a word as Chip lead her past the car gate and out into the surrounding junkyard. It was hot outside and Mal felt sweat bead up on the back of her neck. Mal knew that she was a danger to them now. CoOp was at stake, and she didn't believe that she'd be let go. She knew she was being taken to die.

They stood there in the ruin for a few moments. A rusted-out backdrop to a standoff that Mal didn't want to be part of. That she wasn't sure she even understood. Mal was looking for something to say. She had betrayed them, and she knew it. What had Ramos known? How long had he known it?

Then Chiphead pulled out Mal's service pistol from behind her, in her belt.

"We fought together. Side by side you're not, in your heart, one of them."

"But I am."

"Ever loyal," Chip said.

"Any cost," Mal said.

Mal felt the weight of the moment. There was no protecting her cover now. There was nothing she could do to get back into the mission. Taking out a target like Chiphead would earn her a medal on her coffin perhaps. She would not even be buried. The Commander would know that she had betrayed Axiom. She would be incinerated, and her carbon recycled. There was nothing for her.

"Goodbye," Mal said.

Chip didn't reply. Mal turned around. Her fate was already set. She took a step forward and though she never felt the shot, she heard it. Everything went black.

》·····《

Mal was being rushed in a medical vehicle. She saw screens, and a light, and was in and out several times. Kass was there, though she looked like she does in the Aetherium. She was holding Mal's hand and crying.

"Stay with me," she said.

"I'm trying," Mal replied.

Mal felt pain wracking her whole body. It felt as though every nerve was on fire and freezing at the same time. She screamed.

》·····《

When Mal opened her eyes again she was in no pain; in fact, she could feel absolutely nothing at all. Mal was in a medical room, tiled in white with a single door on one wall and a closed drapery on the opposite one. There was a medical attendant there, the Axiom crossed keys emblazoned on his white coverall.

"Are you in any pain?" he asked.

"I can't feel anything," Mal said. She looked down at her body. It looked fine, covered in a thin white sheet. Nothing major missing, at any rate.

"What's the last thing you remember, Citizen?"

"I was in a ground transport. Kass was with me," Mal said.

"That is not possible, Citizen, you arrived in an air transport and were alone."

"My name is Mal. I am an Agent of Axiom," Mal said.

"I apologize, Agent. What can you tell me about your injuries?" came the flat reply.

"I was hoping you could tell me about them," Mal said.

"You had two projectiles pierce you from the back. An Axiom recovery team found you in the Recyclery, with med patches on your back and chest. We don't know who called them in."

Rat?

"You should rest. Someone will be here to talk with you soon."

"Wait. My injuries…"

"You lost considerable blood, but you were found in time that there will be no lingering effects." He left then, without waiting for additional questions.

〉〉••••••〈〈

After three hours a different man entered the room. He was wearing a pressed grey uniform. His hair was close cropped and the same shade of grey as his uniform and his skin looked deeply pocked. He smiled as he came in. Not an Agent, just an operative.

"I am Andrew," he said.

"I am Mal."

"A transport has been dispatched and will arrive here before morning. There is a guard station attached to this room. You are safe. I am the Citizen Liaison. If you need anything, I will be in the guard station. At your service, Agent. Rest for now and then make yourself ready for travel by 0600. A fresh uniform is available for you."

"Thank you," Mal said. He left the room without another word. There was a clock with an alarm next to the bed which Mal set for 0500. She closed her eyes and was immediately, deeply, asleep.

〉〉••••••〈〈

After Mal woke, she climbed, gingerly, from the bed. She need not have worried; her wounds were healed. Mal stretched, all the way from her toes to the tips of her fingers. Not a twinge. Mal breathed out a slow, long, sigh of relief. To be alive at all was a miracle; to be whole again… Damn these fragile Meatspace bodies.

215

Mal wondered what Ramos was doing at Outpost. Mal wondered if Chip hadn't killed her intentionally. Mal wondered if it was really Rat who saved her. Mal wondered a lot of things.

After donning a fresh uniform Mal made her way to the hall. A medic approached immediately.

"You are to proceed to the helipad, through here. You will find a transport," he said, pointing.

Mal went out and saw it waiting for her. An Agent approached.

"Agent Turner," he said, extending his hand. "I am Agent Lowery." His eyes were sharp and green, his skin pale and freckled. His voice was crisp and official, his handshake a little too firm. "Are you ready to depart?"

"I am," Mal said over the noise of the transport.

"Good. We won't shut down, then. Back in the air in one minute," he said.

They got situated for what turned out to be an almost silent ride through the air. Downtime in the Meatspace was so different from downtime in the Aetherium. Time crawled around them. She sat and wondered about her fate. The inside of the transport was empty; the Agent was sitting up front with the pilot and Mal was alone in a bay that could hold a dozen troops. There are no windows in the rear of these transports so Mal was unsure where they were when they landed several hours later.

The bay door opened, creating a ramp from the rear of the transport. Mal walked to the edge of the ramp, bending a bit to look down.

There were only two people at the bottom. They were in an internal landing bay. It was huge: two other transports were inside and there was room for perhaps four or five more.

"Agent Mal," one man said. "I am Director Weathers, this is Agent Deblin." Mal inclined her head in response. Mal moved down the ramp alone; apparently the Agent and pilot were not coming with her. Mal stepped onto the bay floor and Weathers and Deblin started walking and she followed in step.

"You have arrived at Pinnacle Fortress," Weathers said. Mal almost gasped but kept her demeanor calm. Pinnacle Fortress was a place of legend. It was said that the rigs here were top of the line. It was also said that Pinnacle Fortress was a prison from which there were never any releases. Sculpted of black granite and rising high above a desolate wasteland Pinnacle was a secure location and its location in the world a secret.

"It's an honor," Mal said. Also terrifying. And very worrying. And super-surreal. But, yeah, an honor.

They walked her to a huge lift, something that could take up a squad of Praetorians with room to spare. Standing there, in front of the lift, waiting was Commander Mullen. Mal felt as though the floor were dropping out from under her feet.

"Agent Turner," he said, extending his hand. Mal shook it. They looked straight into each other's eyes without looking away.

He welcomed her onto the lift.

"Thank you, Director, Agent. I'll take Mal from here," he said. The others left them, and the lift ascended.

"We won't be listened to here. We can talk safely. I can't believe you made it out," he said.

"I still don't understand how I survived. What is going on with your beard? It's gone from adequate to inspired."

"Thank… is that really important? Things seemed to start unraveling fast there."

"Ramos became less and less reliable. He was taking more and more risks."

"Ramos has always been a mystery," he said in an odd tone. "Do you know what happened? I mean, is there anything you didn't tell the medic?"

"Deja shot me. I believe it's possible that a Nanomei named Rat saved me."

"So, it wasn't Ramos?"

"It wasn't. He wasn't there."

"Where is he? Listen, Mal," Mullen said, "Whatever happens in here, I've got you. We are going to get through this."

Mal nodded her head slightly instead of answering verbally because the lift was approaching its destination. As they reached the top, he motioned to the exit of the lift and Mal sensed that once again they needed to be careful of what they said.

Mal walked quietly from the lift and into a wide and dark hallway. Shallow alcoves filled with dim orange-ish light that made the hallway murky. Commander Mullen accompanied her. Banners, the crossed keys of Axiom, hung along the twenty-foot-tall walls. They were not the usual printed banners but hand woven, thick and coarse. They looked like artifacts of a forgotten time.

The doorway slid open noiselessly as they approached to reveal a cavernous room, with a ceiling at least a hundred feet high; three circular stairs in the very center of the room lead to a broad platform. Standing in the middle of that was a woman. She was wearing the robes of a Matron of Axiom. Her tall hat stood a foot above her head, her shoulder draperies flowed as she breathed. She'd never seen a full Matron in person, though every citizen had seen holos of them. So, this is what Sim is going to dress like some day? They were often used to deliver proclamations or decrees.

They approached quietly. Something made her put her duffle down at the entryway of the door before she approached. Mal was leaving her weapon. Mal looked at Commander Mullen, directly in the eye. He smiled and then looked up at the Matron.

"Welcome, Mal," the woman said.

Before Mal could answer in kind she raised one hand.

"Let me interrupt you," she said. "I am Head Matron. I am the master of Pinnacle Fortress, and I am very happy you are here. Please, join me on the dais."

Mal walked up the steps. As Mal did, she could see nine huge windows around the entirety of the room, each with a doorway that seemed to lead out to a narrow balcony beyond.

"When I first came to Pinnacle Fortress," she continued, "I was little older than you. I have seen a great many things in my lifetime but very few have I seen who have the capabilities you do. Tell me," she said, "are you loyal to Axiom?"

"Loyalty Eternal," Mal intoned.

"An adequate if uninspired answer," the Matron said. She held up her hand, preemptively interrupting Mal again.

"The Axiom hierarchy is strict and structured, as you can well imagine. We have been watching three Agents with the potential to advance. You are one of those Agents," The Matron said.

Mal paused briefly to process what she was saying. "I understand." Mal felt the Commander standing behind her now, a few steps back. He was still, and silent.

Anything you say now will be stupid, Mal. Say nothing. Do nothing.

"I have known for some time that Mal is worthy," the Commander said.

"It may be. It may not. Please remember - there are three candidates of which Mal is only one," Matron said.

"How is the decision made?" Mal asked.

"The candidates are measured on efficiency, loyalty, and efficacy. Please follow me."

Not trusting herself to glance back at the Commander, Mal followed the Matron dutifully. They entered a long passage and again a door swept open as they approached. This was a Pylon Room. There were only three bays and each one looked like it cost the Value of a small collective or a large corporate entity to build and maintain. Two of the bays were empty. In the third a man lay: Dek. These bays were not the usual open chairs. Instead, they looked more like reclined tubes made of a clear acrylic top and brushed steel bottom. The man inside was suspended in some sort of liquid.

"He rests in a conductive gel," The Matron said as Mal looked on. Dek was naked and Mal could see no wires or connective trodes.

"The gel enters through both the lungs and stomach. It is a ... disconcerting process, but it allows for a very long-time logged in."

"How long?" Mal whispered.

"All things being normal, it can sustain someone safely for a year at a time."

"Holy shit," Mal said loudly, her voice echoing against the black stone of the floor and walls. The Matron raised an eyebrow at her.

"It is extremely costly, but the results are worth it. There is no delay, no neuro decay. These rigs are superior to anything else to which we have access. These are the only three Rigs of this kind."

"You've got a real opportunity here," the Commander said as he rested his hand on Mal's shoulder.

That's when Mal heard the faintest of footsteps. Another Matron, dressed the same way as Mal's guide walked another person in. The woman she was with wore a loose fitting black and orange silken robe. She had pale eyes that were staring directly at Mal. It was Kass.

Mal's head was spinning. But who else could it have been?

"Ah, good. The third is here," the Matron bringing Kass in intoned.

"Yes. We are an hour behind you, I think," she said. "We were just finishing up our little talk and about to head to the decontamination area."

They walked past the other two, Kass staring wordlessly at Mal the whole time. Mal was taken to a small room with a single shower stall. There were two pegs of brushed steel on the wall one holding a silk robe, like the one Kass wore and the other a large, fluffy looking towel.

"Please follow the prompts after I leave. I will await you outside this door," she said as the door closed between them. The Commander stood behind her now and looked at her all the way until the door closed.

Mal stripped off her clothes. It had been almost two months since her last real water shower. Mal stepped in and a kind-sounding voice said: Please prepare for water. Mal waited obediently and water started pouring out of a trough over her head, creating a waterfall. Mal stood under it. It was warm and welcoming. She must have been cleaned in some way at the hospital, but this felt like she was washing away grime that had crept across her from living in Outpost.

Please prepare for detergent. The water falling from the top was joined by jets from the sides and all around her, even the ceiling. The water coming from them was frothy with soap.

Please prepare for disinfectant. The water started to run clear again but now it stung her eyes and burned.

Please prepare for rinsing. The water ran hot and clear and though her eyes still stung a bit, her skin felt renewed, almost like it was humming.

Without warning the shower ended. Mal stepped out and dried herself and then put on the robe. Her other clothes had been taken.

"Please follow me back to the Pylon Room," The Matron said as Mal emerged. The Commander was nowhere to be seen.

Kass was suspended in gel already when Mal got there. Kass' guide was nowhere to be seen. There was one last bay left. It lit up as Mal approached.

"You will find yourself in the Aetherial Pinnacle when you log in."

"Is there anything I should know about the controls?" Mal asked as she removed her robe and placed it on the floor near the unit.

"All will be made clear. Loyalty Eternal," she said.

Mal stepped in and let her feet slide down to the bottom of the bay. The bay inclined further so Mal was almost laying flat. Then the gel started to come up from somewhere behind the padded back of the tube Mal was laying in. It was warm and entered the tube slowly. It was hard not to feel that the ge"You will feel a mild sensation of drowning. Be assured that you will survive the process," a woman's voice rang through the device. The gel was filling about half the tube. Mal was completely submerged up to her thighs and partially everywhere else. Her face was still above the level of the gel. It took every ounce of concentration and focus Mal had to not move. As the gel came up to her face she let it cover her. This wasn't so bad.

"You must breathe the gel in for the system to work," the voice said.

That was a harder sell to her body. Finally, Mal opened her mouth and swallowed some gel.

"That is not breathing. That is swallowing," the voice said calmly. "It may help to expel the air from your lungs."

Everything Mal had rebelled against letting go of what air she had. Panic was setting in. They were trying to kill her. The gel would kill her. They knew she had saved Tok's ship. Mal gathered up all of the fear and anxiety of this mission and screamed it into the gel. Her lungs empty, she breathed in a great amount of gel but she panicked, and it closed again. Her arms and legs started flailing, trying to escape the tube. Black spots appeared in her vision. Everything blurred and Mal blacked out. It was almost instantly that Mal found herself in a White Room. Well, that's one way to do it.

Mal was alone in a white room. She did not have her standard interface so she was unsure of what to do. Mal did not know how to call up any menus or choices. Her body, though, felt more capable in this room than it ever had before. The body she was in was more perfectly herself. She was certain that if she woke from a dream in this rig she would not be able to tell Meatspace from Aetherium.

Mal started to imagine how a Rig like this would work.

"Help," Mal said.

Upon verbalization of a help request an AI spawned in for her. "How may I be of assistance?" a female form materialized in front of her as it spoke those words. It made itself from a glossy white material; its face moved in a life-like, animated way.

"List functions," Mal said.

"Manual, Advice, Mission Briefing, Gear."

"Spawn Mission Briefing and then," Mal said.

"Mission Briefing. Your mission begins–"

"No," Mal said, cutting her off. "Spawn material copy of briefing."

A single piece of paper appeared and hovered a foot from her hand.

"Thanks," Mal said. "Spawn Console." A standard console grew itself from the White Room floor. A black touch screen holo panel atop a white pedestal. "Dismiss AI." She disappeared.

Though the console was preloaded with an Axiom outfit that was obviously meant to be chosen, Mal coded a workable outfit: black hoodie and jeans, combat boots. Mal thought about a blade or weapon but decided only to create the core of a weapon program. Carrying a low complexity weapon program with her would give her something to modify instead of having to create it from nothing. Alone it was almost nothing, but the wings had to be done. She wondered idly if everyone would be waiting for her so she endeavored to move through the process as quickly as possible.

All told, it took her about a minute to pull together everything she needed yet the internal clock read just under fifteen seconds. The coding was fast and efficient, and the hacking was easy, fluid. Mal wondered if this was just a benefit of being in the Pylon's white room or if this was how hacking would always function.

Then Mal did two things more: she let the console fade away into nothing and she thought login.

›› • • • • • ‹‹

Mal called up the display for completing login beyond the White Room. It showed that the white room gave way to a huge terrace high above an Aetherial city. Mal was in the Aetherial version of Pinnacle Fortress. That meant they were in Aegis Prime. Mal had gone to academy here but had never really ventured out into the city. Coming into the Aetherium through the gel rig, though, was taking her breath away. She felt no lag, no hint of anything between her and the Aetherium itself.

Mal's own White Room opened out onto a terrace and as she stepped into it she saw that there were two other White Rooms attached as well. Two forms were already standing at the edge of the terrace looking out over the city. One was Kass and the other was Dek who she'd seen in the gel.

Mal approached.

They were both wearing black on black uniforms: fitted pants and tight black, long sleeved shirts with a wide belt covered in small pouches and fitted running shoes. There was the usual orange piping on the black, running along their outer legs and arms.

"You didn't dress for the occasion," Dek said as Mal approached.

221

Kass moved a few steps towards her and then reached out. Mal held a flinch in check as she hugged her tight. "Isn't this wonderful?" she said loud enough for Dek to hear. But she breathed in Mal's ear, "You owe me."

"So I do," Mal murmured.

"Was your console malfunctioning?" Dek asked, gesturing at her outfit. Mal looked back at him silently.

"Don't bother," Kass said. "Mal is far too arrogant to think rules apply to her."

From behind them a throat was cleared. Another Matron was there, this time in the Aetherial regalia that Mal was accustomed to seeing on billboards and holos, similar to those worn by the Matron in the Meatspace but the hat was even taller, the shoulders more stylized and coming to more of a point. The other main difference was the height. The Matron here was a good foot taller than even Dek.

"Welcome, Agents," she said. In response, they fell into line, three across facing her. Their backs to the city laid out behind them. "You are now all assigned to the same mission where once you each held your own," she said.

"Let me guess," Kass interrupted. "We will be judged and measured during this mission and whoever performs the best will receive the promotion."

"No," the Matron said. "That would be inadequate. The measure of your worth has been going on since before each of your recruitments." Dek was an aggressive head nodder. It was making Mal dizzy.

"You see," she continued, "the educational system imposed by Axiom is a sorting facility for minds. We let a few rise to the top. This is the first step. When you're recruited you are constantly re-evaluated. Some people spend their entire Axiom service years being evaluated for this without ever knowing it. Most people are eliminated from consideration from this position and remain on the level they're on within the first few days of being chipped. Others take longer but very few, obviously, make it this far."

"What happens when someone who has served for years ends up failing?" Kass asked.

"That's when their promotions stop."

Mal let that sink in. Mal had never sought out promotions; she had only been interested in the newer and better rigs. Yet the promotions had come.

"What part does loyalty play?" Dek asked.

"Loyalty is tested on a regular basis both via the loyalty tests and interviews to which you have surely grown accustomed as well as via direct and indirect observation."

Kass looked over at Mal and smiled. It was a crooked smile, full of danger.

"Have you all read the briefing?"

They all nodded silently.

The Matron walked over to the edge of the terrace and activated a holographic display. It showed a map of a Pylon infrastructure. It was a Pylon in The Drain. Mal wasn't sure which one; it didn't look particularly impressive.

"This," the Matron said, "is the gateway to CoOp. From here, you will be able to access the underside of The Drain and find CoOp. It is relatively undefended, though some of the best hackers in the worlds call it home or a rest stop. Though Dek failed in his mission to ascertain the complete extent of the Nanomei plot in the Drain, we are certain that this location is key and without his work this location would not have been found. There are several high Value targets there, including the Nanomei renegades Ramos and Niro," she said. "These fools need to understand that they have no safe place to hide or operate from. Your mission is to destroy this secret hideout, tear it apart, bring down the Pylons completely. Any who flee and survive must tell the tale of an unforgiving and overwhelmingly powerful Axiom force."

She nodded at her then and continued. "This intelligence comes from Mal's recent mission. It was well done."

Dek looked at her with unbridled jealousy.

The Matron broke the silence by moving forward.

"Destroy their Pylons. Leave not a single one operating. Once you have neutralized the Nanomei base, you will return here, and we will conduct final loyalty interviews. In the end one of you will find a promotion and the other two will remain Agents," she said.

"If we fail…, will we be given a chance again?"

"No."

"The last mission before you are judged starts now," said the Matron as she winked out.

Kass and Mal looked again at each other. They held each other's gaze for three breaths. Mal knew what Kass was thinking without a single word. She did not need to respond. They both circled Dek without him really realizing what was going on.

At the last moment he started to speak, "Hey what's," was all he got out before both Kass and Mal acted in unison.

Dek had very little idea what was happening. Mal hacked two knives into existence in a heartbeat, threw one to Kass and executed a hack to bind Dek's hands while Kass made her attack at his head. All this before he could react. He brought his bound hands up in defense, too late. The battle was fast and deadly. Mal and Kass slashed at his form until he started to derez, Kass paused and looked at her.

The gel Rig was more powerful than Mal could make myself understand. Her speed was twice what it had been, her motions smooth, strong, and precise. Mal twirled the knife blade across the back of her palm and hacked it into a full-length blade without giving much attention to it at all.

"We can't kill him," she said.

"Yeah. I know," Mal replied sounding disappointed. Mal hacked her sword invisible, holding the entire hack in her mind at once and making it permanent with barely any effort.

"No. The rules are different in the Gel Rig. We literally can't do enough to him to cause the sort of damage we're used to."

"Oh. I bet that was in the manual," Mal said.

"No. But I've been here for a while, been using one of these gel rigs for a month now. We can make it so the gel takes a long time to reset, though," she added as she slit his throat.

They walked away from there together, to the edge.

"How are you on flying these days?" Mal asked.

"I could hack together something. Nothing like your wings, of course," with a sidelong glance from under her long eyelashes.

"We can get to The Drain through the subnet here," Mal said, popping open a holo display.

"Short flight," she said.

"Any way to make it harder for him to catch us?"

"We have an hour," she said.

))······((

"Pylon seventeen, in the Trench," Mal said. They both reentered their White Rooms and relogged at The Drain.

"We're well ahead of him. He hasn't even logged back in yet," Kass said as they walked up the steps of the subway terminal.

"What? How do you know that?" Mal asked.

"Because I hacked a ping on him when I slit his throat. It'll tell me when he manages to log back in."

They were walking toward the Gateway Pylon. Kass stopped and took her by the elbow and looked Mal dead in the eyes.

"I don't know what your plan here is. I don't know if you're Axiom or Nanomei or what. But I know that we are in this together," Kass said.

"I am Axiom. I have always been Axiom."

"I know what you did. I've been watching you," Kass said.

There was a long pause.

"Why didn't you tell anyone what I did? That I saved her ship."

"Because it would destroy your choice. You can still come back now. End this madness. Get the help you need."

"I always figured you'd want me out of Axiom, anyway. No more competition."

Kass did not reply to that.

And so, they walked toward the Gateway in silence, both stealing side-long glances both wondering. A few times Mal thought Kass was about to speak and a few times Mal had been about to speak. But in the end, they walked together in silence.

As they approached the Gateway which was a rundown warehouse in the shipping district, Mal stopped before going around a corner.

"Look, Kass. I owe you," Mal said.

"We're in this together. Like I said. Now let's get to this."

"I've been there before. We didn't go through this Gateway Pylon, but I've been here."

"With the Nanomei?"

"Ramos took me there," Mal said.

"What do you know? What can help us?" she asked.

They were standing outside the warehouse now.

"Kass... I can't kill those people."

"I know," she said. "Just don't try to stop me," she added. "You and I could have ruled the world."

"I know."

Mal watched Kass walk into the warehouse. In moments she'd be beneath The Drain and it wouldn't take her long to find CoOp. She'd kill them. Ramos, Chip, all of their people. All of them, or at least a good number of them. Mal started walking away, opening her wings, and then paused. On the side of a building, staring at her was the painted Death Angel, holding in her outstretched hands two broken keys. I didn't paint that.

Mal stood there, unable to walk away. Mal turned back to the gateway. The space ahead of her and behind her stretched and grew in her imagination. Mal had to walk in one of these directions. If she walked away, she'd lose any chance at advancement in Axiom. She could even be reduced away from Agent status. She could be hobbled, made a Patch. Or worse. If they were feeling particularly vindictive, they could break her mind in the torture chambers, and she could end up one of the Deleted. If she entered, she'd be faced with choices she wasn't ready to face. Who would she be going to CoOp to help? She did not know the answer to that question as she stepped through.

〉〉••••••〈〈

The Gateway was a simple Pylon, and accessing it only took a moment and then the world spun around her on that one same axis and a door appeared.

"Tok, you out there?" Mal pinged.

There was no answer. Mal didn't know what to say in any message and didn't have time to figure it out. "Ever onward," she said aloud to no one.

Long range comms needed to be shut off during a fight to keep defenses as high as possible, so she cut them. She'd only be able to communicate with those under The Drain during the coming fight.

Mal walked through it and found herself in that same cityscape: the Underside.

Mal flew into the air, the Quantum Noise roiling above her.

She flew high, almost until her wings touched that Noise so she could get a good look at the cityscape below her. Mal saw CoOp and saw also saw that Kass had hacked together some large pieces of machinery. Shit. They were cannons being assembled. Mal was too far to see individuals but she knew her work. This was Kass writ large, across a horizon. The Gel Rig must really be working with her. The Nanomei were doomed.

Mal flew towards CoOp as fast as her wings would allow which almost tore her apart; the gel Rig cranked everything up. Too fast. Too fast.

There was chaos there as the energy blasts from the several surrounding cannons made huge sonorous impacts, rattling bones and shaking the foundations of reality.

Mal dropped down in the central courtyard, chaos all around.

Mal heard Ramos' name yelled, people clustered on rooftops and in the streets. Small groups had gathered in knots and were hacking. So much code was flying that it looked like a celebration. Mal saw Chip coming out of a building; she hadn't seen Mal yet. Mal strode forward and she caught sight of her, rezzing a handgun into her hand as she did and raising it.

"I'm not here to fight!" Mal said.

"You brought them here!" she screamed and let loose several blasts.

Mal rolled out of the way and launched herself into the air. Evading Chip's blasts was almost comically easy. Mal landed atop the building she had emerged from, a four-story place connected to several other buildings. Ramos was there.

"You!" he bellowed.

"Ramos!" Mal yelled.

Ramos bounded forward, pulling an enormous shotgun from nowhere as he did. Mal leapt upwards but that was what the was expecting and he fired the double barrel at her, striking her hard. It burned like Glitch and Mal fell back to the rooftop.

He crossed the space in an incredible speed and leveled his weapon at her again.

"Stop!" a voice yelled. Kass. "Ramos!" she screamed. "Face me!"

Ramos fired another shot, but Kass's distraction had given Mal time to rez a Praetorian shield onto her arm. It shattered on the impact of his shotgun blast, but it protected her too.

226

Kass was on him, then, a hurricane of slashes with her silver katana. That's when Mal heard the explosions start to close on their position.

〉〉••••••〈〈

At some distance, there were six guns lobbing energy blasts into the CoOp indiscriminately. The guns were huge and operated by small teams of operatives.

Kass and Ramos were keeping each other busy so Mal tore towards the cannons. Mal had thought that these were hacked together, but as she approached it became clear they were rezzed programs.

The first cannon Mal approached from the air was solidly constructed and operated by a crew of five. Two targeters, one loader, and two guards.

There were a few derezzing Nanomei on the ground, the guards standing over them.

"You heard what the Agent said! We can finally get some revenge."

Mal landed and shoulder blocked an operative about to blast a fallen Nanomei up close with his gun. They were fighting for kills not simple derezes.

Then shots rang out behind her. Three shots and the loader and two guards fell to the ground.

"Duck," Chip's voice sang out behind her.

Mal threw herself to the ground and a grenade sailed over her head, detonating against the body armor of one of the targeters. The cannon was obliterated and so were the men.

Mal stood and turned to face Chip. Mal didn't know if this was a reunion or a fight.

"I don't know how you're alive or why you're helping us," she said. "But there are four more cannons."

"I'll take the two here you go to the other side," Mal said.

"Good enough for me," Chip said. She opened her mouth as if to start talking but did not say anything. Mal could find nothing to say either. Chip ran forward and slid down the wall to the ground.

Mal wasted no time and took to the air. Between the two of them they took out the four remaining cannons quickly. Efficiently even.

〉〉••••••〈〈

Mal flew across the chaotic battlefield. The Nanomei had Hacking on their side, and the Pylons here were theirs, so their Hacking was significantly stronger than anything the Axiom were bringing. Agents were arriving, though, and that meant things were about to get even more dangerous for everyone. Then in the distance she saw one of the black cubes explode. She veered there and landed atop the cube one over, as if on a rooftop looking down into a crater.

There were Ramos and Kass, still fighting. His shotgun was nowhere to be seen. Ramos' fist connected with Kass' head and she went sprawling out, flying through the air. She slammed so hard into the crater wall that shards of black gridstuff exploded outward at the impact.

She rolled to her feet and launched herself at him, grabbing him under one arm and flipping over his head. He was thrown head over heels backwards from where he had been standing. Mal stood helplessly by. Then she saw a drop ship come through the Gateway Pylon, heading straight for CoOp.

She looked down and Kass and Ramos were nowhere to be seen. "Kass?" she said into comms.

"Dek just arrived with several Agents," Kass said into Mal's ear. It wasn't comms, she had landed just behind Mal.

"Wait, what? Did you kill Ramos?" Mal asked.

"He got away, slippery bastard." Relief.

"Kass, stop this attack. It's not needed. Nanomei can't enact their plan without me and without Tok's ship. It's over."

"No. I will show Axiom that I am loyal, that I am deserving. I am going to stomp out this nest of vipers."

"I sent Tok away. Told her their plan. She won't let it happen and neither will I."

"I don't believe you anymore," Kass said.

"Don't do this, Kass."

"Why? Are you going to fight me?"

"No," Mal said.

"Why not? You could beat me. I know it. You know it."

"That's not what I want," Mal said. "I don't know what I want."

"My mission was to find the traitor. I lied. I did find him. I know it was Mullen. But I can protect you. He'll fall but you won't," Kass said.

"I don't know what you're talking about. Mullen's a good man."

"Mullen's not what you think he is. Maybe you are innocent. Maybe you're just a puppet," Kass said, sounding almost hopeful.

"I am out, Kass. Done with this fight," Mal said.

"But the Gel rig! The promotion! You know Dek's not winning. You can have one of those rigs. I'll make sure of it. Just stay with me."

"I can't, Kass. I just… I can't, I can't fight these people."

They embraced then, hard and long, the length of their bodies pressing into each other. Her hand pulled her close, her fingers laced into Mal's hair at the back of her head. They kissed.

When they let go it felt like parts of her were left behind with her. Mal knew Kass felt the same.

"Well, if you're out I'm in. No way Dek takes it."

"You deserve it, Kass."

"I know. Just stay safe and I'll try to protect you with the Matrons as much as I can."

Below, the battle raged on. Explosions rocked the Aetherial landscape. Axiom troops were massing now, more and more coming through. There was no turning the tide. Mal turned her back on the battle.

Mal stood atop one of the matte black cubes, like standing atop a building looking across to other rooftops and the streets where the fighting continued.

"You're just watching our world burn," Ramos said from behind her.

Mal spun around, flashing her sword into her hand.

He held out his hand and stepped forward, bringing a hack to bear. Mal felt the hack warp around her blade. He made the blade visible before Mal could even counter him.

"How long did you know?" Mal asked.

"From the beginning. You were never looking for me without me knowing it," he said.

He drew out his own blade, a two-handed longsword what he wielded and twirled in one hand.

"We don't have to do this," Mal said.

"Yes, we do. I thought I could change you. I thought I could bring you over," he said. He punctuated his sentences with great strokes of his sword. Mal dodged and ducked instead of parrying. He was fast but the raw strength he brought to each stroke was frightening.

But the shock of that statement jarred her. She started fighting back. She swung three times, driving him back and to the very edge of the rooftop. She raised her sword to strike again but hesitated and, in that moment, he reached out, grabbed her other hand and flung her off the roof and down, half a block away.

She landed in a tumble and could feel damage to her connection. Ramos leaped from the rooftop, landing with a crash twenty feet away.

"You can't beat me," he said.

"I'm going to beat an explanation out of you, you arrogant-"

An errant energy blast from one of Kass' cannons smashed into the building next to them. And the concussive force sent them both flying. She must have respawned the cannons. Damnit Kass. Ramos was up first he reactivated his shotgun program.

Mal was stunned, struggling to her feet, her ears and brain ringing. She saw Ramos raise the double-barreled beast of a weapon at her. She knew she should move but something was stopping her. She was slow. She saw the blast coming and then he was there. Rat from nowhere had launched himself between the two of them and the blast hit him full force. His body slammed back past Mal. She turned and saw him starting to derez.

"That was meant for you!" Ramos screamed. He took aim again and Mal hacked the street beneath him. She held out her hand and the street swallowed Ramos whole. He was gone.

Mal spun, no longer stunned, and knelt down next to Rat. His connection was badly damaged, and he had taken far too much Glitch.

He spoke, and his voice sounded mechanical, strangely pitched. "You can always…"

"Count on Rat," Mal finished for him. Then she stabbed him with her hypospray straight in the chest. As the program started to work, she hacked it as well, making the strands of code sharper, more able to penetrate into his connection, fortify it. He gasped as her hack found purchase and she rebuilt his connection by the force of her will and the aid of her code.

"How?" Rat sputtered.

"You can always count on Mal," she said. Then a look of fear came over Rat's face.

Mal stood and spun around, rezzing her blade to parry Ramos' attack. She pressed a counterattack, mostly to clear away from Rat and they fought their way into the middle of the street.

"You were meant to learn from me!" he shouted.

"I've done alright, thanks," Mal said. "Axiom training and all that."

"You were goddamn delivered to me from Mullen," he said.

Mal reached a tipping point and slashed instead of at him or his blade for the handle in his hand. He screamed in pain as the blade shattered into blue motes.

"What? What did you say?" Mal sliced towards him and he stumbled backwards. Mal kicked him in the chest and he completed his fall, landing on his back. Mal leapt forward and landed with her knee on his chest, her sword tip touching his neck.

"Mullen sent you to me to join me. This has all been part of the plan. You were supposed to question yourself as an Agent. He sent you to your old home, so you'd wake up to what you were, what Axiom was. Show you what they'd done to your family. To your brother." Ramos punctuated that last with a stroke of his blade, sending Mal's away from his neck long enough for him to regain his feet.

More clashing of blades, desperate parries, wide arcing attacks, they were fighting and yelling, and both were on the edge of breaking.

"Who the hell do you bastards think you are?" Mal yelled, drawing her sword up.

"We saw you as possibility."

Mal needed to think. She leaped upwards and backwards, landing on the roof behind her. She looked down at him. Don't follow me.

But he leapt and just barely made it, up the hundred feet or so.

"Mullen and I are friends! We were both watching you for a year before you were even assigned to The Drain!"

"But Mullen? He's as Axiom as they come!" The blade in her hand was shaking.

"He's a good man. He saved me from Axiom."

"But…" Then Mal let out a guttural howl of rage. Mal brought the sword crashing into the rooftop just to the side of Ramos' head. He kicked up, knocking her off of him. Mal stumbled and recovered herself as Ramos reactivated his blade.

"You saved Rat. I thought you were turning then. You didn't need to do that," he said.

"I saved a person," Mal said. Another explosion rocked the area near them, sending shattered bits of program through the air like snow in a hurricane.

"That's not what an Agent would do."

"Maybe you don't understand Agents."

He laughed then and clipped her arm with his blade for the first time. It stung like she'd been cut to the bone. Mal rolled away, almost to the edge of the roof and slapped on a sync patch, letting the program do its work while she focused on not getting cut in half.

"I brought you in. You slept in our camp. You ate at our table."

"It was a job," Mal said.

"I don't believe that it stayed a job!" he said. Their blades crossed and locked for a moment. He was taller by a foot at least and towered over her. They locked eyes. "Admit it, Mal. You're not Axiom anymore.

"I…" Mal had a hard time denying this. "I admire you," Mal said. "I admire how hard your people fight," she gritted, and the swords disengaged, flinging them both staggering back several steps.

"You know the feeling of freedom," he said.

"I was never free," Mal said.

They crossed blades again, several bloodless but impassioned passes, blades clashing and crashing. He started bringing a hack at her. Mal couldn't identify it but Mal moved her own will towards it. They both threw aside their blades then, and between them a thousand lines of code snaked, flew, and howled between and through them. Mal felt him slip ever so slightly, pulling her will harder around her. Mal knew that he was her better, but the gel Rig was working in her favor. They were too evenly matched and they both stopped at the same time, a thousand lines of code crashing in blue strands and shattering all around them.

He took a tentative step forward without menace, without anger.

"Mal. Come with me. Walk from Axiom. We can get you out physically. You can be one of us. You were meant for this."

Then the whole cityscape was rocked by an explosion. Ramos turned and they both saw a cloud rising above the CoOp.

"I have to go. Come with me," he urged, stepping to the edge of the roof and holding his hand out to her.

"You know I can't."

"We'll start again. A new battlefield. My Death Angel. If you go back to your body, they'll kill you for treason."

"Good luck, Ramos," Mal said, and turned away and started walking back to the Gateway. She did not look back. It took him a moment to leave. Mal could imagine the look of disappointment and Mal didn't want to see it.

The desolate cityscape around her got smaller and smaller as she approached the Gateway. Behind her the battle still raged.

〉〉 • • • • • 〈〈

Logout.

Mal regained consciousness in a panic and instinctively tried to breathe in and found her lungs already full. Breathing out felt wrong, yet she knew she had to. Her hands smashed against the inside of the tank. She struggled inside the tank. She instinctively tried to Hack to get out. She panicked when she realized that she was going to die in the Meatspace. The gel and her lungs were equal in pressure, impossible to breathe out gasping with lungs full of concrete. The tank emptied slowly, reducing the pressure around her.

"Delay cycle seven complete. Please remain calm while the tank drains. You will experience discomfort as the gel is purged from your system," a comforting voice said as Mal started to heave and vomited a great quantity of gel. It slid from her throat, felt strangely cool instead of the heat of usual vomit. Mal blacked out for a time while this happened and then woke with the tank open, and in the 45-degree angle position.

"You have recovered," the voice said. "Please await instruction."

Mal stood from the tank, naked and cold, slick with the gel. She looked at the other two tanks. They were both empty. There were no lights. And no instruction was coming.

There were no techs here, no guards, which was strange.

On the black surface of the floor was the body of Commander Mullen, his throat slit, blood pooling around him. Someone had drawn their fingers through the blood and spread it out on the floor to look like wings behind him. Mal did not check his body. She knew Kass' efficiency.

Her tank re-closed itself and Mal stood there, looking for a moment at her reflection in the curved glass. Then she saw a mark on the outside of the otherwise perfectly clean glass: the print of a goodbye kiss.

Mal walked away.

» Aetherium: Primer «

>>Access Point: Usually a Pylon, access points are the safe places in the Aetherium to log in and out.

>>Aetherium: The world between worlds. An alternate dimension accessed by humanity through digital interface. The place where most people live out the majority of their lives.

>>Derez: To deactivate a program or to be disconnected violently from the Aetherium.

>>Glitch: A disturbance in the connection between the human mind logged into the Aetherium and their Aetherial selves. Glitch can come about by mishandling their programs, proximity to Quantum Noise, or even taking damage in the Aetherium.

>>Hacking: If all things are programs, hacking is the magic way of changing those things. A mixture of talent, coding knowledge, and willpower.

>>Meatspace: The world of flesh and blood.

>>Nodal Plane: Areas in the Aetherium where the Quantum Noise is naturally less intense.

>>Node: A Nodal Plane reinforced with Pylons, made safe for humans.

>>**Patch:**   A person who is logged in to the Aetherium who has no weapons, Hack, or complex programs.

>>**Programs:**   Every object in the Aetherium is a program.

>>**Pylon:**   Technological wonders which exist in the Meatspace and the Aetherium. They keep the Quantum Noise at bay and host the reality that people experience while in the Aetherium.

>>**Quantum Noise:**   The substance native to the Aetherium. Toxic to human minds.

>>**Rez:**   To login, and also to activate a program. Programs tend to be invisible until "rezed" into existence.

>>**Rig:**   The piece of Meatspace tech that allows people to login to the Aetherium.

>>**Schema:**   All of the area and programs governed by one Pylon (or group of linked Pylons). Smaller than a Node.

>>**User:**   A person who is logged in to the Aetherium who has a Hack score, can run complex programs.